CURSE OF THE DIVINE

KIM SMEJKAL

CURSE OF THE DIVINE

HOUGHTON MIFFLIN HARCOURT
BOSTON   NEW YORK

hmhbooks.com

The text was set in Dante MT Std.

Cover design by Andrea Miller
Interior design by Andrea Miller and Kaitlin Yang

Library of Congress Cataloging-in-Publication Data is available.

ISBN 978-1-328-63725-3

Manufactured in the United States of America

DOC 10 9 8 7 6 5 4 3 2 1

4500817378

FOR JOHNNY,
MY LUGNUT

WISTERIA
TOWNSHIP

ROVER FIELD

ROVER FIELD

MALIDORA

KINALLEN

ROVER FIELD

LASSINA
SEA

CHAPTER 1

HE'S A DEAD THING.

Celia shivered and wrapped her arms tight around her middle, clutching all her shattered pieces together so they didn't spill out like an overturned cart on the cobblestones at her feet. Watching Griffin from across the busy market square of whatever town they were in, she held her thoughts at bay with knives.

They didn't know for sure whether Diavala possessed him. In all the days since they'd left the city of Asura, Diavala hadn't made herself known; all Celia had was paranoia, suspicion, and nagging, ever-present regret. Perhaps this was what winning looked like, and Celia was just so broken she couldn't recognize it.

Still, the bees in her head insisted, *He's a dead thing.* The words kept buzzing in her mind, repeated and repeated. It might look like they'd overcome the body-stealing devil, but Celia had been fooled by Diavala before.

As a plague doctor, Griffin was certainly dressed the part. His costume was all black—hat, tight leather pants, coat of raven feathers, except for his bone-white mask with its long, stabby beak—and it seemed to give his inner death a face.

Slowly rotting on the inside but whole on the outside, decomposing by degrees. The illness inside him festering, rattling his bones, humming to him: *Diavala, Diavala, Diavala . . .*

Griffin scanned his growing audience—their baskets filled with bread and other market staples under their arms, harried looks on their faces, toes already pointed down the road they'd continue on if he didn't hold their attention—and he turned up the shine of his smile. It looked as if he was trying hard to ignore that he was competing with bread, squash, and butcher cuts of meat, and how equal the match was.

He'd been standing statue-still for a handful of moments, waiting for people to notice him before beginning his performance.

It hadn't taken long.

The town lived in another world. Market day was a bustling affair, with people moving this way and that, laughter and conversation coming from every direction, a steady hum. Tenors—the visible, ever-changing markers that signaled gender identity—shone brightly around everyone's head and shoulders, as individual as fingerprints. The sights, sounds, and smells of innocent daily life. Anything dark and beaked and ominously silent, evoking the plague and death and mystery, stood out like a bonfire.

He hadn't seen Celia yet. She stood on the steps of a bakery near the back, the scent of cinnamon and melted butter enveloping her.

When the attention of his crowd wandered too far, he'd hand

out one cheery yellow dandelion with a dramatic bow. Except for the tilt of his head when he aimed his beady-eyed goggles at someone, his deep bows were his only movement. Soon most of his small audience had one yellow tuft either tucked behind an ear, in a basket, or clutched in a hand.

Who is he? Why would he give me a flower?

And a few, *Hack, capitalizing on fame, trying to wheedle hard-earned coin. There's only* one *plague doctor.*

Most of Illinia knew of him now, and absurdly, his fame had grown so big, no one would have believed he was indeed *that* plague doctor. The one who had stood with the Divine when she'd revealed herself to her followers; the one who had calmly heralded her death.

With the sun miraculously shining despite the crisp autumn season, and with whatever arbitrary crowd size he was waiting for finally assembled in front of him to his liking, he began.

 Celia held her breath.

A slow nod. Unclasping his hands, he swept his gaze, hidden behind those dark lenses, across every intent face. For a moment his goggled gaze seemed to land on Celia, and even though she was well hidden, she had no doubt he'd managed to see her.

He did that a lot: see her.

Always Celia and Griffin, opposite each other, circling, two polar ends of a never-ending abyss. The setting around them didn't matter at all.

He nodded at her before he began. *"'Another dawn brings shadow!'"* he boomed in his performer's voice.

One of the shoppers flinched, and the corner of Celia's mouth quirked up. His volume control was still an issue, obviously.

He shook himself off and adjusted, settling his voice into the rhythm of the poem. Dipping and lengthening and stretching. No longer words: a work of art, a painting, a story. He was used to speaking more with his body than with his words, but it was easy enough for him, animating poems already written.

Celia stopped breathing as she listened to his voice: smooth and deep, soft but strong.

"Another dawn brings shadows
Full of creeping things and claws.
And our love for each other—
Starving us and nourishing—
Has found its perfect home."

Celia didn't recognize the poem he recited, but it seemed as if it were his own composition, just for them. Who else would understand that when love was born from the darkness, sunlight would only make it wither?

Griffin cocked his head at her. The pointy beak of his white plague doctor mask aimed at the ground like a stake, his goggles reflecting the sunlight that mocked them.

The crowd grew as he continued, his voice luring them more than his costume ever could. They tossed coins onto the purple and blue cloth at his feet; they clapped and smiled and gasped where they were supposed to. But many quickly moved on, no one staying for the whole monologue, no matter how much he inflected his voice to pierce them or lowered it to reel them in closer.

A commotion in the crowd drew Celia's attention. An elderly soul with wispy white hair like a dandelion puff shook a cane at Griffin, his peculiar tenor made of bright shades of silver with barely any nuance. Often, it took some measure of training to identify whether the proper pronoun for someone was *he, she, they,* or none at all—tenors were by nature fluid and complex, filled with an array of color and light—but this person's tenor was so uniform it would have been easy even for a Kid just learning the skill.

The plague doctor saw the shaker of the cane from the corner of his eye—Celia felt his hesitation, his reluctance to let go of their eye contact across the distance—and in that silent pause, the intruder said something. One word, over and over again, with a voice as wispy as his hair.

"Abomination."

The crowd cleared space around the old soul, giving him more room to shout his awful word. The plague doctor turned his head away from Celia slowly and smiled at him, not looking upset at the interruption, nor about the word he shouted. The old silver-tenored soul may as well have yelled *Codfish oil!* for all the rise he got from the plague doctor.

Celia had a different reaction.

She pushed out of the bakery's doorway and flew through the crowd, shoving people out of the way as she went.

When the crowd parted just so, the plague doctor looked up, perhaps catching a glimpse of her familiar black top hat, ratty around the brim from overuse, a scrap of ocean-blue fabric pinned to the underside. Because of how tiny Celia was, he might not have seen anything but the disembodied top hat weaving its way through the market crowd, approaching fast. As Celia pushed her way to the front of the group, she reared to a stop. The couple she'd just wedged herself between murmured "Excuse us!" and shuffled aside.

Celia stared at the old soul for a heartbeat, her heart in her chest hot and huge. "*What* did you say?" She stepped toward him. "*What* did you say?!"

With both hands perched at the top of his cane, he frowned at her, then lifted a gnarled finger and pointed at the plague doctor. His lips parted. But before he could utter that vile word again, Celia was in his face, looking up at him despite how stooped he was. "Don't you dare."

Something fierce had risen in her, and she had to concentrate on not unleashing a primal scream. At the old soul. At the sky.

"'For whatever's inside you,'" the old soul said, quoting a passage from the *Book of Profeta* with a defiant tilt of his chin, "'will be revealed in the end. So the Divine knows.'"

"No," Celia snapped. She'd heard enough self-righteous nonsense about the Divine's grace in her lifetime. There was no Divine, only Diavala. The trickster of a thousand faces. The one who possessed souls, used them, and then abandoned them to madness when she was done. There was nothing graceful about her, nothing good. Her religion was built entirely on lies.

Diavala was the true abomination.

But perhaps the old soul had seen something of Diavala inside the plague doctor. They'd suspected that Diavala was inside him for weeks, biding her time, licking her wounds, planning revenge against them.

It had become the perfect torture for Celia: sensing that her enemy was close, so close, but not having it confirmed.

Maybe this stranger had just confirmed it.

And oh, how Celia hated him for that. "How dare you!"

The crowd pushed closer, eyes wider and conversation quieter. The way they looked at her, nervous and skittish, it was as if they expected a brawl. Some tentatively offered murmured explanations: *He's traditional, not a fan of Commedia, thinks art is evil, slightly mad hahaha . . .*

He straightened his hunched back, then looked from her to the plague doctor again. "Abomination," he whispered one more time.

It was a dare. A taunt. He *wanted* one of them to overreact. To prove him right.

Celia's hands clenched, close to giving him what he wanted. Close enough that Griffin took a step forward and put his hand out in front of her, snapping her attention back to him.

With his hand still in front of Celia, the plague doctor tipped his hat to the intruder and smiled wide, defusing the battle with one sentence.

Abomination, the old soul had accused.

"Well, you're not wrong," Griffin said. Then he tilted his head back and laughed and laughed and laughed.

The old soul blinked and shook his head, then hobbled away, casting glares over his shoulder and muttering under his breath until the crowd closed around him, leaving the plague doctor alone again.

With another player, who'd just made a fiery entrance.

Griffin tipped his hat at Celia and stared, silently acknowledging the fiery thing in her eyes. The fear. The sadness. The hate. He tilted his head, his long hair fluttering like a waterfall at his shoulders. "Welcome to the shadows. The creeping things. The claws."

He held out a hand, asking her to join him on that bare expanse of cobblestone he'd claimed as a stage. Celia shook her head. She would have backed away if the crowd hadn't closed behind her, blocking off a retreat.

So she gave them an awkward smile. Too bad for her, she'd placed herself right in the middle of his act, and she knew the plague doctor wouldn't let her leave without a fuss.

She stepped forward into the shadows, where they lived together.

The plague doctor bowed deep. "My shadow bows to you— a tender poison, a sweet deceit—recognizing its one and only ruler."

Instead of dying, the fiery thing inside her grew bigger and hotter. It had started with the old soul and his shouts of abomination. The truth, bluntly stated by a stranger: *There is something foul inside this plague doctor performer.* But it grew and swelled beyond that initial surge of anger.

It was the thing she'd held back for weeks, rising up in revolt all at once.

This was *her* plague doctor, and Diavala couldn't have him.

He reached into his pocket and pulled out an offering: a yellow flower.

"Don't be ashamed, good ruler," he whispered. "I am your land and your possessions, your treasury and army. Claim me."

Celia met his eyes behind his mask. Despite the tint on his goggles, she could imagine the exact depth and breadth of his dark eyes. How they crinkled in the corners from his smile, how the constellation tattoo at his temple would move with the flex of his jaw.

Her plague doctor.

She found herself responding.

Improvising.

She'd been a performer too, once, and she'd been so good at it she'd cast a nation into chaos with her show. She too had been on the stage when the false Divine died.

"I can claim Death himself?" she asked. Wonder lacing her voice, she took the flower, brushing her fingertips against his as she did. Time stretched out like taffy, slowing everything down painfully. When was the last time they'd touched? So close all the time, traveling together, yet such a chasm between them.

But now everything sparked.

She pressed her hand to her chest. Slowly, like something long lost and now found, she smiled at her crowd. "If I am Death's ruler, he must obey me." She waited for people to nod, acknowledging her claim.

She turned back to the plague doctor. "Tell me everything about my kingdom," she commanded. "Tell me what it looks like, smells like, tastes like. For if I am to rule Death's land, I must understand it."

It was her own dare.

You know death. You've seen it.

Tell me. Here. Now.

More than a year earlier, he'd fallen out of a tree and died, then somehow miraculously returned. She'd asked him dozens of times—What is death like? Where are our friends? Where's . . .—but he'd deflected every question. The closer they got to Wisteria Township and every impossible hope Celia had pinned there, the more restless she'd become. He knew exactly what she wanted, but he held his secrets close.

Tell me where Anya is.

"You seek reassurance," he said sadly.

They circled each other, as if dancing.

"I seek understanding." Celia's voice cracked, and her arms wrapped around her middle again, tighter this time. Half of her was gone, and she needed to know what had happened to it.

Where is Anya?! Tiny explosions as Celia's mind bees slammed against the inside of her skull, stinging her, buzzing so loud they drowned out all other sound. *You know what I need to know, and I'm your ruler, and you must tell me!*

They must have looked ridiculous, a plague doctor circling a tiny thing like her and calling her ruler. Her face was made of a pointy chin, small nose, and big dark eyes, all framed with hair like black grass. Her tenor generally toured through hues of red and bronze, *she* and sometimes *they*, in a lazy way, slow and steady, where other people's tenors flickered and sparked. Truly, there was nothing regal or refined about Celia. Yet when she stopped moving with a hard stomp of her feet, staking a claim to the truth, the plague doctor paused, listening.

"I command it," she said. "I claimed you."

Some of the crowd became bored and moved on, but Griffin and Celia were too lost in their act to notice, weeks of tension coming out in subtext that flowed too easily, in innuendo and accusation that cut too deep.

He shook his head, the beak of his mask swinging from side to side like a slow pendulum.

Tell me where Anya is! the confused bees in her mind shouted.

The plague doctor went down on his knees in front of her. "You ask for the one thing I can't give you." It was no longer a performance. He bowed his head. All she saw was the top of his black hat, the nape of his neck where his hair parted, and the movement of his shoulders as he breathed deep. She longed to rest her hand there, on that small glimpse of skin.

She pulled her hand away before it could betray her and touch him.

Death had broken both of them, but hers was a fresh, raw wound where his was an old, jagged scar.

His head tilted, as if he were listening to the cadence of her booming heart.

The ever-present pain behind Celia's eyes got worse. "You're my tender poison, my sweet deceit," she said, her voice cracking. "I'll always meet you here, in our home full of creeping things and claws."

It was just them, and darkness. The most terrible home, but their home now nonetheless.

She barely registered when people began clapping at the finale.

When it seemed that he'd never rise, content there on his knees in front of her, hugged by her shadow, Celia pulled him to his feet. The tinkling of coins as they fell to the purple and blue cloth meant that the curtain was drawn. They accepted congratulations, smiled at their well-wishers, and gathered their things.

She didn't look at him again.

The trouble with every conversation they had now, the reason she had trouble looking at him, was that Celia didn't know who he was at any particular moment.

He could be himself: Griffin Kay of Rabble Mob fame, the person who'd died once, the smiler, the bull-shitter, the flirter, the illusionist.

Her plague doctor.

But the thing Celia hated most might lurk inside him. The thing that had forced Anya into a place so terrible, even a plague doctor couldn't bear to talk about it.

Diavala.

It wasn't Griffin who was the abomination, yet the two — Griffin and abomination — were inseparable.

Celia closed her eyes — one slow, forever blink — before she opened them again and they walked away.

He was a dead thing, and like all dead things, people had trouble looking at him for long.

CHAPTER 2

AFTER HALF AN HOUR OF WALKING IN SILENCE, CELIA AND Griffin veered off the main road. Their camp was nothing more than the edge of a clearing, their small covered wagon the backdrop, and, on the occasional cool night, a fire. Their small horse, Aaro, dozed under a tree while twilight washed out color.

After growing up in the largest temple in Asura, then running away and joining the Rabble Mob, a famed theater troupe, sometimes the silence of her new life still shocked Celia. Where had the rest of the world gone? How had it just fallen away?

Griffin cleared his throat and began humming as he collected stray branches to make a fire. Celia plopped herself near the base of the tree, leaned back against it with her eyes closed, and flexed and extended her fingers.

Her hands were sore from the work she did every day, trying to fill their coin purses with as many kropi as possible before they got to Wisteria Township. With the ban on traditional tattoos lifted for the first time in generations, everyone wanted one, and Celia's nimble fingers and artistic skills were in high demand. Most of her clients were the devout: followers of the religion of Profeta, mourning the death of their Divine. They took ink as a form of religious observance to their dead god.

Others just wanted pretty pictures on their skin.

Either way, the people of Illinia had finally been given permission, and they were taking it.

For the first time in Celia's life she was making her own money, being her own boss. And she hated every minute of it.

Her last client—the one just before she'd encountered the plague doctor in the town square—had looked to be in her forties, sharp-angled and rough like leather, but she'd trembled the entire time Celia had worked on her forearm. She'd asked for a mass of pennyroyal flowers.

"People will begin to experiment with dyes now," Celia had said as she poked the needle into weathered skin. She'd vowed to never use her inkling powers again, so she had to do this the harder, longer, normal way. "Can you imagine if these blooms were actually purple? Tattoos would be paintings instead of sketches." She truly had no personal opinion about where the art should go now, but airy conversation chased away the dark corners of the places where her thoughts were prone to wander. She forced small talk, sometimes too aggressively.

She'd also noticed that conversations like this seemed to increase the amount of her tip, and that was the endgame.

The client ground her teeth against the pain but met Celia's dark eyes with her light gray ones. They had no spark in them, as flat and as dull as sandstone, but something burned there that Celia recognized. "Do you ask people why they choose what they do?" the pennyroyal client asked.

That would imply I care.

Celia bit back her first thought and said instead, "It hasn't been that long since people have had the option of choosing. I'm pretty sure if I asked that question, most people wouldn't know how to answer."

When Celia was an inkling, the only tattoos she'd done were in the Divine's service: Divine tattoos were meant to guide behavior, help you toward heaven. This new reality, where tattoos could be whatever a person wanted, was a sharp shift away from that.

Most of what she'd tattooed the last two weeks were obvious whims, and she was glad. Why would she want to know the secret hearts of strangers? Their insides? But this client had obviously thought about it. She held Celia's gaze a beat, almost daring her. *Ask me, why pennyroyal? Ask me, why seven blooms exactly?* Pennyroyal wasn't a pretty plant—the blooms stomped up the stalk with harsh purple bursts, like a path of bruises. It wasn't a particularly useful plant either—too toxic to keep in most gardens.

Celia knew of only one use for it: to stimulate menstruation and, maybe seven times, to clean out the uterus completely.

The client must have seen something shift in Celia's eyes. "We do what we have to," she said, wincing as another particularly painful tug of Celia's needle scraped into her skin. A tiny drop of blood blossomed, and they watched it together. "We bleed when we need to."

Celia pursed her lips. "Or when we're forced to."

The client looked up again, breaking Celia's concentration.

Her light gray eyes looked ghostly, but her tenor of red and orange shades burned bright. "You're awfully young to be talking like this." She said this not as though she doubted Celia's knowledge, but as if she were sad for the truth of it.

Thankfully, the image was almost done. The client's house was too musty and damp. After being on the road for two weeks, and many weeks before that, four solid walls felt like a prison.

Celia had lived in one most of her life, and she recognized the smell.

"You're a good sitter," Celia said, changing the subject. "Some people act like I'm ripping out their tongues with my fingernails."

After Celia had washed and dried the tattoo, her client admired it fully for the first time.

"I can almost smell the mint," she marveled. "Can almost taste it." And Celia caught her significant side-eye. *How did you get so good at this, considering that two weeks ago it was an offense punishable by execution?*

"I used to be an inkling," Celia offered by way of explanation. She could have gone further—yes, I'm actually *that* inkling, the infamous Devil in the Bell Jar—but the client's eyes were already as round as moons. She dove back into her coin purse for a larger tip. Pity to the homeless inkling, now that her role had been spectacularly burned to the ground and she had no religion left.

It had been two weeks since Celia had ripped apart the religion of Profeta and left the city of Asura behind in chaos.

Everyone knew about her, which made hiding from her fame easy. Just as with the plague doctor, no one expected an exceedingly short, young soul with dark eyes, straight black hair with straight black bangs, and a nondescript black top hat to be *that* inkling.

Now, Celia opened her eyes and nodded to Griffin as he sat down with crossed legs on his bedroll. The entirety of the last hour had passed in silence but for his humming.

He hadn't taken off his mask yet, nor his bullshit plague doctor smile.

"I thought it would feel good," he finally said. His hands, resting in his lap, opened and closed, as if he wasn't sure whether to hold on to the performance in the square or let it go.

Celia swallowed. How he must miss performing onstage, loudly, with his people. Probably so much that it physically ached—a bee sting in the center of his chest, a tight grip around his throat.

And it was her fault.

"And did it?" she asked.

He flashed his wide smile at her. "I enjoyed it more before you cornered me."

"As I remember it, *you* cornered *me*. I didn't name myself your ruler. Really, you asked for it."

"We'll have to agree to disagree on that point." He poked at the fire with a stick. "But really, it was the least I could do after you defended my honor so valiantly."

Abomination. Abomination.

Remembering the part that had brought her into his act, a sharp pain stabbed behind Celia's eyeballs, another headache trying to take over. Sometimes she didn't think it was hyperbole that she would explode from the stress, but fact.

Griffin fell silent as well, the memory of the old soul and his hostility wedging between them.

Celia sighed and focused on the muffled hissing noises coming from the fire. Blessedly, it wasn't raining, but the wood Griffin had used was damp and produced more smoke than flame. "So, we'll be there tomorrow," she said. They'd fled Asura, left everyone behind without so much as a goodbye, with only this vague mission in mind: get to Wisteria, find Halcyon.

"You're headed toward the devil," Griffin replied. But those words didn't make sense coming from him.

A chill settled around her. Unnatural.

Celia forgot her headache. Her head snapped up, her heart stuck in her throat, and she pushed her back into the tree so hard she felt the bark dig in deep enough to cut.

She began to shake.

For all the suspicion she'd had about Diavala—that she was lurking inside Griffin, biding her time, tormenting her with silence, and even Griffin's own admitted feelings of unease—this was different. It was the moment before absolute confirmation. The briefest of moments, where any sliver of hope Celia might have had that she was wrong would disintegrate.

Though she'd tried to goad Diavala into showing herself before this, suddenly it was the last thing she wanted.

And because she was so scared, she wanted Anya.

Anya.

Celia's hands clenched into fists. Her breathing sped up. She ground her teeth. All within a span of a few heartbeats.

Don't lose your composure, Cece. In the far corners of her mind, she let Anya be her practical self. *She's going to try to bait you. Don't fall for it. Be calm.*

"Diavala." The word fell from Celia's mouth like a canister of black powder, landing heavily, loaded and ready to detonate with a spark. Celia pressed her fists to her eyes. She didn't look up, because she would only see her plague doctor. Too painful, to feel like screaming and scratching at a face you loved. "You've been quiet," Celia said, her teeth nearly fused together. With everything in her, she held back the urge to scream.

"You should be relieved I took a moment, Inkling." It was Griffin's gorgeous singer's voice saying the words, but not Griffin saying them. Celia heard the layers of centuries underneath. "You killed my purpose, you took away Profeta, the only thing that mattered to me. If I hadn't controlled myself so well, the collateral damage might have been spectacular."

Diavala said this as if Celia should be *grateful* to her. Celia's eyes were still closed, but she saw bright starbursts as she pressed her fists harder against her eyes. "The collateral damage *was* spectacular," she said. Diavala had taken away Anya, the only thing that mattered to Celia.

Celia didn't even know who she was anymore, without her angel.

"We both know our battle isn't over, Inkling," Diavala said. "But now that we're so close to Wisteria, I think I should warn you about what you'll find there."

Even as the tears began stinging her eyes, Celia almost laughed. "Yes. Listening to you is the perfect plan. I trust everything you say completely." She took a steadying breath. "You can't con me away from Halcyon, but I do appreciate the effort. Did you bury yourself so deep in Griffin that you didn't realize where we were going all this time?"

Toward Halcyon Ronnea of Wisteria Township: the only person on the Roll of Saints who'd survived Diavala's Touch. He was nothing more than a name, but one loaded with promise and hope. Halcyon was the only one who might know how to defeat Diavala—Celia's enemy.

Unfortunately, her *immortal* enemy.

Her immortal enemy who was currently inside Griffin, who couldn't leave without shredding Griffin's mind into confetti with the Touch.

Diavala assessed her for a long moment. The silence between them fell thick and heavy. "Keep hating me. That's fine, and I expect nothing less. But the fact is, I'm stuck in this body for a good long while, and I know how much you love it. You think I'm the threat here, you think Halcyon survived my Touch because he's special, because he has answers you need—"

"All true," Celia interrupted. "What else do you want to

talk about? How about how you killed Vincent? How you were ready to kill dozens more, including *children*—" Celia's voice cracked, thinking of Remy on that stage, defiant chin held high, a mistico's blade ready to pierce the back of her skull. "Or we could go back further, to all the lives you ruined over the years, *centuries,* of messing with people. You stained so many with your ink, manipulated so many, all so they believed in you as a deity. Well, we both know you're no deity. You're a murderer, a con artist, a bottom-dweller."

The world was too small to hold all of Celia's rage. *So much for not losing my cool, Anny. Sorry about that.*

"You didn't mention Anya," Diavala said in Griffin's soothing voice.

Celia's gaze finally snapped up: Diavala leaning forward intently, dropping her hands, shifting her legs, wearing the plague doctor mask. All of it preparing for battle. All of it with *Griffin's* body.

Celia slammed her eyes shut to wipe away that glimpse. "I liked it better when I knew where you were but you didn't open your mouth—*Griffin's mouth*—to speak. How about you go away again so I can ignore you properly?"

Diavala tsked. "So dramatic. I'm trying to warn you, Inkling. I've dealt with Halcyon before. You won't come out of this unscathed."

"You talk as if you care about my well-being. You talk as if I'm listening."

There was a terrible pause, one where not even Anya's ghost

dared tread. Then Diavala whispered, "Maybe you'll listen to this."

Griffin put his head down so his chin touched his chest, the beak of his plague doctor mask pointing straight into his lap like an arrow. For a second, Celia thought Diavala had put him immediately to sleep.

And then he screamed.

The sound shredded Celia. So familiar: *mistico, Vincent, suffering, pain.* So completely Griffin's voice making those terrible sounds, echoing inside her, then swallowed by the night. She launched herself at him, trying to — do what? She clutched at his chin and tried to pull his face to her, she put her hands in his hair and tore off his mask. It was the sound that meant madness, too many memories, a broken mind. It was the sound that always ended with chloroform, then gashes at the sides of the neck, then bleeding out.

Sobs burst from her lips like bubbles. Griffin twisted and jerked away from her, his eyes pressed tightly shut, nonsense words competing with his screams. In seconds, his shirt was soaked through with sweat, and it clung to him as she clung to him.

It stopped as suddenly as it had started.

"Griffin. Griffin?" *Dia,* neither of them could catch their breath. She panted. He panted. She took his chin in her hands and tilted his face up to hers, searching his eyes.

They were glassy and red-rimmed, dazed, but it took only a moment before they focused on her.

"Celia—" he croaked. His head flopped back down to his chest, and he kept falling. Celia caught him in her lap, sobbing freely now.

If she could have thought straight through her panic, she would have known that Diavala wasn't leaving him for good. There was no one else's body close by for her to hop into except Celia herself, and if she'd wanted that particular revenge, she would have taken it already.

No, Diavala hadn't left, but she'd tugged.

Celia imagined Diavala's poisonous essence inside Griffin as if it were a rubber band: stretching out, stretching tight, pulling at his mind, torturing him just enough.

Then springing back.

Celia cradled his head in her lap, brushed sweat-soaked hair away from his forehead, traced the constellation tattoo beside his closed eyes, and cried.

It was the closest they'd been in weeks. They most they'd touched.

And it had happened because of pain.

Their world was shadows and creeping things and claws.

His eyes opened again, and he stared up at her.

It was too hard, that stare.

Without thinking, Celia pushed him away and scrambled back like a crab, squawking in alarm.

Looking at Celia with so much hatred that Celia physically recoiled, Diavala hissed, "Are you listening to me now?"

Celia loathed her with everything she had. As in the square

earlier, her rage rose to volcanic all at once, choking her. Griffin's unique flashing metallic tenor didn't change; it didn't give any indication that Diavala was there with him. In a world where everyone had a tenor, the absence of Diavala's only marked how soulless she was.

Shaking, flushed, Celia couldn't speak.

But she nodded. *Yes, I'm listening.*

"Good," Diavala said. "So here's the predicament I see. Now that Profeta has ended, I cannot leave this body. Well, I *could*, if I had any confidence that you could put him out of his misery to keep him quiet." Griffin's dark eyes were usually as soft as a doe's when he looked at her, but no longer. "But I don't. And so there would be someone in the world loudly proclaiming that everything that had come to pass in Asura had been a hoax. Because how could someone still be Divine Touched? It would make no sense, and people would be forced to rewrite all they understood. You might have taken away Profeta's future, but I will not allow Profeta to be robbed of its past. My legacy will *not* die because of this." She inhaled and adjusted her shirt where it still clung, damp with Griffin's sweat.

"So, to my chagrin and yours," Diavala continued, "I'm stuck inside this one. If there was a way to remedy this, trust me, I would not be keeping it a secret from you."

There was a way to "remedy this," and Halcyon was the one who knew it. Diavala's reaction—showing herself for the first time in more than two weeks—proved that they were close to the one person who could help them.

Dia, how gullible did Diavala think she was?

"I think the answer is a lot simpler than you're letting on," Celia said. "At least from *our* point of view."

Diavala hesitated a moment, then chuckled, shaking her head. "Simple? You think approaching Halcyon will be simple?"

Oh, she did. Celia had never been so sure of anything in her life, especially now.

"Halcyon will never help you willingly, Inkling." Diavala chuckled again, and Celia heard it a little more clearly this time: a laugh laced with pity for how little Celia understood. Diavala's words were heavy with emotion but delivered with such matter-of-fact bluntness that it took Celia aback.

For a moment.

"That's an interesting line," Celia said, infinitely tired of the conversation. "Or maybe, because Halcyon's the only one who's survived your Touch madness, he knows a hell of a lot about you, and he's exactly who we need to talk to."

"He survived nothing. He was never in danger at all," Diavala snapped back. "He doesn't have the information you and I *both* need."

Annoyed that she even had to listen to this, Celia stood to add more soggy wood to the soggy, barely there fire. Diavala had a hundred reasons to lie and manipulate them, and Celia didn't feel like wasting her breath arguing.

"My history with Halcyon is . . . fraught," Diavala said, shaking her head. "I took him over, then left. He wailed long and hard, screamed and wept. For a special, singular moment in time, I felt vindicated." Diavala's lips curled in a happy sneer at the memory, and despite how well Celia knew Griffin by then, she'd never seen his lips make that horrid shape. She turned away, disgusted, her rage nearly overshadowing all that Diavala was telling her.

"But then," Diavala said, "he stopped. He stood up straight, he smiled at me. And oh, how he laughed and applauded. He loathes dramatics, unless he's the one performing." She shuddered, as if to shake his dramatics off her shoulders. "So that's why he's on the Roll of Saints—he screamed loud and long enough to go down in Profeta's books as a unique case, an example of something impossible—just to annoy me."

Celia snorted. If this was true, it sounded like Halcyon hated Diavala as much as Celia did. "If he's able to withstand your torture and laugh about it, then he's someone I want to meet very much indeed."

"You're missing my point," Diavala said. "Halcyon cannot know where I am. For all of our sakes, not just mine."

Then she moaned.

No. It was Griffin who moaned. He put his face down in his hands, his fingers tangling in his hair, clutching hard. He didn't scream, but he began breathing hard through his teeth, actively trying to absorb the pain and not succumb to it again.

Celia didn't have time to react. Just as quickly, his gaze snapped back up to meet Celia's, all panic gone, his stare not his stare. "Do you understand, Celia Sand? Halcyon will not know I'm inside this body. I'm giving you no choice."

The threat hovered in the air between them.

Diavala had moved from silent houseguest to aggressive hostage-taker, just like that, and she wanted Celia to know it.

Celia's nails bit into the weathered skin of her palms. "I understand," she finally said. "I'll keep your hiding place safe." *For now.*

Griffin's eyes narrowed. "I'll know if you veer from our arrangement."

Our arrangement.

As if Celia had asked her to hold Griffin hostage. As if she'd had a hand in choosing this path at all.

With the fire between them, they watched each other. Celia's constant headache throbbed and pulsed, always present, always enough to remind her that she was never again going to be okay. She knew the exact moment when Diavala retreated; Griffin's shoulders went from tight to slumped, his fists unclasped. He tilted his head to the left and looked at her with tired eyes.

"Celia?" Griffin said. His whisper was low, inviting, and weary. His bones hummed from Diavala's presence, a constant song vibrating from the inside. Maybe Celia's headaches were in sympathy—why should he suffer for all her mistakes?

"How do you feel?" she asked.

"Eh," he said, shrugging. "I fell out of a tree once, hit every branch in the world on the way down, and actually died from the thumps. That hurt so much more."

Celia almost chuckled. "I don't think I believe you," she said.

"Yeah, you're right, I'm lying. Diavala messing around inside my head is worse."

"She confirmed it," Celia said. Their running theory about why she hadn't already left Griffin with the Touch in retribution had—fortunately?—been pretty accurate. "She worries that the Touch would spread doubt about the sanctity of Profeta's lore. She won't leave you until she finds an alternative. If there even is one."

Griffin nodded absently at the news that he and Diavala were indeed stuck together, as if it weren't a monumental revelation. As if he'd expected it. "And? There was another reason she wanted to talk to you." He paused, then added, "And make it such a painful experience for me."

Sometimes Celia wished he wasn't astute.

"She and Halcyon have some sordid history," she said, waving her hand. "She says he's powerful, and she warned us against approaching him."

With perfect timing, Aaro nickered.

Griffin, pulling his knees up and wrapping his arms around them, tossed a glance at their horse. "Well," he said. "At least one of us thinks that's funny."

"It's horseshit, Griffin. She's only trying to scare us and gain the upper hand again. She's stuck in a body she doesn't want, stuck without her followers and purpose. Threatening you, threatening me, trying to hold on to what little power she has left. She knows we're on the right trail, and she's just trying to keep us away from it."

If Halcyon hated Diavala, then Celia and Halcyon already had a whole lot in common. He could, in fact, be a fated soul mate.

Wasn't the enemy of her enemy her best friend?

"Maybe," Griffin said.

"Definitely."

He didn't seem half as sure as Celia was. "But there are easier ways she could keep us away from him," he said calmly. "She could take me over and run away, for one. If he's so terrible, why give us the opportunity to approach him at all?"

"She's assessing me, Griffin, waiting to see what I do until the moment she can take advantage. Taking off won't allow her to spy on what I'm doing. Are you suggesting we *don't* follow our only lead? That Diavala is warning us because she cares about keeping us safe? If she says finding Halcyon is a mistake, it means we should do exactly that."

"But it's as if she wants *us* to find Halcyon while staying far away herself. I don't trust her, Celia, but she's definitely scared of him, I can feel it."

Hearing this, the blood roared in Celia's ears. A mixture of loathing that Griffin had to share these feelings in the first place and a grim satisfaction. "Good. I'm glad she's scared."

Celia thought of a blade, quivering, entering her line of sight, her small hand around the hilt.

Anya, shaking, a handspan in front of her. The dagger between them.

Another hand—Anya's—wrapping around Celia's, holding the dagger and Celia both.

Pushing it into her own neck.

Red blood.

Black ink.

And then it was over. A ten-year friendship, a young life, and a thousand-year-old religion.

It hadn't been worth it. Freeing a people from a crooked religion that meddled in lives seemed like such a noble cause, but if people hadn't known they were enslaved, how could they appreciate their freedom? In her daydreams and nightmares both, Celia often revisited that night. Sometimes she tried to make it play out differently: no dagger in her hand, no sacrifice, no plotting. But however hard she tried, it always ended the same way: Anya gone, the only person she'd ever loved so deeply, and by Celia's own hand.

She shouldn't know what Anya's blood smelled like, but it stained everything she looked at. She hated how the people had reacted with reverent shock, as if what they'd watched on that stage had been divine and noble. And she hated, with a bright, fierce longing, the creature who'd made Anya believe that her death was the only way to freedom.

"We need justice," Celia said. "I'm going to get every one of Halcyon's secrets and hope to all the devils in hell that one of them can break Diavala for good and free you."

Griffin assessed her for a long moment. "*'Rage scrapes your judgment.'*"

Celia moaned. "Don't quote Ficus to me. This isn't an epic poem."

"You're acting like all I want to do is survive," Griffin said. "But I want justice just as badly as you do."

Like Anya's name, Vincent's name wasn't uttered either. Vincent, whom they'd watched suffer with the Touch for days. The true Touch, full and deep and permanent, not just an approximation of it that Diavala could inflict seemingly at will.

Both ghosts joined them around the fire.

"All I'm saying," Griffin said, "is that we need to tread carefully here. Don't let your hatred for Diavala cloud what comes next. We know nothing about Halcyon except that he survived the Touch and that Diavala fears him. And think about how scary someone must be for someone immortal to be afraid of him."

The constellation of tattooed stars beside his eye beckoned to her. He'd tattooed himself with nothing more than ink, a needle, and flame, long before tattoos were legal again. The constellation Leonus, nine stars strong, Regulus, the largest star, perched perfectly at his temple. *All around the world, people give this star mighty names,* he'd said once. *The Princett, Heart of the Lion, the Mighty. In a vast world easy to get lost in, Regulus has always been my anchor.*

Celia blinked long and hard, trying to push away the pain of her pounding headache. Griffin's gaze stayed locked on the dancing flames, but occasionally his eyes flitted to her. Midnight black pools, dark eyebrows, impossibly long eyelashes fringing them.

"I'll be careful," she promised. "If only to stop you from quoting Ficus at me again."

It was what he'd been waiting for. With a long breath, he stood and walked over to her, and gently, carefully, as if she were hollow and breakable, guided her down to her bedroll.

He lay down behind her and arranged a blanket over them both, his chest pressed to her back and his arm under her head like a pillow. A day ago, she wouldn't have let this happen, too worried that it could have been Diavala manipulating her, too scared of everything. And she was still scared of those things, but she pretended she wasn't.

She pretended it was just Griffin. The mystery under the plague doctor mask that she'd only begun to know. That she had plans for, had dreamed with, before all hope was sabotaged.

"The stars in Kinallen?" she whispered, watching the embers flash in eddies and swirls. Celia and Anya had daydreamed about making it to that infamously beautiful country, and Griffin wanted so badly to show her his beloved land of stars. On a map, it didn't seem far, but even on good days it had always felt impossible.

"Mmm hmm," he murmured into her hair.

"Tell me about them."

"No words can describe such wonder. You'll just have to see them yourself one day."

"I wish we could go there," she said. "I wish we had a choice."

"There's always a choice." He pulled her closer. So warm. And for a moment she felt safe, wrapped in his arms. "Some choices are just harder to make than others."

INTERLUDE

The plague doctor was more than a bit insulted that Diavala had chosen to talk to Celia first. He'd been trying to start a conversation for weeks.

So rude.

He'd felt Diavala in there, poking around in his mind. A memory—like the time he'd tried a backflip and broken Sky's nose with his heel, or the time he'd run out of Kinallen powder and had attempted to perform with *real* fire—would rise up without any sort of trigger, as fresh as if it had just happened. Or some emotion would surge, discordant with the moment: he'd almost wept while reading a map, his heart had fluttered in fear as he'd fed Aaro an apple. The plague doctor always had difficulty figuring out real from not real, upside down from right side up, and Diavala's increasing agitation wasn't helping matters.

At first he'd fought against the invasion, trying to imagine rooms in his mind where he could keep his most private thoughts hidden.

But Diavala was an expert with the lockpick. Better, even, than he was.

Enough was enough.

Diavala!

He thought the name as loud as he could. Beside him

on the hard ground, Celia shifted in her sleep as if she'd heard his mind-shout. Possible, he supposed. She had a queer knack for knowing exactly what he was thinking, even when he didn't know himself.

Still, Diavala ignored him.

The plague doctor hummed, thought about Wisteria, wondered about Halcyon, tried to ignore the past as he pushed ever forward. But then he drew one clear image in his mind. One moment in time, captured like a still life hanging on the wall:

Nero, the biggest bear of a soul the plague doctor had ever had the pleasure of meeting, smashing a gilded chest full of Divine ink with a sledgehammer.

Nero brings the hammer up, he smashes it down.

The plague doctor repeated the memory, singling out only that part—not shattered Celia pressing against him, not the sound of his thundering heartbeat—but only the giant soul, the sledgehammer, the smashed chest of ink. The grand finale of Diavala's fall in Asura.

When the repetition threatened to put him to sleep, he added other details he thought Diavala might appreciate: the crestfallen expression on Ruler Vacilando's face, the broken sound of that one mistico's wails, the small Kid on their parent's shoulders, so young they likely hadn't even chosen a name for themselves yet, part of the first generation who would grow up without a deity.

Chest, smashed.

Chest, burned. (The plague doctor didn't remember how the fire had started, but the smoke had been spectacular.)

The final moments of Profeta, where the Divine and her ink had left their world forever.

Chest, smashed.

Chest, burned.

"All right, all right . . . enough!"

Satisfied, the plague doctor linked his fingers behind his head and smiled up at the night clouds. *Ah, there you are, Diavala. Finally.* He thought the words slowly and emphatically; it was harder to think in full sentences than he'd anticipated.

He closed his eyes to concentrate, the smile staying on his lips as Diavala muttered something unintelligible.

Hmm? What was that? he asked. *I didn't quite catch it.*

Silence fell, the intrusive muttering falling quiet. But he knew Diavala was close.

I want you to talk to me, not Celia, he said.

More silence, but tinged with curiosity. Her mind was closed to him save for occasional hints of emotion.

"Why is that, plague doctor?" Diavala finally asked. *"Don't you trust her?"*

Diavala was playing a game, trying to rile him up. *You know well that it's you I don't trust,* he said. *But more to the point, I much preferred it when you watched and listened* rather than took over and spoke. *I can't keep you out, I can't stop you from knowing everything I'm thinking and doing and wanting. But when Celia talks to me, I need her to know it's me.*

A strange sound—an echo of a laugh—and then Diavala said, *"Interesting. With your mask and false smile, don't you already deceive her? How does she ever know who she's talking to? You call yourself the plague doctor, but to her you're only Griffin."*

The plague doctor gritted his teeth and kept his smile.

Chest, smashed.

Such a pretty chest, too. Gold and sparkly.

Chest, burned.

So much smoke. Outrageously thick and black and sinister. If he could have found a way to harness it for the stage, the Rabble Mob would have been famous long before.

"You are a frustrating one," Diavala said. A tinge of electricity burned through his bones at a higher frequency than the usual ever-present humming. He felt Diavala's frustration just as he'd felt her curiosity.

You might have made your own deal with Celia, he said, *and you obviously have a vested interest in what happens in Wisteria, but you forget whose mind you're sharing. I can make this stay very unpleasant for you.*

"Are you really in a position to threaten me?" Diavala said.

Are you really in a position to leave? he replied. *We both know you're stuck for the time being. So unless you want end- less reminders of the worst moments of your life—*

The frequency got even higher, and a tear slid down the plague doctor's cheek as he realized that this was how Vincent must have felt for weeks, but without knowing the cause.

He pushed the thought away and focused on another: the moment onstage in Asura when the tide turned. A tattoo on Celia's back that heralded the imminent death of the Divine, who'd just revealed herself.

The moment when Diavala had tried to take center stage and failed, instead being driven into hiding forever.

"Fine!" Diavala said, her thought a scream. *"I'll talk to you instead of Celia if I have something that needs saying. But don't forget I'm here, watching everything. You can't keep anything from me. The moment I suspect things aren't going in my favor . . ."*

The searing pain of the Touch took over. Knitting needles in his brain, poking around. His eyeballs being pulled inward, everything caving in. The plague doctor took the physical pain with shallow panting breaths. He curled into a ball away from Celia, pushing his fist to his mouth to stifle a scream. Sweat broke out all over his body, as if he were on fire, yet he shivered. And all of it in an instant. It would have been a mercy if the shock knocked him unconscious.

But the emotional pain was worse.

As if he were made of everyone's sadness. As if everyone's regret, loneliness, and suffering had been collected—twined into a never-ending ball—and then unspooled inside him.

It was exactly like the other side of the veil; when he'd died and traveled the afterlife, he'd felt this same thing—a sorrow so intense there weren't words for it in this world.

He lost himself to it. He was made only of hurt.

Some of it existed in strange images: snowdrop flowers emerging in early spring, lilies blooming then fading fast. Others were clear: a dying child, a mound of earth.

Broken hearts and suffering minds.

"Welcome to my world, plague doctor," Diavala said as she let him go.

He gasped and bolted to sitting, close to unleashing the scream. His breaths came hard and fast, and he concentrated on slowing them down. The physical pain stopped immediately, but the images and memories, thousands of them and each full of sadness, lingered before fading.

Celia rolled toward him in her sleep, a frown creasing her brow, as if her dreams had taken a dark turn. The fire was close to flickering out, embers pulsing in a slow glow.

Point taken, he said after his breathing had slowed.

They both knew that Diavala had the upper hand, but at least he'd gotten what he wanted.

Dia, but he was weary. He lay back and pressed one hand to his heart. *Now go away, Diavala. I have some happy dreams to attend to.*

A jolt of Diavala's revulsion washed through him. *"Yes, you have the most imaginative dreams of anyone I've ever known,"* she said.

Diavala had meant it as an insult, but it made the smile return to the plague doctor's face. And it was a smile he meant.

He shifted toward Celia and waited until the crease disappeared from between her eyes and her expression was restful again. "Dreams are nice," he whispered to her. "When you're inside one, there's never any doubt that it's real."

CHAPTER 3

CELIA AND GRIFFIN ENTERED WISTERIA TOWNSHIP IN THE late afternoon with none of the parade and pomp that should have come from such a long-awaited entrance.

It was exactly the opposite of exciting: Heavy and lush. That moment in time when you're suspended just at the cusp of sleep—that point you can never remember, but you know it must happen.

Wisteria was a regular Illinian town, albeit quite a bit more intense in color than any Celia had ever seen. Wisteria wasn't only a pretty moniker—the plant grew everywhere: arching over footpaths, creeping up buildings, hanging above door-frames and windows. Clusters in full bloom dripped from every surface, painting the whole town purple.

Strange, for wisteria to bloom in autumn.

"Let's find a room before we ask any questions, okay?" Celia said.

Griffin only nodded. Dark circles hugged his eyes, and a dark-ness eclipsed them, the effects of the pain from the night before still fresh. He needed sleep. In a real bed. With a real pillow.

Without a skin-jumping creature inside him.

They rode through the wide streets, forcing themselves to smile at the two or three people they saw out and about.

"Where are all the Kids?" Griffin asked.

That was strange, Celia had to admit. In every town they'd passed through—on this journey or with the Rabble Mob—Kids playing outside had been the loud but comforting herald of civilization.

The only activity was fragrance-heavy blooms of wisteria buzzing with lazy, saturated bees.

"Excuse me." As Griffin pulled the wagon to a stop, Celia addressed an elderly person wearing a proper suit and holding an elaborately carved walking stick. "We're looking for food and lodging. Can you point us in the right direction?"

The wrinkles on his face smoothed for a moment, as if he'd aged backwards forty years, before settling back into deep, furrowed ruts. "What brings you to Wisteria, good souls?" he inquired.

Was he making lighthearted conversation or did it matter for his answer? This stranger seemed to be studying them with an acuity that didn't fit the situation.

Griffin said, "We're searching for someone" at the same time Celia said, "A vacation."

The stranger lifted his eyebrow, his forehead disappearing into deep wrinkles.

With a good-natured laugh, Griffin chuckled the awkwardness away. "Both are true. We're from Asura and needed to get away from the big city, especially after certain *dramatic* events unfolded there. We've also heard that a friend of ours may live here."

"We'll be staying only a short while and then moving on," Celia added quickly.

The stranger nodded sagely and looked up the street. A person with a basket of flowers—plump wisteria bunches mixed with plate-size peonies and dahlias and dainty baby's breath—appeared from around the corner where his gaze had landed, as perfectly timed as if he'd conjured her. "Rosetta!" he said. "These travelers from Asura say they're looking for someone. Should we direct them to the Outside Inn or to Rian's?"

Her chin high and her shoulders stiff, she waltzed over, feathery light on her feet, the blooms in her basket not shifting with her movement as they ought to. The flowers seemed carved from a light stone rather than something living.

"From Asura?" Rosetta came over, appraised them, and nodded. "The Outside Inn."

"That's what I thought as well. So, at the next block, make three left turns—your first left on each cross street—and you'll be delivered straight to Davi's lovely inn. She makes a fabulous carrot stew. Tell her I sent you, and she'll give you a discount. The name's Garuld."

"Thank you," Celia said, tipping her hat as Garuld and Rosetta stepped out of the way of their wagon.

As they continued on, Garuld shook his head at Rosetta. "I think they are," he responded to whatever question she'd asked him.

"This place is a little strange," Griffin said, but he smiled wide as he said it, as if he understood that level of strangeness and wholeheartedly approved. He scanned the street, peering into windows. "Everything feels . . ."

"Dulled," Celia offered.

"Yes, dulled," Griffin agreed. "But sharp at the same time. Maybe too sharp."

Too stabby.

They turned left at the first street. They passed buildings made of stone and brick, every shutter tight, very few marked as businesses, and no one else in the streets. At their next left, the street got narrower. Celia reached her hand out toward the high fence beside her as they passed, thick ropes of wisteria trailing along the top. She wanted to touch a blossom but hesitated.

"Is this considered a street?" she asked, nudging Griffin. The road was so narrow that if another wagon came from the other direction, they would meet in the middle at a stalemate.

He shrugged, staring hard at the wisteria climbing along the top of the fence, and as if reading her thoughts, he pulled the wagon to a stop again.

Celia stood up on her tiptoes, keeping her balance on the wobbly cart with difficulty, and leaned right over, pressing her face an inch from the closest wisteria bunch. A bee's fluffy body ambled slowly past her line of sight, filling her ears with the echo of its soft buzz. She could definitely smell the flower, a subtle vanilla. Up close, the bunch of blooms had white pistils laced with yellow, everything perfect, everything normal.

"Careful," Griffin murmured. His hand found the small of her back.

She shivered as he leaned forward with her. They studied the plant together.

She shouldn't have called the town dulled. Rather, it felt normal, but *too* normal. An approximation of normal, which made everything stand out. Should she hear a bee's echo? Or notice its fluffiness? "I'm too scared to touch the flower."

There was that sharp stabbiness to it.

"Pardon me?" Griffin shook his head, as if getting rid of cobwebs. "I didn't hear you."

"That bee was too loud," she said, agreeing. "I said, *I'm too scared to touch the flower.*"

They looked at each other, as if realizing that they were acting weird, but had no clue as to how to stop. Griffin's smile only grew wider.

Using his gloved hand, Griffin poked at one of the small purple flowers.

It moved.

As if it had been poked.

"Is it hard?" Celia asked. She still thought it looked too solid. As if, even if she tried, she wouldn't be able to crush it out of shape. But bees wouldn't be attracted to something made of stone. *Would you be so fooled, my precious bees?*

"It felt"—Griffin shrugged—"flowerlike." He frowned again, grabbed the cluster of blooms at the stem, and bent it off, taking the whole bunch. "We're being absurd. I think we're in desperate need of a good night's sleep."

Celia launched into full panic. "Wait!" It felt wrong for them to alter anything. If the town would go to such great lengths to show them one thing, perhaps they shouldn't be messing with the show.

"Rosetta had flowers in her basket. It's fine." Griffin plunked back down on the wagon bench to examine the bunch, and Celia followed suit.

But not before first making sure that the bees weren't rallying en masse for retribution.

She peered over Griffin's shoulder as he turned the flowers this way and that. "They're normal?" she asked.

In answer, the plague doctor handed the flowers to her, but stupidly, she didn't have any idea what to do with them. She didn't dare leave them in the road—that felt wrong. She also didn't want to have evidence of tampering in her hands—that felt even more wrong. She finally stuffed the flowers into her bag and tried not to think about them anymore.

As they turned the corner at the next street, Celia wondered if they were drunk. Maybe some of the homebrew honey rum they'd bought in the previous town had been stronger than they'd thought. They'd had some with their early dinner a couple of hours ago.

Another left turn. The third one. They turned the corner

where the Outside Inn should have been and found themselves on the same street where they'd encountered Rosetta and Garuld.

"We went in a circle?" Celia breathed.

"A square," Griffin said, smiling wider.

"What the hell is going on?" Celia said. "Maybe we made a mistake with our lefts. That narrow one wasn't a street." She expected to see Garuld and Rosetta. If she did, she would ask for directions again.

Then they came upon the Outside Inn.

"Ah, of course!" Griffin said, nodding sagely. "If it's the Outside Inn, we had to turn it inside out first."

Celia looked around, blinking. A second ago it was the same street, but now it was definitely different: this one boasted a clothing shop, and one of the houses was painted a cheery yellow that stuck out like butter on dark rye bread. Griffin was examining the cobblestones, as if fully expecting them to reshuffle under his feet.

Dia, but Celia's head hurt. She pinched the bridge of her nose and inhaled deeply as Griffin tied Aaro up to the hitching post.

With a gentle hand on the small of her back—his sign that he understood and would do the talking—Griffin led her through the double doors of the inn.

Inside, the air felt heavy and as thick as molasses. Celia took in the sight of the rug on the wooden floor, the bright chandelier, the desk with rows upon rows of shelves behind it lined with books and papers.

And more flowers. Everywhere. In pots on the floor, bright fuchsia bloomed. In vases on the counter and shelves, cut daisies and cornflowers. Without the bees of outside, though, the stillness felt more profound.

Behind the counter, someone with a tenor made of metallic reds and highlights of silver sat reading, only the top of her blond head and a portion of the spine of the book in her hands visible. It took a moment before her eyes peeked up over the book and locked on Celia and Griffin standing in the doorway.

"Oh my!" She stood quickly, growing in size before their eyes, like a giant. Celia was short, but Griffin was not, and this person towered over them both. "Welcome to Wisteria, strangers!" Making her way around the counter after putting her book down—*A Study of Carlotta*, it was called—she smiled brightly at them.

"Garuld recommended this place," Griffin said. "You must be Davi of carrot stew fame?" He bowed low, took off his hat, and smiled so wide that a dimple appeared in one of his cheeks. Celia had never seen that adorable dimple, and she thought she'd seen every iteration of the plague doctor's horseshit smile. *Always full of surprises.*

Davi laughed. "I am indeed she, but Garuld is a rascal. I buy his carrots, and he wants my carrot stew to get famous so his carrots get famous in the process." Her laugh was a hearty thing, springing from deep in her belly. She looked to be about thirty years old, with deep crescent wrinkles around her eyes from smiling. Despite her height, she wasn't imposing. Her dress had flowers on it, and as she approached, Celia noticed clover woven into her pinned hair. Davi was the prettiest giant Celia had ever seen.

"We have plenty of rooms to choose from, and after supper hour, the pub will reopen."

They negotiated the rate for a single room, booking it for a few days with the possibility of extension. Celia's temples constantly throbbed, but occasionally piercing pain split through, and she could feel a fresh onslaught approaching.

"Why would the pub close for supper?" Griffin asked.

Celia admired his gentle tone. If she'd asked the same thing, it would have sounded more like, *Isn't a pub's literal job to provide food and drink?*

Davi frowned, as if she didn't understand the question, so Griffin clarified. "We were wondering where everyone was." Maybe Wisteria was some strange sect of the fallen Profeta. Celia didn't know what day of the week it was . . . Perhaps if it was Saturday . . . some places in Illinia had started a kind of observance for the moment their deity was killed on a stage.

If so, how would they feel to have the murderer walk into their inn and book a room?

"Oh." Davi waved her hand, leaning against the counter and putting her hands on the edge as if she were about to hoist herself up. "I suppose I can see why it'd unnerve people not used to it, but it's not a rule so much as a tradition started by our leader. For the two hours just before sunset, Wisteria folk go home and spend suppertime with their families. It began so many years ago, I suppose we forget it's not something everyone in the world does. Everyone's loud enough behind their closed doors, *believe* me. I always use the time to enjoy the quiet with my family." She tapped a finger lightly on the top of her book and waved at the bookshelf behind her.

"That sounds like a lovely tradition," Celia said, pressing the heel of her hand to her temple, trying to release the pressure of her headache.

"Are there any more traditions we should know about?" Griffin asked with the ease of someone well traveled. "We wouldn't want to offend any resident here, nor your leader."

Celia started sweating when she remembered the crunched-up wisteria blossom in her bag. "Do you mean the leader of the officer's brigade?" Celia asked Davi. Her mind went to Nero for a second—her giant of an enemy who'd eventually become her friend. She hadn't said goodbye to him before she'd left Asura. She'd barely said goodbye to anyone, her shame and anger burning too bright. She'd needed, and still needed, to disappear. Nero would have told her—bluntly and with an economical use of words—how selfish she was.

"I suppose *mayor* is the better word," Davi said. "Halcyon Ronnea. You'll probably meet him if you stay long enough— he's been around a lot lately."

"Halcyon Ronnea," Celia repeated, giving Griffin a significant look. The Roll of Saints hadn't mentioned his occupation, so Celia had assumed it hadn't been anything noteworthy.

Diavala herself hadn't mentioned him as an important figure. Yet he was the mayor? "What do you mean, he's been around a lot *lately?*"

"He travels. Sometimes he's gone for months at a time." Davi went back to her chair, picked her book up off the counter, and disappeared behind it again. "Watch that you don't get lost as you wander. The streets can turn you all around," she said. "When the pub reopens, you'll see how not quiet Wisterians can be. It's a ruckus—tonight's Stomp Night—everyone sings loud and bad, and the crowd stomps along. Another thing Ser Ronnea started."

"Do you think he'll be there tonight?" Celia asked.

Davi shrugged. "Probably."

"What does he look like?"

Griffin elbowed Celia in the ribs and shot her a withering look. Okay, so she was being a bit obvious, but the topic of Ser Ronnea had already come up . . . why wouldn't she ask?

"It would be nice to meet him," Griffin said, walking quickly back to the counter and peering over at where Davi had resettled in her reading nook.

Celia joined him, barely able to peer over the edge of the counter. Stupid being short.

With her nose already in her book, Davi lifted a finger, her eyes scanning the page, trying to find where she'd left off. "If he's there, you'll know who he is when you see him."

They looked at each other as Davi continued reading. She

wasn't being rude, necessarily, but was acting as if the conversation had reached its natural conclusion. What did that even mean? Did he wear a flashing name tag?

Celia closed her eyes, pressing on them for a second, trying to suppress the hiss of pain that wanted to escape her lips. To Griffin's concerned look, she nodded. *I'm fine.*

Griffin wrapped his hand around her upper arm and pulled her away from the counter. "Maybe we'll see him at the pub then. After a long day on the road, we definitely need drinks."

Celia wanted to ask more questions, start a full-on interrogation, but Griffin was aggressively tugging her out the door, the key to their room clenched tight in his free fist. "Stop it. You look like you're going to pass out."

"My head." Celia gestured at . . . her head. "I'll be fine, just tired." And, if she was being honest, she was still scared of the flower in her backpack.

"Part of me recognizes this place," Griffin said, a crooked grin curling his lips as they went in search of their room. The entrance was at the rear of the building, and Celia had little confidence they'd be able to find it without traipsing around the whole town again. Griffin tilted his head up, exposing the long line of his neck, his chest expanding under his dark trench coat, and added, "There's a hint of madness in the air." He looked eager to breathe it all in.

They found their room eventually—four walls, two beds, a small table with an oil lamp, two rickety chairs, a jammed window, a cold fireplace, and not much else except insect vermin, probably.

The floorboards creaked under Celia's weight as she pulled back the covers on the bed with a wince, prepared for the worst. After a thorough inspection that thankfully didn't reveal evidence of bugs, she collapsed into a chair . . . which promptly shattered under her weight.

"Of course," she mumbled, picking herself up.

That was when a burning sensation on her thigh jolted her: another inked message from Dante. She muttered under her breath—he truly had the worst timing. If he kept her awake all night again with his nonsense, she was going to find a way of flying to Asura to snap every one of his pretty inkling fingers. He'd messaged her every hour in those first days after she'd left.

At first she'd responded, just quick updates about where they were going, what they were doing, thinking that might placate him. She ignored him anytime he expressed concern, every shred of sympathy or offered understanding, and each *I'm so sorry, Cece*. She couldn't handle those.

His messages had slowed to once or twice a day lately, but she hadn't responded in so long, she wasn't sure why he wasn't getting the hint. She never wanted to use her ink again, which she'd told him with her last message. Yet he still tried to poke her into responding.

Griffin added his pack next to Celia's in the corner and busied himself with inspecting the other bed, humming under his breath. Where she was close to collapse, Griffin looked liberated and free, his movements less stiff, as if the fresh, mad air had fed him well.

Celia closed her eyes against her headache (and her Dante-induced thigh ache), sitting on the edge of the bed and trying not to whimper. Sometimes she could almost, *almost* forget about her headache; other times it flared and took her by surprise. Either way, the near-constant pain was making something inside of her shrivel. It was so hard to be strong, continue on, and *hurt* all the time.

Griffin's next words were softer, though she still heard a lingering smile in his voice. "Now that we're here, you need to find a healer. There's no need for you to suffer if the headaches are getting worse."

"*I'm* not the one who needs a healer," she said. "And they aren't getting worse." *They're just always bad.*

Griffin cocked his head to the left, as if listening to her unsaid words.

"Let's check out Stomp Night," Celia said. Halcyon—and all the answers he had about Diavala—was closer than ever. A headache wouldn't stop her.

But before she left the room, she made sure the bunch of wisteria blossoms Griffin had stolen was well-hidden at the bottom of her bag.

CHAPTER 4

CELIA WAS THE FIRST AT THE BAR TO PLACE HER ORDER, leaving Griffin at the door, examining who he would corner first for information.

Many of the locals examined him right back, with appreciative smiles and nods to friends. *Hey, hey! Look at that stranger . . .*

Celia hadn't forgotten the way people tended to respond to him, but there hadn't been a time for him to shine in weeks. He would have no trouble getting people to talk, although staying on topic might be a different matter. He'd already launched into a loud soliloquy—a stranger in a strange town, a vagabond in search of adventure—and a lengthy narration of his impressions, as more and more people turned their eyes to him.

The bartender was even shorter than Celia, with long hair and dainty features. "What can I get you?" they asked, unsmiling, as they watched the pub quickly fill up and eyed Griffin with undisclosed fascination.

"Absinthe, and a description of Halcyon Ronnea."

They arched an eyebrow as they poured the drink. "He'll be here tonight, most likely."

"So I've heard, but I'd love to know what he looks like so I can find him."

The bartender slid the drink toward Celia without answering, stealing glances at Griffin, perpetually ready to take his order.

Celia turned on the barstool to the person sitting next to her, a rotund soul with dark smudges on his face and hands that looked as if he'd been working in a mine. Or perhaps he was an artist and worked with charcoal. "Hi," she said. "I'm new in town and would love to talk to your mayor, Ser Ronnea."

After a brief interaction, the same result.

Then another. And a fourth.

With each person she talked to, she slammed back a drink. Everyone was friendly enough, and apologetic about it, but no one could tell her what Halcyon Ronnea looked like, even though he'd apparently run the town "for quite a while" as the miner/charcoaler had said. From the roundabout descriptions and reverent tone of the locals, Celia imagined a much-loved grandparent complete with fancy suit and floral hat. Perhaps a few bonbons in one pocket and a handkerchief embroidered by his own grandparent in the other pocket. A wink and a story for anyone willing to pause a moment and listen.

But instead of elderly Halcyon getting confused once in a while—forgetting he'd already told that story, misplacing the handkerchief—it was the entire town around him that was suffering from memory loss.

Celia and Griffin had decided on a divide and conquer approach, but every once in a while he slid up next to her and reported that he was having the same luck. His smile grew with each non-report, as if this were a Most Fun Puzzle instead of aggravating as hell.

Celia moved from table to table — "Do you know Halcyon?" — her frustration mounting and her drunkenness following along like a diligent puppy. Many Wisterians started to express worry about her well-being, which only pissed her off more.

Griffin's loud, booming laughter cut through the din. He was talking to someone at the bar — a young person with a shaved undercut of brown hair, the longer hair on top flopping over one eye, and a vivid black sunflower tattoo on their shoulder — whose stiff body language was the polar opposite of Griffin's.

Something about the cut of their frown felt familiar to Celia. They sat backwards on their stool, leaning against the bar, slamming back drink after drink with a scowl that got fiercer and redder with each drink and the longer Griffin talked. They were frightening in a caged animal kind of way, looking to pounce, nodding absently at Griffin's happy conversation.

Leave it to Griffin to find the one person in the room who couldn't be swayed by his charm and to take it as a challenge.

Turning away, Celia fell into a chair at one table without even asking if she could join. Two people stared at her, their faces frozen mid-sentence, their laughter cut off abruptly by her entrance. "I'm looking for Halcyon Ronnea."

One of them was rough-cut and jagged, with oily hair and sharp features bordering on hawkish. The other was different in every way: as polished as marble, not a hair out of place. A duo of opposites, Celia couldn't fathom what they had in common. Her sentence had been slurred enough that the one with the oily hair asked her to repeat herself.

Before either of them could answer, the stomp part of Stomp Night began. People beat out a rhythm with their feet, reminding her painfully of the Rabble Mob shows, where the performance itself has a heartbeat. Griffin whooped and jumped on a table, feeding off the familiarity, earning laughter and applause. A few people pushed at one another to join him.

Griffin was clearly enjoying himself, but to Celia it felt more like the bang of war drums, the sinister beat of illness or revenge.

The pair across the table from her glared at her when she didn't join in, their hands banging on the sturdy tabletop, adding different beats to the underlying steady thump of feet.

With a weak smile, Celia banged on the table a few times. And then a few more. The "song" seemed to stretch on forever, with hoots and hollers adding a melody. More people hopped up on tables, wearing intense looks of concentration inside their smiles, as if the movements of their bodies had to perfectly match the rhythm and nothing else in the world mattered.

The intensity rocked her. Sweat soon glistened on foreheads and necks, everyone, including the bartender and, surprisingly, Sunflower Tattoo, eventually taking part. It wasn't musical or artistic as much as vigorous exercise, everyone exerting themselves to their capacity.

Abruptly, Griffin launched himself off the table, and with

one final smack on the tables and one final stomp of feet, the song ended. Unprepared for it, unsure how she missed the signal for the end that everyone else, including Griffin, seemed to recognize, Celia continued her tapping two beats too long.

The polished gentlesoul sitting across the table smiled at her as everyone cheered around them, congratulated each other, panting and sweating, and went to refresh their drinks. After the boom of the beat, the chaos of conversation and laughter was a soft, feathery noise.

Celia's gaze found Sunflower Tattoo just as Sunflower Tattoo's found hers. Griffin had flopped onto the stool next to them again, resuming his unrequited chatter, and it *almost* looked as if Sunflower Tattoo were beseeching Celia for help.

Celia tried unsuccessfully to hold back a snicker.

"I know what Halcyon looks like," the person across from her said casually. "But it'll cost you."

His long fingers tapped the table with feather-light precision, playing a piano concerto on the splintered wood. It wasn't the same as the beat of Stomp Night, but as if he were playing the unheard melody accompaniment.

Celia was drunk by that point, but not drunk enough that she didn't catch the look of confusion his greasy friend shot him, which was quickly covered. "Oh look, there's Kosta," the friend said, standing and taking his leave. "I'm going to say hello to them. We need to schedule another night for Imp tiles."

Piano Fingers nodded, a crooked smirk playing at the corners of his lips. His tenor had given Celia pause when she'd first sat down: too much bronze for the *she* pronoun, too few golds for no pronoun, and a mix of reds and silvers stirred in and flickering. Nothing was unusual in and of itself—there were as many tenors as people in the world, and pronoun classifications were a fabricated construct of linguistics that didn't always match up easily to reality—but for the first time in a long time, Celia had hesitated before landing on *he.*

"Finally, someone who's willing to help me." She matched his smirk with a look of wide-eyed innocence. "What payment would you need? I'll give you anything."

His eyebrow quirked at *anything,* and his fingers stilled for a minute. His fingers were long and fine, looking as if they hadn't worked a day in their life. And they perfectly suited the rest of him: smooth skin, short, light brown hair graying at the temple in a way that didn't match his age, wide lips slightly curved into a smile, green eyes that didn't care, and a suit so well fitted it had obviously been made exactly for that one body and only that body. Everything about him felt finished to perfection. For a second something tingled up Celia's drunk spine: caution, maybe, her self-preservation whispering *careful.*

"I'm sure we can come to some arrangement." He leaned forward again, whatever perfume he wore giving the subtle scent of pine needles, and locked his eyes on hers. His hands had crept up the table, tapping closer. "But first, traveler, your name."

"But first, how about *your* name?"

His smile got wider. "Ah, she's not as foolish as she looks. Fine, then. Tell me why you want to talk to him."

I need him to help me defeat Diavala for good.

But now she didn't believe this stranger could help her. He was a con artist, and she'd presented as an easy mark (*curse you, absinthe!*). Celia regretted the lineup of glasses she'd emptied, at the same time wishing there were more of them.

"We have a mutual acquaintance," she said carefully. "Can you help me find Halcyon or not?"

"Oh, I can help you," he said. "How about we make a game of it? I'll give you five answers to five questions."

Celia blinked. That's exactly what she wanted, so why would he call it a game? A con artist and a fool, then. Or perhaps he was trying to be charming.

"For some answers I'll be lying," he said, "and for some answers I'll tell the truth. You'll have to judge for yourself which are which. Uh-uh—"

Celia stood, pausing a moment, but only because she'd gotten momentarily dizzy, not because she cared to listen to more of what he had to say.

"I'm the closest you'll get to Halcyon—that, I promise, is a truth. Your only free one in this game." He leaned back in his chair and crossed his arms over his chest, enjoying himself. He glanced over her shoulder toward Sunflower Tattoo and nodded a greeting. Sunflower Tattoo snorted fire at him in response.

Celia sat down heavily, turning her attention back to Piano Fingers, knowing that Griffin had noticed the brief exchange and would ask Sunflower Tattoo about it. "All right, let's do this," she said. "Is Halcyon Ronnea a real person?"

"Yes."

"Why can't anyone tell me what he looks like?"

"Everyone else here has remarkably poor vision or poor memory, or there's some sorcery afoot . . . I haven't figured out which it is, but I'll let you know if I do."

"Why are you different?"

He shrugged. "I wasn't born in this town. I don't have the same affliction."

"Describe exactly what Halcyon looks like."

"Well, he's a charming fellow, always dressed in the latest fashions, with a keen appreciation for well-made shoes and long leather skirts. He has brown hair with a dashing shot of gray in it and green eyes—most of the time—and everyone who meets him wonders at his eloquence."

Celia processed the information, her eyes roaming over his brown hair, the gray at his temples, his green eyes and regal posture. She glanced under the table to confirm his footwear and ankle-length leather wrap. "Are you Halcyon?"

He smiled. "Yes."

Celia wanted to punch him. She shouldn't have wasted her time. She *really* shouldn't have trusted that this would get anywhere. And she really *really* shouldn't have had so many drinks. Her chair scraped the wood again as she stood up. "Enjoy your night."

He grabbed her wrist, and she blinked down at his hand. "But we were playing a game," he said, clicking his tongue with a hint of aggression. This was someone who wasn't used to being walked away from. "And you don't yet know whether you won or lost."

She yanked her hand away, and he smiled, his canine teeth too pointy and biting into his lower lip. Sharp and dark.

"Celia," Griffin said, suddenly there. "Introduce me to your new friend."

The sharp, dark stranger shook his head. "We were done here anyway, weren't we, Celia?" he said as he strode toward the bar.

Even after she'd turned her focus to Griffin, she felt a lingering unease: the slow dance of fingers along her spine and the back of her neck, the hoarse whisper of her name.

Celia let out a long, slow exhale. For whatever reason, Griffin did the same. His light joviality had disappeared, and now it looked as if he were trying to summon it back.

"How's your headache?" he asked, his head tilting to the left.

"The same."

Then, with a laugh, he said, "That person with the sunflower tattoo on their shoulder haaaaates me."

"Did you get their name?" Celia would have loved to stop referring to them as Sunflower Tattoo. Her mind bees hated the mouthful.

He nodded. "Lyric."

They both looked toward the bar. Something poked in Celia's mind, her bees murmuring something about *names, introductions* . . .

"That's a nice name," Celia said absently. All Illinian children chose their own names when they got old enough, and the convention was to select either family names or traditional ones. Celia loved it when someone's chosen name showed something of their personality: Griffin, Anna-turned-Anya, Lilac, Sky.

Lyric.

Lyric was still perched backwards on the stool, staring daggers at Celia and Griffin as an elegantly put together soul in a sharp suit and long skirt whispered in their ear.

Celia had been talking to someone. They'd played a game, and she'd been convinced that he was lying when he'd said he was Halcyon. He'd described himself.

"I found Halcyon," Celia said. "I think. I don't know."

She looked to the table where she'd been sitting a few moments ago: there were three people sitting there now, deep in a story, laughing loudly. She scanned each of their faces carefully, then moved on to the others mingling about.

She couldn't find him.

Lyric took their friend's arm and they walked past Celia and Griffin to the door. Everything about Lyric's movements looked annoyed. "Don't worry," Lyric said, bumping Celia a little too hard as they passed. Their voice was gruff but melodic at the same time. "It happens to everyone."

"What does?" Where the hell had he gone? Griffin was scanning faces carefully too, returning the many smiles of his new friends whenever he made eye contact.

Lyric's friend gave Celia a smile, his crisp green eyes, perfectly smooth skin, and fancy suit all far too dandy for a Stomp

Night at the Outside Inn pub. "The forgetting," he said. He tipped an invisible hat to her, and she noticed his long, lean fingers—pianist hands, fingers crafted like slender master-pieces—before he scooted toward the door with Lyric.

Celia wanted to laugh, but the stranger was right. It wasn't that she had lost the person she'd been talking to. He hadn't left the pub, slunk away, or joined another group.

It was that Celia had no idea what the person she'd been talking to looked like anymore.

Neither did Griffin. "He grabbed your wrist?" Griffin said, as if he needed confirmation that his memory was sound.

Celia nodded. "That *was* Halcyon, then," she said with something like wonder.

For the first time, Griffin didn't look like he appreciated the madness. "This feels like the stage I know—theater tricks and deflections and sleight of hand—so how can it be fooling me?"

The bell above the door tinkled as Lyric left with their friend, and Celia let out a long exhale. The only thing Halcyon had lied about in that conversation was that only those born in the town were afflicted with poor memory.

Because Celia and Griffin were afflicted, too.

CHAPTER 5

CELIA PACED CIRCLES AROUND THEIR ROOM AT THE OUTSIDE Inn, banging her knee against the rickety table every time she passed it. "We need to flush him out."

After three days of questioning the locals and getting nowhere, she was in a *mood*. Every time she looked at Griffin now, she saw Diavala laughing, mocking her. *You think approaching Halcyon will be simple, Inkling?*

Not only was Celia unable to talk to him, she couldn't figure out who he even *was*.

"You're making me dizzy," Griffin said, sitting cross-legged on the bed, watching her pace. He'd made some contacts in the town — Davi and the bartender, Giada, among his new friends, but none of them were the particularly helpful variety. Griffin was convinced that they were the best players in the world, despite not claiming membership in any Rover troupe. "They're all in on it!" he'd said with glee. He delighted in the mystery of being fooled. His biggest issue was that they still hadn't seen any Kids. In fact, there were very few young people at all in Wisteria: Lyric, Giada, and the town's tailor, Michali, among the rare exceptions.

"We've tried the cautious approach," Celia said, ignoring him and continuing her pacing. Her nails were chewed ragged. "We need him to *want* to talk to us. And what could do that?" She stopped. Looked at Griffin. Truly, she had no idea.

He stared back, then sighed. "My answer to everything is a performance."

Another beat passed. They could come up with some stage show to pique interest—something about Diavala, Profeta, and the Touch, perhaps—but most of the town already knew they were *that* inkling and *that* plague doctor from Asura. Word of their identities had reached Halcyon's ears, she had no doubt, and it still hadn't been enough to coax him out of hiding. Nothing they could come up with would top what they'd already done.

No, it would have to be a performance of a more intimate variety.

Shuddering with revulsion, Celia rifled through her bag, pulling everything out until she found her inkling quill. She paused slightly at the bunch of wisteria flowers from their first day; they hadn't wilted despite being stuffed in a bag all that time.

Griffin flew from the bed in a burst of agile movement, snatched the quill just before she could press it to her skin, and was back on the bed playing with it before she could even blink.

"I meant we should go the main square in costumes and play with some purple and blue fire. I meant we should be our incredible selves and embrace our celebrity again." He stopped lightly moving the feather through his fingers and looked about ready to snap it. "I didn't mean we should be stupid."

A hot flush took over Celia's face. *Always so stupid, Cece. You're always such a mess.* Anya's favorite lines.

The pain behind Celia's eyes flared, sending waves of stabbing agony through her skull. Her breath came in gasps, and she twined her fingers together, trying to still the way her hands shook.

Anya had wanted Celia to be free, she'd wanted to stop the oppression of a crooked religion, but if Celia *wasn't* free, and if the people of Illinia didn't know the crookedness of their religion, Anya's sacrifice had been for nothing.

I'd give anything to go back in time, Anny. I wouldn't go back to that stage and still my blade, I wouldn't go back to the first day at the temple, or to our final inkling test when we thought there was no turning back. I'd go to that day before meeting Kitty Kay and make sure Lupita didn't get you that message. I'd have never tried to escape in the first place.

This prison was worse. Cold and lonely.

With constant pain.

Her headaches were penance for what she'd done. She knew she'd never be rid of them. They were manifestations of her guilt, the poison she was, her inherent *badness.*

Sitting down on the bed, Celia bit her lip, chewed on it, breathing through her nose and trying to calm the mad fluttering of her heartbeat. "Theater won't help us now."

"I thought you weren't going to use your ink again." Griffin's hand hovered near her face as if he wanted to cup it, maybe stroke her hair, maybe bring her into a hug. But the last time he'd tried to do something like that during one of these attacks, Celia had lashed out and they hadn't spoken for days.

Inside his hesitation, Anya's name became a refrain — *An-ya, An-ya* — as Celia fought to quell the wave of pain.

It was a lullaby, a whisper, a plea, a question. *An-ya . . . ? Should I?*

The ink was the only thing Celia could think of that could command attention. She'd done it for ten years.

"If he and Diavala had a falling-out," Celia said, inhaling a ragged breath and snatching the quill from his hands, "he'll know about the ink. He'll think this is intriguing or infuriating, but either way, it'll get his attention."

She lifted it, pressed it to her skin, and drew, but paused after a few stokes; the black lines on her arm, in the form of a picture frame, gaped at her, distressingly blank, full of potential. "What should it be?" she asked, her voice quivering.

Griffin looked up and met Celia's gaze. "Are you sure about this? It's the exact opposite of careful. Divine ink shouldn't exist any longer. Beyond your personal stance on using it again, it also doesn't fit in this world anymore."

"We need him to listen, and in order to get him to listen, we need his attention. So yes, I'm sure." Celia wasn't sure at all, but at the end of the day, the ink was the only thing she had. She was exceptionally unexceptional, except for the ink in her blood.

Griffin cleared his throat. "Well, he clearly loves his town, and the town loves him," he said, collecting the still-fresh (yet three-day-old) wisteria bunch Celia had tossed aside earlier. "Give him an innocuous image—something that can be seen as a gift."

With the quill in her hand, the familiar movements calmed the last of her shaking, the panic attack fell away, and she immersed herself in the drawing. She traced each tiny floret with care, shading them to create depth, until a hanging bunch was captured in the frame like a still life. Her stomach revolted from using the ink, but she couldn't deny the feeling of contentment that surged through her for creating her art again.

Griffin stared at the image for a long while. "It's perfect," he finally said with resigned acceptance.

Celia sent the tattoo to Halcyon, transferring it to his upper arm. Griffin didn't blink the whole time the image disappeared, line by line, from Celia's skin.

"Is that what it looked like when you gave me Chappy?" he asked.

So unexpected, her bark of laughter, that it momentarily stunned her. "You named your plague doctor tattoo Chappy?"

He graced her with the old plague doctor smile—the one that took over his face, wide and brazen. "Of course not. That's ridiculous."

"Hmm," she hummed, savoring that small burst of warmth, even though, for some reason, it also made her eyes prickle.

When her forearm was bare, she severed her link to the ink

and gave it to Halcyon. She'd debated making it temporary, pulling the ink back into herself so it didn't stain his skin, but if she was going for a statement, it had to be as loud as she could make it.

This would either go very badly, or it would work and he would listen.

"Let's go then." Celia's headache raged as she walked to the door, the small burst of warmth already gone, but in order to capitalize on the tattoo's message, she couldn't stay hidden in their room.

As soon as they were out in the street, they sensed something wrong.

Deep rumbles rolled through the air around them. A dog barked in answer.

Looking up at the sky, Celia pulled her sweater around her tight as the wind picked up. "Thunder?" It hadn't been anything but clear and sunny the entire time they'd been there, but the clouds were forming and darkening at an alarming rate, swirling above their heads and blocking the sun. Another dog began barking in the distance when a second rumble of thunder boomed. A few people scurried for shelter, watching the skies with undisclosed alarm.

The wind pulled Celia's top hat off her head, and with a shout, she tore after it as it rolled along the cobblestones, pulled this way and that with every swirl of wind. She heard Griffin call after her, but it was a distant shout, swallowed by the howling wind. She finally caught up to it where it was trapped against a metal gate barring a private courtyard, flopping left and right and looking very much like it was demanding entrance.

Despite their endless rounds of the town over the past three days, Celia didn't remember ever seeing this gate. Beyond it, a wide cobblestone path led to a serene garden. Though most of the garden was hidden around corners, she glimpsed a bench, a large stone water fountain, and a series of torches and lamps, freestanding or hanging from the sides of the bordering building.

Along the length of the path that led to that garden—climbing up the walls and arching overheard—was the thickest, tallest growth of wisteria she'd ever seen: wisteria wallpaper, a wisteria ceiling.

Griffin pulled up beside Celia and quickly assessed the garden beyond the gate. "I wish I thought this was coincidence!" He bellowed the words so Celia could hear him over the wind, his hair whipping up and around his face, coils of black, loose curls writhing like snakes.

"Look," Celia yelled, grabbing her hat and holding on tight as she gestured to the courtyard. "Nothing's moving in there!"

Shingles screamed off of rooftops, window shutters banged and tore from hinges, and shouts from frightened Wisterians added to the cacophony. Yet the courtyard remained blissfully untouched: the plants didn't sway, a butterfly flew by without trouble, and when Celia pressed her ear right up to the gate, she heard the soft burbling of the fountain.

She pushed herself up the gate, putting her foot on the top of a NO TRESPASSING sign for leverage. "Come on," she said. "This is where he is."

Celia jumped over, landing hard on the path. The wind still screamed on the other side of the gate, she could see its destruction, and when she reached her arm through the wrought iron bars, the wind bit into her skin. The clouds swirled in a heavy mass, black and crackling with energy.

On her side, everything was calm. The fountain trickled, birds chirped, the sky clear above her head. The high tunnel created from arching wisteria vines was a luscious, inviting purple.

Impossible. It was the same world, but the gate separated it into two distinct parts.

Griffin was up and over the gate in a flash. "I love being guided by a hat," he said absently as he looked around the different space they'd jumped into. That almost made her laugh again, despite her headache, despite her churning stomach and disorientation. Griffin wasn't being sarcastic; he *literally* loved that they'd followed her hat.

"I followed a dandelion seed once," he continued, "but that adventure took a grim turn." He didn't expand, but his eyes darkened and his voice lowered. "As I suspect this one might. As skilled as I am with illusions, I can't fathom how someone can manipulate weather. Are you sure we want to talk to Halcyon while he's in a mood like *that?*" He gestured to the other side of the gate as the clouds finally unleashed their spoils: heavy rain pelting sideways from the wind, with the added *ping-ping-ping* of hail hitting like miniature cannonballs.

After the chaos of the storm they were now separated from, even his quiet words sounded harsh and out of place. It unnerved Celia too. Halcyon could control the weather, disguise himself in plain sight, and frighten Diavala. This was no stage show. All of it was impossible. Who exactly were they demanding an audience with?

Celia turned toward the wisteria archway as a tiny bird flitted among the flowers.

"Part of him is also in a mood like *this,* though," she said. "Whatever's going on here, we're behind the curtain now, plague doctor. He's allowed us backstage."

Light footsteps sounded from the direction of the courtyard. Celia forced her shoulders to relax, dropped her hands to her sides, and straightened her spine. Inhaling and exhaling with exaggerated calm, she waited, each footfall clomping along with her heartbeat.

Framed in the archway at the other end of the wisteria tunnel, Sunflower Tattoo—Lyric—faced them.

Celia and Griffin shared a questioning look.

"That's not Halcyon," she said. But truthfully, she didn't know for sure. Everything was mixed up in her memories of that first night at the pub. Scrambled and opaque like the town itself.

Griffin's hand found the small of Celia's back. "Hello, Lyric! Is your true name Halcyon, by any chance?" he called.

As if summoned, a taller, much fancier person walked grace-fully to Lyric's side. The purple of the flowers acted as a filter, dulling his glowing—and quite confusing—tenor. Through the tunnel of arching wisteria, the two couples assessed each other.

"What part of *go away* did you not understand, exactly?" he called. "I was pretty clear."

Griffin looked sideways at Celia, cocking his head. "So it wasn't an invitation-by-hat after all," he said.

The storm, still raging behind them, had been their warning.

Still, this was the most progress they'd made in three days. They couldn't lose the opportunity, because Celia was positive they wouldn't get it again.

All in.

Even if it was a most confusing play so far.

"Did you get the tattoo I sent you?" Celia called back to Hal-cyon. "It was a gift."

He frowned.

She'd gotten his attention, now she had to keep it. "I know you have something to do with the trickster deity I killed in Asura."

"You killed her? Or you convinced others you did? Don't try to deceive me with wording, former inkling. There's a big dif-ference between the two, and you're smart enough to know that." After assessing her a beat, his hands fell, and he shoved them into the deep pockets of his sharp-cut black skirt, a ges-ture so unthreatening and normal that it shocked her.

"I have a suspicion about what you want from me." Halcyon turned and walked around the corner, disappearing from sight. "Come. Let's get this over with."

Celia swallowed and took a step forward.

"Not you," Lyric said with a scoff to their words as Griffin stepped forward to follow. They held their hand up as if to push him back. "You are nothing. You have nothing he needs." They smirked. "And you're annoying as hell on top of that."

Celia looked back in time to catch Griffin shaking his head and smiling. "Honestly, what did I do to them?" he mused.

"We work together," Celia said. She reached out, trying to take Griffin's hand in a show of solidarity, and . . .

Her hand traveled *through* his.

She couldn't touch him.

It was as if he'd disappeared, yet he clearly hadn't.

"Interesting," Griffin said. All merriment gone, he frowned at the tunnel, at Lyric, at the corner where Halcyon had disappeared, before turning back to Celia, who was having a hard time remembering how to breathe. *Impossible, impossible.* She could see him, but her hands found only air. "This might be worse than the dandeli—"

And then even the specter of Griffin was gone, taking the rest of his sentence with him.

It was only Celia and Lyric at either side of the tunnel now. "Let's go," Lyric said, walking away.

"How did you do that?" Celia demanded, her voice cracking.

Distantly, Lyric chuckled. "If I'd tried to do that, he would be splattered on the bricks." Their words were immediately swallowed by the flowers.

In a panic that she might lose both Lyric and the one who'd made Griffin disappear, Celia ran through the tunnel.

She reared to a stop at the other side, turning to the right, where Halcyon stood in front of a bright cherry-red door leading into a large stone building. Lyric strolled inside and vanished.

"Where is he?" Celia said, her voice a shriek. "What did you do to him? How did you do that?" She looked around for mirrors even though she knew she'd never find them: he was too good to give away his secrets with carelessness.

Halcyon laughed, a gruff sound like an avalanche of boulders.

Panic rose in Celia as he spoke, but instead of letting it take over, she focused on the headache, the familiar thumps of pain against the inside of her skull. She welcomed each bolt, each torturous stab. They grounded her, reminded her of . . . Anya.

Of everything she'd already lost.

And what she could gain.

She closed the gap between them, stopping only when she was within arm's reach, and looked up. Damn, he was tall. His suit was perfectly cut, the buttons sparkling strangely, as if they were made of gems rather than metal. His features were angled and cunning, his chestnut hair speckled with gray that served to highlight his youth rather than detract from it.

Celia's gaze darted to his hands: long-fingered, slim, and

fine, unused to work. He looked very much like he belonged on a throne — folding the long lines of his thick skirt over crossed legs and sitting back disinterestedly, burdened by the demands of his people.

Celia tried to commit every angle of his face, clothing, features, and tenor to memory in case he managed to disappear on her again.

He took a step even closer, his slender frame towering a full head and half over her. So close, she could see flecks of something moving in his irises: a tornado of variegated greens and browns, like fresh leaves mixed in a compost pile but flecked with bursts of moving darkness, like imploding stars.

"So are you going to come in?" he asked. He smiled, and the movement in his eyes disappeared, the black swirls resting on the greens and browns so they looked like normal eyes again.

She must have imagined it. A trick of the light.

Still, she hesitated.

"Rest easy about your friend, Celia. He's safe and sound in your room at the inn, but he is in for a mighty frustrating day if he tries to find this place again."

Celia exhaled. Nodded.

And stepped through the door.

CHAPTER 6

As Celia followed Halcyon, no words passed between them. She didn't know what to say now, but instinct told her to shush and let him lead. She was dealing with a specter, a phantom. His town loved him so much they performed flawlessly . . . as if they really didn't know what he looked like and weren't acting at all.

And here Celia was, following him into the deep recesses of some secret place.

The brightly lit hallway had rows of closed doors on either side, each a bright cherry color that matched the main door, but these were rimmed with white carved borders. Masterfully crafted wrought iron sconces at the apex of every door were each of a different design: a tangle of ivy, a carnation, a rose, and, of course, wisteria. Celia had never seen such attention to detail, and she knew that whichever blacksmith had been commissioned to make them had devoted the better part of their life to the task. Everything about Halcyon whispered elegance: his clothes, his manner, his surroundings, his appreciation for the beautiful for beauty's sake. She had a feeling that not many had walked this hall, which meant that every gorgeous detail was for his enjoyment only, as if he couldn't stand the thought of living alongside anything other than perfection.

Large paintings hung at regular intervals, each illuminated with its own light angled just so. Many of them featured Halcyon himself, but most were portraits of another person: tall, as elegant and refined as Halcyon in their bearing, and although their clothing and hairstyle changed dramatically between portraits, they always wore the same expression, with sharp, calculating eyes that seemed to bore into Celia as she passed. Whoever that person was, they were important enough to Halcyon that he looked upon their image every few steps. Judging by some of the racier depictions, the two were lovers, but Celia didn't recognize them as any of the Wisterians she'd encountered over the past few days. Halcyon must have spent a fortune commissioning all those portraits, and Celia was simultaneously creeped out by that devotion and intrigued by it.

Even the floor was a masterpiece: a complex parquet that somehow muffled footsteps and cushioned her feet, as if she were floating. Like a ghost. Following another ghost.

Insults burst onto her tongue about pointlessness, wasted money, and arrogance, but each one died before springing out. She stared at Halcyon's back as they floated along—the nape of his neck where his hair rested, the multiple colors in his tenor, the stiff set of his shoulders—and knew that anything she said would bounce right off of him. He didn't care for her or anyone else's opinion, that much was abundantly clear.

He turned his head, offering his profile. "Are you wondering what's on the other side of these doors?"

"I'm guessing" — she pointed to a few as they passed by — "armory, library, aviary, and . . ." She met his eyes and held on. "Bordello?"

He turned away first. "Amazingly, two out of your four guesses are right." But he didn't mention which ones.

Celia wondered which door Lyric had disappeared behind, because they were nowhere to be seen.

At the far end of the hallway, double doors stretched all the way to the ceiling and touched both walls. Positive that this was their final destination, Celia had her hand on the doorknob — which was crafted in a sunflower shape that would have matched Lyric's tattoo perfectly — before realizing that Halcyon was opening a door to their right.

It swung open wide, and she could see nothing inside but blackness. He turned to face her, the slight smirk on his face falling off completely when he noticed where her hand rested. "Never," he said as she dropped her grip on the sunflower doorknob. "Never go in there."

She laughed off the chill in his tone. "Ah, so *that's* the bordello."

He gestured for her to go into the open room, and as she passed him, she felt the warmth of his body melting the chill. Almost to the point of burning her. "Your playthings are safe from me," she said. "Don't worry."

Celia didn't even register that he moved. Without warning, Halcyon loomed above her. Her back was pressed painfully into the door frame, and her breathing came out in clutching gasps, as if she were emerging from the familiar water torture of the temple. So close, she couldn't escape the swirling in his eyes, the vortex, the flecks like a dying constellation. The heat was unbearable, all air disappeared, and she would have collapsed to the floor if not for the strong hand pressing her shoulder into the doorjamb and pinning her painfully in place.

"You're a guest in my home," he whispered. The darkness from the open door melted around her, swallowing up the hallway, the bright lights, the cherry and white trimmed doors, until nothing remained but the swirling darkness of his eyes: black on black. "You'd be wise not to forget that."

Celia's eyes bulged from lack of air, her hands clawed at her throat. She didn't remember the moment Halcyon released her, only that she felt him there and then felt him not-there, a few steps away and beckoning again into the dark room, the hallway as normal around her. She didn't gasp the air into her screaming lungs, because her lungs weren't screaming.

Warily, she eyed him, reaching her hand up to the spot on her shoulder where she'd felt pinned to the doorframe. Had he even touched her, or had that been part of another illusion? No wonder Griffin was impressed—as the plague doctor, he created a special purple and blue fire, he levitated, he seduced like a siren—yet this was another level of performance altogether. But to what end? And why involve the entire town?

Oh, Celia . . . her mind bees whispered, trying to get her attention again. Where Griffin had opted to believe the rational explanation, Celia's bees had only gotten louder and more persistent. *What if this isn't a performance at all?*

Halcyon's lips cocked up—not a smile, maybe a smirk—as if he could understand her thoughts. His eyes still seemed to hold those specks of unnatural darkness, undulating and pulsing, but nothing like the swirling, terrible vortex of moments before.

She stepped past him and into the dark room.

It took only seconds for her eyes to adjust. Like emerging from thick fog, the room materialized outward as a series of lamps flickered to life in a circular pattern. First she saw the floor under her feet, the same parquet as the hallway. Then more lamps lit up a few surfaces: tables and desks piled with books; glass containers and vials, some full of various liquids and some empty, many of them with suspended dead creatures inside. Then the sconces on the far walls illuminated lines of bookcases, art supplies—canvases, blocks of marble, and a pottery wheel—and paintings and art of various mediums and with different subject matter: landscapes, sculptures of faces, textile art, more images of the person in the hallway portraits, and bizarre pieces that were more color than substance. The room danced from the light of a dozen different lamps now, each casting a globe of pale, pleasant light around them and meeting so that, while not overly bright, nothing was in darkness.

It felt as if it should be chaos, so much in one space, but everything was organized with precision. It wasn't the contents of the studio that struck her as much as the methodical *rightness* of everything having a place. She knew nothing about what she was actually looking at or what purpose most of those things would serve, but if Halcyon told her to find a flint, or a blue book, or lamp oil, or a thick piece of parchment made from layers of onionskin, she had no doubt she'd be able to find any random thing with little trouble. The space made nothing but sense to her.

She almost forgot about the door with the sunflower doorknob, Halcyon's menace when she'd almost opened it, the feeling of drowning.

Almost.

Halcyon swept over to a large, puffy lounge chair, looking as soft as feathers, but instead of folding himself into it, he perched on the edge, rested his elbows on his legs, and leaned forward with his hands clasped.

Whatever peace Celia had felt being surrounded by such a lulling, familiar space disappeared, and she was back in the hallway, pressed up against the doorjamb. From panic to peace back to panic again. But Halcyon was clearly waiting for her in the puffy chair, not choking her, not pressing, the smirk on his face brash and cold, his large, slender hands pressing together slightly in a delicate dance of fingers as he waited.

She knew with certainty she could not mess this up. There would be no second chance with Halcyon. There would be no take-backs or do-overs. Everything about his bearing showed that he was humoring her, that he didn't expect anything more from her than a bit of entertainment.

Certainly not that she would surprise him.

You know what to do, Celia's bees whispered. *You've dealt with big egos and people stuffed with self-importance before.*

There were other seats in the room—stools and another reading chair in the corner—but with steps surer than she felt, Celia floated across the parquet and melted down until she was sitting in front of him, legs crossed, like a child at story time. She knew from her time with the mistico that the best way to approach an inflated sense of self is to pretend to bow to it, so people in positions of power don't see you as a threat. His eyes widened for a moment, but he patiently waited for her to speak.

Trouble was, Celia didn't know what to say. Her tongue stuck on a hundred different questions. *How did you survive the Touch? What's your history with Diavala? Why is Wisteria so strange, and what do you have to do with that? Who, exactly, are you?*

But first and foremost she had to earn Halcyon's trust.

Swallowing, beginning to sweat, she looked up at his face and examined every line—the sweep of his eyebrows, the cut of his jaw, his totally normal eyes that he could make look not-normal. Now that she'd seen the vortex he could turn them into, this regular, placid movement within their green depths was almost appealing. Almost attractive.

Almost.

There were a lot of *almost*s about him.

Almost human, but not quite . . . her bees whispered, and Celia commanded them to stop helping.

Carefully planning her words, watching his eyes for a reaction, Celia finally settled on, "Why did the tattoo finally get your attention?"

"Ah," he said, leaning back, as if that were precisely the question he'd been expecting. He rubbed his face with his hands and sighed dramatically, his poise evaporating into a gesture of melodrama: legs spread under the leather of his skirt, arms flopping down over the armrests, spine curved into the back of the chair. "Now, that *is* a good question, isn't it?" Abruptly, he stood and walked around Celia to one of the worktables. On top sat rows of bottles, assembled from tiny to large, each filled with a rainbow of colorful liquids.

Celia unfolded herself and joined him.

"Take the contents of this jar, and add two drops to this one." He handed her the required bottles as she cocked an eyebrow. What did this have to do with anything? Not willing to risk annoying him, she followed his instructions.

A flat-bottomed translucent jar, ornately decorated with etchings, rimmed with gold, and almost as big as Celia's head, sat on the table, filled with something that looked like water. Using an eyedropper, she carefully added two drops of a green, slimy substance from a much smaller bottle. Neither had a scent that she could detect, but as soon as the liquids merged, a plume of gray mist rose up, smelling so strongly of rot that Celia gagged and let go of the eyedropper. It clattered to the table as she put her head between her knees and tried not to throw up.

"Holy hell, that is vile." She couldn't stop gagging, the smell crawling up her nostrils and staying there.

Halcyon laughed—a stormy sound, full of broken branches and vicious wind this time—and she wondered if there was a version of his laugh that didn't sound like it wanted to kill her. "That it is," he said. "Lyric once told me they thought it smelled like the devil's ass, and though I haven't personally smelled the devil's ass myself, I bet they're right."

Celia tilted her head toward him without raising it, still not trusting her stomach and not wanting to get another whiff of that stench. It would do her in.

Halcyon stood, spine straight, shoulders back, chin tilted up, and—with his elegant pianist's forefinger and thumb—plugging his nose.

A laugh jumped out of Celia before she could stop it. "I've never seen someone so dignified look so undignified."

"Well"—he kept his nose plugged so his words came out nasally—"The scent of the devil's ass makes fools of us all."

She laughed harder, not trusting the sound of it and hating how it felt, but unable to stop. Delirium, maybe, from the stench. She followed his lead and plugged her nose before rising. "You should have some spare clothespins lying around."

"I wanted to see your reaction." He inhaled through his mouth, held his breath, and reached under the bench for a thick bandanna, tying it around the lower half of his face. Above the midnight-blue cloth, only his eyes were visible, the swirls in them pulsing in a steady beat, maybe matching his heart. He cocked his head toward where he'd found it, indicating that she could help herself. There was an army of thick bandannas, ready for use.

"Wow, that was low," she said.

He nodded, appreciating her look of outrage. "You have no idea how surprised I am that you didn't vomit. If I was a gambler, I'd have lost a fortune." His voice was now muffled slightly, softened.

As she tied the bandanna around her face, the terrible stench gave way to a new smell: the tender sweetness of wisteria in full bloom, pleasant and subtle, like vanilla or honey. The bandanna wasn't only a barrier, it was infused with the scent, refusing to let anything else win against it.

"Better?" he asked. By the way his eyes crinkled in the corners, Celia could tell that his smile was wide under the cloth. It was basic merriment, a shared joke between them.

Normal enough to startle her.

She cleared her throat and turned to the infusion on the bench, gesturing with a waving hand. "So? What are we doing here?"

"You've just helped create a poison that will kill a person in less than a minute. All it takes is one drop — on the tongue preferably, but on the skin works as well — and they skitter toward the afterlife like a rat escaping to the sewers."

Halcyon said this with such a charming lilt to his voice, the corners of his eyes still crinkled, that it took a long moment before Celia registered the meaning of his words.

"What?" She backed up a step.

Still smiling from behind his bandanna, he said, "I simply wanted to let you know I'm no fool. I know why you came, and I won't allow it." He gestured toward the poison with his slim fingers, as if she'd missed his threat.

Celia swallowed, looking from the jar on the counter to Halcyon and back again. He'd said one drop was enough. "I don't know what you're talking about. What won't you allow? I came to talk to you about the fall of the Divine—"

"You said that already," he said, stepping forward. "But I know what you're truly after." And this time, when his slender fingers gestured around the room, they pointed at a gilded box.

Celia backed up and nudged another table with her hip in her haste, causing some glasses to clink against each other.

Her eyes wanted to snap back to his, demand an answer, but she couldn't look away from the box. All that was left was rising panic. Her breathing tempo increased, the pain behind her eyes throbbed, and she was close to running.

It was the Chest Majestic.

But that was impossible. They'd smashed it. They'd destroyed the terrible ink inside.

Leaving her, Halcyon took three strides and grabbed it, hefting it in his arms as if it weighed nothing. Opening the lid, he all but shoved it under her nose, not letting her recoil the way she wanted to, forcing her to look inside.

"This isn't what you came for?" he said. "Are you sure, Celia Sand? Because I know a lot more about you than you think I do." But his voice was far away, so far away she could barely hear him.

Inside the Chest Majestic, the substance was dark, sticky, and thick, something resembling molasses. It moved within the chest of its own volition, turning itself over and swirling around. The last time she'd seen Divine ink was when it had stained the stage in Asura, leaking out of Anya's body along with her blood. Anya lying in a pool of it, Celia trying to soak it up with her dress in a single-minded pursuit to get it as far away from Anya as possible.

"Where did you get it?" Celia shut her eyes tight, the throbbing in her temple beating to the same tempo as the thick, undulating glob, as if it moved to her pain, danced to her grief. *How did he get it?!* Her thoughts rose to a shriek, and when she opened her eyes, she found herself on the other side of the room, clutching the back of Halcyon's puffy armchair and hiding behind it, as if to keep a hefty barrier between her and the substance of her nightmares.

From above the dark bandanna Halcyon's now-frowning eyes bore into her, but he'd placed the chest on the workbench beside the jar of poison and had moved to block her view of both with his body. Whether he did it as a kindness or unintentionally, Celia wasn't sure.

"The reason the tattoo got my attention, Celia"—he still sounded far away, the chair between them acting like a boundary between reality and nightmare—"is that the ink is my life's work. And when your life's work shows up on your arm unannounced, taunting you, demanding answers, when someone has the gall to use it against you, well, let's just say I took notice." He loomed bigger, as if his shadow were billowing out behind him like a black cape, blocking out the circles of light as Celia shrank down.

"This doesn't make any sense," she whispered. Her clutching hands let go of the back of the chair, and she sank to the floor, pressing her spine to the chair and curling around her knees. Where was Anny now? Anny, who could always tell her which way was up and which was down.

The ink had so much power: Diavala had used it to take over a nation. An entire religion had been born from its blackness, generations of people manipulated by its messages. When they'd taken down the religion, when Profeta had fallen because of the sacrifices of Vincent and Anya and countless others along the way, the ink should have disappeared. The Chest Majestic, the one and only source and the only container that could hold it, had been smashed spectacularly weeks ago. Nothing but the ink in inkling veins should have remained—Anya had given her life for that.

But it was all a lie.

"You can stop panicking, Celia. I'm not going to pour it down your throat." So far away, so muted. But it sounded like he'd considered it.

Everything had flown away from her. Every consideration,

every thought, every drop of control, all reason. Anya had died to get rid of the ink, to strip away Diavala's power, and yet there was more ink.

Why? What did it mean, this was his life's work? Had he and Diavala worked together? He seemed to care so little for power, except what he had here in one little beautiful town. So what did the ink do for him?

Breathing heavily, gasping for air, Celia pulled the wisteria-infused bandanna down from her face, noticing how damp it was from sweat or tears, or both. Immediately, she gagged. The smell of the freshly mixed poison, even from so far away, was enough to make her eyes water. Part of her was amazed that she had the faculties left to pull the bandanna back up.

Trying to summon Griffin (*find me, I don't know what to do*) and trying to harness Anya (*I need you, I need you, I need you*), Celia peeked around the side of the chair. Maybe her headaches were giving her hallucinations. Maybe her broken mind had shattered so badly the cracks were filling with madness.

Halcyon's long, lean form was bent slightly at the waist as he peered into the glass container, examining the deadly poison they'd mixed together, his black bandanna tightly in place. He looked like he was reconsidering its usefulness, as if her reaction had confused him and he wasn't one easily confused. His profile was so sharp—nose, cheekbones, chin—it was at risk of cutting anything that came close. Sparkles in his eyes reflected off the glass jar.

Still bent at the waist, he turned those eyes toward her again.

"Please stop cowering." He straightened, held out one of his long-fingered hands as if offering to help her rise from across the room. "I'm intrigued by you, your effort, wondering about your endgame. I'll be honest, I thought you were here to steal from me. But this reaction of yours tells me that I might have been wrong."

Halcyon took a step forward, then another, his hand still held out, his eyes above his bandanna still swirling and hinting at an abrasive smirk hiding under the cloth. "Unless you're such a good player that you can fool even me?" He clearly didn't think that was possible, which might have been the only thing that saved Celia from tasting a drop of that poison and fleeing to the afterlife like a rat.

The shadows behind him had retreated to normal shadows.

What do I do, Anny? In truth, it was a lot easier to stay quiet than to try talking. If she tried making a sound, she'd probably scream.

Halcyon stood above her, where she still cowered behind the chair. Only his lower legs were in her line of sight, heavy black skirt and fancy shoes. The fanciest shoes she'd ever seen; Dante would have swooned at their elegance. She didn't look up. Didn't take his hand when he offered it.

He fell with a *whomp* of extra flair into the armchair again. "This is taking a tad bit longer than I expected. You're walking a fine line between intrigue and irritation with me, Celia, in case that unsticks your tongue." She probably imagined it, but she could feel his body heat through the heavy plush chair. His arms flopped over the side, long fingers dangling in front of her, palms open and pointing up at the ceiling in a relaxed curl.

"I don't understand how you have Divine ink," she said. Her hands were cursed with tremors, and she clutched her fingers, trying to still their shaking.

He scoffed. "Please, Celia. Of anyone, you know the Divine is not divine in the least. Stop playing games."

She untangled herself and, not looking at Halcyon, crept slowly around the chair, toward the open chest on the bench. The fact that it swirled so close, black and viscous, with only a container holding it at bay from seeking out a host, terrified her in a way she couldn't put into words.

"You should be honored," he said. "Not even Illinia's great ruler — who is it now? Erannio? —"

"Vacilando," she responded absently. How isolated was this place, that he didn't know Vacilando's name? She'd ruled for more than two decades.

One foot in front of the other. The ink beckoned her even as it repulsed her.

"Right, Vacilando," he said. "Not even she knows I have this."

With her trembling hands weaving together in front of her, Celia bent toward the swirling ink, adjusting her bandanna and focusing on the scent of wisteria.

"But one creature does know, doesn't she?" he said slowly. "One immortal devil who you've had some recent dealings with . . ."

When Celia was close enough to confirm that it was indeed Divine ink, it made her insides curl. Swiveling away, she went back to her place at Halcyon's feet.

"I can see why you'd jump to the conclusion you did," Celia said. "But you can keep your poison well stoppered. I'm certainly not here to steal from you."

"Aren't you wondering what I do with it?" Halcyon said.

Celia shook her head, but her heart rate jumped, fluttering like a hummingbird against her ribs. What Griffin had assumed were stage tricks she now knew were ink tricks: the strange way the town turned itself around, the manufactured windstorm, his swirling eyes.

She'd seen the ink's power. She'd lived with it for ten years. If a tiny bit of ink on someone's ankle or chest or back could affect the course of their lives forever, what could someone with a full chest of it do? Maybe they could ensorcell an entire town or make wisteria bloom year round. Maybe they could disguise the entrance to their home, make someone disappear, create a vicious storm.

If Celia could command the ink in her blood away, pull it back, change the shape, and manipulate it out into the world as a tattoo, she could only imagine how far it could go when someone made it his life's work.

But damned if she said any of that out loud.

Halcyon tilted his head. "I think you might have figured it out . . ." he said. "Your face gives everything away."

Crap. She bit her lip and dropped her gaze, a flush rising up her neck. "I think it's the fuel for your—" She paused, unsure how to continue. *Fuel* wasn't the right word: her tattoos weren't fueled by ink, they *were* the ink. She started over again. "I think the ink is the substance of your illusions. And we're in the middle of a bunch of them."

"Interesting." His smile widened. "And correct."

A flare of pride burst in her chest . . . for being clever, not from his praise.

She sat there in front of his fancy shoes and tried to sort through her thousands of questions for the ones that would give her what she wanted the most.

"I didn't come for anything to do with . . . *that*," she said, flicking her fingers toward the chest. If he thought she'd come to steal it, she wanted to put his mind at ease immediately. Not only was the threat of lethal poisoning still permeating the air, but handling the ink again was the last thing she wanted. "But I know you have some history with the one everyone called the Divine. That's why I'm here."

He sighed, as if sorry to abandon the topic of the ink so quickly. "Out of curiosity," he said, leaning forward, "what did she tell you about me?"

Diavala had threatened Griffin with torture to make sure Celia didn't disclose where she was, but even if she hadn't, Celia would have kept her location secret. Everything they knew about Halcyon had come from Diavala's point of view—Celia needed to know more from Halcyon's before playing her hand.

"Not much, truthfully. I found your name on the Roll of Saints as the only person who'd survived the Touch, and from my interaction with Dia — the Divine," she corrected, "I know she fears you. Other than that, I had no idea what I was walking into here."

Halcyon looked disappointed. He might care nothing for fame, living so apart from the rest of society in this perfect town, but it looked like he wouldn't have minded being the topic of a *little* gossip.

He leaned back, lacing his fingers together in front of his face. "I know all about your convincing act, the story you sold to all of Illinia about the Divine's death. I also know it was a hoax. You might not have come here to steal the power of the ink as I first thought, but I fear our goals are still fundamentally at odds. If you want to finish what you started in Asura — kill her, punish her, whatever revenge you've daydreamed about — that's your business. She's scared of me for good reason, and I *could* help you, but I have no interest in getting involved in this. I dealt with her three years ago, and I'm enjoying my freedom immensely."

Celia inhaled hard and looked at her hands, wringing themselves into knots in her lap. She'd been foolish to think that finding him would translate to unconditional help.

"She's still out there," Celia said, "and she wants revenge for what I did to her and her religion. She'll take it out on everyone I love, one by one. You're right that I want to finish what

I started in Asura, but my only goal is to make sure she never hurts anyone ever again. If you can just tell me how to save my people from the Touch, I'll leave and never bother you again."

His eyebrows arched, skeptical. "No revenge? Are you sure? I told you I know what happened between you."

"That's not why I came," Celia said, pressing her lips together. *Although revenge would be nice* sat there on the tip of her tongue.

Halcyon assessed her and nodded slightly, though it didn't look as if she'd fooled him. Tap-tap-tappity tapping his fingers on the arm of the chair, he met her eyes.

He'd said he didn't want to get involved with Diavala again, and Celia had nothing to offer him; if their dynamic was a scale, she was underground while he was among the stars. What could she possibly offer him to balance it out?

Perhaps the same thing that had gotten his attention.

The ink in her blood.

She closed her eyes and whispered, "I'll do anything." That phrase felt familiar on her tongue, as if she'd said it to him before, recently.

"Anything . . ." He said the word slowly, quietly, and she imagined his steepled fingers tapping together for emphasis. It took him a long time to answer, and as she waited in silence and darkness, her headache screamed back with force. There were so many thoughts skittering around in her head that her bees had passed out, mumbling and kicking each other in a stupor.

"I don't have any skills beyond inking, but they're the stuff of legend now," she said, forcing herself to open her eyes and meet his.

"But clearly you hate it," he countered. "And I'm trying really hard not to take that personally."

"I do," she admitted. "But when I said *anything,* I meant it."

Surely skilled inklings didn't come through Wisteria often, if ever, and to someone who'd made the ink his life's work, her one talent had to be appealing.

"What you did in Asura was impressive," Halcyon finally said. "Your talents with the ink, even without any real training, show promise . . ."

She waited, holding her breath.

"I travel a lot, and it would be nice to have someone look after Wisteria while I'm away. Fix roof tiles after storms, for example, tend the flowers, and make sure my people stay content. A caretaker, if you will. But you must understand by now that Wisteria needs a special kind of caretaker. One who has mastered all aspects of the ink and knows how to apply them in accordance with a specific artistic vision."

Tears prickled at her eyes. A few moments ago she'd thought he might be drawn to having a messenger or a town tattoo artist. Of all the solutions to save Griffin and others from Diavala's Touch, this was the most vile one imaginable. Everything they'd done against the ink, and now she'd have to use it to sustain more lies?

"What I'm asking is no small thing, Celia Sand. It would take a commitment of the lifetime variety, one you couldn't walk away from. But more important, it would involve you getting over your deep revulsion and using the ink in a number of ways. I think you're willing to offer the first—you seem desperate enough to save your friends, even at your own expense—but the second?" He tapped his fingers along the length of the armrest, playing an unheard symphony.

He was right. She'd lived her entire life in a prison, and Wisteria was a far prettier one than the temple. Running a town when he was away was a small price to pay to know that Griffin would be safe from Diavala's wrath. She would never see the stars in Kinallen, but she'd never deserved Kinallen to begin with.

He was also right about the second part being far more loathsome an idea to her. "So that I'm perfectly clear—" she said. "I have to prove myself to you. Then, in exchange for pledging my life to taking care of Wisteria, you will tell me how you survived the Divine's possession? And it's not some unique, impossible thing—your answer will be helpful, and it will protect my people from the Touch. No tricks?"

He nodded. "Much like the poison we made together only moments ago, it's a little of this and a little of that, mixed together into a tea. It's not painless, but it will buffer the mind against an onslaught of memories. Protection and immunity from a brain flood, so to speak. I'll even mix the dose myself. In addition to being dashingly handsome, infinitely clever, and remarkably creative, I'm also a passable apothecary."

Well, that sounded perfect, which made Celia instantly suspicious.

"I'll give you a day to think about it," he said. "Either you show up here tomorrow and we get to work, or you leave Wisteria with your beautiful friend and all your problems, and never look back."

He stood abruptly, towering over her. She felt a tingling in her center that had nothing to do with anxiety or elation, and when she looked down, her hands were a little less defined, a little erased.

"Understand, this is a unique courtesy I'm offering you, Celia," Halcyon said. "I don't give everyone the opportunity to simply walk away."

Just before she disappeared completely, she looked once more at the jar of lethal poison and the chest of Divine ink next to it.

She imagined the ink waving at her with long, beckoning fingers.

INTERLUDE

"Stop pacing, plague doctor," Diavala growled. *"You're making me dizzy."*

The plague doctor looked through the front window of the inn just in time to see Davi glance quickly away, caught staring. Earlier, when he'd asked her for a map of Wisteria, she'd stared at him with a look of *What is this* map *thing you speak of?* So rather than go in circles (which he'd already done for an hour), he paced a trail back and forth in front of the inn, waiting for Celia to return.

He'd never been fooled this way before. No sleight of hand, mirror trick, or misdirection had ever confused him for more than a few minutes. Ever since he was six years old, his one talent had been seeing through any stage trick. When Celia and Anya had swindled most of Illinia (and, embarrassingly, most of his own theater troupe) with their Devil in the Bell Jar show, he'd known that they were somehow communicating with their ink, even though he'd understood next to nothing about how their ink magic worked.

But he had no idea how he'd been *there* only to end up *here*. It was like an invisible Obi the Giant — the hero of Bicklandian folktales — had come along, plucked him up in his massive hand, and set him down in a different spot. But Obi wasn't invisible, so even that unlikely scenario couldn't be true.

Halcyon Ronnea had managed to stump him, and it was driving him to distraction.

"Ah! Michali!" The plague doctor bellowed a greeting across the street, grateful that a diversion decided to walk by. The town's tailor, a tall, reedy soul who always wore as much color as possible, inclined their head and sauntered over. Their wheatlike hair—an unusual color in Illinia—flowed down to their waist, and every time the plague doctor had seen them, they'd had it loose. The two of them had bonded the day before over a love of leather, and Michali had offered to mend the plague doctor's favorite pants free of charge. A fast friendship was forming, when you could bond over leather.

Michali clapped him on the back, matching the plague doctor's grin with one made of all teeth. "You look worried, my friend," they said. "What plagues you?" Michali flipped their hair over their shoulder and chuckled at the pun. The plague doctor had shown Michali his mask the first day and they'd been enthralled by the craftsmanship.

The plague doctor smiled wider. As much as he loathed the reason for their visit to Wisteria, the townspeople were lovely. How had he and Kitty Kay never thought to veer off the main road with the Rabble Mob and perform there? It was as if invisible Obi guarded the place well, warding off visitors without their even knowing. "You have a certain flair that would fit so well with Rovers," he said. "Tell me, do you like Commedia?"

Michali shrugged. "I might like it more if so many story lines didn't extol Profeta."

Then they hadn't seen a Rabble Mob show. "Not a believer?"

Michali huffed and looked dramatically affronted, their light features pinched as if they'd tasted a sour cherry tart. "Do you take us for fools here? You'd be hard-pressed to find a more secular town in all of Illinia." They said it as if it were a point of fierce pride among the population, and the plague doctor imagined it on a playbill: *"Come! See the Rover troupe that doesn't Rove! The most secular town in all of Illinia beckons you to join their illusion!"*

The plague doctor felt Diavala's anger—only a simmer at first—surge with Michali's declaration. "I'm not a believer either," he said slowly. "But fools are those who think they know everything, not those who claim the unknowable."

Michali cocked their head, trying to puzzle out the plague doctor's meaning. Celia called it Riddlish, but to the plague doctor, his Riddlish words were often the ones he thought made the most sense. "I just mean," the plague doctor said, "that any soul who knows anything knows he doesn't know a thing."

Understanding dawned on Michali's sharp-featured face, and they laughed. "And any soul who knows nothing knows he knows everything," they added.

The plague doctor's smile widened. "Exactly so!" How was it he'd manage to find someone exceptionally fluent in Riddlish in such an isolated town?

After promising to deliver the pants to the shop later for mending, Michali left, their long hair swishing against their back as they walked away.

Diavala's irritation at Michali's secular views felt like a wasp's nest swarming inside him. He held up his hand, wondering if he could *see* his bones humming from the outside. Lately he'd felt her emotions so much more.

For someone who's existed a thousand years, the plague doctor thought to Diavala, *you're quite sensitive.*

"*Profeta is a religion of caring. Of love,*" Diavala said. "*You of all people understand what lies at the end of life. I know you see my work as the mercy it was.*"

He cursed out loud, startling the horse tied to a post nearby. Profeta reassured believers that they would get the afterlife they deserved: follow the ink, rest assured you're making the right choices, all will be rewarded.

He'd do anything to believe that what he did in life actually mattered, rather than to know that everyone got the same afterlife, regardless.

No reward for virtue, no punishment for sin.

Everyone gets the same helping of that same nothingness . . .

He shuddered, remembering that place for only a moment before he slammed that door shut.

It's so damned inconvenient that I can't lie to you, Diavala. If Celia ever found out that he sympathized with Diavala's intent, she'd never speak to him again.

But if the plague doctor was tired of one thing, it was of Diavala acting like a blameless victim. *I think you might have started in a good place, but that doesn't discount that you ordered throats slit and unwavering obedience.* He resumed his pacing after scanning the side streets for Celia.

"You know so little about me. I am entirely separate from what the religion Profeta became. I didn't tell the mistico to be so harsh. I didn't tell them to mercy kill those with the Touch."

At any point, you could have stopped it, the plague doctor pointed out.

"I couldn't. Before I knew it, I had acolytes ready to do anything. You probably won't believe it, plague doctor, but the beginnings of Profeta had very little to do with me." She laughed without mirth, the sound echoing in his temples like tinny bells. *"I've been powerless for much of my own story."*

That resonated with the plague doctor more than he wanted to admit, but memories of Vincent screaming with the Touch were seared into him. Those pained screams, and those blades that silenced the screams of his dear friend. His first crush, years ago, which he'd never admitted to anyone, let alone Vincent himself, and now, infuriatingly, only Diavala knew about.

Diavala might have thought she was powerless, but she'd taken a lot of people down with her. *You still gave people the Touch,* he said, breathing through his sadness. *That was a power you wielded indiscriminately.*

Diavala didn't say anything for so long, the plague doctor thought their conversation was over. People began scurrying home for the supper hour, and the sun began to set. How long should he wait before getting truly alarmed? He trusted Celia, but he couldn't decide if it was a good thing or a bad thing that her conversation with Halcyon was stretching into the night.

He took some Kinallen powder out of his pouch and played with a small flame, bouncing it in his palm as he paced. The purple and blue fire helped chase away dark thoughts and sad memories.

"Not indiscriminately," Diavala finally said. *"Never indiscriminately. I wasn't always this way."* Diavala was uncharacteristically quiet, as if she were confiding in him.

The plague doctor snatched the flame from the air and snuffed it out, his fist as hard as a stone. *Are you talking about your life? Your human life, before you . . . changed?*

He pushed against part of the redbrick wall of the inn and slid down, ripping the fabric of his jacket and giving Michali another thing to mend.

"My human life was as short as a blink. No, I'm talking about the beginnings of my curse."

He'd never thought about the origins of her body-stealing powers; she was just Diavala: a nuisance that would eventually drive him mad and kill him. But he had to admit he was intrigued, and what an excellent name for a Commedia production: *The Curse of Diavala* — the *Curse of the Divine* . . .

"At first I stayed in every body until they died of natural causes," she whispered. *"I couldn't control where my soul went next. It was always the closest body. So I lived and then died with one person, then lived and died with the next. There was no decision on my part, and because I didn't leave them until the end, no one wailed with the Touch. But take the time to understand, for a moment, that I wasn't just inside their body. I was also inside their mind. I felt everything they did."*

For the first time, the plague doctor saw the child she must have been so long ago. Her eyes were wide. They were scared. According to Profetan doctrine, she'd been only ten or so when she'd been killed, so the curse that brought her back to life — of a sort — had been inflicted on someone considerably younger than himself.

Diavala had died over and over again. He'd only

died once, and he was the first to admit it had all but wrecked him.

Despite the surge of sympathy he'd briefly felt, the plague doctor couldn't keep the scorn out of his thoughts. *But at some point you decided it was better to have control.* Even if the Touch was an unintended consequence of leaving a body before their time, it was still a choice she'd made, over and over.

Torturing Vincent had been a choice. Not keeping the mistico from slashing his throat had been a choice.

This Curse of the Divine is the curse of everyone who's ever encountered you, he said, opening his hands and lighting more Kinallen powder. The merry flame danced in his trembling hands. *It's my curse now. It's Celia's. It's a curse with a long trail of bodies and mourners.*

Without any warning—like casting open a window to let in the breeze—the barricade between their minds came down and Diavala cycled through a series of her memories. Some were blurred with the passage of time, some were crisp brands that would never fade. But all of them were so viciously inside him, they could have been his own memories. The flow of Diavala's consciousness trying to penetrate his had been a trickle before. Now it was a flood. She was him, and he was her.

The flame snuffed out with his gasp.

In a moment, he lived death upon death: lung infections that took a long time to squeeze out that last breath, accidents with horses, or falls that had everything to do with fate, even death by poison, in one person who'd made one too many enemies.

And with them, he felt their fear of the unknown, he felt every grief and regret.

Then a plague struck.

His soul went from sufferer to sufferer, death after death, all in quick succession. No lapses without pain. No family.

All around him, over and over again, only death.

"What was the purpose of all that suffering?" Diavala asked, letting him go.

He gasped again, putting his hands to his eyes and ducking his head to his knees, panting. *It was the plague that broke you,* he said. Maybe she would have continued on living with each soul until their natural passing, if not for that unnamed plague, centuries ago. Even though she'd closed the window between their minds again, he still smelled the stench of rotten flesh, felt the despair of parents holding their dead babies, knew the horror of eyeballs that oozed blood. In one of her memories, a plague doctor with a mask exactly like his had bowed his head and offered a lily — the flower of death — before walking away. And she'd turned away from the gift because she'd already received so many lilies before.

"Maybe you'll see now, plague doctor, why I turned my curse into something Divine," Diavala said. *"I stepped*

forward and claimed my role as deity. I vowed to bring comfort to those who needed it. Through Profeta, I gave people hope. In me and those tattoos, they found solace. A few casualties will never outweigh the good I did for thousands upon thousands of souls."

Still reeling from the onslaught, his heart thundering fast, the plague doctor brought out his purple and blue fire again, tossing it up and down in his palm like a feather, trying to calm down. The purple was like the shadows under grieving eyes, the blue was like the lips of the dead . . .

He snuffed it out again and stood. Scattered. Shaking. It was taking too long for him to feel like a plague doctor again. He flicked out his hands and jumped up and down in place, briefly considering running. If he ran fast and far enough, maybe he could outrun Diavala. He had youth on his side, after all.

That thought made him laugh, earning another concerned look from Davi through the window of the inn.

No, he thought, still jumping. *You'll never convince me that Profeta was more good than bad.*

Maybe Diavala had started out with good intentions —he could certainly see the appeal of fervently believing the afterlife wasn't a terrifying place—but that couldn't erase what Diavala had done, going from host to host, adopting their lives, taking over. If he entertained the idea that Profeta was a blessing for Illinia, that would cast him and Celia in the roles of villains for bringing it down.

That wouldn't do.

You're selfish, he said. *You should have suffered your curse alone and kept right on dying with everyone.*

That would be his final judgment. For Vincent.

He had no doubt he would be Diavala's next casualty, and he dreaded everything about the place he would be visiting again soon, but he would rather die a thousand deaths than torture innocent souls with madness.

As if sighing, her thoughts weary, Diavala said, *"Well, I hope you don't have to face that choice, plague doctor. I hope you never realize what a bullshit sentiment that is."*

The plague doctor barked out another laugh—a discordant sound to the wasps still rattling around inside him—as Diavala retreated.

What an odd thing for her to say. Not real and upside down.

Then he did what he did best when he was confused.

He smiled.

CHAPTER 7

CELIA APPEARED IN FRONT OF THE OUTSIDE INN. THEIR horse, Aaro, nickered with faint alarm and tugged at his hitch, confused about where she'd come from. *Same, Aaro, same.*

She didn't know what to make of the meeting with Halcyon. Her body tingled with adrenaline—the crash was coming—because it had been so much more than she'd expected. In hindsight, following him into his home had been an exercise in stupidity.

Knowing what she knew now, she could have just as easily not come out. Anyone with the ability to rearrange a town at will, move people from one place to another, and mix a lethal poison in a matter of seconds wasn't someone she ever wanted to upset.

It was also what made her zing with possibility. He'd confirmed in a handful of ways that he was more powerful than Diavala. That he had answers.

Celia had acted on impulse at every juncture of that meeting, following emotions rather than calculating responses, because there'd been literally no time to think. New information piled on top of new circumstance, and she'd gone from one step to the next without any thought to where the path would go.

You got lucky, her bees whispered. *From now on, beeeeeeeee smarter.*

She giggled, appreciating the pun, and then had to grab the hitching post so she didn't keel over, lightheaded from whatever had just happened.

Too bad his power came from the ink she hated so much.

"Celia?" Griffin bolted to standing; she hadn't seen him there, leaning against the front of the inn. "*Dia,* what happened?" he said, wrapping her up in a hug made of pure panic. "It's been hours. I thought Obi—"

"I'm fine. It worked out fine," she said, pushing him away and almost toppling over, still wobbly. She had thought Halcyon had made the town disappear, not *her.* A vortex of rearrangement, with her inside the eye of it, untouched. As if the town were a changing maze and he was in charge . . .

She could be in charge, if she agreed to his terms. She hated to admit it, but she was curious as to how he'd done it. She could wrap her mind around illusions, even complicated ones, but transporting a person from one spot to another seemed more akin to folktale magic than to illusion. How powerful was the ink, truly? How far did its capabilities stretch?

"Well? What did you find out? Can he help? How does he do his"—Griffin waved his hands in a poofing motion—"tricks?"

Griffin, in a bit of a state, grabbed her arms again and held on tight, as if to make sure she didn't dematerialize again.

"What's wrong with you?" she asked. "I said everything was fine. Relax."

"Diavala said that if you didn't come back within the hour, you *wouldn't* come back, and it's so hard to ignore her when she's right inside your head—"

The smile fell off Celia's face. "Wait, you're *talking* to her?"

Griffin stepped back. "Don't you dare lecture me, Celia. It's not like I have much choice."

"When did this start?"

Griffin flushed at the accusation in her voice. When he spoke again, his voice trembled. "We both know where she stands. Nothing's changed. What I *don't* know is what you've been doing for the last three hours, why you smell so terrible, why you have a wild look in your eyes like you saw Obi the Giant himself, and whether or not the director in charge of Wisteria's stage is going to help us."

"It surely hasn't been three hours," she said. But the sun was a little too low on the horizon . . .

"Oh, *Dia*, save me," he muttered, looking to the sky. "Of all the things I just said, that's what you're going to focus on?"

As they walked around the back of the inn and up to their room, she stared at Griffin, wanting to tell him everything, tortured that she couldn't. Hoping a few details could appease him, she told him some of what had happened.

To anyone listening—to one creature in particular who was definitely listening—Celia had encountered an eccentric artist.

One who somehow had his own batch of Divine ink and had raised Diavala's wrath a few years ago because of it. One whose hatred for Diavala ran deep, but who wasn't at all interested in getting involved in Celia's current quagmire.

Most of that was true at least, but she said nothing of Halcyon agreeing to help her if she agreed to help him.

There, see? she told her bees. *I'm already being smarter.*

If Celia decided to stay, Diavala couldn't know about their true alliance until it was too late to do anything about it.

With every word, Griffin moved from panic to curiosity to revulsion and back again, cycling through every emotion just as Celia had. "The *ink*," he kept mumbling. As if that explained everything and nothing at the same time. "If he's not going to help us, we need to leave. Anya would hate this."

At any mention of Anya's name, Celia's stomach went into knots. "You think I don't know that?" she said.

Griffin trembled, his eyes shining fever-bright as he stared at her. And his reaction was merely at the idea of her *conversing* with someone who used the ink. How red would he be if he knew the rest?

"If Halcyon had told me how he survived the Touch, trust me, I would have led with that," Celia said. She had to sit down. Bare floor planks for a seat and hard bed for a backrest. The lies were starting again. Her life was made of them. "But this is a good start. I just need more time to convince him to help us."

More time as in by tomorrow, when she had to make a decision.

Griffin didn't look reassured by this in the least. "More time with someone who almost blew us out of town with a wind-storm? With someone who plays with the ink you supposedly hate so much like it's a toy?"

"The only person who's ever used the ink as a *toy* is currently the one I'm trying to get out of your head, Griffin. Diavala is the one who used the ink to manipulate most of the country. She's the one who used it to enslave people like me." Celia inhaled and puffed it out quickly. She needed time to think, not talk in circles. "Halcyon is a weirdo, a hermit, an eccentric, but it looks like all he does is use it for this town. We're here because *we* need *him*, remember? And he almost blew us out of town because he thought we were here to steal from him!"

Griffin stood over her, his hands resting on his hips, looking anything but convinced that this was the right move. His head cocked to the left, but his eyes were narrow slits. He looked as if he were debating whether to shake sense into her or haul her out of Wisteria over his shoulder like a sack of potatoes.

Did he see how all her reassuring words covered her unsaid ones? And more important, did Diavala?

Griffin ground his teeth. "Your stubbornness is infinite."

"Think about our options here," Celia said, trying to quell her building frustration. "None of them are good. But at least with Halcyon there's hope of more than just running forever." As the words left her lips, she realized they were for her more than for him.

If she didn't commit herself now, there was no hope at all. Diavala would live inside Griffin until he died, threatening and hurting him. Manipulating everything he did to suit her own ends.

Or Diavala might succeed in finding a way out of Griffin without harming Profeta's legacy. She could find a bounty hunter, someone who had no trouble slitting Griffin's throat when he started wailing with the Touch.

Either way, Diavala would then possess someone else after Griffin. Maybe she'd go after Zuni or Lupita or Dante, back at the temple. Maybe she would get Kitty Kay or Lilac or Seer Ostra from the Mob. She had a long list of people she hated nearly as much as Celia. On and on, she would continue, ruining lives indiscriminately along the way. And it would be forever. One day she might find a way of rising from the ashes like a phoenix and reclaiming her faithful devotees. She'd overcome the impossible before.

Time was on Diavala's side in this fight, and it always would be. If Celia walked away now, she was giving up. Who else would have the answers she needed—if not the only one who'd ever survived Diavala's possession, who knew things about her no one else did?

Celia's headache reared up again, fierce and terrible, and she had to lie down. Griffin didn't press her—she didn't have the energy for any more discussion anyway—and eventually his stressed-out mumbles transformed to humming before eventually falling into silence.

And yet, aggravatingly, she couldn't sleep. Too many thoughts swirling through her head, competing with the headache, which only grew as the night stretched on and on. It was always there, always present, but something about the meeting with Halcyon had fed it until she saw stars. Long after Griffin dozed in the next bed, Celia lay awake, her eyes pressed together tight, trying not to throw up from the pain.

She'd finally met Halcyon. After weeks of travel to find him and even longer pinning every hope she had on him, she'd finally met him . . . only to find him irrevocably tied to the thing she hated most in the world, aside from Diavala.

Celia whispered into the darkness of the room, the darkness behind her eyes, "Why does everything need to be so hard, Anny?" She felt like the world was spinning off its axis, trying to pull itself out from under her feet.

If Celia hadn't thought a tattoo might have caught Halcyon's attention, she would have lived out her days without ever using the ink in her blood again. She didn't need to. She didn't want to. But in order to continue down this path, she would have to work with the ink for the rest of her life. Could she do that?

Griffin was right, Anya would hate it.

From the moment that slim tattoo had wrapped around their ankles, she and Anya had been shackled. To rules, to punishments, to isolation. They'd been forced to spread the ink around in Diavala's name and to forward Diavala's goals. None of it had been their choice.

But, Anya whispered. *Is it really the ink we hated so much, or only how Diavala used it?*

Anya always had good points.

They'd used the ink to communicate, to decorate the Rabble Mob with meaningful art, and for their show, which had amazed and delighted people. None of it had hurt anyone.

Celia reached a hand toward the ceiling. "Thanks, Anny," she whispered. Celia would have to learn to live with the ink, but no one said she had to love it. And she certainly had a good reason: he was in the next bed.

Just as she'd made her decision, Griffin's breathing changed. From deep and even, the steady rise and fall of a peaceful sleep, to a shallow, hollow-sounding pant.

When Griffin whimpered, Celia sat up and looked at his sleeping form. It took many moments before her eyes adjusted, the faint moonlight coming in from the window not illuminating much beyond the outlines of vague shapes. He lay on his back, a tangle of blankets wound around his lower body, one arm flopped over his eyes, the other drooping off the edge of the bed. Griffin always slept like that: in some manner of disarray. He moved about like a fish out of water sometimes, tossing this way, settling, then tossing the other way, usually accompanied by weird sounds: fighting off monsters in his nightmares or enjoying luscious dreams. Then he'd settle again, peaceful, the monsters slayed for a time.

Celia had spent a lot of time alone with sleeping Griffin. It was almost easier. In the night, when they were each in another world, she felt she could finally be with him. It was the only time Diavala wasn't between them.

Another whimper, scared and sad. Celia was sitting at the

edge of her bed before making a decision. She was at the side of his bed next, looking down on his sprawled form. Lifting his tangled blanket, she tried to cover him again. The room was cool, the shirt and pants he slept in ragged and torn.

He exploded in a flash of movement, fighting off some invisible demon, crying out with a voice that didn't sound like his own. Eyes open but unseeing, he struggled against her soothing hands and *shh's* of comfort.

"It's okay. You're okay, Griffin. It's just a nightmare." But was he okay, really? She'd been so preoccupied that she realized she hadn't actually talked to him in forever.

Despite traveling alone with him for two weeks, she *missed* him.

Celia sat beside him as he panted and slowly emerged from the dreamworld. Tentatively, she put the flat of her hand on his back between his shoulder blades. She put her other hand on his chest, feeling between her palms every gasp of air his lungs tried to pull in, every flutter of his hard-thumping heart. His body was hot, damp from sweat despite the coolness of the room. He'd been struggling in that nightmare longer than she'd thought.

"Celia." He didn't look at her when he said her name, but pulled his knees up to his chest, wrapped trembling arms around them, and tucked his head down. "It was the plague."

She rubbed his back in small circles, put pressure on his chest, and rested her chin on his shoulder.

Just as Anya had always done for her.

"I'm here," she said. "You had a nightmare."

A slight nod from him without his looking up. In the dimness of the room, with the warmth of him seeping into her hands, Celia felt cocooned, safe. She was the one trying to give comfort, but she was receiving it as well. Not talking, not planning, not thinking, just breathing. Even her headache receded to a dull background roar.

Then a hoarse whisper. "That wasn't my nightmare."

She froze. "What do you mean?"

She knew what he meant, but didn't know what it meant. Was his mind becoming enmeshed with Diavala's now?

Griffin moaned, a shiver racing up his spine, then leaned into her closer. A space for secrets.

He shivered again, pulled the blankets up over them both, inviting her to lean back with him. She surprised herself by doing it, snuggling into his side like a puppy, with his arm wrapped around her, pulling the blanket up under her chin.

His hand absently stroked her back, fingers dancing along her shoulder and spine. She couldn't tell if his eyes were open or closed, but he seemed to be deep in thought.

The silence fell between them again, but it wasn't awkward. It wasn't loaded. Griffin gave her arm a squeeze, then tilted his head enough to press his lips to her forehead. It wasn't a kiss as much as a reminder of him.

So close together, with a prime front-row view, Celia watched his lips. They'd changed since Asura—no longer so subtle in their expressions—and she was still learning their new language.

"Devil's hell, Celia, you have to be careful," he whispered. "Don't promise him anything you can't deliver, keep your head low, don't make any decisions before talking to me first, and for—"

"I got it," she whispered back, putting her hand on the side of his neck and snuggling closer. "I'll be careful. I promise."

I promise to do everything I can to save you.

ACT 2

CHAPTER 8

THE GATE WITH THE 'NO TRESPASSING' SIGN WASN'T IN THE same place the next day. Celia stared at it, positive she'd passed this exact spot already—at least a dozen times—and it hadn't been there. After winding aimlessly up and down the alleys and roads on the north end of town for an hour, Celia had been about to give up and head back to the inn, hoping that Griffin had had more luck with his quest.

"I need to do something more useful than pace circles around the inn all day," he'd said. "Who is Lyric to him? Maybe an assistant? I'll try to get some information from them while you work on appealing to Halcyon. Maybe they can tell me where all the Kids are. I don't know if you noticed, but they're quite in love with me."

Griffin really wouldn't let that go.

"I'm sure Lyric will come around." Celia had chuckled but silently doubted it, from the way Lyric's eyes flashed with annoyance every time Griffin talked, breathed, or moved, but better that he keep trying to win them over than stew about it endlessly.

Now the gate beckoned in invitation. Although it was still locked, it felt like it had waited for the right moment to appear.

Celia wondered if anyone else in the town who walked by just then had even seen it.

She suspected not.

The wild storm the day before was keeping them busy. Not with cleanup—every broken shingle and torn shutter had been miraculously repaired, every tree had regrown its snapped branches, every bit of litter had disappeared—but with gossip. As Celia searched for the gate, she kept catching bits of the townspeople's chatter: *Wasn't a bad one like that in years! I hid in the basement with nothing but my barrels of wine as company. Hardy har har.*

Nothing about how the town had repaired itself overnight.

Halcyon must have stayed up all night dealing with the damage, receiving no accolades. Celia's new indenture would have just as much anonymity as her previous one.

At least it would be prettier.

And more important, it would have meaning.

It had to.

She shivered, debating again whether this was a good idea, the bees in her mind urging her on, with a few outliers whispering warnings. She couldn't trust Halcyon, but she had to trust Halcyon.

Pushing aside the cautious bees, Celia scaled the gate again and thumped down on the other side.

She walked through the tunnel of wisteria, then the empty courtyard with the fountain bubbling peacefully and the plants in lush abundance, and rapped her knuckles on the bright cherry door.

It opened with a soft moan, and Lyric stood framed in the doorway, continuing their habit of glaring at everything. "Foolish move, former inkling," they said. "Foolish move."

They turned around and strode away, making Celia hustle to keep up with them. "This is the kitchen," Lyric said, gesturing in the general direction. "I'm not cooking for you." Another hand wave. "That's the pantry, over there is some storage. Don't go poking around in any of these rooms. I have a system."

Every word Lyric uttered came with another glare, and their pace increased with each step, making Celia sweat to keep up. "Down that hall there's a library, a greenhouse with access to the courtyard, and an aviary. The rest of the rooms won't interest you. Don't bother me about them. Don't bother Halcyon. A lot of things are going to stay none of your business."

"I can wander around myself, you know," Celia said, out of breath. She was irked about the tour. She didn't care where the flour and sugar were kept, she needed to get working. The quicker she mastered "all aspects of the ink" and made Halcyon happy, the faster he would give her the inoculation for Griffin.

Lyric set their jaw. They were wearing a sleeveless shirt over loose trousers, and everything about them *seemed* casual, down to their undercut and weather-browned skin. But Lyric was proof that looks could be deceiving; they were, in fact, perpetually coiled like a tight spring. "There's a good chance you'd get lost, which Halcyon would kill me for. Then years from now Halcyon would come across your skeleton in some back room somewhere, and he'd curse me in my grave for the inconvenience of having to deal with your bones." They leveled a look at Celia that reminded her of Anya. The same eyebrow tilt, *How stupid do you think I am?* The same curve of lip, *Do you know how stupid I think you are?*

"Sorry I asked," Celia said, running her hand along the stone of the hallway. "It just doesn't seem like you want to be here."

"And it seems like you want to be here too much," Lyric snapped back.

"Wrong. I don't *want* to be here at all."

"For now, Halcyon is intrigued by both your passion and your natural talent," Lyric said. "Until you disappoint him, apparently you're my inconvenience too."

"Wow, you're not subtle, are you?" Celia said, irritated. But also with a fair amount of appreciation. She'd had to watch her words so carefully for so long, it was refreshing to be with someone who spoke their mind, however fanged.

"Hey, what's in there?" Celia asked casually, pointing to the double doors with the sunflower-shaped doorknob at the end of the hall. She didn't mention that she'd already tried to go in, nor how volcanic it had made Halcyon.

Lyric paused — significantly — and looked at Celia sideways. "You know about Martina?" they finally asked.

Not at all. "The person in all the paintings?" Celia guessed.

Paintings of one person decorated every corner of the huge

house. In most, they were regally posed, formal and stiff, but there were a few Celia had seen with them and Halcyon posed together, and in those, they were both smiling and casual. As if, together, they were completely different people.

Lyric snorted. "Yes. The person in all the paintings. Halcyon's partner, his lover, the only thing he cares about in the whole world aside from the ink. Dead because of your Divine."

Celia tripped over her own feet. Interesting, and unsurprising, that Diavala had left out the fact that she'd killed Halcyon's lover. The showdown between them three years ago had had more casualties than simply Diavala's pride. "I'd really appreciate it if everyone stopped referring to her as *my* Divine. She will always only be Diavala to me."

"Diavala, then."

"Martina's in there?" Celia felt foolish even asking, but she knew that people did funny things with their beloved dead. The crypts at the temple, lined with skulls, were proof she'd lived right on top of for years. Celia's friend Zuni had been Profeta's skullkeeper. It had been her life, her entire world—tending the dead.

Lyric shook their head. "Halcyon doesn't know where Martina is, but he made Wisteria for her—this place is made of all of her favorite things—for when he finds her."

So Wisteria was a great, grand, beautiful town-shaped . . . mausoleum.

A twinge of pity hit Celia. He'd created Wisteria as a mausoleum, morbid as that was, but it was empty of the one it was meant for. No wonder he didn't want her going into that room; it was a private place, an empty reminder that he couldn't even mourn the way he wanted to.

But it had been three years since Diavala had confronted him here in Wisteria, and if he hadn't found Martina's body yet, Celia doubted he ever would. His mourning would always be incomplete.

Lyric saw the look on Celia's face. "It's not our place to judge. It *is* our place never to set foot in that room if we want to continue breathing." It should have been a statement of finality, but the way Lyric looked at her, Celia couldn't shake the feeling that they wanted to say more.

"Fair enough," Celia said.

With a sigh, Lyric pushed open the door to Halcyon's studio so hard it knocked into the wall behind it with a loud bang. Halcyon looked up from the armchair he lounged in. His eyes were a near-normal shade of green, but they still had the tangles of ivy and vines inside them.

"I hope this isn't a waste of my time" was the first thing he said. He closed his book with a snap and strode to the workbench.

Lyric all but pushed her in before slamming the door shut behind them, trapping Celia in.

"It won't be," Celia said, following him. Thankfully, he'd removed the vat of stinky poison she'd helped him mix the day before. The other Chest Majestic was also out of the way, but it stared at her accusingly from a high shelf in the corner of the room.

Celia hovered, silent, following his lead and polishing some equipment to a gleam, wrapped up in doubt.

What could she possibly do to impress him and convince him she could take care of his town, especially in light of the fact that it was an homage to what he held most dear? The tattoo of the wisteria flower was about as far as her known talents stretched.

He considered her. Then gently put the vial he was holding down on the table.

"Try."

Celia blinked. "Try what?"

"Use your ink to craft an illusion for me."

"Now?!" She didn't want to polish empty glass jars for an age, but she'd assumed there would be some preamble, perhaps even a little guidance.

"This isn't a social call." Patience, clearly, was not one of his strengths. "You're here to prove yourself. So prove yourself."

She put down the glass, the cloth, and walked to a relatively shadowed corner of the room, all in an effort to make herself look confident.

Without saying a word, she rolled up her sleeves and took her quill out of her pocket. Her stomach writhed with unease, violently churning, and her head pounded with angry thumps. She didn't want to do it. She hated the ink, wanted to be rid of it forever, not *use* it.

But sometimes you have to go backwards in order to move forward, her wise bees said.

And remember, it's not the ink you hate, it was how Diavala used it, Anya added. *Make something pretty.*

Celia now believed that most of the tangible things in the town were illusions created from the ink. How else could everything repair itself overnight and the streets and buildings turn themselves around? If Halcyon could do all that with ink, she could too. Maybe not right away, and certainly not to such an extent, but they shared the essence of it inside them, and she had some fierce will.

She'd promised to save Griffin and everyone else on Diavala's eternal revenge list. What she did here would matter.

She'd just start small.

Small and fuzzy.

First she concentrated on the wall in front of them: a bare expanse of stone with wood details. Instead of thinking a person's name as it would be written on a Divine order, she memorized the new canvas. Its grain and texture. The light and color. She would command the tattoo to the wall like a shadow.

She pressed the quill to her arm and drew the rough outline of a bee: tiny wings, fuzzy body, stinger. Nothing more complicated than a child's sketch, with big, bold, recognizable features.

She'd learned one thing during her travels and performances with the Rabble Mob: if you don't know what you're doing, at least fake it well. Every stroke of her drawing was embellished by grand movements. She hummed as she drew, marking her work with a song, giving the impression of ease.

When the image was done, she inhaled and focused on the wall in front of them. Halcyon's face gave away nothing; whether he was amused by her ineptitude or impressed with her approach, she had no idea.

Instead of willing the image to transfer to another person, ink in her blood to ink on their skin, she willed the ink to the wall.

A brand-new thing would exist, coming from completely within herself.

"Just like our experiments, right?" she whispered to Anya. They'd poked at so many edges with manipulating the ink—in the temple and then with the Rabble Mob tattoos—this was simply another test to see what they could make the ink do. Despite their shared ability to think in detours and crooked, untraveled paths, it hadn't occurred to either of them to try to manipulate the ink onto anything other than skin.

Halcyon, and perhaps Martina, were their more advanced predecessors. Perhaps they'd been inklings once, years ago, and had smuggled the ink out of Asura in a teenage act of defiance that Diavala hadn't noticed until many years later. Surely, in all the time Profeta had existed, Celia and Anya weren't the first to escape the temple.

With another ragged breath, Celia willed the bee on her arm to go to the wall. Like splattering paint, like casting a shadow, an imprint.

A dark splotch appeared, looking nothing like the bee on her arm. She gasped and took a step back, shaken. The lines on her arm disappeared one by one as usual as they transferred, but they weren't being transferred the same way. They didn't appear line by line on the wall. It was no-splotch and then splotch, so subtle she had to look twice to see whether it was a trick of the light.

It wasn't a trick of the light. It was spreading, enveloping the wall like an oozing stain.

And when the last line disappeared from her arm, it kept on spreading down the wall to the floor, up the wall to the ceiling. As if Griffin's favorite Bicklandian giant, Obi, had spilled his huge paint pot over the house.

Celia knew she needed to call it back, but she was frozen in place. Did she really want that stain back inside her? The thing deep inside her body was right in front of her, looming large, and the idea that she would summon that stain, that huge dark void, back into her was frightening.

She stepped back. *I don't want it.*

She took another step back, banging into a table. *I hate it.*

What am I doing here?

Out of the corner of her eye, she saw Halcyon watching hungrily, his hands clasped in front of him, his fingers tight, his eyes wide open and swirling manically as they had the day before when she'd pissed him off trying to get into his secret room. In the growing darkness—or was she only imagining that the light was fading?—his eyes glowed a deeper black.

The shadow had marched its way across the ceiling, congregating above her head. It had crept over the floor, inching its way toward her toes.

The ink was still drawn to blood. To warmth. It needed a host.

Somehow that little bee Celia had drawn on her arm had morphed into something hungry. Spreading. Searching.

She closed her eyes and tried to force the ink back to the wall. *I gave you a shape. Obey it.*

She pushed it away with her thoughts, like sweeping it back with a broom, trying to contain it to the wall as she'd intended.

It didn't drop down on her. It didn't swarm up her legs, so, shaking from the concentration, she cracked her eyes open to see if it was working.

The creeping shadow had retreated to the wall. It looked vaguely like a bee, but only because Celia knew what it was supposed to be. The edges of the image flickered like black flames in a fire. It wanted to be fed, reaching out for more.

She glanced at Halcyon again, a wide smile on her face. It was nothing—a blob on a wall, moving slightly—but she'd put it there. She was holding it there. He didn't look all that impressed, but he gave her a slight nod, as if saying, *Okay, it's not terrible.*

Turning back to it, struggling to hold on, she commanded the bee to move its wings. *Movement,* she thought. For effect, she drew her own arms wide and moved them up and down, as if she herself would take flight with her creation.

Too intent on her bee blob to care, she ignored it when Halcyon began laughing at her.

Tentatively, the blob stretched out on one side like a fledgling testing a wing. Celia felt a surge of triumph. It was listening to her. Without any training beyond what the temple had given her and what she and Anya had discovered on their own, she was commanding it to obey her. What else could she make it do?

The black blob paused in its flickering, as if it were listening . . .

Just before it exploded.

Celia ducked to avoid the spray. Because that's what she was expecting after that loud squelch of failure: a splatter of thick ink coating her, the table, the supplies, and, embarrassingly enough, Halcyon himself. For a moment she pictured herself picking thick strings of goo from his hair and off his fine coat, mumbling apologies and trying hard not to meet his eye.

But nothing hit her. Celia peeked out from under her arm. The ink had disappeared. Maybe she'd called it back into her without thinking, maybe Halcyon had dismissed it in some way, but all evidence of the bee blob was gone.

She dropped her arm. "I meant to do that," she said.

"Of course you did." Halcyon looked amused. His lips were curved into something that could have been a smile. "I admit I quite like you. There's just as much hate inside you as love, like a perfectly balanced scale." He inhaled, searching her eyes for something. "The trouble with such a balance, though, is that any little thing has the ability to tip it the wrong way."

Which way would he consider wrong, she wondered. Tipping toward hate or love?

He strode over to her, planting his feet squarely in front of her, an arm's breadth away. "It began well, but the most important thing is knowing the exact consistency of your canvas. You were almost there. You knew to study the wall, get its shape and texture, but you looked superficially, and you need to look deeper. In order for the ink to latch on to something, in order for you to control it, it needs a solid anchor."

Was that her first lesson? It sure sounded like a lesson. "How do you make unsubstantial things like clouds, then?" she asked. "What are they latched on to?" For his illusions to extend over the entire town, there must have been thousands of anchor points. How did he know them all?

Celia's heart sped up. This was a turning point.

Halcyon paused, as if considering how to answer her question, not whether he would bother to answer it. A big part of her had thought he would kick her out after seeing all the things she couldn't do.

"You only need *one* anchor in the real world, and you can craft an entire painting around it. Even a floating cloud in the sky will be attached to another cloud, then to another cloud, then to a treetop, and on and on, the entire thing crafted together and interconnected. Think of it like a painting made of a thousand brushstrokes, or like a sweater knitted from one long strand of yarn. You need a starting point—the first splash of paint, the first knot—but you can build everything from there."

"It's the weak spot," Celia said.

Halcyon shook his head. "Depends on your perspective. I've always thought of it as the strongest spot." He gestured at the now-blank wall. "Your bee got confused when you asked it to fly. It was attached to the wall, but in order for it to take off from the wall, you needed to give it something else to connect to. If your illusion is to move across distances, like a bird flying or a wolf attacking, it needs to be tethered to more illusion at every point across the spectrum of movement. The quickest way for the ink to die is if you rob it of its connection to itself."

"Got it," she said. But did she? "Wait. What was the tether point? Me?" Maybe that's why it had wanted to get back to her so badly.

"No," he said, but he didn't elaborate.

Okay, so she didn't get it after all.

He'd said the bee got confused when she'd told it to leave the wall . . .

As if the wall were something it had understood and accepted.

"The wall is part of your illusion," she said slowly. She'd added another stitch to *his* sweater, she hadn't created a new one at all. "That must be why I didn't physically feel it leave me. That must be how you can do so much . . . *this*."

Every inkling tattoo came with a side effect of fatigue,

depending on how large the design was, but that was because they were literally giving part of themselves away. Ink to skin, then severing the tie between the two.

The way Halcyon worked didn't ask the illusion to exist on its own, it simply connected itself to other bits, ink to ink.

They were exactly like the temporary messages Celia and Anya had sent to each other for years, which Dante still infuriatingly delivered on a regular basis.

Celia had already *done* this.

With Anya.

With each message, they'd commanded the ink to be a temporary illusion; there had never been any actual ink transferred between them. And it had been hard, impossible, to hold the ink in place for very long because they hadn't thought to anchor it.

Inadvertently, and without understanding how it worked, they'd already done this.

Halcyon smiled at her and nodded. Even though she hadn't said anything out loud, clearly he'd noticed that she was having some kind of grand revelation. "Practice more with your bee," he said.

He moved in and out of the room all day as she practiced. At one point he came in with tea for her. "This might help your headaches," he said, setting a mug down in front of her. "It's only linden flowers and honey, but Rian and I swear by it for nearly every ailment."

"Rian?"

"She's the town's healer," he said brusquely.

Celia began yet another sketch on her arm but watched him from the corner of her eye. He was keen to talk about the ink, but if anything remotely personal came up, he shut right down.

As Halcyon leaned over the table, a pendant around his neck swung out. Celia caught only a glimpse of it, but the pattern etched in the top looked much like the swirls decorating his Chest Majestic. Just before he tucked it back into his shirt, he pressed his lips to it with a gentle kiss.

Celia's heart fluttered madly, and she had a hard time reconciling the tender image. And so soon after bringing her tea, at that. "What is it?" she asked, gesturing at the pendant.

His gaze snapped up to hers, as if he'd forgotten she was even in the room. Instead of tender, he looked about ready to bolt her to the wall like a piece of macabre art. "It's infinitely more precious to me than you are, Celia Sand. I'd keep your curiosity in check lest it wanders into unwelcome spaces."

Point taken. The only space he wanted her in was ink-related. Celia went back to work.

CHAPTER 9

AFTER THE INITIAL DEBACLE WITH THE BEE SPLOTCH, THE day went well enough. Celia quickly learned how to fully cast visual illusions, and bolstered by a series of small successes throughout the morning, she tried to show off. She sketched a bat house on her arm, attaching it to the room via a long pole to the floor. Instead of glimmering, shimmering, and appearing slowly, the room was empty of bat homes one minute and had a bat house in it the next.

Her wee little bats took a bit of doing to get right, but she finally had the size and shape she wanted.

"Are the bats wearing tiny *robes*, Celia?" Lyric had asked, making Halcyon look up from his book.

"They sure are." Celia gestured at the bat house, darting a quick look at Halcyon to gauge his reaction; it was a pretty good replica of the Profetan temple in Asura. "They're misti-bats," she said proudly.

Lyric, absolutely *heaving* with laughter, said, "You're so ridiculous! How are bats with clothing going to help your case here, Celia?"

Celia saw Halcyon's frown, then. Because Lyric had drawn such attention to it.

Celia bristled. "Maybe I'm nervous, all right? This is all new to me, I'm getting little guidance, and it doesn't help that you're so damn judgey." Celia summoned the misti-bats back into herself in an effort to wipe away the evidence, what she'd thought had been clever attention to detail now looking like an infantile prank.

Halcyon snapped his book shut and stood. "More tomorrow," he said before disappearing from the room. It was close to supper hour—family time. Celia didn't know for sure, but she suspected that Halcyon went to his locked room with the sunflower doorknob and missed Martina, alone.

"Did you have to do that?" Celia said to Lyric through her teeth. It would have been nice to have an ally, but barring that, it would have been really nice if Lyric didn't actively make her look dimwitted.

"Fine," Lyric said, rolling their eyes. "Your bats were okay." That was probably the only kind of apology Celia would ever get. "Come on then," they said, standing abruptly and beginning to clean up the disaster of a studio, a playful smirk playing at their lips. "Let's get this place tidy and then I'll buy you a drink. We should celebrate the evolution of bat fashion."

By the time they arrived at the Outside Inn pub, it was already lively and full of chatter, with a small three-piece band playing in the corner. As Lyric went to get their drinks, Celia collapsed into a chair across from Griffin and then sprawled on the sticky table, moaning.

"Sooooo, how did it go?" he asked.

Celia tapped the table and pointed toward the bar without looking up.

"Got it," he said, chuckling. Sounded like he'd had a better day than she had.

Celia tried to enjoy Griffin's good mood. He'd made new friends in town and had even spent some time that morning with Lyric, helping them run errands. "Lyric tolerates me now, don't you?" he said with a wide grin as Lyric appeared with the drinks.

"Barely," they said, passing out a round and sliding into the seat next to Celia.

"They hate everyone equally," Celia mumbled. "Don't take it personally."

"Oh, come now," Lyric said, waving a hand. "I said I was sorry."

"Did you though?"

"What's between you two?" Griffin asked.

"It's hilarious—" Lyric started, jumping on the chance to relay Celia's embarrassment.

"It was nothing," Celia interrupted, sitting up and catching her error just in time. "I thought I found Halcyon near the bakery, but it turned out the person I was telling my life story to wasn't him." She poked Lyric in the shoulder. Hard. "Lyric thought my embarrassment was funny."

Probably not the best idea to antagonize the one person Celia needed a favor from now, but Lyric only smiled a little wider, assessing her from the corner of their eye even as they nodded. "Yeah," they drawled.

"If it softens the sting," Griffin said to Celia, "they won't tell me what Halcyon looks like either."

Her stomach churning, Celia then told Griffin (and Diavala) that she'd spent the day endlessly walking around the town, getting lost in the labyrinth that was Wisteria, and hadn't spoken to Halcyon at all.

Halcyon wasn't willing to talk, she said.

She couldn't remember what he looked like all over again, she said.

And that part, at least, was true. Even after spending all day with him, she couldn't call up any of his features.

Lyric listened patiently as Celia told her story, even batting their eyelashes when Celia accused them of being deliberately unhelpful when it came to tracking Halcyon down.

"Celia has a point," Griffin said, treading carefully around Lyric, thrilled now that they "barely tolerated" him. "I understand you're his assistant and your loyalties lie with him, but I'm sure there's something you could do. Arrange another meeting, perhaps?"

Griffin was being willfully naive. They'd discovered that the reason they hadn't seen Kids around was because Halcyon didn't like children. Families with young ones lived in a separate area of town by choice, well away from where Halcyon would be likely to run into them.

Anyone with that much power wouldn't be swayed unless he wanted to be, no matter how reasonably Lyric appealed to him.

But how would Lyric respond to Griffin's question? With a fresh drink in hand and a wide smile on their face, Lyric shifted toward Griffin.

Celia stiffened. If she wasn't so damn tired, maybe she could have sorted out her story beforehand. Now she was at the mercy of the thorniest person to ever draw breath, who could ruin everything with just a word.

"So how long do you think you'll be here?" Lyric asked, ignoring Griffin's comment entirely.

Griffin looked at Celia. Celia stared at Lyric. Lyric watched Griffin.

"Looks like we'll be here forever if we can't even find him again." Celia tried to sound irritated, but her relief came out in a long sigh. Whatever Lyric's deal, at least they took secret-keeping seriously.

But how long could she keep this up?

Celia and Griffin were keeping Diavala a secret from Halcyon and Lyric; Celia was keeping Halcyon a secret from Griffin and Diavala; and Lyric, Halcyon, and Diavala were all keeping secrets from her and Griffin. These alliances would crumble eventually, as all alliances did, but which one would go first?

And more important, even if Diavala didn't suspect that Celia was making any progress, how long would she tolerate being so close to the one who scared her so much?

"Sorry I poked you," Celia whispered to Lyric later, while Griffin was deep in a raucous game of Imp tiles with the tailor, Michali, at another table. "And thanks for covering for me. Things between us are . . . complicated."

Lyric shrugged and took a sip of their drink, unbothered. "Until everything explodes on you, at least you'll be entertaining."

Griffin looked up from his game as Celia glanced over at his table. Their eyes met and held. Her heart fluttered when he smiled. It was one of his genuine smiles: soft and feathery light, as if he knew the world's ugly secrets and had made peace with them. The constellation of stars tattooed beside his eyes represented his anchor, he'd said; no matter where he traveled, he could count on those stars to show him a familiar light. Sometimes, as in that small moment when he cocked his head to the left and graced her with a knowing smile, Celia thought that the tattoo on his temple worked a subtle magic. Despite the fact that he sometimes talked in Riddlish and others claimed that he got muddled, it felt like he understood everything perfectly.

Especially Celia.

Celia didn't want to be entertaining, and she certainly didn't want everything to explode. Most of all, she wanted to have moments like that with Griffin—the sharing of a smile—without Diavala between them reminding her of all she'd already lost and all that Diavala could still take away.

If ink was the answer, she'd have to try harder to accept that.

She turned back to Lyric and forced herself to smile. "Sasti-mos futura," she said, holding up her drink. *To a future where the ink gets us out of trouble instead of being the cause of it.*

Across the room, Griffin held up his glass, as if that unsaid sentiment was one he needed too.

CHAPTER 10

ALL OF CELIA'S TUTORING FROM HALCYON CAME IN STAGES over the next few days, and she quickly learned that making educated guesses rather than asking direct questions was a better approach with him. Instead of *How does this work?* she would come up with a theory—*It works like this . . .*—and then wait for him to respond.

She was often wrong, but she was right often enough that at least he kept answering her, and she made sure to master each new aspect before moving on.

It was all about linking the pieces to something that was already there. The ink listened to nonverbal commands better than the most disciplined army fighters listened to the words of their commanding officer. The hardest part for Celia was figuring out a way of communicating what she wanted properly, so the ink understood her.

After fumbling her way through various random tasks and experiments, Halcyon instructed her to focus her skills. "You need to fool all the senses in order to make a convincing illusion," he said. "Choose one thing and perfect it in all ways."

Celia had become determined to make the perfect bee (and one that didn't explode). Throughout every stage of training, she worked on her bee: first shape, then substance, then color, then sound, then animation.

And it worked. Celia made the perfect bee.

Of all the tricks and illusions she'd done already, Xinto was her most treasured creation.

She made him big on purpose: a bright yellow and black bee as big as her hand, adorable and soft. Something to keep her company.

At first she couldn't master sound, the booms of Halcyon's false thunder far beyond her current capabilities, so Xinto had been a *silent* giant bee. But sound came to her when she considered the notes and cadence. Xinto made a beelike noise only when she stopped thinking *buzzzz* and turned his buzz into a song, following natural dips and peaks.

And the simple thin string around his fat, fluffy neck was like a leash dragging along the ground, literally tethering him to the town. He could fly only as long as that string stayed connected, ink to ink. She eventually figured out how to have him move from illusion to illusion, but by then the leash had become an integral part of him. He'd protested with a loud buzz when she'd tried to take it off. It was sparkly, and he liked sparkles.

Most amazing of all was that even when Celia wasn't consciously commanding him, he'd begun behaving in beelike ways all on his own, as if the ink knew what she ultimately wanted and was able to adapt accordingly.

Scent was the only sense still out of her grasp, to the point where she was beginning to believe she'd never used her nose before.

"Should you even have a smell, Xinto?" she asked him as he zigged and zagged above her head. "No . . . didn't think so. Yet Ser Ronnea insists."

Celia gritted her teeth and went back to her task for that day: Halcyon had thrown a dozen ingredients for a stew into a pot, brought it to a boil, and told Celia to sniff them out individually.

That had been hours ago.

Hours and hours and hours and getting nowhere.

After days and days of getting nowhere.

As if sensing her frustration, Halcyon entered the lab with another pot of tea. "You have to learn the shape and form of each scent before you can master it," he said, setting the mug down in front of her. She suspected there was something else besides linden flowers and honey in the tea, no matter what he claimed, because it worked so well. Her headaches had subsided to the point where she could sometimes forget about them completely, and she hadn't had a piercing flare-up for days.

"You can't mimic the smell of a cooking broth without first knowing exactly what the ingredients are," he added.

Celia had made notes on the scent of the carrots: *earthy, bland, sweet.* How can something be both bland and sweet? Halcyon leaned over her shoulder to look at her list. The proximity bothered her—it was too familiar—and she inched downward, shrinking in on herself.

He didn't seem to notice.

"Deeper," he said, the word booming loud in her ear. He was just as frustrated as she was that she couldn't get this last piece. His instructions had become more insistent and regular, which made her more nervous. "Don't bother trying to put it into words, because words put everything in a box. There can be no sides, bottom, and top to this. A scent cannot and should not be confined." If she'd been at the temple, Mistico Lupita would have slapped her upside the head and yelled *Get it together, Inkling Sand!*

Celia was picking up a new scent now: a little too perfumed, as fresh as pine needles, what some people might find appealing—but it cloyed its way up Celia's nose and stayed there.

When Halcyon leaned away, Celia exhaled hard.

"It's the hardest of the senses to recreate," he admitted, "because it's often the most personal. Scents trigger memories. They live inside us by association. One person will gag because carrots remind them of poverty, of resources pushed too thin. Another will think of their grandmother's garden. *Earthy, bland, sweet* aren't nearly enough."

Celia contemplated throwing the soupspoon at his forehead.

She placed the spoon down gently, slowly. "Even Xinto is bored," she said, gesturing to where her pet bee had made himself comfortable amid a colorful nest of papers. "Are you telling me only now that every illusion is personalized?"

"No, that would be impossible. But you have to understand perspective. Believability comes from reinforcing worldview. If you can't give people what they expect, you're working against yourself."

"Maybe in striving so hard for believability," she muttered, "you're missing a mountain of opportunity." How sad that he didn't have more patience for her "whimsy," as he called it. That might have made all of this more tolerable.

Even keeping Xinto had been a fight. Halcyon had agreed to let her keep him only because she'd convinced him that it wasn't too far out of the realm of possibility. "Your people don't even blink at the town repairing itself overnight, and they've seen bees before. This one's just bigger!"

She'd won, but barely.

Halcyon ignored her comment about missed opportunity. "Although the ink is boundless in its capabilities, you have to work within a believable framework. It's nonnegotiable."

Celia sipped her tea, forcing herself not to get worked up over his use of the word *nonnegotiable,* then gingerly set the cup back down.

This believable framework was what they'd done with the Rabble Mob: given people a plausible story and nudged them into believing it. They'd extended real life and added new layers, but hadn't added a new dimension.

Halcyon tended to underestimate her. She'd already put these pieces together and used them to her advantage: that's exactly why her argument to keep Xinto had worked.

But scent was the last piece, and that was one she could decidedly *not* get to work.

"So, the ingredients?" Halcyon asked, his slim fingers dancing through the steam rising from the pot.

"Carrots, turnips, potatoes," she said, "bay leaves, peppers of some kind, but I can't tell which, and . . ." The one ingredient that didn't belong in a basic stew and the one that left her doubting herself. It had actually been the first thing she'd smelled, so strong was the odor, but because it made no sense, she'd searched around it for the rest of the smells.

"And?" He didn't look at her. Waiting.

"Grimfruit?" she said, trying to sound sure but inflecting it like a question all the same. The root of the plant *could* be eaten . . . if you wanted uncontrollable stomach cramps for many hours on end. Celia and Anya had snuck some into one of Teresia's soups once, thinking it was the mistico's meal, accidentally causing an unprecedented shutdown of Divine tattoos for a day when they'd made all the inklings — themselves included — sick.

Halcyon nodded. "It fattens up the meal, but unfortunately, the smell gives it away."

"O-kay?" Celia didn't know where he was going with this.

"Instead of creating a new scent," Halcyon said, "begin with amplifying existing ones. Take the ones underneath, pull them over, and you should be able to disguise the grimfruit."

Celia was adept at the visual because she'd always drawn the images in her mind. This was a new skill set entirely. It wasn't about sketching something realistic, it was completely abstract: pulling threads, teasing them, folding them over.

"When Lyric returns," Halcyon added as Celia concentrated on how she could possibly do this, "they'll want something hearty and warm for lunch. Make it smell appealing."

Celia looked up.

"It's for the pursuit of science," Halcyon said absently. "They won't mind."

When Celia remembered how it had felt—like her guts were twisting into literal knots, how Yusef and Dante had both passed out from the pain—she thought Lyric would mind very much indeed.

She stared at Halcyon long enough that he lost interest, humming offkey under his breath as he worked at carefully transferring another clay creation into the large kiln. He could create anything with the ink, but he played with more traditional art forms regularly as well. The picture of calm, even while asking Celia to mildly poison his assistant.

Xinto buzzed over and landed on her shoulder, preening himself calmly while she grappled with a moral dilemma.

Celia did what Halcyon asked, working with the scents and strengthening them in order to mask the offending one, but when Lyric walked into the studio later that morning, Celia immediately said, "Don't eat the stew."

Halcyon tsked, exasperated, and threw a clay-stained rag down on the bench. "Scent is the *only* thing you have left, and you insist on sabotaging your own progress." He strode past Lyric, barking at them to clean up as he left.

Probably to go talk to the empty room. Complain about Celia to someone long dead.

"Wow, what did I walk into?" Lyric said with wide eyes, but they walked to the pot and began cleaning it up without asking anything else.

"I just saved your ass, *literally*," Celia said. She stood up so fast she knocked over her chair and forced Xinto up from his cozy nap. "And now I need some air."

Stepping into the hallway, she glared at the door with the sunflower doorknob. If Halcyon was frustrated with her, she was ten times more frustrated with him. He wanted mastery from her and had refused to move forward until that happened. After all the hope and promise that first day, she'd been doing nothing but spin in circles.

Unlike Diavala, Celia didn't have an eternity to piss around. Griffin was as happy as a puppy lately, and Celia was positive it had everything to do with Diavala's being happy . . . happy with Celia's lack of progress in getting Halcyon to help, happy with Celia's endless errand runs as she tried to get on Halcyon's good side, happy it started all over again each morning. With Lyric offering some distractions and the occasional white lie, Griffin and Diavala were both under the impression this was a dead end and Celia was just being stubborn about it.

Maybe she was.

Celia strode toward the front door. Every time she passed

a portrait of Martina, she nodded a hello. Every time Halcyon appeared in one of the portraits, she glared.

Opening the red door to the courtyard, she closed her eyes and inhaled deeply, cleansing the studio air from her lungs, focusing on the feeling of the sun on her face. In a soggy country such as Illinia, where rain fell from the sky much more often than not, it was as if Wisteria's sky didn't know what a rain cloud looked like. The days were bright and blue, the nights clear and twinkly with stars.

It felt like she hadn't been outside in a lifetime.

But as she lingered in the garden, trying to calm down, Halcyon found her.

Shifting from foot to foot, abnormally hesitant, he finally cleared his throat and waited for Celia to meet his eyes. The variegated greens swirled together, placid and calm. No black. "I came to apologize."

Hmm, interesting. He didn't strike her as the apologizing type.

"It's just that you show so much promise, it's difficult for me to watch this . . . floundering."

Celia barked out a laugh. That was a Dante compliment. It sounded nice at first, until you realized it was an insult.

Xinto had landed in an adjacent shrub of lilacs, butt up, head down, and Celia had to help him right himself. "You're the clumsiest giant baby bee in the world," she cooed. He peeked out from the flowers and wiggled his nose at her, most definitely agreeing.

Halcyon ignored her laugh. "I've been thinking maybe you need a little more inspiration. What if Anya was here?"

He seemed to know everything about their last show in Asura, but it still surprised her to hear Anya's name on his lips.

It took a long moment before she registered his meaning.

And even when she did—when the words found their mark right in the center of her chest and spread like a wildfire—she couldn't do anything more than feel them burn. Paralyzed in place, she planted her feet and tried to keep the world from tilting upside down.

Halcyon's expression softened. "Death is . . ." He paused, searching for the right word. "It's unfair," he finally said. "But it's also not necessarily the end. Not here."

Celia turned and stared into the swirling liquid of the water fountain. The want inside her had moved outward, so thick it dripped from her skin, puffed out with her breaths, rang in her ears. In the glimmering eddies and swirls of the water, she saw her face reflected back to her, distorted from the movement, waiting for calm before coming into focus.

In between the ripples (because time had slowed to measurable heartbeats), Celia saw someone standing a few paces behind her—tall, long hair falling over her shoulders, the shadow of a top hat perched perfectly straight . . .

Her next inhale stuttered as she whirled around.

"Anny?" Celia squeaked. Everything hurt, and she swayed, landing heavily on the stone rim of the fountain behind her. It was Anya . . . except it wasn't. She had no fierce red tenor, her eyes were the wrong hue of deep blue, her expression was too disinterested, and she stood wrong, shifting her weight from foot to foot instead of planted firm and stable. It wasn't *her* Anya, but a replica of Anya as made by an artist who'd never met her.

"If you created her," Halcyon explained, noting Celia's critical frown, "she would be perfect." He dipped his chin and lowered his voice. "All I'm saying is that your version of her could be here with you, if you wanted her to be."

Celia had created so much with the ink already — the rough texture of stone, the unique sparkle of water in the sun, the sound of the wind rustling leaves, the taste of sour cherries hitting your tongue — but this was something else completely. The thing she wanted most, the thing she could never have again.

He was suggesting she could have Anya.

Even the whisper of her name in Celia's mind was an explosion, because now it was loaded with promise instead of finality.

So much time spent daydreaming about what *couldn't* be, and Celia had never considered this other possibility: what could.

She knew it wouldn't truly be Anya.

She knew it, she understood.

But maybe, if Celia brought every tiny treasured detail about Anya to the surface instead of keeping them hidden away because they hurt, a thousand complicated parts could become a whole.

The crinkles by her ocean-blue eyes when she smiled, the ruts between her brows when she frowned . . . Celia knew the landscape of her face better than she knew her own. Dark hair that felt like a waterfall between her fingers when she braided it, the shimmer of midnight blue that occasionally glimmered when the right light hit it.

Words in the cadence of Celia's favorite song falling from her lips. *Relax, Cece . . . Think about it . . . Remember the time . . .*

The laughter in her eyes when she teased, the pinch of her lips when she was disappointed, the soft crook of her neck where she invited Celia to rest her cheek.

Warmth.

And the scent of her: soft and reassuring, subtle, like petals in a pond, enveloping Celia in love.

Celia allowed all those tiny bits to rise up and overtake her. Xinto landed on her shoulder, and six fuzzy legs tickled along her neckline as he got comfortable, as if reminding her that *he* was as real as anything . . .

It would be easy.

It would hurt.

It would be marvelous.

What if all of this—coming to Wisteria, meeting Halcyon, working, and learning—was meant to open this path to her?

Celia examined the ink-Anya. Near perfect to anyone who didn't know her well. As she took a step forward, the ink-Anya approached as well. Celia glanced down at Anya's hand, her littlest finger ready to hug Celia's. It could be she and Anny once again, linked pinkies since the beginning.

With a gulp of air, she turned back toward the fountain. She wanted it so badly, even though she knew it was wrong. The only thing stopping her from shouting *Yes!* immediately was the thought of what actual Anya would say about this.

"I'll think about it." Celia felt like she hadn't spoken in years, her words came out as a croak, as if her voice box were shredded. Perhaps her words weren't even heard over the sound of the fountain, it was so loud suddenly.

The ink-Anya disappeared, the feeling of calm presence behind Celia vanishing as if it had never been there to begin with. Because it hadn't.

But oh, the lure of it still teased at her.

Halcyon intruded into that space behind her and looked down.

"I would have done this for my Martina already, but I know in my heart she's still out there, waiting for me, and I'm going to bring her home one day." He paused, hesitated, lifted his head away from their reflections. "With you here, tending this place, I'll finally be able to search in earnest. And if I get what I want, it's only fair that you get what you want."

Celia was suspended in some other place, surrounded by things that became real with wishes.

She turned around, finally, and peered up at him without shame. She already knew he would be the one person who wouldn't judge her for what she wanted.

The bright sunlight, his miraculous Wisterian sun, shone down and cast shadows along his face. She still didn't know what to make of him, whether he was a friend or a mentor or a manipulator. He was just Halcyon—everything and nothing at the same time, and whatever he was, she was going to be forever bound to him, and to this place. He'd never let her leave, not with the ink in her blood and the secrets she knew, that much she'd already surmised from his let's-make-deadly-poison-together encounter. He was entrusting her with so much.

"When this is over for you," he said, "and your friends are safe from Diavala's Touch, you'll have a lot of time here. And Wisteria has always been a place of perfection."

Perfection would be having Anya back again. Perfection would be mastering scent, protecting Griffin from the Touch, *and* defeating Diavala for good. They hadn't spoken of revenge again since that first day, but it lingered in the far recesses of Celia's mind like a thorn: *if Halcyon knows how to kill people so efficiently, perhaps he knows how to kill immortal Diavalas as well.* He was, after all, a passable apothecary.

"Maybe we all need a break," Halcyon said, stepping away from her. "It's Stomp Night tonight."

Celia's gaze snapped up to his, her reverie shattering.

She couldn't show up with Halcyon. "I don't really feel like getting drinks."

He cocked an eyebrow as he moved back toward the house. "Lyric tells me you're at the pub every night."

Damn it, Lyric!

"My headache is pretty fierce today . . ."

His eyebrows turned frowny. "The tea should be helping."

She couldn't think of any other excuse, but she'd have at least a two-hour head start to figure something out. He'd disappear to chat with Martina's ghost; she could try to keep Griffin away.

Celia nodded. "It is helping. A lot, actually. I'll see you there, then. Maybe you can tell me why you started Stomp Night, what it means." She was already walking away as she rambled, poor Xinto startled by the movement so he flopped over into the flowers again and nearly plummeted to the ground.

Celia had to come up with something to avoid a meeting between Griffin and Halcyon so all her lies didn't blow up in her face the way Lyric had predicted.

"Lyric," Celia called when she was back in the house, running down the halls. "Lyric!" She sent Xinto to scout up ahead, but he was a slow giant bee, unused to heavy exercise, so he ended up back on her shoulder soon enough.

Lyric popped their head out of one of the libraries.

"Lyric!" Celia called again. "Heeeeey, Lyric." Celia stopped, bent, and tried to catch her breath. Lyric had already gone back into the room and closed the door on her.

Celia pushed the door back open and strode in. "I might have a problem."

"You have many," Lyric responded as they reshelved all the books Halcyon had pored through that day. Xinto, the traitor, mustered up the last reserves of his energy and abandoned her shoulder for Lyric's.

"Halcyon's planning to go to Stomp Night. Tonight. Shortly."

"Of course he is. He always goes if he's in town." Lyric kept on shelving, frowning at the spine of a book as if doubting the letters they were reading.

"Griffin will be there."

"Okay?" They dropped the book on the bench to deal with later.

"Halcyon and Griffin will be there *at the same time.*"

"They won't," they said, brushing the dust from their hands. "I already took care of it. You don't have to worry."

"What does that mean?"

"I mean Griffin's at the lakes with Michali right now, harvesting river lobsters."

So little of that sentence made sense to Celia that she didn't know what to address first.

"Look, I know you two have some" — Lyric waved their still-dusty hands around vaguely — "domestic issues, but I've been under the impression for a while that it's not in anyone's best interest for the two of them to pal it up. And if I can do one thing really well, it's look out for anyone." They pointed at themselves, with the emphasis on *anyone.*

Celia exhaled and doubled over again. "Oh, thank mercy."

"Now either get out or help me shelve the rest of these books."

Celia helped. She even allowed Xinto to nuzzle into Lyric's neck, giving them a fuzzy bee hug.

CHAPTER 11

THE OUTSIDE INN WAS EVEN MORE LIVELY FOR CELIA'S SEC-ond Stomp Night. By the time she and Lyric walked in, people were already on tables, their noise echoing into the night. It looked like the entire town was packed into that one room: there was barely any air or any space to move, yet they were moving.

"Is that . . . " Davi motioned at Celia's shoulder, her mouth open.

"Oh, him?" Celia said nonchalantly. The giant bee sitting there, as big as a teacup, vibrated his wings in greeting. "This is Xinto. Don't worry, he's harmless." Celia laughed, riding the high of her creation. "Unless you get between him and some flowers."

"He's so cute! Can I pet him?" Davi tittered as Xinto leaned into her attention, snuggling up to her hand like a striped puppy. "What a darling! Celia, where did you find him?"

In the real world, people would be running away, screaming at the unnatural creature on her shoulder. But this wasn't the real world, this was Wisteria. The people here were accustomed to seeing strange things all the time.

Celia tilted her chin, and Xinto pressed his wee nose to

her. "It took some doing, but I finally convinced him to come out." Without Griffin around that night, she could finally show Xinto off.

With Davi still cooing over him, Celia looked around the busy room. "Is it someone's birthday?" she asked, yelling to be heard over the din.

"No," Lyric said, their lips stretching into a genuine smile for the first time since Celia had known them. "But Aspen and Blue have been together for fifteen years today, and this is a celebration of their commitment to each other." Lyric waved to a couple in the corner, unstomping but with drinks piled high in front of them like offerings at a shrine. "They're well-loved here," Lyric said before leaving Celia to greet them.

Fifteen years with one person. That was a lifetime. Celia daydreamed for a moment, about a different life. Maybe, in fifteen years, she and Griffin would have a couple of goats and read books together by the fire on chilly nights. Zuni and Dante would come over for the occasional drink, perhaps with Kitty Kay and some of the Rabble Mob. Maybe they'd started their own miniature Commedia troupe, using fresh characters, telling new stories, where no one knew of the plague doctor or the Devil in the Bell Jar. Where no one cared anything about trickster deities, and it was all for fun. She'd always imagined that place would be Kinallen, but perhaps Wisteria would work just as well. Maybe, maybe, he'd choose to stay. Maybe he'd like helping her take care of the town, although *his* whimsy would be decidedly too much for Halcyon's sensibilities.

What would Griffin look like in middle age? Celia imagined his stubble peppered with premature gray—because the past couldn't be entirely undone—with an echo of gray at his temples, highlighted against his dark hair. A few more lines, laugh lines, living among the constellation tattoo by his eye. Weathered hands, but deft. He'd still be able to amuse her with his purple and blue flames.

Maybe, at the hearth, there would be a dark-haired Kid, almost ready to choose their name . . .

"Another headache?" Halcyon asked now, his face etched with concern. "I really have to talk to Rian about our mixture."

The imagining had been almost painful, she wanted it so badly, and he must have seen it on her face. She forced herself to relax. Forced the happy images away. "No. I was just visiting another world," she said. *It was nice there.* "*Dia*, but you got ready quick," she said. He was dressed in a different suit from the one he'd worn all day, his hair freshly washed and combed. Either she'd been standing alone and daydreaming for a long time, or he'd somehow made the clock wind faster. Time was different around him, she'd noticed.

"And you've brought your friend out," he commented.

Celia panic-looked around the room for Griffin before realizing that Halcyon was referring to Xinto.

"Your people are okay with him," she assured him. *Told you!*

Celia shook off the last of her fond daydream and found them a table near the back. Since most people were already standing and stomping, they had their pick.

Davi had said that Halcyon had started Stomp Night, yet Celia couldn't imagine him dancing or bouncing around. There was an almost religious observance to it; amid the hoots and hollers and laughter was an undercurrent of necessity.

Halcyon ordered them drinks as Xinto made his rounds, snuggling into whoever seemed interested. "Stomp Night actually started when Diavala came a few years ago."

Celia became very interested indeed. Halcyon rarely talked about the past. "What happened?" she asked. She tried to mimic Lyric's detached composure about everything, taking a sip of her beer and looking around as if she weren't wholly invested in his answer.

"I was ever out of the reach of Diavala's mistico. I made sure I never broke any rules of Profeta, because nothing of my work has to do with tattoos."

Ah, the dance of skirting Profeta's doctrine. Celia knew it well.

"She came and tried to deal with me herself."

"With the Touch," Celia said. Another sip of beer.

"She came," he repeated, "then I pushed her out and slammed the door."

He clapped and stomped his feet for emphasis, matching the beat of the song people were still pounding out around them.

So Stomp Night was an anthem for besting Diavala and driving her away. It was his claim to Wisteria, and all the ink work he did there. Celia loved the sentiment behind it with her entire soul, but that story really needed a better delivery. There was nothing about Martina, for one. Nothing of his heartbreak. And no juicy details about how Diavala had run away scared, realizing that someone more powerful than herself existed.

Lyric turned the extra chair around with a flourish and sat on it backwards, joining them at the table with their drink, still smiling. "Aspen and Blue are so happy right now," they said.

Another song had started in earnest, making it difficult to carry on a conversation. The stomping echoed in Celia's heart, beating like a drum in her chest. She stood, pushing her chair back so the legs scraped on the floor. She listened for the beat of the music created by the happy people of Wisteria, and she caught it, pulling it into herself. The thumping of their feet and the clapping of their hands infused her. It was a powerful sound, made all the more powerful now that she understood what it meant.

Every thump was against Diavala. Every stomp beat her down. Altogether, it was a warning for her to never set foot in Wisteria again.

Celia moved her feet, tentatively at first, then with more surety when she didn't misstep. She reached toward Halcyon, inviting him to join her.

Halcyon stood, towering over her. With a *stomp stomp,* he joined the beat, mirroring her movements.

They stomped together in the middle of happy Wisterians celebrating fifteen years of commitment between the elders, Aspen and Blue, and with each strike of her boot into the floor, Celia imagined Diavala's faceless face underfoot. Perhaps sensing Celia's ardor, Xinto flew across the room and joined her, zigging and zagging in between her and Halcyon, begging to be part of the fun.

"You're so close to creating your own stomp, Celia," Halcyon said. "Scent is giving you a hard time, but if you can do it—"

"I'll do it," she said, her voice hot. "Stop doubting me."

She'll do it! Xinto agreed, landing on the top of her hat in solidarity.

Halcyon smiled and climbed onto the table.

"People of Wisteria!"

Celia saw the exact moment when Halcyon allowed them to recognize him. Their faces transformed from guarded to delighted, and even with arms tangled together and drinks in hand, everyone began clapping for him.

"We have another something special to celebrate!" He turned in a circle, yelling loud enough so that all of Wisteria could hear him, and his gaze landed significantly on Celia. "For the past little while, you might have noticed her around the town. Celia Sand has been helping me, learning, and proving herself. At long last, I've found an apprentice. She's vowed to take care of our home when I'm traveling, and she's perfectly suited to the task in every way. I'm delighted for all of us!"

Everyone smiled and hooted. Cheers and applause rose up.

"You're all invited!" he shouted. "Five days from now, bring your stomping shoes and clapping hands to the main square, and we'll drink, eat, and dance all evening and formally welcome her to our town!"

"Congratulations, Celia!" Davi skittered closer, with the

bartender, Giada, in tow. "What an honor. And Halcyon throws the best parties!"

Giada responded with an excited squeal, offering Celia a drink on the house and spilling most of it in their excitement. "Does that mean Griffin is staying too?"

"I'm counting on all of you to make her feel welcome here," Halcyon continued, stepping down from the table into the swarm circling him. No wonder he disguised himself most of the time; he couldn't handle all the people trying to talk to him at once.

Celia tried to keep up with Davi and Giada's chatter, all the people who wanted to shake her hand and tip their hats to her, and the drinks people plied her with. In a daze, she gravitated toward Lyric, hard back pats urging her along at every turn.

"A celebrity in our midst!" Lyric said.

Celia's smile faltered. She had no idea what was going on in Lyric's mind half the time, but she'd become a master of catching their Contraryish. Different from the plague doctor's Riddlish, where meaning was hidden in vague nonsense, Lyric's language was saying the exact opposite of what they meant.

"Five days is plenty of time," Celia said.

Then Griffin would be protected from Diavala's torture. From her threats. And he could take the inoculation to others, protecting them. Diavala truly would have nothing on Celia then.

"Halcyon just gave you a very public deadline," Lyric pointed out.

Looking up mid-conversation, Halcyon nodded at her and tilted his head.

"He gave me motivation." Celia bowed to Halcyon across the distance. A couple of Xinto's legs dangled for a moment, and he nearly fell before he righted himself up on the hat.

"He *also* just gave everyone in the town a heads-up about what you've actually been doing all this time," Lyric said with an arched eyebrow. "How long do you think it will take Griffin to hear the gossip himself—immediately, or immediately?"

The answer turned out to be even more immediate than immediately, because that was when Griffin walked in.

CHAPTER 12

G RIFFIN'S GAZE ROAMED AROUND THE LIVELY ROOM. EVERY-one was arranged in swarming, swirling clumps.

"Doesn't look like he caught many river lobsters," Lyric said offhandedly. "He'd be a lot more muddy."

When Griffin's gaze landed on Celia, his eyes widened. He should have smiled. He should have started moving toward her.

Something was wrong.

With one thought pounding through her head—*Everything will unravel if Diavala finds out!!!*—Celia shrank into herself. She had no idea what to do to head this off, so she just stood there, mute and unmoving.

Lyric shoved Celia toward Griffin, hard enough for Celia to spill her drink all over the front of her shirt. Reluctantly, she pushed her way through the crowd and approached him, hoping, praying, that everyone stayed occupied long enough so that she and Griffin could leave.

"So this is where your dandelion seed is leading you," Griffin said slowly. His words weren't cold, exactly, but they were guarded.

Celia laughed, trying to figure out what he meant. He couldn't possibly know what the commotion was about.

The noise around them was a roar of laughter, conversation, and music all jumbled together, and it was impossible to separate the details. Halcyon was engulfed in a swarm near Aspen and Blue's back table, Lyric had turned back to the bar, and it wasn't unusual to find Celia with a drink in her hand. No, he couldn't yet know about her partnership with Halcyon.

Then she realized he wasn't looking her in the eye.

His gaze was aimed a little too high. Higher than her hair, higher than the brim of her hat, at something right at the very top.

Oh no, Xinto.

"What's a river lobster?" Celia asked with as much enthusiasm as she could muster. Maybe if she didn't acknowledge this, it wasn't happening. So much for herding him out before someone spilled the tea—she'd done that all on her own.

Griffin continued to stare between Celia and the huge bee on her hat, all while soaking in the heightened celebratory feel of the night. As he pieced things together, his eyes shadowed, and it was clear he didn't like the picture. "It seems you're the face of deception now," he mused aloud, and his soft words landed like a brand.

"Give me a minute to explain—"

"You've had so many minutes already," he said, laughing, "and didn't take advantage of any of them."

That was true, but with very good reason. Surely he understood that.

"I didn't realize you'd be so good at this, Celia." He gestured to Xinto with a careless swing of his hand.

It didn't sound like a compliment. His voice was so hard it could have shattered glass. Even as Michali came in and slapped him on the back for his "prime effort, with the lobsters! They're wily little shits," before moving on, Griffin didn't shift his gaze. His eyes bored holes into Celia.

It didn't sound like him.

It wasn't him.

With a shudder silently quaking up her spine, Celia hated that she didn't know the exact moment Diavala had come forward and taken over. When, exactly, had Griffin left the conversation? How big would the gap in his night be?

Celia's concern now had nothing to do with Halcyon and Griffin chatting, nor with the townspeople giving away her impending indenture. The evidence of Celia's lies and misdirection was peeking over the brim of her hat, cocking his wee black head at her as if asking if she was okay.

Not okay, Xinto!

Celia forced herself not to stiffen. "I'm glad you're here now," she said, casually tilting her half-spilled drink in an unreciprocated cheer. She had to play it cool, pretend it was Griffin without letting on that she'd realized Diavala had come forward. She'd made an epic mistake bringing Xinto along, but it wasn't too late to fix it. "We have a lot to celebrate."

Celia nudged Xinto to do a flyover of the crowd, earning

claps and cheers from the locals. Diavala flinched when Xinto dove close.

"I know it's a lot to take in, and I'm sorry I've been cagey about it, but how can you not love him, Griffin?" she said as Xinto perched on her shoulder and looked up at him innocently.

Diavala forced a strained smile. "I must have been stung as a child," she said.

Maybe.

Or maybe because Diavala could no longer touch the ink, she loathed the black and yellow striped reminder of it.

Xinto nuzzled into Celia's neck and tried to disappear down the front of her shirt.

There, there, Celia cooed silently, stroking his fat body. *She can't hurt you.*

"Okay, so I know you're probably pissed off," she said with a long, weary sigh for effect. "But let's just have a drink or two. Come on. It'd be rude to leave now." Celia made her way to a long table where Davi, Michali, and a few others sat. "After all," she added over her shoulder, "it's my party."

Please follow, please follow. Would that carefully placed bomb of information be enough to keep Diavala there a little longer? Would she decide it was too risky to stay, now knowing that Celia had been lying about working with her old enemy, or would her curiosity win out?

Griffin had been right, many days ago, when he'd said it was as if Diavala wanted *them* to encounter Halcyon but stay hidden herself. If Diavala wanted to stay far away from the one who scared her so much, it was far easier to run than to hide.

Diavala must have expected the meetings between Celia and Halcyon to benefit *her* somehow.

It was clear from the way Diavala side-eyed the furry puff, she hadn't expected Xinto. Things had progressed without her knowledge, and not in the way she'd hoped.

Diavala had *every* reason to flee now.

Celia took a long swig of the fresh beer Garuld had shoved in her hand, blanching at the blandness of it, and wiped her mouth to hold in the sigh of relief that Diavala hadn't run away yet.

"You drink too much," Diavala said, sliding into the seat next to Celia. "It impairs your judgment."

Celia smiled at Griffin, but all she saw was an enemy. A stab pulsed through her heart, and her throat closed. *I'm sorry for what I'm about to do.*

Diavala watched Xinto from behind Griffin's eyes, continuing her survey of the people in the room, perhaps looking for one particular face. If she suspected a trap of some kind, she wasn't letting on, but she would have her bearings soon. She would understand exactly how far things had progressed without her knowledge, and she wouldn't like it.

Garuld clapped Griffin on the back quite hard and launched into a story from his childhood, his face flushed from too much wine.

"I don't mean to cut you off—" Celia said to Garuld, doing just that. "But Griffin has no idea what this night is about."

After a brief pause, everyone tried to tell him at once: "Celia is Halcyon's apprentice!" "She knows his secrets and has vowed to take care of Wisteria!" "She's one of us! And look at her adorable bee!"

"I'm going to get us all a round," Celia said, standing.

Diavala gifted Celia with a furious smile. With so many people now eager to share the biggest gossip in years, everything Griffin had missed in his quest for river lobsters, Diavala couldn't rightly make him stand up and leave, but there was only so long Diavala would tolerate this.

After ordering drinks, Celia shuffled her way to Lyric's side. "I need your help," Celia whispered from the side of her mouth. She dipped her chin and smiled at Halcyon when he looked over, then went back to watching Giada prepare the round of drinks.

Celia had never been more grateful for all the coin she'd made while on the road. Their table was mercifully packed with thirsty friends, and Giada's work mixing and pouring them all would buy her enough time to fill Lyric in.

"I can't keep them apart all night," Lyric said, low. "Why didn't you shuffle Griffin out when you had the chance?"

"Things have changed. I don't have time to explain everything right now. But—" Celia hesitated only a moment before telling Lyric what she needed.

Lyric's eyes widened. "You have a strange way of treating

your friends," they said slowly. "Trust me when I say I don't really want to be involved in your business—"

"Then don't be," Celia snapped, immediately regretting it. "Look, it's not what you think," she said, quieter. "Can you help me or not?" She discreetly pulled the tiny packet of jipep seeds from her inside breast pocket. She'd carried them all the way from Asura, even sleeping with them pressed against her heart, always within reach. After Diavala had Touched Vincent and he'd collapsed into wails, tearing out his hair and scraping his skin while lost in a miasma of horrors and pain, the tonic made from these terrible seeds had been the only thing to sedate him.

Celia had hoped she'd never have to use them. After seeing what had happened with Vincent, she had a terrible suspicion that the seeds worked only on the outside—calming bodily function, but not the mind—and she couldn't think of a worse torture than being stuck inside your own body, thoughts storming and hallucinations chasing you into every dark corner.

If she made this too strong, Griffin might be stuck trying to outrun those nightmares forever. She'd gift him with hallucinations powerful enough to drive him just as mad as from the Touch she was trying to save him from.

If she didn't make it strong enough, Diavala would seize control and run, taking all hope of Griffin's freedom with her.

Trembling, hiding her movements, Celia dropped one tiny seed, the size of a speck of dust, into Griffin's rum.

Seeing that Celia was serious, something changed in Lyric's face. Disapproval melded to confusion, their eyebrows knotting. Maybe they saw the truth: it wasn't a callous move, but a desperate one.

Lyric turned their back to the room, nodded to Giada, and ordered a couple more drinks. Their lips pressed together into a tight line before they spoke. "I don't expect Halcyon will ask too many questions about this, but I have a few for you later."

Celia nodded and exhaled in relief. Having Lyric as an ally made this easier.

After adding all the drinks to her running tab, Celia made a few trips to deliver the round, then shuffled back onto the bench beside Griffin.

She slid him the glass of rum, tinted with poison.

As conversation buzzed around them, Diavala leaned close, pressing her lips to Celia's ear. "I know you know it's me."

"Yes," Celia said. "I know it's you."

To everyone at the table, it must have looked as if Griffin and Celia had retreated to lovers' whispers: heads bent close, murmuring in each other's ears. Diavala even tucked a strand of hair behind Celia's ear tenderly, and Celia's responding shudder might have looked like a shiver of pleasure. No one interrupted.

Almost everything could change in the blink of an eye, but Diavala's self-serving behavior would never be one of them.

"What did you think would happen when I met Halcyon, hmm?" Celia asked. "That he would hurt me? Kill me? Something worse me?"

Xinto snuggled against her chest, appreciating the rhyme.

"All of the above, in relatively quick succession." Their foreheads nearly touching, Diavala's lips stretched into a smile, showcasing white teeth clenched together. It made Celia's stomach turn, that looking at Griffin could revolt her so. "But I was hoping it would be his ink that finished you, as a sort of poetic justice."

Charming.

Celia felt the familiar massive hate wash over her, pitch-dark and heavy. She took it in like fuel, barely hanging on to her calm façade. Part of her wanted to scream about how well everything was going, how quickly the ink had listened to her, how even Halcyon himself was impressed, how she had the answer to protecting Griffin . . .

The ink would save Griffin and others, and eventually it would avenge Anya. *That* would be poetic justice. The thing she'd always hated would be their savior; the thing Diavala had always treasured would be her downfall.

Celia took a moment to breathe, letting her hatred flow through her veins like a soporific, powering her.

Motivating her.

Celia stood and raised her glass, offering a toast.

"To Aspen and Blue," she said, finding them in the crowd and smiling wide. "To another fifteen years of health and happiness."

Lyric pressed their lips together in a tight line again, their face in its usual scowl, but resignedly raised their glass with the others.

"And to the future," Celia said, seeking out Halcyon's eyes, holding her drink up higher.

This is for you, Anny, and for you, Griffin.

Celia slammed back the drink as cheers rose up, people drinking, coughing, slapping tables, and laughing before rekindling their previous conversations.

Diavala drank.

Only few minutes later her eyes widened. "Do you care about your plague doctor not at all?" she whispered. Eyelids already drooping, she put her head down on the table.

"Lightweight!" Michali roared, shaking Griffin's shoulder, trying to rouse him. "If I'd known you were so precious, I wouldn't have invited you to the lakes today!"

Laughter surrounded them.

Celia pressed her face close. "You thought you'd win," she whispered. "That's the only reason you were humoring this escapade with Halcyon. Don't tell me you would have stuck around to see how this new path played out. I'm doing this *for* my plague doctor, Diavala. If you'd known that Halcyon and I were working together, you would have taken Griffin and run from this place, you would have found a way to rip him apart and kill him without harming your precious legacy, and you would have spent a lifetime in hiding, out of my reach, biding your time all over again. I will not let that happen."

Diavala's eyes flashed as she struggled to stay conscious. She looked angry enough to set the table on fire with her rage. "This is the biggest mistake of your life, Inkling. You have no idea what—"

"All I see is a win on the horizon," Celia said, leaning in even closer, her lips tickling Griffin's ear. "And it's glorious."

Interlude

"We have a problem."

It took the plague doctor a while to understand that this wasn't his own thought. He was, after all, trapped in a room with no door and trying not to hyperventilate. He could pick any lock and escape from any binds, but only if there were locks and binds.

Closing his eyes, he focused on separating Diavala out. Every time she intruded now, he made sure to give her form and substance. He imagined a conversation with someone in front of him.

Another performer.

Diavala had been ten or so when she'd been drowned, so he imagined a ten-year-old child. Long brown hair in a simple braid. Threadbare pants and sweater. Unexceptional, except for her purple eyes. Striking. A violent shade of violet. He made her real with just enough not-real to remind himself of the truth; otherwise she could be any young player who'd ever come through the troupe—Remy or Maude, Coral or Ivan.

We have so many problems, he agreed. Namely, that Celia had been the one to put them in this doorless room, at the mercy of a near-toothless stranger who'd named herself after a war criminal. That Celia had drugged him to get him there (and not the nice kind of drug) was the worst part. Perhaps Celia believed that protecting him, no matter the cost, would banish her guilt over not saving Anya, but both he and Diavala knew better: certain ghosts lingered forever.

He squeezed his hand into a fist and scraped it down the doorless wall, grimacing. Celia was so close to being consumed by Anya's ghost. Anya lingered in every move she made, every breath she took. Ghosts are strange that way; they're supposed to be made of love, but they're oh so hungry all the time. Insatiable.

"Your mind wanders around more than a hummingbird seeking nectar, plague doctor," Diavala said. Impatience made her thoughts hiss. *"Don't waste time grieving. If Halcyon has seduced her, she's already lost."*

Seduced her . . .

All I know for sure is that Celia made a big bee out of ink, he reminded himself.

But he'd never been a convincing liar, and no matter how much he wanted to, he couldn't force himself to swallow that one. Celia had done far more with Halcyon already: they'd become allies, confidants, an apprentice and a master. And it was the ink that Celia claimed to hate that had brought them together.

Forcing himself to unclench his fist, the plague doctor pressed his palm to the smooth marble walls. So opulent and ridiculous. He couldn't even name the closest nation that mined for marble.

Was everything in Wisteria an illusion, then? Was this wall even real? If Celia could make a giant bee now, what else could she do under Halcyon's tutelage?

He crept toward the only window, not quite trusting the tiles under his feet nor the roof over his head. It was a large enough window for him to fit through if he smashed each of the dozen small glass panes and ripped apart the frame. He had his trusty hammer. Maybe it would work . . .

Then he'd only have to deal with the impossible four-story drop into Rian's flower bed.

"Are you listening to me, plague doctor?" Diavala shouted.

Why should I? he asked absently, mentally weighing how much Kinallen powder he'd need to bounce himself down. If wind speed and direction were on his side, he could do it. People assumed that the plague doctor's levitation was an optical illusion — wires or some nonsense — but he could, when pressed, do something akin to flying. It was one of the biggest trade secrets he'd ever been gifted with, from an old player named Stash before he'd retired. "Kinallen powder usually combusts into flame," Stash had told him. It had been the one and only time he'd ever spoken offstage, despite working with the troupe for years. "But under the right conditions, that point between stasis and combustion, it can also create pockets lighter than air. And if you train enough, you can master them. And *fly*."

At twelve years old, Griffin had believed him. Even after he understood, logically, that it had more to do with manipulating a chemical reaction, he still believed him. He could fly.

"You should listen because I'm saintly next to Halcyon," Diavala said. *"Halcyon will waltz Celia—and you, if you don't heed me—into the deepest pits of hell before she even realizes what's happening."*

As he stared into the darkening fields, the plague doctor thought of dagger cuts, bleeding, applause, and a broken Celia on a stage. He thought of his role in creating the worst memory of her life. *Oh, we're already there, aren't we? And if I recall correctly, Halcyon isn't the one who started this particular act.*

To Diavala's simmering silence, he tested the glass by rapping his knuckles on it, hoping it wasn't as thick as it looked.

It was.

He'd just decided to make a series of increasingly loud noises, culminating with smashing one windowpane, to test the decibel level that summoned Rian the Toothless, when Diavala intruded. *"Do you know anything about Martina, plague doctor?"*

Dia, but her timing was the worst. His mind was a hornet's nest at the best of times, and Diavala wasn't helping.

The Ides of Martina? he said. *Poet Martina Buggatin? The*

Plains of Martina's Tears? I know a lot about all kinds of Martinas. You'll have to be more specific.

Diavala didn't respond to his agitation. If there was one thing she was very good at, it was ignoring inconvenient emotions.

"The most important Martina to our story is Martina Donesse. She was Halcyon's lover. His obsession. His muse. Halcyon blames me for her death."

Interested despite himself, the plague doctor stopped cataloguing his list of noisemaking diversions and turned his full attention to the purple-eyed player in his head.

He knew that Diavala had come to Wisteria three years earlier to confront Halcyon about the ink he wasn't supposed to have, and poor Martina must have gotten in the way. Just like Vincent had gotten in the way. Just like Anya, ultimately, had gotten in the way. *You know I won't stand for you excusing Profeta's atrocities. In that, I agree with Celia completely. As I said before, the Curse of the Divine has fallen on all of us, and there's only one to blame for that, Diavala.* He drew out her name for emphasis.

"Martina's death had nothing to do with Profeta. If anything, Halcyon killed her."

His hands clenched, and he started pacing. After a moment's hesitation he decided he may as well multitask: he allowed his words to come out, starting out Griffin quiet and ending plague doctor loud. *When will Rian the Toothless come a-knocking? A-knocking?*

"So everything we're doing here is based on a . . . misunderstanding," he said. "You never came here and tried to possess Halcyon. Martina didn't die as collateral damage in your fight. Halcyon never wailed from the Touch and got his name entered on the Roll of Saints. He never recovered from said Touch, thus becoming the only one who knows how to survive you."

Not even the plague doctor's bellows summoned Rian. Almost as if he weren't a patient at all, and the healer already knew it.

Damn. Toothless was in on his captivity just like Celia and Halcyon.

"*Yes, all of that is true, in a sense. I did possess him, but for only a brief moment in time. All his thoughts revolved around Martina, Martina, Martina. She was a saintly soul, the way he saw her, and could do no wrong.*"

"Get to the pooooint," he sang, flopping dramatically onto the bed. He rolled over, stared at the ceiling, and laughed. "You're being almost as obtuse as I usually am. I'm starting to understand how frustrating it is." He resisted the urge to punch the wall. "If you have something to say to me, then say it."

"*The point is this: Halcyon will say and do anything if he thinks it will help him get Martina back. Whatever's he's promised Celia is a lie he thinks will help him meet that end. I have a feeling Celia bargained for a cure for the Touch to try to save you, of which there is none. Unless you can find a way*" to break my curse and allow me to die, you and I are stuck together for the rest of your days."

Angeli help him, there was so much nonsense to unpack in those sentences. He pinched the bridge of his nose and tried not to scream at the purple-eyed young player. "You just told me Martina is dead."

"Plague doctor, you and I both know that death isn't always final."

For a moment the plague doctor didn't know how to respond. He didn't know if he even believed her, considering all the things he sensed she was still withholding. But if what she said was even remotely true, Halcyon's quest was a particular atrocity. Hoping to bring back the dead was an abomination of nature.

"'Allow you to die?'" he finally said slowly. "That's an interesting choice of words."

"I know you fear the afterlife, plague doctor, but I've lived a thousand years too long."

He didn't like how wistful the purple-eyed girl sounded, playing on his sympathies. "A few weeks ago you were on a stage claiming life at all cost." They were so embroiled with her only because of her fight to be seen as the absolute and marvelous head of Profeta.

"On that stage I witnessed the beginning of the end of my legacy," she said, her tone hardening. Then it softened into a sigh again, disarming him. "Now there is an appealing beauty in all that nothingness."

Tantalizing whispers of new story lines were everywhere lately. Inspiration brushed up against him, offered a hand, took a seductive bow. *The Appealing Beauty of Nothingness,* a Rabble Mob production starring only two players: the Palidon and the Plague Doctor. But he had no Palidon, he had no stage.

The plague doctor grabbed his mask and held it up over his head, inspecting the sleek whiteness of it, making sure it was still amazing. Considering the glitz and shine of the lamps, the paintings, and the furniture, it was by far the most hideous thing in the room, and therefore perfect. "So this feud between you and Halcyon boils down to you wanting an impossible death and Halcyon wanting an impossible life."

He pulled his plague doctor mask on. It settled on his cheekbones, the world tinted darker through the lenses. For the first time in weeks, he felt complete.

"You and Halcyon both have ink," he said, running down all the things he was certain of. There weren't many. "You hate each other. You both play god, only on different scales." He paused, thinking about ghosts, and death, and performances. There was only one other thing he was sure of. "All of this is happening because gods shouldn't exist," he said.

"Or maybe that, Griffin," Diavala said with a sigh. *"Maybe that."*

CHAPTER 13

WHEN HALCYON ENTERED THE STUDIO THE NEXT DAY, Celia looked up from her pacing. "Let's get going," she said, holding out the bouquet of ink-flowers in her hand as an offering. Everything was about flowers in Wisteria. If she could just figure out flowers, maybe that would be good enough for him.

"Your friend's regained consciousness and is nicely set up with Rian," Halcyon said, referring to the healer's home where he'd taken Griffin the night before. "You can visit him whenever you'd like." Halcyon untucked a ledger from under his arm and gestured for Lyric to come over and look at an entry with him. Business, accounting, perhaps a grocery list.

As Celia, Lyric, and Halcyon had hauled Griffin outside the night before, he hadn't stirred. Halcyon placated the people concerned for Griffin's welfare with a charismatic smile and platitudes. In the short amount of time they'd been in the township, Griffin had made a lot of friends, but no one could dismiss and handle a Wisterian crowd the way Halcyon could.

"I feel like this is crossing all manner of lines, Celia," Halcyon had said just before they'd parted. "I can't claim to have much authority over morality, but—" And with a graceful shrug, he'd left it at that. When he shrugged, Griffin's head lolled onto his shoulder and rested there. They were nearly the same height, with the same slim build and angular features. Despite their differences in hair and eye colors, they could have easily been siblings. That observation bothered Celia in ways she couldn't explain, and she'd been all too willing to let Halcyon deal with setting Griffin up in his new accommodations.

Temporary accommodations, Celia told her rioting mind bees.

"I need more than what I'm getting," Celia said now, jostling the bouquet. "These all smell the same to me, I've sniffed them so much."

Halcyon leaned toward Lyric but kept his gaze on Celia. "She's suddenly quite impatient, isn't she?"

"I think she's feeling a little guilty for locking her friend up," Lyric replied.

Celia bristled. *She* was still in the room.

"I hate that he has to hide here," Celia said. "It makes me angry that someone I care about can't live his life like he wants to. I'm not impatient, I'm eager." Celia had explained that they'd had an argument and that Griffin wanted to leave Wisteria, but considering his role in the takedown of Profeta in Asura, Diavala would be after him, and he'd be in danger as soon as he left. "Given how much Diavala fears Halcyon," Celia had said, "she won't come here looking for us. Wisteria is the only place we're safe, but Griffin's too stubborn to see that."

It was all for his own good, which was true, just not in the manner she described. From across the room, Xinto shook his head at her and turned away, as if he were thoroughly disappointed in her.

"I want you to succeed here, Celia," Halcyon continued, snapping the ledger shut, nearly cutting off Lyric's nose. "Having someone tending to affairs when I'm away, even with your little strange embellishments, will put my mind greatly at ease. It will allow me to be away longer and explore further, so perhaps don't snap at me for your failures. I'm giving you everything I can. How fast we get what we both want is *entirely* up to you."

Halcyon went over to his vast bookshelves and took down tome after tome, stacking his selections into three piles. "Try these," he said. "Maybe academic learning will jog this last piece loose. Lyric can show you the proper sections." He left with his ledger tucked back under his arm. "And I suppose *I* have to deal with *this* then," he muttered, adding a door slam for good measure.

"Guess taking a break didn't work out for either of us," Celia said. She stared at the flowers in her hand, hating every one of them.

Lyric tossed their hair and looked up at the ceiling, as if waiting for patience to fall from it and cover them.

Whatever the ceiling provided worked for a little while, because with infinite patience and measured words, Lyric helped Celia sift through the mountain of books for hours. Anything to do with scent, from the known science of it to detailed descriptions in fiction, Celia read and tried to internalize. They debated. Lyric asked pointed questions. Then, when they'd gone through the stack Halcyon had set aside, they urged her to apply anything she'd learned.

But nothing worked.

You locked him up for nothing, Cece, Anya said.

For nothing, for nothing, Celia's bees echoed.

She refused to see Griffin — ashamed of what she'd done — until she had the inoculation against the Touch to show for her betrayal. Would he ever forgive her? It had been the wrong thing to do, but Diavala had stripped away all other options.

Not for nothing, Celia rebutted, clenching her teeth. So help her, the end would justify the means.

Although Celia set her mind to the task of learning scent, she wasn't getting any closer. Her grasp of scent wasn't reliable; it was too weak or too strong or too off, always giving away the illusion in some way. Everything else, she could do. In every other way she was just as adept as Halcyon, to the point where she'd been altering the town on his instruction: refreshing the color, restocking the insects or sunbeams, correcting flaws in texture. She and Xinto made rounds of the town, Lyric documenting everything Celia said needed to be fixed or changed, and along the way, Celia sniffed at everything like a ridiculous hound dog.

She had made some progress, enough to be heartening, but not enough. It wasn't good enough for Halcyon, who insisted on perfection.

Celia had only one thing to do — master scent, appease

Halcyon—and Diavala would have to find a new host to torture and manipulate.

One impossible thing.

Suddenly, five days didn't seem like enough time. By the time she looked up at the clock, bleary-eyed and half delirious, she had only two days left.

Celia had tried to argue with Halcyon that it wasn't important. She'd proved she could do everything else, the ink was hers to control in every way. What did it matter if she had to wait for him to return from his travels before fixing up the scent of the flowers?

Desperate to prove both Anya and her bees wrong, she'd also tried to bargain for more ink, thinking that all her experimentation had depleted the ink in her bloodstream or dampened its powers, or *something*. With her mind bees whispering how terrible she was, she had to prove them wrong, even if it took more ink in her blood to do it. Halcyon was constantly replenishing his; she'd seen him put his hands into the chest more than once already. "I'll just put my hands in for a second," she'd said. "Just to freshen everything up. What can it hurt?"

And wow, had *that* had been a mistake. He'd promptly moved the chest of ink that had been in the studio since the very first day and hidden it from her. "You will not steal from me," he'd said.

So now, along with being obsessed with capturing scent properly, Celia was also obsessing over where the ink was. Where he'd taken it. Was this all a game? Was he setting her up to fail by keeping it from her?

When Celia went to fetch something from the kitchen, Lyric looped their arm through Celia's and led her away from the door with the sunflower doorknob. Celia didn't even remember stepping in the wrong direction, let alone reaching for the knob to open it.

"Is it in there?" Celia asked.

"Is what in there?"

"The ink." If Halcyon was holding it hostage until she met his standards of perfection, it made sense that he'd put it in the forbidden room.

Celia looked at Lyric sideways, waiting for their answer.

At the fourth side glance, Lyric had had enough. "Before you bother," they said. "I'm loyal to exactly one person in this life, Celia, and it isn't you."

Celia had to hand it to them, Lyric was a fantastic liar. Lyric might stand beside Halcyon, but there was something keeping them there that wasn't loyalty.

As if Celia couldn't recognize false devotion.

Lyric's jaw flexed, and they ran their hand along the shaved bit of their hair, ruffling it with aggressive jerks. "If I were you, I'd *definitely* keep the door closed," they said. If Lyric said "don't," they usually meant "do," all part of their Contraryish charm.

And Lyric used door metaphors far more than anyone else Celia had ever known. They'd been encouraging Celia to open the door for a long time now.

"*Definitely* don't tell me the *opposite* of what's *not* behind that door, Lyric . . ." Celia said, still side-eying them. Was that a double negative? A triple?

Lyric barked out a laugh—a miracle. "What?" they said through their chuckles.

"I'm trying to speak Contraryish," Celia said, nudging them. "Is it working? Did you understand me?" Celia tried to wink playfully, but she was so tightly coiled, it probably looked frightening.

"Okay, you've officially lost your mind," Lyric said.

"Will this silly party still happen, even if I haven't figured it out?" she asked.

"Halcyon won't be made a fool of, Celia. There's no option for you *but* to figure it out."

The fact was, everything was supposed to be settled by the day of the party. A celebration of an exchange: indenture for inoculation. Celia looked up. "But what if I *don't?*" Their conversation had been laced with jokes for its entirety, but Celia heard the desperation in her own question.

Lyric heard it too. "Honestly, I don't know. He thought he was giving you plenty of time. Part of the reason he's deep-dived into party planning is to distract himself from the possibility that you won't pull through."

They stared at each other a beat.

"You still have time," Lyric said. "And you are getting closer. You just need that one piece to click, and you'll have it."

That was, in all honesty, the nicest thing Lyric had ever said to her. Through her fatigue and hunger and desperation, Celia felt her eyes tearing up.

Lyric rolled theirs and turned away.

"What do you get out of this arrangement?" Celia said, swiping at the tears on her cheeks. She was still puzzled by Lyric's role. They seemed indispensable to running the town, on one hand, but at the same time, Halcyon wouldn't be so eager for Celia help him if Lyric filled in all the gaps. "Why wouldn't you learn to use the ink? Be Halcyon's apprentice rather than his assistant?"

"Well, that's insulting on so many levels."

"I didn't mean anything bad. I just don't get it."

Lyric glared. Any bonding they'd done had been fleeting, and now, judging by the heat in their eyes, was over completely. "You don't need to 'get it' — you need to focus. Halcyon won't entertain this forever, and you're running out of time to figure it out. The door of opportunity will stay closed if you don't get around to opening it soon." Another door reference. Funny. Lyric straightened and rolled their shoulders, as if trying to calm down. "If you're not going to do any actual work here, let's call it a day. It's late, and you tire me right the hell out, Celia Sand."

They walked shoulder to shoulder toward the front door. By then, Xinto knew the labyrinthine house inside and out and could easily lead the way if Celia got lost, but Lyric always insisted on escorting her to the exit. Perhaps they really were worried that Celia would die in a back room somewhere.

And Celia hated to admit that she was distracted. Halcyon had given assurances that Griffin was fine, if a "tad emotional" about the ordeal, but she still hadn't visited him.

She refused to see him empty-handed.

Which meant she needed to be full-handed.

Celia snorted a laugh, making Lyric glance over at her. "Opposite of empty-handed is full-handed?" she muttered, then quickly looked away. When was the last time she'd gotten any sleep? She spent her evenings wandering the streets, smelling everything, practicing.

Lyric rolled their eyes, and as soon as Celia stepped outside, they slammed the door.

Celia knocked, and it flew open again.

"What?" Lyric barked, as if Celia had unceremoniously woken them rather than seen them moments before.

"I just wanted to say I like you."

Lyric's head tilted. "You can't out-sarcasm me. Don't even try."

They tried to slam the door again, to leave Celia alone with her giant bee friend, but she rammed her foot in the door. She wasn't being sarcastic at all. Lyric reminded Celia of Zuni—a tough friend with a soft center. She'd physically ached for Zuni lately: the somehow reassuring smell of death that always clung to her skullkeeper friend, the games Celia used to play with the shimmering rainbow of Zuni's tenor, the whispers and confidences they shared. Dante had messaged Celia—before Celia had stopped reading his messages—that Zuni had left Asura, so Celia liked to imagine Zuni out in the world for the first time in years: adventuring, bird watching, laughing even, but probably with a bag of her favorite skulls tucked against her hip.

"I wasn't being sarcastic," Celia whispered.

Lyric frowned, but it wasn't their usual sharp one. More like confusion. Or discomfort. As Xinto perched on Celia's top hat, Lyric laughed, as if grateful for the distraction. "I'll never be as devoted a friend as your bee, sorry."

"Eh," Celia said, shrugging. "As cute as he is, Xinto's not real. You are."

Celia didn't know how long the two of them stood there awkwardly. Long enough that Xinto got bored and flew away.

Although she wasn't full-handed yet, Celia straightened her spine and made a snap decision. Maybe it was fatigue getting the best of her, maybe it was thinking of Zuni and friendship. She needed to push aside her shame, be brave, and check on Griffin. She was doing what she had to for him (even though he might not see it that way), but it wasn't fair to him that she hadn't visited to explain herself.

"Can you give me directions to Rian's, pretty please?" Celia finally asked. *Ree-un.* The pronunciation fell off her tongue strangely, like it was covered in cotton. A weird name, fiercely dated. Rian had been the first ruler of Illinia after the civil war ended, a much-hated figure from history whose grandest claim to fame was not in restoring peace—that had been her predecessor, Iadanza—but for pissing off both sides and almost inflaming the war anew. "Why would she choose that name for herself?" Celia wondered aloud.

Lyric waved a dismissive hand. "She lost her mind years ago."

"What?" Celia exclaimed. That was where Griffin was supposed to be safe.

"Relax, I'm teasing." Lyric shrugged and wouldn't meet Celia's eyes as they stepped out the door to lead the way. "She does her best."

Celia was glad that Lyric accompanied her; otherwise she would have wandered around in circles for an age. The healer's house lay at the outskirts of town on a large swath of farmland. Picturesque, with rows upon rows of carefully tended crops: orange pumpkins, green peas, blood-red tomatoes, purple-topped beets. Celia knew next to nothing about farming, but enough to know that no one growing season could bear all these vegetables at once.

The path passed through tall corn and sunflowers, yellow and bright against the evening light. Despite the perpetually clear skies of Wisteria, Halcyon either couldn't be bothered or couldn't quite manufacture stars properly. A few twinkled against the darkening canvas, but not nearly as many as should have been there.

Xinto flew ahead and returned to Celia, back and forth, thrilled with the adventure no matter how many times Celia or Lyric swatted him away, his buzzing a low, comforting hum.

A gnarled old soul appeared on her front porch as they approached. She looked them up and down with one gimlet eye.

Raising a shaky hand, she pointed to the road they'd just come down. "Begone, peddlers," she grunted, her breath raspy with age. "We make my own tinctures and tonics here, thank you very much."

"Hello, grandmother," Lyric said with a forced smile.

Grandmother.

Grandmother?

At that, the old soul waddled with great speed toward them, proceeding to inspect Celia from head to foot. "Yes, this one needs my help," she said, her murky eyes glistening with something like glee. "You did well to bring her to me, Lyric. The pallor of her skin, the slight sheen of fever in her eyes. Yes." She nodded, placing her weathered palm on Celia's forehead, then the back of her hand on her cheek. She grabbed Celia's wrist and felt her pulse. Celia had never known a healer to be so thrilled at the idea of illness in her midst. Rian clicked her tongue and shook her head. "And not a moment too soon. Poor dear."

"She needs nothing from you. She's fine," Lyric said. "We're here to visit the traveler Halcyon brought to you the other night."

Halcyon had told Rian that Griffin needed to be quarantined for a spell. Nothing serious, but he was a potential danger to himself and others and needed protection and solitude in order to recover.

Rian eyed Celia dubiously, as if sensing that the "she's fine" part was debatable. "Right. Well, he's inside. Though he looks perfectly well to my expertly trained eye, if only a little tired and sad. He did request no visitors, however—particularly, and I quote, 'a small, shattered soul in a top hat.'"

Flushing bright red, Celia looked toward the fields. Xinto flew in tighter and tighter circles around Rian's pumpkin patch.

Something about Rian was off, not in any sinister way, but she reminded Celia of Lupita: both absent-minded and deeply traumatized. Lupita had tortured Celia for years, doled out punishments, regimented her life, but had somehow become one of her only friends. She was the one Celia often missed the most; her unpredictability had become so perfectly predictable.

But the image of Lupita's wrinkled hands on a dagger, helping Celia do an unspeakable thing, rose up in her memory, unbidden. The stark contrast of pale white cracks and crevices of age, filling, filled, overtaken by the warm, crimson red of life . . .

Celia bent in half, hugging her head to her knees, trying to hold her insides in, breathing through it until she managed to push the images away. She could run from Asura, everything that had happened there, everything she'd done, but it still managed to sneak up on her and land a punch. To Lyric's concern, she gasped out, "She reminds me of someone from the temple," but then couldn't continue.

She concentrated on not curling up in a ball. She listened hard for Anya's voice. *Stand up, Cece. You're such a disaster. Stop feeling sorry for yourself.*

The hollow space inside crawled with rot, and Lupita had helped put it there. Most things could be forgiven, but there were some that lingered like a fungus, growing over time rather than healing.

Lyric rubbed her back tentatively, but with a kind of understanding that was deep and full. "I understand more than you think I do," they whispered.

Celia grabbed Lyric's hand without thinking. She squeezed. After a few heartbeats passed, she was able to straighten and walk toward the farmhouse. She didn't let go of Lyric's hand, and Lyric, surprisingly, didn't pull away.

CHAPTER 14

GRIFFIN'S KNUCKLES HAD DRIED BLOOD ON THEM. HE WAS wearing his plague doctor mask, his feathered cape, his black coat and pants, and, most infuriating of all, his wide, brazen plague doctor smile.

But all Celia could focus on was his knuckles.

She hadn't expected a huge smile and a hug, given the circumstances, but she *definitely* hadn't expected blood on his knuckles. They were alone, Lyric and Rian doing their own awkward dance in another part of the farmhouse, with Xinto buzzing circles around their heads until Celia summoned him.

The room was lavish: high ceilings, comfortable furniture, a bookshelf stocked with more books than Celia had ever seen in her life, enough space to jog around for exercise, and a big bed heaped with pillows. Somehow the room was ten times bigger than Rian's entire farmhouse appeared from the outside. Celia was almost jealous of the luxury, except that it didn't look at all like Griffin had enjoyed any of it. The door Rian had led her through had disappeared. No matter how luxurious, it was still a prison, and she'd put him there.

Griffin stared at Celia through the glass lenses of his mask. Arms crossed, feet planted apart, he waited for her to speak first, explain herself. His hands pinched tight on his arms, the scabs over his knuckles threatening to draw fresh blood with a crack. His hands were meant for playing with purple and blue fire from Kinallen, mined in some magical way he'd once hinted at when they could still sit with each other and talk. They were meant for fixing wobbly floorboards on a stage or the wheel axle of a wagon. They were meant for tenderness, for gestures in the air as he told stories to the Kids.

Nothing about his body language said that he would entertain any horseshit.

"Diavala was going to run," Celia said. She commanded her feet to walk toward him, but they were stubborn as hell and didn't move, other than shifting from foot to foot. It was as if there were a gaping crack in the ground between them, perilously deep, rather than a few steps.

"I figured that part out," he said. Up close, Celia could see his fatigue more clearly: his head and shoulders sagged uncharacteristically, his mouth a tight line. How much of it was a result of spending a few nights in captivity, and how much from housing a monster? She wished she could see his eyes, and at the same time she was thankful for his mask.

"I needed to keep her here," Celia said. "This was all I could think of to do." She begged him to understand. To forgive her.

"Look at how much power he has over you," the plague doctor said. He shook his head, his beak swiping left and right slowly.

Celia bristled. *She'd* made the choice, however terrible it had been. It hadn't been Halcyon. "I can undo any of this whenever I want," she said. In essence, the whole of Wisteria was one giant, interconnected life form—like a bloom of algae on a pond or a bed of lichen covering a rock—it could spread, retreat, and change. Halcyon nurtured it like a topiary: snipping away imperfections, molding it into an ideal.

And it was, in fact, easier to unravel than to create, as she'd already learned. Like swiping your hand across an image in the sand. All she had to do was call her ink back and the knot she'd tied in the sweater would unravel and return to her.

"I can undo it and let you out, but I won't," she said, meeting his eyes.

Because Diavala will still run.

Because now, perhaps, you would run too.

The plague doctor smiled ever wider. "At least Halcyon cuts his prisons from the most extravagant cloth." With a sharp laugh, he opened his arms to encompass the room. "When you inevitably join me, when whatever scheme you're orchestrating blows up in your face, we'll live like the richest rats in the world. Unless, of course, we die for our trouble."

The way he said it sounded very much like he believed that death was the expected outcome. "This is the only road that has a way of protecting you, and I'm happy to walk it," she said.

"But what is this road you've hidden from me, Celia? What have you bargained for? Where is all of this going?" He leveled a look at her, his manner weary and angry at the same time. "Is it possible he might indeed be a bigger problem than *she* is?"

So careful not to say her name, as if the walls had ears and could hear their secret alliance. Celia had come to make sure the jipep seeds hadn't harmed him, not to be confronted with the vile idea that Griffin and Diavala were *bonding*.

"I'm working on it," Celia snapped. She would master scent, start her service, and get the inoculation. "And whatever lies Diavala is feeding you, you need to stop eating them," she said. "She's had a thousand years to perfect the art of manipulation."

"I can discern her lies easy enough. I am sharing my head with her, after all."

The crack between them widened, threatening to swallow them both.

Turning away from her, Griffin examined the expanse of wall where Celia had come in. Griffin's hands trailed along the wall with an intensity of concentration she hadn't seen since he'd performed with the Rabble Mob. Moving to another space, he examined another section of wall, the evidence of her choice highlighted in the blood on his knuckles as he compared every dip and crack in the stone faces. "The door is in a different spot every time," he mumbled to himself. Bending, he examined the floor.

"Griffin, I—"

"I know you don't want to listen," he said, cutting her off, "but we made a big mistake coming here." His words were swallowed by the stone, but there was a manic edge to them that echoed back to Celia's ears. When he said, "We have to be prepared next time Rian comes," Celia wasn't sure he was even talking to her.

And if he wasn't talking to her, he was talking to *her.*

"Griffin," she said, louder, trying to overtake the poisonous voice in his head. He couldn't possibly be aligning himself with Diavala. The thought was unconscionable.

Still, he didn't respond.

"Plague doctor!" Celia yelled.

His jaw tightened, but he didn't look at her as he tried to pry a section of stone up from the floor. Judging from the amount of scraped-away mortar and the state of his fingernails, he'd been working on that section for a while. He acted as if she'd made the wrong choice, but then what was the right one? Celia wanted to scream at him until he told her. To leave Wisteria, chase Diavala around and doubt everything Griffin said and did forever, and *hope* that Diavala didn't hurt him? To wash her hands of everything, leave him behind, and try to start a new life with everyone destroyed in her wake? Those weren't choices, they were failures.

"Your jailer is bigger than this one room," she said, "and it isn't me!"

"Stop," he said, hissing as his raw knuckles scraped against stone. Whatever he was doing was causing more harm, one knuckle freshly bleeding, but he didn't seem to notice. "Didn't

Diavala always claim to have noble intentions? Didn't she claim to be saving people? And here you are, doing exactly the same thing."

"How dare you," Celia said, her voice pitched low. She clenched her hands, resisting the urge to ink a hand slapping his perfect jawline or a bird swooping in and stealing his precious mask. "I would never take away your choice—"

"But you *did*, Celia. The moment you drugged me, put me in here, and decided not to let me out. I may have resigned myself to a certain fate—death is no mystery to me—but there was a freedom in that resignation. A freedom you've now stolen from me."

"It isn't *you* I locked in here!"

"Okay, but what if I refuse?" he said, standing. "What if I say I don't trust Halcyon's promises and I want to leave and deal with this on my own?" Griffin took a step closer. "You know what I think would happen? You'd convince yourself that I was under Diavala's control, you'd force me into whatever web you've spun with Halcyon, you'd continue using the ink you hated only a few weeks ago, and I think you'd justify it to yourself every moment until it was done, and then all the years after."

She shook her head. "All of this has been for *you*." How could he toss it back at her like this?

He turned and stared her down. "It hasn't been for me in a long time. Your ghosts are taking over your reason."

Just then a door appeared, on a different section of wall from where Rian had let Celia through, a dozen steps away from where Griffin was trying to pry up the floor.

He took three graceful leaps over to Celia's side and put his hands behind his back as Rian eyed him suspiciously. "I made you some biscuits." Her milky gaze skittered between them. "Is it a good visit?" Concern laced her voice, and Celia wasn't sure who she was worried about.

"Fine," Celia said.

"Fine," Griffin echoed.

"Well, this tea should help," she said, placing the tray on a side table. "Linden flowers and honey."

It was likely the same tea Halcyon had been serving Celia, though Celia had yet to see a linden tree in bloom. "Help with what?"

Rian straightened and blinked, already on her way to the magically appearing door. Because Rian wasn't an inkling, Halcyon must have worked the door into the illusion for her. "Well, your headaches have been better since you started drinking it, haven't they?" And she tapped her temple with a smile. "Stress always aggravates things. Let's call this preventative medicine."

"Yes, things are definitely aggravating in here," Celia said.

Beside Celia, Griffin had turned into a statue. Only his eyes moved, assessing Rian's movement. He whispered something, too low for even Celia to hear, that sounded like a garble of sounds together, ending with ". . . *not now.*"

With one more appraisal of them standing there side by side and staring at her, Rian nodded and left the room. As the door closed behind her, Griffin launched himself to it, grasping at the wood and scrambling to find purchase on any of the ridges even as it turned to stone and disappeared from under his fingertips.

A line of blood from one of his fingers marked the wall where the door had been, and he stared at it, shaking his head at some unheard words.

"Don't listen to her, plague doctor," Celia said, choking on the name she used to address him. Whatever was going on with him, he'd fallen back into his plague doctor role. Hiding, scared.

"She isn't manipulating me—"

"She's doing exactly that," Celia said. Her hands began to shake. "She's inside your head, like you just said." Tears had sprung to her eyes, but that only made her angrier. "She knows exactly what scares you the most, what would make you panic and listen to her and want to leave. She's using your deepest fears to turn you against me."

He watched her. He was still beautiful, but in a fractured way now, as if something were scraping at his insides, hollowing him out bit by bit, like a sculptor carving into wood or marble, creating something new by omitting. The plague doctor mask highlighted his deep wounds so clearly now. It was his protection in the face of death.

One thing was obvious: Griffin had spent too long alone with only one toxic creature for company. He'd spent his whole life free, on the open road, without any walls around him. Leaving him here, as lavish as it was, had been a mistake.

The plague doctor had moved to the lone window, staring out, his palm pressed to the glass. Old, dried blood tainted most of the panes, as if that was where he'd tried to escape first. "It won't be much longer," Celia said to him. "I came to tell you this is almost over. Just a few more days."

He nodded without turning around, but his reflection off the glass stared at her, a ghostly version of an already ghostly plague doctor. "I doubt that very much."

Celia created a new door, unsure of how to manipulate the one designed for Rian, and closed it behind her with a click. On the other side, Griffin was probably standing there, watching it disappear. She imagined him pressing his palm to the bare wall, putting his ear to it, listening. "I'm sorry," she whispered, tracing her fingers against the grain of the wood on her side. For so many things, but, in that moment, mostly for the wall between them.

Downstairs, voices mixed together in a jumbled conversation. Celia hadn't thought Lyric would wait around for her to finish visiting with Griffin, but their voice was pitched the highest, talking over Rian's.

Xinto had responded to Celia's summons but was eager to rejoin the party, leading the way in loop-de-loops, buzzing loudly. Celia followed, pressing her fingers to her lips, urging quiet. It didn't sound like the kind of conversation they should barge into, and if Lyric and Rian were rehashing old wounds, Celia hoped to avoid intruding. Xinto listened, buzzing over and landing on Celia's shoulder, tickling her neck with his fuzzy legs. She had no doubt that if she threw a twig, Xinto would fetch it. Such a good bee.

"Maybe it's better if you don't come round again," Rian was saying.

"Or maybe I should 'come round' more often," Lyric bit back, "to make sure you remember what a conscience is."

Although Celia couldn't make out the details of their disagreement, it sounded like an age-old difference of opinion. Something bone-deep that had created a wedge between them.

If Rian was Lyric's Lupita, their relationship was fraught.

Unless Celia altered the home to give herself another exit—which wasn't fair to Lyric, who'd waited for her—there was no way to avoid the front room. She cleared her throat as loudly as possible. "Uh, I'm sorry to intru—" She stepped around the corner and stopped, as if she'd hit a wall.

Lyric and Rian, standing in the middle of the sitting room, turned to face her. In Rian's hand was a bottle of something Celia had seen only once before. It wasn't the bottle she recognized—stark white and gleaming with the triangular symbol on the front—but the smell of the bottle's contents.

Even muted with a stopper, even such a small amount, the vile scent of the poison still clawed its way up Celia's nose, giving itself away. She'd made it herself, the first day in Halcyon's studio.

One drop could kill a person in moments.

And if Rian had laughed it off before tucking it immediately away, if she'd dismissed it as "nothing to worry about," or "a personal matter," Celia would probably have believed her. Rian was a healer, after all. It made sense she would have both poisons and antidotes.

But Rian didn't do those things. Instead, she flushed bright red and gently placed the bottle on a nearby table. She and Lyric stared at it, then glared at each other. "Lyric believes I have no heart," Rian said, looking right into her grandchild's eye. "When everything I do — everything I've ever done — has been for them."

Only then did Rian laugh it off. She said all the right things as she hustled Celia out the door, but it was too late. Doubt had snuck in.

CHAPTER 15

I N A GONDOLA, CELIA TRAVELED DOWN ONE OF ASURA'S MANY canals toward Lupita's floating home. The sound of the water lapping at the sides of the boat and the soft, distracted humming from the gondolier were the only sounds of the night. The other person in the boat was wrapped in swaths of dark fabric, like a spool of thread. It was a strange sight, every limb pronounced, features hidden but not menacing. The figure leaned forward and held their hand out—every finger tightly swaddled, the cloth looping around their palms, wrists, up their arms—offering her a stoppered glass bottle.

"Remember Salome," they said. Their voice was kind and soothing, sympathetic.

Celia took the bottle, uncorked the stopper, and remembered one of her first childhood friends at the temple. Salome's fiery red hair rose up first, then her crooked smile, then the entirety of her friendly, freckled face. When one solitary tear fell from Celia's eyes, she put the bottle to her cheek to catch it.

"Remember Monroe."

The child's laughter floated through the still air around her, and she added two more tears.

"Remember Lupita's crisp blue eyes."

"Remember Vincent."

The small bottle was nearly full. Celia was in a place of quiet remembrance, the tears cathartic because she'd never before let them escape in such quantity. A small, grateful smile tugged reluctantly at her lips.

"Remember Zuni."

Celia's melancholy smile turned to a confused one. This was about remembering the dead. The casualties of Diavala's false religion. She held the bottle toward the wrapped figure.

They didn't take it. "Remember Dante. Remember Zuni."

Celia pushed the bottle more forcefully toward the figure in black. It was meant for the memories of the dead and gone. Dante, Zuni . . . they weren't dead.

Were they?

As if they knew her thoughts, they nodded their wrapped head and urged her to continue spilling and collecting her tears. "Remember Dante. Remember Zuni."

"No," she whispered. She corked the bottle and dropped it into the canal, where it bobbed and floated beside them in the inky nighttime water.

Unfazed, the figure held out another bottle. "Remember Lupita."

Celia smacked the hand so the bottle went flying, landing in the water next to the other before coming to the surface to float beside it.

Another bottle Celia refused to touch. "Remember Wallis."

She would not collect these tears, though they fell from her eyes like rain.

"Remember Wallis, the sloth Seer Ostra, Griffin . . ."

The offered bottles were endless; each time she batted one away, it was added to the cluster in the water.

The figure's agitation rose slowly. First, a more forceful tone. Then trembles. Then head shaking. "Remember them," they insisted.

When Celia glanced beside the boat, she saw the bottles bobbing in the water. Perfectly spaced apart, holding their positions, row upon row, each a curved swell springing up from the dark water. The canal was wide and long, bottles glinting all around them in parallel lines, toward the hidden banks and into the horizon.

Grave markers in the biggest cemetery of them all.

The gondola rocked. The gondolier's soft song became louder, and instead of a lullaby it became a lament. They moved their rowing oar with precision, finding the water between grave markers, careful not to disturb them.

"Remember Zuni," the wrapped figure said, scooping one of the bottles from the canal. They pushed forward, holding the bottle to Celia's cheek themselves. As soon as the glass touched her skin, she was powerless to move away. The figure collected a full bottle of tears for Zuni as the gondolier sang his lament, then they returned the bottle to the water.

"Remember Lupita and Dante." Another bottle, pulled out of the water, filled with tears, and replaced.

"Remember Griffin. Remember Wallis. Remember Lyric."

Celia's eyes burned with a dry, stinging heat. She couldn't use them for seeing anymore, they were only for making tears. The sobs coming from her throat burned their way up, and she buckled, wrapping her arms around her waist to keep her insides from spilling out. She cried with her whole body, everything hurting with unparalleled pain.

Many of the bottles were full, but not all.

The gondolier sang for her, for the bottles of tears, for the people attached to those tears. Their voice was as deep as the water they floated in.

Celia had nothing left in her to give, but the wrapped figure was not yet satisfied. They pushed two bottles against Celia's shattered skin, one under each eye, and waited for Celia to look up.

The fabric wrapping the figure's head had loosened, peeling away just enough to reveal the face underneath. Despite being featureless—a blank canvas of a face without eyes, a nose, or mouth—she knew it would be Diavala.

When the fabric peeled away, a darkness oozed from the hole, staining the cloth strips as it dripped. Trembling, Celia reached up to wipe the ink away, to see her tormentor's face for the first time.

Black eyes as dark as the ink met hers, and Halcyon demanded, "Remember Anya."

"Anya," Celia whimpered, and shattered.

She had enough tears to fill the rest of the bottles after all. And then even more tears came, pouring from her eyes.

They coasted down the canal, surrounded by the markers of the dead, until the boat was pulled under by the weight of her never-ending tears, and Celia joined all of them in the water. Surrounded by ink, floating in a pool of it, captained by Halcyon.

CHAPTER 16

THE NIGHTMARE HELD ON, THE BONE-DEEP PAIN PINCHING Celia tight. When she gained enough sense of her surroundings through her gasps, she pushed Xinto away from where he'd been snuggling in the bend of her knees, her heart pounding against her ribs.

With a squeak, a decidedly non-beeish noise, Xinto flew off, hurt, to pout on the cold fireplace mantel, staring at her accusingly. But he was made of ink, and she'd just drowned in it. He was made of ink, and everyone she loved would end up drowning in it too.

Celia sat up, wrapped her arms around her knees, and stared into nothing as she tried to get her breathing under control. Admitting that the visit with Griffin the night before haunted her was like swallowing a jagged shard of glass. Diavala's manipulations were contagious, spreading from Griffin and then to her.

Leaving Rian's farmhouse with the sinister image of a bottle of poison seared in her mind hadn't helped things.

A shudder rocked through her at the memory of her nightmare. Trusting Diavala unequivocally would be stupid, but perhaps she'd put too much trust in Halcyon. In the ink itself.

She'd convinced herself that the ink wasn't evil, only how one used it, but what did she really know of Halcyon's intentions? She'd made a plan to take down Diavala without knowing all the facts, and it had cost her Anya. She couldn't do that again and risk losing Griffin. She had to figure out the whole truth first.

And all of Halcyon's secrets hid behind one closed door.

Celia walked through the main square toward the gate earlier than usual that morning, but there were already people out and about, thrill tainting the air. To say that Wisteria was excited about Halcyon's upcoming party was an understatement. The square was undergoing a massive transformation: torches had been hauled out, a stage was being erected, and garlands hung from doorframes and windows. Halcyon had been overseeing everything. The other day she'd found him standing with his arms crossed over his chest, watching the construction of a low platform stage. A dozen sweaty people were hammering and sawing.

"Couldn't we just do that with the ink?" Celia had asked, gesturing in their direction.

"Once in a while they need purpose. Coming together is good for morale." It sounded like he was talking about errant children, a herd to manage.

"I'll keep that in mind," she'd said slowly. If he was so precise about ink mastery, he would have specific requirements for Wisterian management too. She should have taken notes.

That morning, Celia skirted along the periphery of the square, sticking to shadows and side streets, with Xinto—who'd forgiven her for earlier—tucked inside her shirt to keep him quiet, praying that no one looked up from their work long enough to spot her.

Especially Lyric, who stood in front of the bakery with a few Wisterians, going over an order with the baker.

Celia didn't see Halcyon, which was troubling. He should have been there already. Walking around another corner so no one could spot her, she pressed herself against a wall, counting out sixty seconds five times exactly, no longer trusting her ability to accurately comprehend time.

If Halcyon wasn't in the square by then, she would reconsider her plan. The risk of being discovered would be too great.

When the allotted time was up, she peeked again, letting out a sigh of relief when she saw Halcyon striding toward Lyric and the baker. His punctual, perfectionist tendencies were handy for something.

Celia made it to the gate, scaled it, and darted through the tunnel of wisteria.

Every other time she'd gotten to the cherry-red front door, Celia had knocked and waited for Lyric or Halcyon to let her in, but it had been a courtesy. It was never locked. Why bother, if no one could see the gate except those who were invited?

So far, so good.

Walking down the long corridor toward the back room

where she worked most often, Celia's heart hammered in her chest. Every footstep echoed back to her as loud as thunder.

She hesitated at the door to the forbidden room. As soon as she broke in, she'd burn her and Halcyon's verbal contract to ash.

Xinto, innocently astute as ever, emerged from inside her shirt and buzzed loudly near the door to the studio, as if trying to pull her in that direction.

Pressing her ear to the door, she listened, as if unheard whispers could tell her what to do. Her gaze landed on a portrait of Martina across the hall, one of the formal ones that made her look noble and stern. "What do you think?" Celia asked. "Are you okay with this?"

The idea of intruding into a space Celia wasn't welcome didn't bother her very much—that wasn't what had kept her from trying the door all this time. It wasn't even Halcyon's anger.

Disrespecting the dead bothered her.

She didn't know Martina and never would, but it was her space, even if she'd never found her way there.

Celia's hand went to the sunflower doorknob, her fingers just dancing on the top, while Martina looked down on her.

Come on, Celia, haven't you done enough? Celia imagined her saying. *Leave me some dignity.*

She hadn't touched the sunflower doorknob since that first day, hadn't asked Halcyon about it. Her bees had been smart. Something had told her to hide her interest in what lay beyond.

Her hand covered the sunflower, gripping tight. The

doorknob was warm in her hand, and strangely malleable. Like if she squeezed hard enough, she could transform its shape.

She ground her teeth. Nothing was *right* here. Not even doorknobs.

It turned easily. The fact that it wasn't locked showed how much Halcyon trusted her not to cross him. Another one of her bees scooped up that tidbit and held it close. *The more trust there is, the bigger the betrayal,* it warned her.

But she needed answers.

Celia pushed the door open and stepped in before she could change her mind, leaving Xinto waiting outside.

He cowered in the corner of the hallway and wouldn't look at her.

CHAPTER 17

THE UNNATURAL WARMTH OF THE DOORKNOB WAS NOTHING compared with the oppressive heat inside the room. Celia's breath caught in her throat, the air thick and suffocating. It was too dark to see anything clearly, but it was a strange darkness: just as stifling as the heat and humidity, and one that a lantern or candle wouldn't help chase away.

She stepped farther into the room, and behind her, the door swung closed.

She swiveled at the sound of the slam, and the handle on this side — a rose — stared at her.

Okay, that's fine, she thought. *I'm probably locked in now, but that's fine. Everything's fine.*

Celia waited for her eyes to adjust. She could see only a few steps around her in any direction, the rest of the room swallowed by a void. It wasn't black, but *empty.*

The heat tugged at her skin and burrowed into her lungs.

She should have been sweating, or shivering, or panting in gulps of air. Her heart should have been skipping ferociously.

That was a lot of *should haves,* and when she realized that her body wasn't reacting at all like it *should have,* she froze.

She stopped breathing in the damp, hot air. And her lungs didn't struggle, even after many minutes passed.

She put her hand to her chest slowly. No sound, no taps. Nothing but more empty.

"Okay, shhhhh, calm down," she whispered. She would have liked to inhale a big, steadying gulp of air, but her lungs were broken, just like her heart.

Celia stifled the urge to laugh, knowing she was bordering on panic and trying hard to stay levelheaded. So her heart wasn't beating—so what? So her lungs weren't breathing and her skin wasn't sweating, that was all fine. She didn't *feel* dead, only a bit broken.

Most broken things could be fixed.

She'd expected a room of secrets, but it looked like she had to hunt for them and hope she could find her way back. The idea of losing the doorway out of that broken place made her very, very nervous.

The ink in her veins—was it still there if her blood wasn't pumping?

With a clear thought (thank goodness her brain was still working) and a nudge, Celia pressed her quill to her wrist and commanded the ink inside her into the illusion she needed.

It began as a thrumming, unheard but visceral. The ink was still there, somehow, and it was listening hard.

Just like many of her other creations, the thread she created was not-there, and then there. Solid. Real enough. And in the palm of her hand.

With another nudge, she moved the thin, near-transparent line from the rose doorknob to around her wrist, unwinding it slowly. It was as insubstantial as spider's silk, but indestructible, no matter how far it stretched. She believed it to be so, and so it was.

That'll have to do, she thought, turning to face the dark empty.

A few steps in, the space around her erupted with light all at once. She swiveled around, but the doorway and the rose doorknob were gone. Her slim thread disappeared into emptiness at the end, hovering there as if attached to a ghost. She followed it back again, panicking, and her hand wrapped around the knob. She would have exhaled if her lungs worked. The way out was invisible now, but it was still there.

Steadying herself, she turned around and stepped away from the door, trusting that the thread would lead her back.

The light wasn't sunlight, but a dappled gray washed-out blurriness, more like a thick fog. It disguised most of the room, with only the space immediately around her having any substance.

In the distance, muted and soft, she heard singing, a haunting lullaby from someone with a voice like an angel. Instead of comforting her, the sound chilled her, and she had no desire to wander in that direction. But even as she made up her mind to keep away from the sound and the person making it, the song crept closer—although she hadn't taken a step.

I'm Celia Sand, a former inkling of Profeta, she said to herself. *I love Anya and starlight and drawing.*

She took a step back. The direction the lullaby was coming from had switched places, now behind her. Closer.

I'm Celia Sand, former inkling of Profeta. I love Anya and starlight and drawing. Over and over, she said that simple refrain. She had no idea what else to do. Her mind was in full panic mode, yet without her body reacting as it was supposed to—no fluttering heartbeat, no labored breathing, no nervous sweating or swiveling eyes—there was a strange disconnect.

As if she were there but not there.

A stranger in her own existence.

I'm Celia Sand, a former inkling of Profeta—

As she repeated the refrain, she commanded the ink to form a cage around her. Strong silver bars on all sides, with room enough for her to move within them comfortably. This was different from the devil's bell jar: instead of trapping her, it trapped everything else. It kept the outside out.

Immediately she felt better. She believed it to be protection, so it was. She took another step backwards, and the cage moved with her.

With the creation of the cage, the thrumming of the ink inside her had become fiercer. As if the ink itself were singing, echoing the haunting song of the faceless, bodiless singer in the fog.

This was no ordinary room. There was no altar to Martina, no candles, no personal treasures.

This place was a prison.

Everything about it felt like Halcyon's illusions, but where he created beauty and light in Wisteria, this was the opposite.

Was it illusion to keep someone—like her—out?

Or was it intended to keep someone—like the singer—in?

Celia had asked Lyric if Martina's body was in this room—if it was a crypt of a sort—only to be told *hahaha, no*. But perhaps Halcyon had created and trapped an illusion of his dead lover here. Or memories of her. Or . . . something. If Xinto had been there, he would have fainted from the idea.

It didn't sound like a natural voice, but Celia had yet to try using hers, so maybe she'd sound as hollow as the singer.

"Martina?" Celia whispered. She pitched the word so quietly she could barely hear herself. With the cage around her as protection, she continued taking steps. No matter which direction she moved, the singing became louder.

As if they had no choice but to meet.

The fog began peeling away, as if a spotlight were shining down to illuminate the space as she moved. As she walked, more of the fog evaporated. She squinted into it, trying to strip it back farther, and slowly, the outline of a person materialized. The mental image of Martina from any one of the dozens of portraits rose up in Celia's mind: brown hair, sharp expression, clever, calculating eyes.

So when the singer's form finally became fully visible, Celia had to blink hard.

It was a child, but they had no tenor.

Squatting near the ground, the child had long, copper-colored hair which was trying viciously to escape their braids. The braids trailed along the dirt floor like paintbrushes. Swiping their hand in the dirt, they looked as if they'd lost something small, their tiny fingers flitting over the dusty ground and turning it over. The melody of their song continued, so whatever they'd lost, it wasn't an emergency. Maybe they were just drawing in the dirt.

But she had no idea what to say to this child, because she had no idea what was going on. Between that and the humming inside her from the ink calling out in response to the song, the only rational thought she had was, *Figure out all his secrets.*

"Hello?" she whispered, moving to the back of her self-inflicted cell even though she was still a good distance away.

But the child didn't answer, nor did they look up. Getting closer might startle them, but she needed the child's attention.

The ink shouted to be let out, and Celia considered what might work in the situation. Halcyon's voice echoed. *The ink wants to belong,* he'd said. *To make any illusion more believable, make sure you disguise any inherent wrongness with something right.* Believability came from giving people what they expected to see. Filling in the blanks.

Because the child looked as if they were searching for something small, Celia drew and cast a marble. She made it blue and bright, shiny and glossy, and placed it under a thin layer of dirt in front of the child.

The child squeaked, their song cutting off abruptly. They stood and looked around, as if knowing that someone had put it there but alarmed at the possibility.

"What's your name?" Swallowing, Celia also asked, "And what are your pronouns?"

She wondered, with dread, whether *she* still had *her* tenor. Her heart didn't beat and her lungs didn't work, so was she soulless, like the ink-Anya Halcyon had created in the courtyard?

The only person Celia had ever known without a tenor was Diavala. Soulless, once-dead, body-stealing Diavala.

"I'm Terrin," the child said. "She." Her gaze finally swung around and landed on Celia. Terrin giggled as she approached.

Instead of being swallowed up by the fog, the sound of her giggle carried, echoed, and got louder as it surrounded them. Her clothing, from a fashion of hundreds of years ago, when all children wore dresses made of thick, homespun wool, was in tatters. Threads of wool hung from her skinny shoulders.

Celia gagged as Terrin moved closer. Like her clothing, Terrin's skin was shredded underneath, large swaths of it hanging down, sticking to the thick wool.

Terrin swiped a hand across her forehead to push stray hair out of the way. Her face was relatively unmarred, but this movement smeared blood, gore, and dusty dirt just above her eyes. "Did you give me this?" she asked, holding up the marble, which was no longer bright blue, but the deep red of old blood. "It's so lovely, thank you!"

Terrin clutched the marble to her chest and smiled, her face cracking nearly in two, her smile was so wide. But with the clumsiness of childhood, she bobbled and dropped the marble.

With a sickening squelch, the marble fell *into* her chest cavity.

Alarmed, Terrin rooted around, moving flaps of skin out of the way until, triumphant, she lifted it out of a small pocket of flesh, where something had carved more deeply into her.

Oh Dia. Dia, Dia, shit. With no heartbeat to give her away, Celia nodded and smiled through her horror.

Terrin had been flogged, and there was no way she could have survived those wounds.

Terrin had been flogged, and Celia knew of only one child who'd died this way.

Griffin had once talked about his experience in the afterlife, on a level that was so abstract it hadn't made much sense to Celia at the time. "The afterlife is vast, but its pain feels intimate." He'd said it like a warning. As if the intimacy was the worst part.

If this was the unnamed child from Profeta's history, she'd been the first person Diavala had stolen after being cast out of the afterlife, and her death had created the idea of Diavala in the first place: the trickster, the evil, the wrong. This child had been an innocent victim, but her spectacular death had left a legacy in the living world.

For her to appear to Celia exactly as she might have looked when she died—that was definitely intimate. The thought nudged at Celia, sent her mind whirring. She didn't know what she'd expected to find, but it certainly wasn't this vast nothingness. The only place where tenors didn't exist was the afterlife: the land of the dead. Celia reached out and gripped the silver bars in front of her, feeling their substance against her skin. They grounded her, calmed her. She was still in Halcyon's forbidden room, she reminded herself.

His forbidden room just happened to be the afterlife.

I'm not dead, though? Celia tried to think in facts, but her thought was tinged with doubt.

Would Diavala recognize this place? Would Griffin?

Celia checked her wrist to make sure the shining thread was still attached. It shone in the fog, a shimmering tether to the land of the living.

Steeling herself, Celia addressed Terrin again. "Is there something you want to show me?" If Griffin was right, there was a reason Terrin appeared for her.

Terrin held out her hand, dark red and flaking, and offered the marble. "This?"

"No. You can keep it." Celia swallowed. "I made it for you."

Why did the ink still work in the afterlife when nothing else did? Celia would have done anything to feel her heartbeat again.

Something about the child was changing, but Celia couldn't quite put her finger on what. Was she growing? Getting closer? Alarm bells began ringing in her head. The silver bars dug into her back as she pushed farther away.

"You made it?" the child asked, confused. She looked down at her ripped-apart chest again.

"There's a special ink," Celia continued. "I can control it and make things, like your marble."

And then Celia recognized what was changing: Terrin was getting angry. Or frustrated, perhaps. Either way, it was aimed in Celia's direction.

Terrin locked eyes with Celia as Celia quickly conjured a toy bear.

It was almost a feverish response. She had only one way to protect herself: ink.

What would an eight-year-old, maybe ten-year-old, like? She couldn't tell how old Terrin was—not with her features obscured by blood and any hints of body shape ripped into tatters—and that detail, like her name, had long been lost to history.

Terrin had the bear in her hand for only a moment before she tossed it to the ground, stomped on it, and marched toward Celia, eyes blazing and nostrils flaring. Was Terrin's heart beating? Celia didn't think so, but it sure looked like it should be. Beating so hard, in that tattered chest of hers, that it might fall right out and be trampled underfoot.

"Where did you come from?" Terrin demanded. She wore no trace of innocence anymore. If Celia didn't know better, she would have thought it was a different child altogether.

"I—" Celia stopped, then backed up a few steps. The smell

of the child was overwhelming. The smell of death. Her cage didn't work against it, which felt like a cruel taunt after all her struggles to control the sense of smell in her illusions.

She registered more voices approaching in the distance. More than one conversation, back and forth, getting louder. Lured by the noise Celia and this child were making with their conversation.

Terrin grabbed the bars and pushed her face close. She tilted her head as she assessed Celia from top to bottom. "There's something different about you." She pierced Celia with a narrow gaze. "And don't lie to me."

Celia put her hands up. "I didn't mean to upset you. I only thought you might be able to help me." She licked her lips, tried to reason whether this was a very stupid idea or just a stupid idea. "You might know someone who comes here, someone who feels different, like me, who uses the same special ink—"

Turned out, that was a very stupid idea.

A primal scream tore out of Terrin's mouth and she lunged toward Celia. Fingers tearing, teeth gnashing, her short arms still somehow managed to reach through the bars, and she hit Celia with everything she had left in her to hit with. Celia had no time to think of an escape plan, too busy trying to keep the child from tearing her limbs off.

"It's ours!" Terrin screamed. "Martina says the ink is supposed to be ours, but *you* have it!"

With a mighty shove, Celia pushed her back and shuffled

away with her cage, panting without taking in any air. The approaching voices were almost near, louder and closer. The fog would reveal them soon.

I'm alive-ish, alive-ish, Celia thought, putting her hand on her chest, trying to remember what a heartbeat felt like.

"I was good, I remember," the shredded child said. "It shouldn't be like this for me. I deserve heaven, but all I get is nothing." She'd fallen over on her backside, the marble still clutched tight in her hand, and she stared up at Celia with nothing but hate in her eyes. "Your *friend* brought the fog for everyone. Your *friend* makes all of this nothing. It's not fair!"

"Martina said this?" Celia had a hundred clues but couldn't fit them together. Was Anya there? Surrounded by wasteland, knowing you're dead or different in some way, miserable without quite knowing why. Was this where Celia had sent her best friend for all of eternity?

This was far worse than anything Celia could have imagined of the afterlife.

Anya was too beautiful to be there, amid all that nothing.

"Anya?" Celia screamed.

Those approaching souls, so many of them, were illuminated all at once. Standing in a semicircle, they stopped their conversations. They stared and glared.

They were all Profetan mistico, with long robes and throats slashed open. High Mistico Benedict was front and center, his ice-cold eyes boring into Celia just as they'd done in life.

Celia closed her eyes against the sight of them and began

backing away quickly, hoping her steps took her away instead of right into the middle of the throng. "I'm alive, I don't belong here," she chanted. Her panic was a wild thing, untamable. *Dia,* why couldn't she hyperventilate like she wanted to? Her body wasn't her body, wasn't reacting as it was supposed to. Maybe she was dead after all . . .

She thought of the door and tried to pull herself toward it. The thread around her wrist tightened like a mini-noose and yanked her back. Her eyes snapped open, but she wasn't close enough to the door. It hadn't worked.

The crowd of people, all gruesome, macabre victims of Diavala, paused in their approach, each one creating a puddle of blood under their feet, the drip, drip from the wounds in their necks the only sound.

The door! Celia thought again, concentrating on the thread around her wrist, willing it to work. Another yank, more powerful this time, and Celia crashed against the bars of her cell, crying out in alarm. She dissolved her only protection to avoid being torn in two, and the thread continued to tighten and pull, reeling her in with impossible speed until her shoulder slammed into the door with a sharp crack.

CHAPTER 18

A LURCH, AS IF SOMEONE HAD GRABBED A HANDFUL OF Celia's skin and yanked her through a narrow tube, and the nothingness of that terrible place disappeared.

Celia shouted as the door slammed behind her. She was in the hallway, collapsed on the parquet floor, and a cold chill had settled deep under her skin, making her shiver uncontrollably. Her breathing—monstrous inhales and exhales—and her heartbeat—mad thumps that pounded behind her ribs—felt strange after that hollow emptiness of moments before.

Xinto flew overhead in zigzags, his buzzing as loud as high-pitched thunder.

"They were so angry," Celia said aloud, putting her face in her hands, trying to erase the memory of the shattered dead child and the vicious way the mistico had stared at her, far more threatening than they'd ever been in the mortal world. Before, they'd treated her as an inconvenience. Now they would have torn her apart and left her a husk. "How?" Celia said. "How is there a doorway?"

With one turn of a doorknob, everything had changed.

Celia couldn't wrap her mind around it: a gateway where one could freely go from the realm of the living to that of the dead. Halcyon's forbidden door with the sunflower doorknob led to the afterlife. How had he done such a thing? His pining for the dead Martina made so much sense suddenly. *One day I'll find her. One day I'll have her back.* Halcyon wasn't wandering through Illinia looking for Martina's body. He was searching for her soul in the afterlife. He wanted the real thing.

If Celia wandered through that gloomy fog, could she peel it back far enough to find Anya, Vincent, even her long-dead friend Salome?

Her mind flew around wildly, trying to put everything together. Panting hard, she had to gulp air in. Her mind bees were so scattered—confused about what was truth and who to believe and where to go next. When Celia thought back to everything that had happened behind that door, another blast of panic overwhelmed her. Her eyes blurred, as if she wanted to cry, but her chest was hot, like she wanted to scream. With everything in working order again, her body wanted to do it all.

She tried to convince herself for many long moments that it was a hallucination of some kind, delirium, another nightmare, or even the most complex of all of Halcyon's illusions.

But that made even less sense.

It didn't feel real, but more than that, it didn't feel right. She felt the *wrongness* deep in her bones. The souls she'd seen—full of desperation, with hunger in their eyes—they were all starving.

Celia took a deep breath and closed her eyes. *Anya? What would you tell me right now?*

And she pictured it in her mind's eye as clearly as if Anya were standing across from her.

Anya narrowed her eyes and squared her shoulders as she assessed the new information. She didn't waste time on shock, diving straight into logic. *We were told that the Divine's ink fell from heaven, Cece,* Anya said. *And most rumors have a seed of truth, don't they? Think about it: the ink might not have fallen from heaven and into Diavala's lap, but it did come from somewhere* Other.

Celia nodded.

Diavala had even lied about Profeta's origin story, crafting a sympathetic tale about an innocent child to make her mystical messages appear more wholesome and pure. And that original lie, delivered via thousands of tattoos, had manipulated an entire nation.

In truth, she was nothing more than a thief. She'd stolen the ink from the afterlife and had manipulated with it for a thousand years.

Halcyon, too, could craft illusions that defied all logic, but he was content in his little purple bubble of Wisteria because he'd somehow gained unrestricted access to the afterlife as well. He passed between worlds no one should traverse.

Diavala and Halcyon had both played a game of false gods with their stolen goods.

And all of it came from something that didn't belong here.

The souls Celia had encountered—Terrin and her shredded body, the mistico with their slashed throats—all of them had wanted the ink. They fought for it, were miserable without it.

Terrin had made it sound like the ink would have given her the heaven she deserved, that without it, they were all in hell.

They knew the ink was missing, and they knew who had stolen it.

Celia eyes snapped open.

She'd been so set on blaming Diavala, but Halcyon was the only thief they'd accused. Though they'd all been put there through Diavala's actions, they hadn't said anything about her. She wasn't the one who had stolen the ink. And if Diavala had possessed the ink for a thousand years, but hadn't stolen it from the afterlife, where had she gotten it?

Not from where, Anya said. *From* who?

But that would make Halcyon older than Profeta. Older than Diavala herself. Could there be room in the world for two immortal devils?

He uses the ink on the living side to be a beloved ruler, Anya said, *But there, he's the enemy.*

The afterlife was a wasteland because of Halcyon.

He was the reason Anya was condemned to an eternity, without the angels she deserved, and why Griffin was so afraid of death.

Celia's breathing, finally under control, began speeding up again. She was steps away from peeking behind a curtain that shouldn't exist. It led to a backstage no one should ever see.

And she'd promised to serve the soul who'd stolen from one side to feed the other.

It was all clear to Celia now. Whether serving one devil or

another, Diavala or Halcyon, she needed to stop depending on any semblance of truth or purity. Everyone was crooked, and she needed to match them breath for breath.

She put her face in her hands again, tears threatening to spill.

Lies everywhere. Always. Her entire life had been made of a revolving door of people with their own agendas, using her to get what they wanted, big or small. She was a means to an end, a tool to wield. As her breathing settled down from the fright, her body flushed red with rage.

She was tired of being used.

She wouldn't be used anymore.

"Celia?" Lyric turned the corner and raced over, trying to haul her to her feet. "Are you okay? What happened?"

"*You,*" Celia said, yanking her arm away. She sprang up and pressed her back against the door to the workroom, digging her fingertips into the doorframe. Why had Lyric wanted her to go through the door? What sadistic pleasure would that have given them?

Lyric frowned, took a few steps toward her, and then . . .

Bent forward and sniffed Celia's shoulder.

"Hey!" Celia shrieked. "*Dia,* what is wrong with you?"

Their gray eyes darted up. "You smell like him, right after he comes back. Like ash or dust." They swore under their breath, and this time when they grabbed Celia's arm, they pinched hard enough that Celia couldn't wrench free.

Lyric hauled Celia to a room she'd never seen, shoved her in, and closed the door behind them, telling Xinto to keep watch in the hallway.

As if she'd stepped outside and into a forest, Celia was surrounded by trees, shrubs . . . and birds. So many of them, the room was full of discordant songs—trills, chirps, and cries—and more color—reds, purples, blues, yellows—than could be found in Seer Ostra's bursting wardrobe.

Celia almost laughed. "This pretty room won't erase the one just down the hall. I barely escaped with my skin still attached." Her imagination, inconvenient as always, played it out for her: ripping, peeling, dead fingers raking across her body, scraping away her skin and flesh until the ink inside her was exposed and the dead souls could feed . . .

She put her hands to her eyes, trying to stop the images. If Anya had been there, would she be one of the hungry masses tearing Celia apart?

The idea of being ripped apart for her ink was terrifying, but she couldn't help but think it was the punishment she deserved. If it would make Anya content in that terrible place, if giving her the ink she needed would make it bearable, maybe that was exactly what Celia needed to do . . . At least a decision would be made for her. All her questions, her wanting, her regrets, they would be out of her hands. Opening the door again and getting swept up by fate appealed to the part of her that was tired of fighting.

It was so exhausting, to survive all the time.

If she were ripped apart, all this would be over. There would be no Celia left for anyone to lie to.

Lyric rounded on her, snapping her out of her daydreams. "I never for a moment thought you'd go in. Not without protection. That amulet around Halcyon's neck is the only thing that keeps him from being devoured, and last I checked, you don't have one. What the hell is wrong with you?"

"Why wouldn't you think I'd go in?" Celia shouted, close to laughing. "You all but told me to! I had no idea about the pendant!" The matching swirls on Halcyon's chest of ink and his pendant made more sense now: both were tied to the afterlife.

"This is one of the most private places in Wisteria," Lyric said through their teeth, "but *not* if you keep shrieking."

Shut up, Celia Sand. Shut up before this is all over for both of us.

Celia pressed her back against the rough bark of a gnarled oak tree, settling in, trying to hold her temper in check. Above her, a messy nest of fledgling ravens peered at her curiously, the rest of their family scattered on branches, sending up the occasional caw. A black feather fluttered down gently.

Zuni would have loved everything about that room. She would have collected as many feathers as she could, patiently waiting until they floated into her palm.

And that one thought made Celia square her stance. "What I saw there . . ."

"Look," Lyric said. They stepped forward as a starling alighted on their shoulder and began nibbling at their ear. With exaggerated calm, their hands casually trailed a gentle path over the soft leaves of a shrub alive with birds. They stilled, allowing a small, unexceptional wren to peck at their fingertips and hop onto their hand for a closer inspection. It sang happily, as if calling its friends. Lyric was turned toward the bird, the bush, but they watched Celia carefully. "I know this is a lot to take in. I didn't want to distract you before you met your end of the bargain with him—"

"So you wanted to ease me into it with riddles?" Celia said, interrupting. "Lie to the inkling until she has no choice, is that it? Hint about the door, pretend to be her friend. Don't tell me you stayed quiet for my benefit, Lyric. You've always been open about looking out for yourself."

A defiant chin tilt. "You're right, I do look out for myself. The only reason I'm tangling myself up with you at all is because you're the first one who's come along who I think can help me."

Celia barked out a laugh, startling the starling on Lyric's shoulder. "What could I possibly do for you?"

"You're more naturally talented with the ink than even Halcyon," Lyric said. "I've been trapped here my whole life, and I want out."

That sounded so familiar, but where Celia's imprisonment was on Diavala's hands, full of water torture, daggers, and screams, Lyric's was at Halcyon's hands, full of wisteria flowers, happy people, and sunshine.

Celia snorted, fighting the surge of resentment. "You know what, Lyric? I'm not really in the mood for this. If you want anything from me, you're going to have to stop with the bullshit. Fully and completely and without convenient gaps. And whatever you tell me, know I probably won't believe you."

"Damn, but you've gotten under my skin," Lyric said with appreciation. They smirked, but it was an expression without humor. "My entire life has been serving him, running errands, spying, which would have been bad enough, but I have something even worse waiting for me." They paused to collect themselves, their teeth rattling, as if this was the first time they'd dared speak against him and they were preparing to face their biggest nightmare of all. Too bad Celia's sympathy had disappeared in a depressing fog of dead people. "Halcyon's a fan of apprentices, so when Rian dies, I'll take over her position. He likes having his lines nice and straight."

Celia gritted her teeth. Lyric's problem wasn't even a problem.

"Rian isn't a healer," Lyric said. "Halcyon calls her that only because she takes care of the illness and ugliness of life so he doesn't have to look at it. She's very much the opposite of healer; she's the culler, the butcher, the disappearer. He makes poison, and she administers it."

Lyric paused. Swallowed. The look on their face was pure shock, as if they'd never believed they would say these words aloud. "I nicknamed her the Spectator when I was little. Because all she does is watch, and poison, and watch some more. Always on the lookout to complete Halcyon's bidding, whatever it is. Completely detached. Like a shadow on the wall."

"A killer is a hard person to have sympathy for," Celia said. The way Lyric described Rian now felt exactly like the mistico: aligning with a warped sense of duty rather than individual conscience.

Celia didn't doubt for a minute that in this, Lyric was telling the truth. When they'd first arrived, Garuld and Rosetta had debated whether to send them to the inn or to Rian's; they must have been weighing whether the newcomers could stay or had to be disposed of.

"You can't walk away from Wisteria," Lyric said. "Neither can I."

Some of Halcyon's first words to her—*It's not a courtesy I offer just anyone, to be able to simply walk away*—had never been far from Celia's mind, but with Lyric's blunt sentence, other hints screamed into focus. Her mind bees—who'd so far spent their time flying in a tangle and had been easy to ignore—had now become more organized. They stood in a soldier's row in her head, at attention, each one in charge of a particular oddity.

The first bee reminded her that visitors didn't come to Wisteria, and if they did, they didn't stay long. Despite its access to this beautiful lake country, despite the fact that it was a gorgeous destination for the Illinian rich to vacation in the sun. No one Celia had talked to could name someone who'd been born outside of the town.

The second bee saluted and mentioned the sharp, stabby feeling Celia and Griffin both had when they'd first come. How frightened she'd been of the wisteria bunch they'd plucked from the vine.

The third ticked off some boxes about Halcyon himself: his obsession with his dead lover; the absolute loyalty everyone showed him, to the point of hiding their children; the way he disguised his face from even his own people and talked about them as if they were a gaggle of Kids rather than freethinking adults.

Few came to Wisteria, and no one simply walked away. Halcyon curated this town and its secrets like a museum.

Meeting Celia's eyes, Lyric crossed their arms and squared their stance. "You're right, Rian's a hard person to have sympathy for, unless you understand that she's spent years living with someone who can make nightmares come true."

Celia laughed. "You're simultaneously telling me that Griffin has been at her mercy for days *and* that I should feel sorry for her? Bold of you, Lyric. Bold as hell."

One of the ravens fluttered to a lower branch, staring at Celia with an inquisitive head tilt. Then it cawed and fluttered back up toward the high branches, making her notice that all the birds in the room had stopped their fluttering in order to stare at her. Dozens of sets of eyes and beaks pointed her way. The starling she'd scared off of Lyric's shoulder was downright glaring.

Celia met Lyric's worn, weary eyes. "Stop making the birds do that!"

"They're reacting to you," Lyric said with an impatient huff. They turned to the quivering, glaring starling and held their finger out, trying to coax it back to them. "They're ink, and you command it. *You* tell them to piss off."

The birds behind her had erupted into a flurry of wings and screeches, mostly drowning out Lyric's words.

"You've had a knife to your throat since you came," they said bluntly. "Griffin's life has been leverage, in case you refused to cooperate. All Rian's been waiting for is the order, and she'll pour him the tea that will send him to the other side for good."

Celia couldn't stop laughing, the birds around them making a discordant symphony. Lies, lies everywhere, but it was refreshing to hear the sharp truth: Celia was alone there. She'd come for help but had stepped into a hornet's nest.

Lyric hesitated only a moment before adding, "Rian also has a slight soul confined at her place — freckled, frowny, with a bag of skulls. A second knife to your throat that you don't even know about, in case one wasn't enough."

Zuni.

Celia's laughter stopped abruptly, and the birds quieted. Stray feathers floated around, and in another life, Celia would have grabbed at them. She would have tucked them into her pocket like the treasures they were and saved them for Zuni.

Zuni, who worked in the crypts at the temple, who rarely saw the sun and never saw birds. Zuni, who's wings had been clipped when she was old enough to remember freedom but too young to appreciate it.

Zuni, who'd left the temple weeks ago and had, apparently, made it to Wisteria just in time to land in a new prison. Dante hadn't said anything about Zuni's destination. Maybe he hadn't known she'd gone looking for Celia.

Lyric jumped forward and grabbed Celia's arm, but when Celia tried to yank it away, Lyric held on tight. Their eyes blazed, and for the first time, it didn't look like anger. It was desperation: toxic and full-bellied. "You need to concentrate on only one thing right now: your end of the bargain. That's it. That's all. You know how to act, so do it. Pretend everything's going according to plan. Pretend you're still on his side completely. When he trusts you, he'll leave, and you'll have free run of this place."

Lyric's eyes begged Celia to listen. Their grip tightened. "Don't ruin what you have here by being rash. All he wants is a puppet for when he looks for Martina in the afterlife, so for now, just continue being a puppet, Celia. It's the only way any of us can get out of this."

Celia managed to yank her arm away and made for the door. "Stay far away from me, Lyric."

The birds erupted in a cacophony of shrieks and caws, tossing the branches around in the wind they produced with their frantic wingbeats. When Celia opened the door, Xinto joined the fracas, thinking it was a game.

"Disguise your smell, Celia!" Lyric called after her. "Unless you and your friends want to join the souls on the other side of the door, he can't know that you went in."

Celia gritted her teeth. Smell would be her undoing in this

place, whether it was because she couldn't mimic it properly or because she smelled like hell itself. Just as she'd done with the stew, she covered the offending smell by layering over the scent of the first herb she saw in his garden: rosemary.

She raced toward the main square, disheveled and full of fire, making people stop and stare. With her quill clutched in a tight fist, she jabbed into her skin, sending fireworks up over her head, bursting in a million bright colors but all melting to black and red. She added a gargoyle to the peak of each roof: ugly, misshapen things, twisted up, clawed, and snarling. The clouds above her turned gray and angry, the wind kicked up. She moved the quill along her arm in nonsense strokes, activating the ink to listen to her inner thoughts and become real.

All the time she and Anya had covertly messaged each other, they hadn't had to worry about images or words: the ink responded to what they wanted, not what they drew.

Even their devil and angel act with the Rabble Mob, where Anya had walked through the crowd under scrutiny and inked commands to Celia, who'd been trapped under a bell jar, hadn't been a measure of their artistic skill. Anya hadn't been overly clever with her images.

Even that, in the end, had been a lie.

The ink always listened to intent. It had heard what Anya *wanted* to draw and had made it real.

And just then Celia's intent was a jumbled mix of ugly and beautiful, of chaos and order.

Her footsteps boomed on the cobblestones, the same echoey sound as that of a mistico hunting her down in the bowels of the temple.

She created a sloth, born from the image she'd once seen in one of Lupita's books, and had it hang from a window upside down, smiling at her lazily as she ran past.

The fireworks rained down in sparkles of red and black, coating the streets in colorful dust.

Celia could undo it all, and would, but for the time being, she needed to let her insides out or risk exploding.

Being a puppet is something I've always been good at! She screamed it in her head, shouting her mind bees down until they settled enough to stop shrieking.

Celia forced herself to slow to a jog, and with a thought, she undid all her beautiful chaos, restoring the serenity of Wisteria all at once.

No one had borne witness to her tantrum; she'd done it all behind a false curtain, shielding it from outside eyes. She knew how to hide illusions too.

So easy.

Everything with the ink was so simple for her.

And that's when she knew she could mimic scent. She had only to *believe* she could do it, and the ink would acquiesce.

"Beautiful day!" Celia said, tipping her hat to Garuld as she loped past where he sat on his front stoop. The sun was too high in the sky; she'd been behind that door only a few moments, talking to Lyric a few more, yet hours had passed. It should have still been early morning, but Garuld himself was a late riser; she'd never seen him out and about until well past noon.

Nothing was *real* there, not even time.

"That it is, Celia!" Garuld responded warmly. "Everything in Wisteria is just as pretty as everything else in Wisteria, isn't it?"

Her stomach turned over, squeezing itself into a knot, but she managed a nod and a smile.

In addition to being deceptively clever, infinitely angry, and remarkably talented with the ink, she was also a passable actor.

CHAPTER 19

THIEF, *THIEF, THIEF,* **THE SHADOWS WHISPERED.** *ABHORRENCE,*
liar, miser, lost soul . . . Celia could think of a hundred words to
describe Halcyon now, all of them distilled down to the fact
that he was not on her side and never had been.

He had Zuni and Griffin under his thumb, and he thought he
had Celia—poor, naive Celia—squashed there too. She would
have bet her soul *(and I have, haven't I, Anya?)* that there was no
cure for the Touch. That there'd never been any hope for Griffin
to outlast Diavala with his mind still intact. That Halcyon had
survived her probably had something to do with the ink, and a
thousand years, and maybe he didn't even understand it himself.

It didn't matter. Now that Celia knew where she stood, she
could formulate some offense. Her rage would be fuel.

Good things came from having everything stripped away
from you. There was a certain freedom underneath. When the
worst has already happened and you'd lived through it, what is
there to fear?

Halcyon needed her, and she would use that.

Celia barged into Rian's farmhouse without knocking and
made her way up to Griffin's room, Rian hobbling behind, looking about as much like a serial killer as Xinto did.

But in Wisteria, everything was just as pretty as everything else.

Where was Zuni in this maze of a home? It looked so humble from the outside, yet inside was a palace.

Celia pretended she didn't remember exactly where Griffin's room was, and she used the ink to create a door every few steps. She threw them open one at a time, from the downstairs sitting room to the kitchen and down each hallway, all the way upstairs to where she knew Griffin was.

No Zuni.

But she was there, somewhere. Zuni hadn't been directly involved with anything that had happened in Asura; she wasn't famous like Lupita, Anya, the plague doctor, and Celia. Lyric couldn't have made it up.

When she finally threw open the door to Griffin's room, she rounded on an out-of-breath Rian.

"We're going out for a bit," Celia told her. Knowing what she knew now, it was hard for her to look at Rian. Were her eyes so wide all the time because she was used to peering around corners in search of hidden nightmares? Was she so stooped from fighting off years of literal demons?

Despite herself, pity tugged at Celia's heart.

She'd seen displays of Halcyon's anger exactly twice, and both times he'd been restraining himself: once with the storm, and once when she'd put her hand on the sunflower doorknob.

She could only imagine what his true displeasure might look like, given how adept he was with the ink.

If he could create a paradise, he could easily create a hell.

Griffin was in his plague doctor costume, casually sprawled on the giant bed. He sat up slowly as Celia burst in. Whatever he'd been doing moments before (it clearly wasn't sleeping) was disguised by a dramatic yawn and stretch routine.

"Halcyon didn't tell me anything about this," Rian replied, clearly unsure whether to let them go. Her eyes darted to Griffin as he straightened his mask.

"I'm telling you it's fine," Celia said. "I just spoke to him." She laced her arm through Griffin's and led him past Rian. Not toward the new door, but to the window. "Let's go."

Rian deferred to Celia's authority, bowing her stooped form even more as they passed.

Like a spectator in her own life. Waiting for the next order.

Killer, disappearer, knife to her throat. Rian could be overpowered by a strong breeze, yet poison didn't require strength.

The window was four stories up, with nothing but a straight drop into Rian's garden.

"Ah, are we flying away?" Griffin said, smiling down at her and not meaning the smile at all. "Finally! I've tried everything else."

Celia ignored him, concentrating on bending the window into the shape of a door and then calling up the stairs that would lead them down safely. She still used her quill, but one day soon she would be like Halcyon and not need to draw on her skin anymore. She would move the quill in the air and draw on the wind. Or she would need only to think it, as he did, and it would come to pass.

For now, she saw the stairs in her mind's eye and traced the outlines, filled in the shadows. Just like the series of doors, the stairs appeared without applause, without sound. One moment there was nothing but a terrible fall ahead of them, the next was a circular wrought iron staircase with gilded Commedia masks decorating the banister every few steps. Xinto, always trailing behind Celia even when she was doing grand things, landed on the nose of the sparkling Gemello mask and began preening his fuzz.

Griffin turned and bowed to Rian. "It's been a pleasure, dear healer, and I will miss your cakes and tea, but it's time for us to fly."

Celia elbowed him in the ribs and scowled. "I'll bring him back in an hour or so," she said apologetically. "He clearly needs some air."

Relief washed over Rian's haggard face. It had looked, moments before, as if she were weighing the cost of reporting a legitimate escape against showing vast disrespect to the almost-second-in-command with a false alarm.

"I *could* fly from here, you know," Griffin said conspiratorially.

"Save your tricks," Celia said as they started down the stairs. Something told her they would need them later. She subtly added glitter to the steps, so with every footfall, the stairs under them sent periwinkle-blue and plum-purple sparks up in glittery plumes, soon coating their lower legs.

Rather than carefully choosing their steps to avoid crushing Rian's flowers, Celia moved them out of the way; bending the tall sunflowers, shuffling aside the azalea. It was still amazing to her how much she could do with only a thought and a stroke of her quill—how powerful the ink actually was.

She caught Griffin's tight jaw of disapproval, even though he still smiled. "It's my imagination come to life," she said defensively. "Sometimes it's actually *fun*." Fun wasn't what she had in mind just then, more like honing her skills, but she didn't elaborate.

As the garden resettled behind them, Griffin turned to her. "So, where to, jailer?" His tone was deceptively light, considering that his new nickname cut her like a blade.

With a quick look around and a wave to Rian, who was watching them from the top of the ornate stairs, Celia led him toward the far end of Rian's farm, past the large barn, opposite the main road. "You need to leave. Now," she whispered. "There is no help for you here. I was wrong."

So very, very wrong, her bees agreed.

Griffin's demeanor changed immediately. He dropped the stage smile, and his strides got longer as he altered his path in a deliberate way. Part of her wondered why Diavala hadn't run immediately after they were out of sight of Rian's.

"Griffin. Listen to me," she said, trying to keep up. They followed the wide road that skirted along the western edge of town. Small homes with large gardens dotted the right side, while grassland gave way to thickening trees to their left. The path was rarely used by the townspeople, and Celia had yet to see another traveler pass through, so it was overgrown with tufts of knee-high weeds. "Be mad at me, go ahead. You were right about Halcyon, right about this place. But I'm begging you, you have to leave. Now. Before the celebration tonight. Are you listening to me, Diavala?" Why, when she *wanted* Diavala to leave, wasn't she doing so?

"This way," Griffin said. He turned abruptly down a faint path of trampled grasses. "To the lakes, in search of river lobsters," he said far too loudly.

Ever since Celia had fetched him from Rian's, Griffin had been in performance mode, as if he knew they were being watched.

"I need to talk to *her*," Celia whispered as she followed. Her stomach knotted—demanding to speak with Diavala?—how things changed.

"Ah, yes. Sadly, that's not possible. We've come to an arrangement where she talks to me, and I talk to you, and you two never talk to each other. But never fear, she heard you." With each word, Griffin made flamboyant gestures with his hands. If there was someone watching, they'd see a casual conversation. Two people, perhaps catching up after a long period of fighting, both finally coming to their senses and feeling remorse for how they'd acted.

Celia blinked and pasted a smile on her face, following suit. "And why would you make that arrangement?" She added a soft chuckle and trailed her fingertips along the tall grasses at either side of her, keeping up the ruse of *nothing's wrong, of course nothing's wrong.*

"I want you to know it's me." He stopped and turned around so suddenly she bumped into his chest. He grabbed her shoulders to help her regain her balance, and his hands stayed there, gently holding her.

A soft breeze swished the grasses, their hair. A few paces away, the forest beckoned with the distant sound of lapping water at the lakeshore. With careful movements, he removed his mask, letting it hang at his back, and looked down at her as Griffin. Serious, unsmiling. His hands moved from her shoulders to her upper arms.

Her breath hitched. When he removed his mask, it was always the constellation of stars beside his dark eyes that caught her attention first. An act of rebellion when traditional tattoos were still banned, a way of making his sharp features even more so, the symbol that something more lived under the mask.

"It will always be me from now on." He searched her eyes again. "Know that." Though he whispered it, there was heat in his words. It sounded like a demand. "I need you to know it. By far the worst part of being possessed by a devil," he said with wry tilt to his mouth, "is the way you look at me."

She inhaled and tried to look away, but his hand went to her chin, cupping it gently, not allowing her to move. His lips tilted into a faint smile. "You only just started to look at me, Celia Sand, before you started to look away."

Celia knew that none of this was his fault, but knowing it hadn't made it easier. She couldn't even imagine how she must have looked at him, what her body must have told him these past weeks. So much hatred, coiled and ready to strike.

"So what would you like to ask her? I will be your messenger, Ce-li-a." He stretched her name out into three distinct syllables. A whispered song on his lips. He bent a little closer, his gaze dropping to her lips, then meeting her eyes.

Her heart beating madly, Celia flushed. That familiar push and pull of him flooded back.

As much as she still loathed the idea of Griffin talking to Diavala, it meant everything to have him back. A weight had lifted from her shoulders, and she was surprised by how fully and completely she trusted his words: that he would always be him and she had no need to worry about Diavala's taking over again, pretending to be him.

She stepped up on her tiptoes and leaned closer, and he bent obligingly, offering his ear. "Where did she get her ink?" she whispered.

As he relayed Diavala's answer, with pauses in between sentences as he listened, he didn't let go of Celia's eyes. *It's me,* they said. *Even though these words are not.*

"*I found the Chest Majestic,*" he relayed.

"You found it . . . in this world?" Celia choked out.

Griffin blinked at the question, but responded, "*Yes. Near the small settlement that would become Asura. And I began using the contents to ink tattoos, which became the start of Profeta.*"

Griffin paused longer than normal. He swallowed before continuing.

"It didn't take Halcyon long to find me, the way my notoriety spread."

After what Celia had seen behind the door, she had expected this, but hearing it confirmed still took her breath. This meant that Halcyon was just as old, if not older, than Diavala herself.

Somehow, Celia and Griffin were embroiled in a feud that had started centuries ago.

The small smile had fallen off Griffin's face. "Is she saying what I think she is?" he asked. None of his casual act remained. Blunt and angry, the question was equal parts shock and understanding.

With stuttering words, Celia whispered to Diavala, "Let me make sure I understand this perfectly. It was Halcyon's chest? His ink?"

"Since the beginning, it's been the two of us."

Griffin was having a difficult time relaying Diavala's words now. With the way his posture had stiffened, it looked like he regretted being the intermediary.

"But technically, the chest I stumbled across was Martina's. He still has his own chest to this day, as I'm sure you're aware, Inkling. He insists that I stole it from her and killed her, when in reality, I was simply in the wrong place at the wrong time, and here we are, a thousand years later."

It was harder for Celia now, too, to pretend at the intimacy. She knew it was Griffin in front of her, but the words Diavala spoke through him triggered her fierce hatred. How blithely she spoke of centuries of pain, how easily she dismissed her role in it all and painted herself a victim.

Just like Halcyon, who would have Celia believe everything he did was out of love.

A few hours ago, Celia would have laughed at this information. Now she felt the truth of it, even if she didn't understand all the details.

She'd seen the ink's origin point behind a door in his home, in his town full of strange and perfect. There was far more to Halcyon's story than an ink-loving, artistic hermit. He'd somehow figured out how to steal the ink from the afterlife and extend his life unnaturally. As a child, Diavala had pissed him off by taking his toy and using it as her own.

Three people, two chests of ink, and one doorway. Everything was there: Celia just needed to put it in the right order.

The most important thing was already confirmed: Halcyon had started everything.

Griffin put his hands on Celia's shoulders again, squaring his body with hers and forcing her to look up at him. "Tell us what happened. What changed?"

She hesitated, wanting to tell him everything: what she'd seen behind the door, where the ink had come from, that the souls on the other side were suffering. But just because she suspected Halcyon of treachery now didn't mean that she trusted Diavala.

"I need to ask her one more thing first," Celia whispered. "If she took the ink from Halcyon, where did he get it in the first place?"

Xinto finished his examination of the field and flew over to snuggle into her chest. *The afterlife, of course!* he seemed to buzz. *I'm made of something that comes from the other side of the door. Everything here is made of death, Celia. Buzz buzz buzz.*

After a moment's hesitation, Griffin said with a frustrated tone, "She says she doesn't know." His grip tightened, and he pulled Celia closer. "She always assumed that he and Martina made it with alchemy. She's not lying, Celia. I would feel at least a hint of it. But she's definitely leaving gaps in what she's relaying . . . *Aren't you, Diavala?*" He was speaking as much to Celia as he was to Diavala with that last statement, his words a low growl.

Griffin laced his fingers through Celia's and began walking again. Slower this time, an intense look of concentration on his face that he covered with his mask again in short order. "Give me a minute to deal with this devil," he whispered.

So Celia walked through a perfect grassy field beside a perfect town toward a perfect lake with a perfectly unnatural bee now sleeping in her shirt; and she was holding hands with a plague doctor who was having a silent conversation with the immortal creature who'd killed her best friend and now possessed him.

If only Celia were still in the Commedia and this was all just make-believe.

Always such a mess, Cece, Anya whispered. *Everything is always such a mess.*

INTERLUDE

Just when I thought we were starting to get along, the plague doctor said, shaking his head at the purple-eyed child in his mind. *It turns out you've omitted a fair amount, Diavala. Like the bit about Halcyon being an ancient scourge. Just like you.*

"You know, I liked you much better when you were scared of me," Diavala said. *"When your mind trembled at my presence and worried what I could do. Now it almost feels like you don't care that I'm here at all—except for the inconvenience."*

He ignored her. *I sense your happiness.* He loaded as much mistrust and accusation into his thought as possible, lobbing it at her like a perfectly delivered line of dialogue. If she was happy all of sudden, something had changed, and he needed to know what.

"If Celia is asking these questions now," Diavala said, *"if she's trying to get you to leave, it means she doesn't trust Halcyon anymore. Obviously I'm happy about that. Halcyon is an untrustworthy scoundrel."*

He grumbled. She'd said variations of that so many times, it had lost meaning.

Tell me everything, he demanded.

When he looked down at Celia, she arched an eyebrow. One dainty little eyebrow, bending from its usual stern *v* into a mountain peak. "Griffin?" she said softly.

He turned away, but his wasps settled for a moment, hearing that name on her lips. It wasn't one the plague doctor recognized often, but it always sounded right, coming from her.

No, don't tell me, he said to Diavala. *Show me.*

He took Celia's arm for support as Diavala opened the window into her memories again, and they walked toward the lake together. He became the young, purple-eyed child and saw a hazy memory through her eyes:

A gilded box lying under a bush, abandoned. A pinched feeling in his stomach, a hunger he'd never known. The brief debate about whether he should take it, hunger soon winning out.

The plague doctor ground his teeth. Halcyon's extravagance wasn't a new trait, then. And in this case, it had acted as a lure for an impoverished child and began a series of events that would take over a nation and last a thousand years.

You did steal it then, he said. *It wasn't yours to take, Diavala.* But if a starving soul had happened along a loaf of bread, he would hardly blame them for taking it.

The memory continued.

Inside the chest was no treasure he could sell, but he learned to use the ink inside. At first the tattoos were ornaments that people paid well for, but that changed quickly: he listened to the people and made sure to give them images that would be precious to them.

"*Regardless of what you and the inkling might think,*" Dia-vala said, intruding on the memory, "*I've always cared. I know you imagine me as a poor ten-year-old child, and except for the purple eyes, you are very close to the truth. I was exactly that, in the beginning. I was a child inking art onto people and making those people happy. I helped them realize themselves in this life, so they were unafraid of meeting the afterlife.*"

Irritation hummed in his bones now. Distantly, he registered that Celia was asking if he was okay.

No, he wasn't. The sun was too bright, and he missed his people. He ached for the stage. It was like a wasp sting in the center of his chest, and the pain of it spread every day.

But he nodded. "Diavala's doing a lot of justifying without giving me actual information," he explained to Celia. When would Halcyon enter the script?

"*It was a thousand years ago,*" Diavala said, affronted. "*But fine, we can condense it.*"

So you became famous for your tattoos quickly, he said, doing the condensing for her from what everyone knew of Profeta. *People start to believe you're an oracle of some kind. And then?*

A brief pause, and then he was plunged underwater. His nose and mouth filled with water, and gasping for the breath he needed only made his lungs burn more. Panic consumed him, and he twisted to the side, try-ing to get free. But he couldn't struggle long, the hands holding him were too strong. As the world stilled, he noted the snowdrops growing on the bank of the lake: clumps of small white flowers arching their heads down toward him. Swimming in his vision, they beckoned to him like nodding promises of life. If only he could get to those snowdrops . . .

But he didn't. They disappeared into blackness as his eyes closed forever and the water won.

"*My story should have ended there,*" Diavala said. "*Profeta should never have been named, and it shouldn't have grown. It should have died with me, underwater, that day.*"

The plague doctor pushed Celia away and bent over, gasping for breath, coming out of the memory with force. Lilies and snowdrops. Death and life.

With the snowdrop memory came Halcyon's face: unchanged from then to now. His hands—pushing, holding, pinching—had been the ones making sure the water claimed her.

"Halcyon is the one who killed you," he said. With those words, Celia—who'd bent with him, trying to figure out what was wrong—reared back.

Their charming host was a child killer.

"Because he blamed you for his lover's death," he finished. He kept speaking to Diavala aloud because there was no part of him that wanted to explain this to Celia over again. He would live it once and then banish all thought of lilies and snowdrops and child murder to the rooms in his mind that dealt with death and pain, and he'd shut them in tight.

"*Yes,*" was all Diavala said. A simple word, and the truth.

Still, although Diavala was finally being clear about the cause of their hatred for each other and how long it had festered, the plague doctor knew she was still withholding something.

"*You know the place I went, plague doctor. You were a visitor there too.*"

The afterlife.

All it had taken was one orange and white cat in a too-tall tree, and yes, he'd been a visitor there. He'd seen death before, he knew what to expect of the afterlife, and he wasn't eager to return. The nothingness, the sorrow. An abject feeling of being lost while knowing there would never be a way to get unlost . . . Yes, he knew the place. And every moment Diavala possessed him, he was reminded of it. Every second his bones hummed, he felt Death calling him back: *You belong with me . . .*

He shook his head to drown out Death's call.

"I escaped the afterlife through sheer luck, Diavala," he said carefully. "How was it that you returned to us?"

The plague doctor braced himself for her answer by reaching for Celia's hand and clinging hard enough to crack her knuckles.

"*Ah, good question,*" Diavala said slowly. "*You see, I*

*didn't know it was Halcyon who'd killed me until he visited
me in the afterlife to gloat."*

Given his experience with saving a cat stuck in a tree
and dying and coming back, he'd known it was possible
to see the other side and return. That was something he
and Diavala had long had in common.

But who could "visit" the afterlife intentionally? The
way Diavala so casually inserted Halcyon into her story
suggested that he had the ability to travel back and forth
at whim. That he was not a person nor a dead soul, but
someone who straddled the line between worlds.

"I was not afraid of him there," Diavala said. *"He'd
already killed me, how could I die again? And oh, that irritated him so: a child flaunting her bravery, defying him by not
trembling at his feet. He'd come to revel in his power over me,
but his revenge quickly turned sour."*

Diavala's pitch had risen alarmingly. It was entirely
possible that she hadn't talked about this to anyone since
it had happened more than a thousand years ago.

*"Part of me remains there, in the afterlife. He pushed the
rest of me out. I am not alive. I have no body of my own. My
memories, my wants and fears, that's all I'm made of now.
That is my curse, and it will go on forever. Maybe you can see
now why I wish for death. Only in death will I be complete.
Only in the afterlife will I be whole. Yet it is the one place I will
never see again."*

Celia was shaking him, and from the wide-eyed look

of panic on her face, she had been doing so for quite some time. "Griffin, what's wrong? Answer me! Griffin!"

What could he say? He'd never trusted Halcyon's motivations, but the story he'd just heard—the truth of which he could feel in his bones just as clearly as Diavala's constant humming—told him he'd underestimated his mistrust.

They were dealing with the overlord of the afterlife, the devil himself.

The plague doctor had seen his domain, and a worse place didn't exist, even in his vast imagination.

"*Oh, plague doctor,*" Diavala said. The laughter from the purple-eyed child scared him, how wild it sounded, even in its silence. "*Honestly. I didn't emerge from the womb an immortal body stealer. Who do you think cursed me to begin with?*"

CHAPTER 20

CELIA PULLED GRIFFIN ALONG TOWARD THE SOUND OF softly lapping water. Every muscle in his body had fused into rock, and the smile had been smacked off his face; she'd never known him to fall out of character so fast and so hard.

She couldn't imagine anything worse than finding out that Halcyon could travel to and from the afterlife, and that's precisely what she suspected Diavala had just told him.

At least it saved her the trauma of being the one to break the news. *Oh by the way, dear plague doctor, you're now embroiled in a dispute that spans centuries AND worlds, including the one you're so terrified of! Sorry I brought you here, my mistake!*

Celia inhaled, readying herself.

He confirmed everything she already knew . . . and then some.

They'd come to Wisteria on the hope that Halcyon would have a way of saving Griffin from Diavala's possession, and Celia had bet everything on it, including her future.

But it turned out that Halcyon was the one who'd cursed Diavala to begin with.

Celia might have laughed at the irony, if she didn't feel like throwing up.

"I'm not going to say 'I told you so' about Halcyon," he finally said, "but know that I'm thinking it."

That was fair.

"And every few hundred years he hunts me down," Griffin quoted at one point. It sent quivers under Celia's skin, hearing him talk as Diavala. *"He has a bottomless amount of hatred for me, but his anger is a glacier . . . it builds over such long stretches of time that the force of it when unleashed is unparalleled. Your worst nightmares realized. Your fears, in the flesh. Though you might not believe me, plague doctor, there are so many things worse than death, and I've seen them all by Halcyon's hand."*

And Celia reached for sympathy harder than she'd ever done before: if Halcyon became displeased with her, she might have exactly the same story to tell one day.

Both of them were tied to monsters now.

But why wasn't Griffin's monster leaving? This was her opportunity for freedom. The road out of Wisteria lay around a few bends. The horizon beckoned.

Celia's suspicion flared anew.

"Does Halcyon still trust you?" Griffin asked Celia.

"As much as he trusts anyone, yes."

"Make sure you keep it that way," he said, squeezing her hand again. For all the shock this must have been for him, Griffin was handling it shockingly well. Only the briefest stutter, and he was back to swaggering and smiling as if he'd never gone off script.

Celia didn't know who could possibly be watching them, but

she suspected that at least Rian was. Maybe the entire town was in on Halcyon's duplicity.

Celia tried to tell him about Rian—how she was, apparently, Halcyon's executioner—but he cut her off. "I know," he said with a wry grin.

"What?"

"There are no sick people here, no overly elderly ones. Illness and age aren't exactly perfect, are they? Travelers are carefully screened. It makes sense. But the most obvious hint was that Lyric told me not to eat or drink anything Rian offered. They've been sneaking me food and water for days."

Celia hissed through her teeth. "Well, isn't that nice of them." Hopefully, they were doing the same for Zuni. "I didn't have time to grab any supplies, but I have a bit of money, and with how distracted everyone is by the party tonight, you'll be able to make it pretty far before anyone notices."

Griffin cleared his throat. "You want me to leave *before* a party? It's like you don't know me at all." Anger rolled off of him in waves, but he skillfully hid it behind his fake smile. "You're making it sound like you want me to leave without you."

"You have to."

He chuckled, as if she'd just told the most hilarious joke.

Celia yanked him closer to her side. "Nothing about this is funny," she whispered fiercely. "If you're staying because of some sense of duty or obligation to me, trust me, it's not needed. I'm going to be fine here. He needs me, but you and Zuni are leverage."

Griffin squeezed her hand tight again and brought it to his lips, as if apologizing for his noise. It was dizzying, living inside chaos and pretending everything was normal. "Ah, so Zuni's here," he whispered, as if that explained everything. He must have assumed there was something else keeping Celia there, and now he had his confirmation. "At Rian's?" he asked.

"Don't get any ideas," she responded, glancing over her shoulder. No one seemed to be following them, but the show had to go on. *I'll find her.*

"Or," he said slowly, "you can stop being a stubborn mule." Louder, he said, "Let's put the past behind us and enjoy this expedition, shall we?"

Celia grumbled. *How would you think this through?* Celia asked Anya. She brushed Xinto away and put her hand to her stomach. *How would you make him leave?*

They approached a copse of trees toward the promise of river lobsters. The path underfoot had changed from dry grasses to damp moss, the surrounding landscape stretching out into trees and shrubs, all of it much more familiar to Celia and Illinia-like. They crested a small hill, and the forest opened up to a huge expanse of calm water. Even with the sun high in the sky, Celia could barely make out the opposite bank. The trees that dotted the far side looked like twigs.

Shimmering in the sunlight, the water looked nothing like the grungy canals of Asura, nor even the glimpses of sea Celia had seen at the port, with its bustle of ships, docks, and rough sailors. Celia's breath caught at the beauty of it.

"This is the kind of hunt that's better to do in pairs," Griffin explained. "One stays on the shore, quiet and meek and completely still, while the other dives into the water and stirs it up, with the aim of making the most commotion possible. The instinct of a river lobster when faced with an unknown threat, Michali explained to me, is to seek out the familiar. They rush toward shore, where they breed and nest, and—hopefully—into waiting hands."

Griffin didn't stop to admire the view, but immediately jogged down the bank and stopped at the edge, where the moss gave way to mud and then deeper, reed-filled water. "They're fast as hell," he said, taking off the dangling plague doctor mask, his boots, his coat, and his shirt, and rolling up his pants. Damn, but his speed was impressive. He could be undressed in a matter of seconds if he wanted, which, she supposed, he'd learned through rapid costume changes with the Mob.

Then he squelched through the mud until he was in ankle-deep water. "If you try to catch them, they'll only dart away. They're smart and can't be caught with conventional traps. So smart, Celia, that people call them river lobsters when they've never been known to live in rivers, only freshwater lakes." He turned and smiled at her, admiring those clever, wily river lobsters. She recognized that false smile; it spoke of a hidden meaning, just for her. "It's as if they fooled everyone, even the cleverest, by pretending to be one thing, only to be another thing entirely."

Tears prickled at Celia's eyes, and she had to look away from Griffin's smiling face and shocking amount of bare skin, instead examining the lakeshore and surrounding forest. With Diavala between them, their relationship was impossible to nurture, but the hint of forgiveness was there. And more important, it amazed her how familiar his Riddlish was. How easily they fell back into understanding each other.

He'd led her here for a reason.

"Michali told me the far easier job is the catcher," he said, "although I don't think that's true. I had much more success out there, causing chaos, than on the shore. You try it first." He held out his hand as she shook her head. "Don't worry about your clothes. I have no trouble with a little nudity."

His tone was so light, but his offered hand was insistent.

Tentatively, she took off her hat and boots, added her folded coat and shirt to his strewn pile of clothes on the shore, and rolled up her pants. She hadn't worn a corset since leaving Asura, so she matched him, skin for skin.

Their eyes didn't leave each other's, but it was a struggle. Griffin looked like he would combust. He grabbed her hand and pulled her in farther. At every handspan she walked deeper into the water, mud squelching between her toes until it turned to silt and then to pebbly rocks. She gasped at the shocks of cold water. When they hit her kidneys, she hissed and tried to turn around.

He didn't let her. His grip had turned viselike.

"But I can't do the chaos causing," she said to his back, "because I can't swim." Illinia was as waterlogged a country as one could find, yet swim lessons had never been on the mistico's list of priorities to teach little inklings.

Griffin laughed like he didn't believe her. His hair hung loose, and she had some trouble looking away as it moved in waves across his bare shoulders. "You'll have to learn," he said.

He turned, scooped her up, and threw her into deeper water. Her scream didn't have time to leave her throat before she went under.

Her eyes slammed shut while her arms and legs windmilled and kicked. She stretched out, reaching for the ground she knew had to be there, but she had no idea which direction it was. A bolt of pain knocked through her leg as she kneed a large rock, and she grappled for it, trying to orient herself to up. It was so cold, so dark. Her heart raced and her lungs screamed for the air they knew they couldn't have, but she forced herself to open her eyes. She forced herself still enough to notice where the glimmers of sunlight came from.

Directly in front of her, two legs, one boasting a beautiful plague doctor tattoo. The water was clear. Crisp. Perfect.

Like everything else in Wisteria.

Celia twisted and put her feet under her, then scrambled up. "You *ass*," she said, sputtering and spitting, her hair dangling in her face. The water was barely to her armpits. "What part of 'I can't swim' didn't you understand?" It was a good thing the temple had taught her how to hold her breath, but then again, they'd also taught her it was possible to drown in a tiny amount of water.

"That was how Georgio taught me," he said. "Don't worry, I was ready to haul you out if you panicked even half the amount I did when they tossed me in." Griffin's laughter was full-bodied but sharp around the edges.

She shoved a wave of water at him, but all he did was step into it, coming closer. "I won't lie," he said. "I feel much better all of a sudden."

"Vindicated?"

"A bit." He was infuriatingly hard to stay mad at, with water droplets falling from his hair and down his chest, with a smile that, for the first time in a long time, looked completely genuine. Even if it was at her expense.

Her breathing had calmed enough from being underwater that it hitched again when he stepped closer. Right in front of her. Nearly chest to chest. Their tenors flickered against each other, pressing close enough to mix: his silvers with her bronzes and reds. If they edged even a bit closer, all manner of colors would tangle together beautifully.

He bent and whispered in her ear, drops of water from his hair falling on her exposed shoulder. She'd frozen like a rabbit, shivering from the cold, but not minding it too much at all. "I'm staying, but I'm not just staying for you. I'm also staying for Diavala, because there may be a way to help her. And I'm staying for me."

He paused to let the words sink in.

Hints of forgiveness weren't in the air after all. That had been a part of his act. And he'd wanted her to know, unequivocally, that it was he who was saying those words.

"You were right—there are answers here," he said, so low she had to tilt her head even closer. "But maybe you're not asking the right questions." His words brushed against her neck and ear. "And Celia, just so you're perfectly clear, I don't expect to survive this. Stop trying to save me."

His words stopped, the silence filled with the sound of water dripping, of faint ripples, of light wind in the leaves. The warmth of his breath, of his closeness, made her shivering stop. The water pushed against her skin.

It was as if the entire world paused, allowing them a moment to breathe together. Even the setting was perfect for a false reconciliation. The few frayed threads that remained of her heart snapped, one by one.

His hand went to her cheek. "I hate this," he whispered. The look in his eyes was a fiery mixture of anger, confusion, and betrayal. "I hate how much I want to kiss you, and how much I want to fly away. I hate how well you know me, because that means you know how to hurt me."

Celia was having trouble concentrating, couldn't look away from his dark eyes. One drop of water trailed from his damp hair, across his tattoo, and down his jawline, and she watched it, still partly caught in the world's pause. They hadn't been this close in weeks. So many nights, too many days.

His words flooded over her, wave after wave. "I hate that

I still want to trust you even though you've proved I can't trust you. I hate that I understand your ghosts, I hate that you understand mine. You've always been both my beginning and my end."

His chest, pressed against Celia's, was warm with his thundering pulse. She wanted to explore every inch of it with her hands, press her lips to where the heartbeats came from. Despite what he'd just said, the pull of him would never go away. She should have hated that herself, but she didn't.

One of his hands slid under the water and his fingers traced lightly along Celia's hip. His gaze roamed over her face slowly as he moved his hand from where her pants clung to her, and upward to her skin.

His gaze landed on her neck, just before his lips followed. Celia nudged her face until he turned his head, his lips tracing gentle kisses along her jawline until they found her mouth. It began as a sweet kiss, slow and leisurely, his lips dancing with hers. She could pretend, for a minute, that he hadn't scripted this in. That it was real, and he meant it.

The sweetness didn't last long. A moan in the back of his throat, and both of his hands were wrapped around her, caressing the small of her back and her shoulders with increasing urgency. It felt real. His tongue, his taste, everything about him overpowered her. Celia's fingers stroked up his arms and along his neck until they tangled in his damp hair. She twined a leg around his and pressed their hips together.

"Celia," he moaned against her lips. Then he broke away

from the kiss. Panting, flushed, fully in character and able to harness lust and passion and hate and fear, all at once. To outside eyes, their reconciliation was complete.

Under the water, where no one could see, he took her hand significantly. "I don't expect to survive this, but I hope you do."

Then just as fast, he dropped it, darted away like a fish, and sent up a wave of water at Celia's face. She swallowed half of it.

His laughter, slightly deeper than normal, told her he'd really enjoyed that too.

ACT 3

CHAPTER 21

A NEW PLAY WAS BEGINNING. ONE WITHOUT A PROPER stage, and one without a known ending. "From here," Griffin had said by the lake, pulling his plague doctor mask back on over his damp hair, "we work our improvisation skills." Celia understood now why Griffin had permanently donned his plague doctor persona after his death and miraculous resurrection: he'd been performing the part of someone who wasn't scared of death.

Rian had found them shortly after their confusing, incredible kiss, waving her arms and out of breath, as if she'd climbed a mountain. Celia didn't buy it for a minute; she'd heard rustling in the bushes almost as soon as they'd entered the lake. Griffin had been right: Halcyon's spy had been lurking around long before she'd made her dramatic appearance. "You are taking much longer than an hour!" Rian pointed out. "And I have a suit to squeeze into for the party, so I'd appreciate if you hurried it along!"

With Griffin determined to find Zuni, and Diavala intent to stay the course for some unknown reason, Celia's first improvised task was to make sure that Halcyon was happy enough with her that he would leave on one of his find-Martina quests.

Celia needed to prove to him that she was capable, prove he could trust her completely. In that regard, Lyric was exactly right. If Celia was in charge of Wisteria, she would also be in charge of that door and its secrets, the ink and its power, the whole of the town.

As much as she wanted to stay with Griffin, to find Zuni, Celia had to be clever about strategy. She needed to keep the upper hand as long as possible, where Halcyon had no idea how much she knew.

Celia made her way toward Halcyon's home with quick steps. She'd thought the portraits of Martina were beautiful, once. Now all she saw was a partner in deception, long dead but no less to blame. With every stride, she cursed Halcyon and Martina both.

They'd messed around with the natural order of things. Whether they'd been the ones to actively pierce through the barrier between life and death or whether they'd stumbled upon a breach already there, they were the ones responsible.

They'd stolen the ink from the place where it belonged and brought it to the place where it didn't, wreaking havoc on both sides. Halcyon acted without thought to consequence, yet the consequences of his actions were everywhere. They stretched out over hundreds of years, to all corners of Illinia, and even beyond, to the world of the dead.

That Diavala had gotten in the way of their plans had earned her a drowning and a flogging and an eternity of straddling life and death—belonging to both and neither at the same time. A curse, not a blessing. Part of Celia, a small, teeny part, could hardly blame her for trying to make the most of it.

The fountain burbled quietly as Celia made her way through the wisteria tunnel toward the courtyard. She created a family of sparrows for Xinto to play with and then stretched out the clumps of lilac bunches so they were as large as pumpkins, snapping one off and pressing her nose into it to drown out the scent of wisteria. She was just about to make the cluster in her hand orange when she saw him.

At a stone trough full of crisp, cool water—the aqueduct that fed the fountain with a constant supply of fresh water—Halcyon stood, his back to her, dipping a cloth in the water and washing his face and chest with an abundance of care. Even the way he cleaned up was elegant; she would have bet a hundred kropi that his favorite shoes wouldn't see a drop of stray water splash on them. How beautiful he was, with his chestnut hair veined with silver, his perfect skin and strange eyes. But surreal somehow, as if he'd stepped out of one of his paintings and hadn't thought to bring along his heart and soul.

Thief, thief, thief . . .

Celia silently called on Xinto and his new sparrow friends to play quietly behind her so they didn't startle him, and she backed away slowly, the giant lilac bunch still held up in front of her face like a big purple shield. Instead of the awkward feeling of intruding on an intimate human moment, she felt a shuddering unease crinkle its way up her spine, crunchy and harsh. It wasn't shock at seeing his skin: that might have made her flush and turn away, embarrassed at her intrusion.

But she hadn't realized that Halcyon wore a mask until that moment when she saw him without it.

Seeing him so *normal* only accentuated that he wasn't normal at all. There were layers of him she didn't understand and didn't want any part of. She'd wanted only the mentor, the recluse in his studio, the means to an end.

Not to be so hit with all the things she'd chosen to ignore, all the backstory she didn't know.

With his obsession with ink, Halcyon was more like Diavala than anyone else. It shouldn't have been a shock.

And yet.

He turned his head to the side, listening, and Celia froze. In mid-flight, poor Xinto and the sparrows froze too, Xinto's very stylish leash dangling to the ground like an unfurled ribbon, connecting him to the rest of the town.

Halcyon dropped his chin to his chest, resting there a beat with his eyes closed, then carefully hung the rag on its hook. Every movement precise, methodical, stiff. *Child killer, thief, immortal narcissist* . . .

Celia took a careful step back, her heart pounding against her ribs, still holding the lilac shield in front of her face. So much damn skin lately! By the end of the night, everyone would be dancing around naked.

As Halcyon pulled a loose shirt on, Celia realized exactly what unnerved her so. A small thing. A big thing.

His upper arms were unmarked.

The wisteria bunch she'd carefully drawn to get his attention—the tattoo she'd sent him that had started all this—wasn't there.

There were only two possibilities Celia could think of that would explain it. He might have created an illusion of fresh skin to cover it. If so, that meant he was part of the grand illusion too.

Impossible.

Or he might have wiped it away somehow. But getting rid of Divine tattoos was also impossible. It was a dead form of the ink. Totally inert and untouchable compared with the sweater of live ink sustaining the town. He shouldn't have been able to do it.

It was shocking to see something that should have been permanent just *gone*.

He didn't face her, only turned his head to the side, offering his profile, waiting for her to explain herself.

"What happened to the wisteria tattoo?" she asked.

He waited a beat, as if surprised by the question. "I didn't like it. I got rid of it."

"But how?" It hadn't been an illusion, it'd been real.

"That doesn't particularly matter, does it?" He turned to face her slowly, the pendant laying against his chest in plain sight between the wings of his shirt as he slowly buttoned it up.

"What matters is whether you're ready for tonight. What matters, right now, is how much more time I should waste on you."

A shudder knocked through her, and she carefully tried to keep her face neutral as she stepped forward.

What was bothering her so much about the tattoo not being there? She should be shuddering at the fact that he could traverse the worlds of both the living and the dead. She should be cowering at the idea that he was somehow a thousand years old, or raging that he'd trapped Zuni somewhere close. Yet it was the missing tattoo she fixated on.

Celia called Xinto and made the sparrows disappear. One thought—those sparrows shouldn't exist—and they were gone.

But the sparrows were different from a Divine tattoo.

Quivering, she finally parted with the lilac bunch in her hand, restoring it to the shrub she'd plucked it from. "I'm ready. You'll see."

As she walked away, she made the mistake of looking back at Halcyon once more. And right then, when a sunbeam sliced through the taller shrubs across his face, Celia decided that she liked clouds and rain very much. Sunlight made things wither. Made things ugly. Creeping things and claws lurked everywhere, but in the sun, they stared at you with a glinting smile.

CHAPTER 22

As the sun set, Celia made her way with Xinto to the main square. She hadn't had much time to get herself together, but she'd inked herself to perfection: a glittering opalescent gown, her dark hair swept up with silver clips, such elegant taste that Dante would have been proud. She'd even covered her regular buckled black boots with slippers that looked like they were made of pearls. So much easier and faster to get yourself into costume when the ink did all the work.

She was opposite-Celia that night, an inside-out version of herself.

Perfect.

The giant platform the town had built together had an arch of flowers stretching from one side to the other. Every person in the square would have a good view, and the expanse of cobblestones around it would make sure that everyone had plenty of room to dance. Wisteria dripped in heavy bunches from the arch, all along the periphery of the platform, and hung in planters around the square, painting everything a splendid, delicately textured purple. It was a lighter shade than the plague doctor's signature rich plum, and Celia hated it to her bones. She had a feeling that Halcyon had spent a lot of time on those particular flowers, and they wouldn't have that offness she'd seen in the other bunches around the town. They were the showcase, and they would be perfection. Hideous, tacky, and perfect.

She wondered about music: Would everyone make the music with their stomping and shouts? Then how would they dance? Or would Halcyon cast an illusion of music? But then a band began assembling in one corner of the square, answering that particular question in the most mundane way.

Lights twinkled in the night sky, bigger than fireflies but smaller than lanterns, and for the life of her, Celia couldn't figure out what they were or how they glowed. It seemed as if Halcyon had taken each star and pulled it closer.

Thoughts of Kinallen entered her mind for a moment, but she pushed them aside, blurring them back into the maelstrom with everything else.

"Well, don't you look beautiful, Celia!" Michali announced, their pale hair swishing like silk. In a way, Michali reminded Celia of Vincent, in coloring at least, definitely not in personality. Then Michali spied the bee on her shoulder. "And Xinto, my good soul! I'm amazed!"

Xinto wore a sharp black bow tie instead of his usual leash and, to complete their paired look, a wee top hat that matched Celia's. With Michali's praise, he shuffled back and forth on her shoulder, as if embarrassed by the attention from one so charming themself.

"The square is absolutely stunning," Celia said with awe in her voice. "Everyone did such a good job." Full of lavish opulence, it was a repellent kind of beauty to her now: a golden throne for a starving ruler, or the jeweled sword of a dead soldier.

If the ink of the dead had created it, there was no beauty here at all.

"Yes," Michali said. "It looks like someone's getting married, doesn't it?"

Celia's choice to dress so fancily suddenly didn't feel very clever.

Halcyon was already onstage, dressed in his finest of all his fine suits: a formfitting indigo jacket and long indigo skirt, threads of silver woven in subtle tessellations. His hands waved gracefully, as if he were a conductor, urging people to begin the night with dancing.

When Celia was close enough to take his offered hand, she forced herself to do it. "You look nice," she said. Underneath his clothing lay fine, unmarked skin. Just as he had with the tattoo of a wisteria flower, he could wipe away any indication of his true age. She still didn't know what it meant, but the thought sent shivers dancing up and down her spine.

"As do you," he replied.

Shoulder to shoulder with him, she turned to face the milling people. It was a sight she hadn't seen since taking the Rabble Mob's stage: hundreds of people in front of her, their tenors shining bright and rich.

"Shall we dance?" Celia asked Halcyon, taking a bow.

He looked startled that she would ask, and every time she

startled him, something soared inside her. Small triumphs she savored.

She was still determined to match Halcyon beat for beat. He was done surprising her.

He took her hand and turned her around so they were back to back, not touching. Celia knew about the Dance of Latessa only in theory, she'd never tried it. But because of his gesture and the signal to the band to start a song of the right tempo, she'd have to fake it.

In the dance, the couple didn't face each other until the very last beat: they spun and circled, stepped away from each other, then back, and only at the end did they turn around to see who their partner had been. It was supposed to be mysterious—you got flashes of your partner as you spun, the heat from their body as you brushed by.

The spaces around them filled with people, and when the last bar sounded, every couple turned around. One last step, finally into the arms of your partner, ending the dance face to face. Because Celia was a bit behind, she heard the sighs and whispers as the other couples came together just as she turned to face Halcyon.

He smiled down at her, as charming as ever, but she couldn't bring herself to smile back. She extended her fingers to avoid piercing his fancy suit with her claws.

"Another dance?" she asked.

He nodded and held his arms out again, but assessed her shrewdly. "You wouldn't by any chance be stalling, would you,

Celia? When you told me you were ready for tonight, I assumed that meant you had everything in hand, including scent." The line of his false smile hardened. "You wouldn't dare make a fool of me."

Celia laughed, her gaze inadvertently finding Rian's in the crowd; Griffin needed as much Rian-free time as possible in order to look for Zuni, so the longer the night went on, the better. She was definitely stalling, but not for the reason Halcyon assumed.

"No. I'm celebrating. I figured it out. Why scent gave me such a hard time."

"Oh?" That piqued his interest. He pulled her to the side of the stage and folded his arms across his chest, waiting for her to prove it.

"You confused me when you said that scent was tied to memories, that it would mean different things to different people. I thought that meant I had to crawl into someone's mind and figure out what they expected and then deliver that expectation to them." Celia huffed out a breath through puffed cheeks and got her quill ready. "But it's tied to me, as the artist."

He shook his head but looked interested. "To be honest, I have no idea how it works anymore, which is why I couldn't help you. But that makes some sense."

Ah, yes, it would be hard to remember details when you're a thousand years old, wouldn't it? She bit her tongue against everything she still didn't understand and focused on what she did.

The ink.

He'd said that scent was closely tied to memories, and literally the only thing she hadn't tried yet was drawing on her *own*.

"So? Show me," he said, stepping back.

Celia inhaled. *You've performed without practice before,* Anya reminded her. *On a stage in front of hundreds, with everything to lose, and you did it fabulously. You can do this, too.*

The scents she could call to mind best—damp mold, rotten apple, blood, ink—weren't ones Halcyon would appreciate in his town.

But Celia had had a shirran once, a buttery breakfast pastry that smelled strongly of the ground anise that peppered the glorious insides. It had stuck with her, the lusciousness of the scent, and she'd never smelled it in Wisteria.

It reminded her of Vincent and his preciously rare ghost of a smile.

It reminded her of peace and happiness.

For her, it was the scent of safety.

She drew the shirran on her arm, imagining the anise smell taking over the flower smell slowly. She knew she didn't have to draw the actual pastry for this exercise, but it helped focus her. It gave her purpose, a shape she could understand. Lines disappeared from her arm as she dismissed the ink, invisible, into the breeze. To be safe, she was using the gentle wind *and* the underlying scent of wisteria as anchor points, to be sure the shirran scent spread everywhere.

At first she couldn't tell if it worked. She was imagining the scent, and the sight of Vincent's placid, beautiful face that she associated with it, with such determination that the smell could have easily been in her own mind.

Then she noticed a couple of people stop dancing and a few more conversations taking place before even more people changed course and headed toward the refreshment table at the far end of the square, as if they assumed the smell came from there.

Celia's own stomach rumbled. The image of a shirran had disappeared from her arm, the ink dismissed to create the scent that would linger until she or Halcyon decided to override it.

Halcyon shook his head in disbelief. The pride in his face shone, and for a moment she felt like puffing out her feathers and strutting. It took a lot to impress him, and it took even more to surprise him. After all these days—how many?—of work, she'd grown accustomed to moving on to the next task without fanfare.

But this was what they'd both been waiting for.

She'd found the way to force the ink to listen to her intent.

"Won't they be disappointed when there aren't any fresh shirrans on that table," he said, his tone amused.

"So now that you know I can be the caretaker Wisteria deserves when you're away, it's your turn." Celia turned away from the duped masses and faced him. "The cure for Diavala's Touch." *Pretty please.* She smiled.

She expected him to bargain for more time, somehow. To promise it after the celebration, or after he returned from his first trip. But he nodded and smiled, still facing the refreshment table. "I knew you wouldn't let me down," he said. "I'll begin making it tomorrow morning. After all, a promise is a promise."

Celia still managed to be shocked. "There really is a cure, then?" she blurted out before she could stop herself.

"I am many things, Celia, but a liar isn't one of them."

With that bold lie, delivered straight to her face with no hint of remorse, Celia flushed.

"Be warned, though," he added, distracted, perhaps already planning a trip to find dead Martina. "That it is a delicate—and lengthy—process. If I begin tomorrow, it may still be a week or two before the cure is ready."

There it was: bargaining for more time. He would dangle the possibility of a cure over her head for as long as possible. Celia had a hard time not ripping his pretty, swirling green eyes out of his head. Somehow she managed a tight smile and a deep bow.

Song after song, they danced. They danced on Halcyon's illusion, under his illusion, through his illusion.

Celia wondered what Wisteria would be like if the illusion were stripped away. Dancing on dust, everything made of bones. The smiles and laughter of the Wisterians was innocent and ugly at the same time. They cared nothing about the outside world. To them, there was no outside world. It was a privileged life, full of luxury and self-indulgence.

Celia even danced with a shadow. How had he managed to

cheat his own death for so long? Time passed strangely when-ever she was around him, so perhaps he'd found a way to make the ink command the clock. He was nature, time, and the reaper, all at once.

By the time Halcyon signaled for the band to stop playing and gestured for everyone to leave the platform, Celia wasn't entirely positive it was the same night.

"This will only take a moment," he said, "and then you can all go back to the revelry." He scanned every face, and when he was sure he had everyone's attention, he continued. "I've taken care of Wisteria for a long time, and as most of you know, I've finally found someone capable of taking up my mantle and working alongside me. It's no small thing, to assume this responsibility. Wisteria is my home, my masterpiece, and I care deeply about it and everyone who lives here."

He turned to Celia.

"Celia Sand doesn't have the same history with you that I do, but she will learn to love Wisteria with time and care, I have no doubt."

Tentatively, Celia bowed as all of Wisteria clapped for her. They seemed even more thrilled at the news than they had when he'd first told them, though she didn't understand why. Until one person's loud exclamation reached her: "This is won-derful! He's been alone for so long . . ."

They weren't happy for her, for themselves, or even for their town.

They were happy for Halcyon.

As she rose from her bow and Halcyon took her hand, the applause became a deafening roar.

She met Halcyon's eyes and held on. "To prove my commitment," she said quietly, "I will expand Wisteria's borders."

As the crowd continued their hooting and hollering, oblivious to Celia's declaration, Halcyon leaned in close. "You might have mastered giant bees and baking scents, but nothing so grand as everything. If you feel the need to show off for them, what about fireworks or little mistico bats?"

"Misti-bats," she corrected. "But you're a very good teacher, and I'm an exceptional student."

Her mind bees rallied to boost her confidence while her real bee made his way to her palm like a little ruler on his throne. *You're an aloof ink master,* she told herself. *You have nothing to worry about. You're more naturally talented than even Halcyon himself.*

Celia's imagination had conjured a barren landscape of death and decay under the pretty covering, and her stomach roiled against the idea of stretching it farther, but if her goal was to get him to trust her completely, expanding his beloved town was the best way.

She also needed to know she could do it.

Running her mind through every lesson she had had with Halcyon, she kept coming back to scent. He'd been overly focused on it, to the point of absurdity. She'd thought all the wisteria in Wisteria was for aesthetic appeal, but it was deeper. If all illusions needed to be tethered to another illusion, all those links would quickly become cumbersome. But perhaps the birds could fly and the clouds could roam and everything could feel more fluid and connected if the tether were invisible. Connected by scent.

Shifting so that she had a line of sight down the one straight road that led out of town, Celia took out her quill, Xinto holding tight to the back of her wrist like a corsage so she had freedom of movement. The road she focused on was illuminated with sparkling hanging lights, just like the main square, as if Halcyon had lighted the way for her. Though there was no visible boundary between the illusions of Wisteria and the outside world, he'd created one there: the lights stopped abruptly partway down the road.

In that particular direction there were no farmhouses or properties, nothing but the forests and lakes of the west, where mysterious wily creatures called river lobsters lived in lakes.

She focused on the trees in the distance, just past the line of lights, and pushed the scent of wisteria blossoms outward. In order to give the ink some direction, on her arm and in her mind she sketched a rough landscape image of the tree line, the road—first cobblestones, then dirt—as it wound through the pale trunks and disappeared. With the scent of wisteria all around her, real and delicate, she nudged it farther. *There,* she thought. *I want you to stretch there.*

But in order to grab it properly, she had to imagine what wisteria smelled like to her.

She thought of that moment of unexplainable dread when Griffin had snapped off a bunch when they'd first arrived.

The thrill of hope she'd had when she'd tattooed an image of it for Halcyon.

The way the scent was connected to Anya, because everything was connected to Anya.

To most, wisteria smelled like subtle vanilla, but to Celia it was the scent of her darkest side: the confused one, the desperate one. The part of her that would do whatever it took to overcome Diavala and Halcyon both, and be free of the devils that played such games.

She sent the command away after sketching on her arm. There was no way to *visibly* tell if that bend in the road was now part of Wisteria until they tried to embellish it.

"Go ahead," she said to Halcyon. "Feel free to check my work." She dropped her head, waiting. For a brief moment she was suspended under her bell jar, nothing but a devil onstage, waiting at the mercy of her jailer, who believed he was an angel.

A slice of noise cut through the silence, the heavy roar of cheers and applause as the audience reacted to whatever Halcyon had done.

The lights extended farther down the road now, sparkling like fireflies, illuminating the once-dark trees.

"You added a section as large as a house," he said with wonder.

As part of Wisteria now, it could be manipulated in any way they wanted: with shrubs, a sign of welcome, the façade of a building, another garish fountain if they were so inclined. More ink had a place to attach to more ink, and on and on.

"Now you can add to that, Celia," he said, admiring her work. "And embellish it however you'd like. Wisteria is an homage to the souls we love and have lost. This beauty is for them. You can add things Anya would have liked: a particular plant or animal—style the buildings as she would have appreciated." He smiled down at her, as if that offer were kind and generous, given with love.

"What a wonderful idea," she said in a whisper. It sounded like awe in her voice, so that was good. His smile turned softer at it, his shoulders relaxing as he looked out into the distance.

With the relative ease and unobtrusive way of using scent as a tether, Wisteria's expansion was limited only by desire. If she wanted, she could walk down a road, adding to Wisteria as she went. If sixty copies of herself and Halcyon walked outward from Wisteria, they could take over Illinia in the amount of time it took to traverse the landscape.

He put her thoughts to words. "We can expand ever farther, you know. There are no limits."

With a prodigy such as Celia at his side, anything was possible.

The applause had died down, and the people were silent, as if waiting for some sort of public acknowledgment from their leader. Even the whispers, speculating what was going on between them onstage, hushed. Halcyon shook his head and smiled at them.

"To mark the occasion, I have one favor to ask," he said. "I ask that every courtesy you extend to me, you now also extend to Celia. She is the key to a thriving Wisteria for many years to come, and I expect everyone to understand this and act accordingly. When I travel, she is in charge and has my full support.

"She will have to earn your respect, of course, and you don't have to like her—goodness knows I don't like her much of the time—" That earned some laughs, of course. "But it's in everyone's best interest that she succeed, and you know what to do to make that happen."

His people nodded and clapped. Celia didn't see what they could do differently—they'd all been remarkably pleasant.

"What are you asking of them, exactly?" Celia asked.

"Well, now there's an entire town to make sure you stay focused," he answered lazily.

Celia looked out at the crowd again. Their happy smiles had more teeth, their waving hands were claws. They looked at her, as hungry as the dead souls on the other side of his forbidden door.

She blinked the image away, and when she scanned their faces again, she saw nothing but eager, wide-eyed appreciation, their claws and teeth hidden now, looking again like wayward children—never leaving, never questioning, taking everything Halcyon said and did as fact, regardless of truth.

She'd grown up in an insular place, indoctrinated by those more powerful, so she felt she should understand these people a bit better. Then again, the Profetan temple and Wisteria had little in common. She'd doubted Profeta because she'd hated Diavala. These people didn't doubt Wisteria, because they loved Halcyon. However toxic their admiration looked to her, they thought they were in love: with Halcyon, with their town, with beauty they didn't know was tainted.

Unless they were made of ink, too.

That was certainly a disturbing thought, but their tenors looked normal enough. Halcyon's tenor—with its confusing jumble of hues—was the only one that looked different, but that had to be because of his unnatural life span.

No, they couldn't be made of ink. Lyric? Impossible.

Celia shook the thought away and turned to Halcyon.

With dramatic flair, he bowed to her. The pendant escaped his shirt again, always taunting her now, and she saw it more clearly than she ever had: made of heavy stone, smooth and flat, its face etched with an abstract design of swirls. She'd only caught glimpses of it over the weeks, but the design was one she recognized. It matched the eddies and swirls of the design on his Chest Majestic.

Lyric had said it protected him from the dead souls on the other side of the veil.

Celia bowed to him just as deeply, holding back the urge to snatch it from around his neck and yank it off so he was in for a surprise next time he went for a trip.

Addressing the crowd, he commanded, "Now, continue with the party, have fun, and dance all evening!"

Everyone took the dismissal with grace and started up their noise again. Halcyon offered his hand, and like a good acolyte, Celia took it. This time, she was even able to produce a genuine smile.

If she could add to the illusion, she could also tear it all down.

CHAPTER 23

Lyric sat hard right by Celia's head, rocking the bed, making it feel as if it were caught up in a hurricane. "Wake up."

Celia gasped awake and scrambled for purchase as Lyric laughed.

"You're mean as hell," Celia mumbled, rolling over. She hadn't been drunk nearly enough since they got to Wisteria and had tried to remedy that all in one night. Her head buzzed as if Xinto had crawled in and rallied her other bees to bellow a drunken chorus. She didn't even know where she was, come to think of it. The pillow was too soft for her bed at the inn. Closing her eyes even tighter, she realized that maybe she didn't want to know. It wouldn't be the first time Celia had awoken in a bed of regret.

Oh, she missed Dante sometimes. Because she'd spectacularly broken her vow about never using the ink again, she'd finally broken down and messaged him the night before. It was mostly a blur, but she remembered solemnly vowing that Zuni would be okay and then taking a few jabs at Dante's hair. Their relationship was a lot of things, including regularly bonding over his vanity.

"You're in my room," Lyric said. "I hauled you here late last night just before you passed out."

And Celia missed her fleas — the little apprentice inklings she used to tell stories to. Wallis, most of all, with their soft hair like a dandelion puff and aggressive cheerfulness. The way they snuggled into Celia's side late at night.

And she missed Lilac, Caspian, and Sky. Seer Ostra. Georgio. Vincent.

Zuni . . .

Celia sat up in the too-comfortable bed, trying to snap to attention. Barely functional, her head screaming in protest, she dressed as quickly as possible. *"Dia,* the sun is barely up!" Celia exclaimed as she tugged on her pants. No wonder she was still so wobbly. "Has Halcyon left yet?"

Halcyon had announced that he would leave that morning, convinced that his prodigy would have things under control while he darted away for a few days.

The best thing about immortal creatures like Diavala and Halcyon was that the centuries made them overconfident. All it had taken was a little dancing, a few smiles, and a boundary extension on his beloved town.

One would think that living so long would make you more amenable to human nuance, but that certainly hadn't been Celia's experience when dealing with immortal creatures.

If this was to be her first solo run taking care of Wisteria, Celia couldn't mess up. She started a list in her head of all the things she'd have to do as a bare minimum: fixing anything broken, making litter disappear, removing the decorations and lights, sweeping the cobblestones to near gleaming. The square needed to be back to normal when people woke up, as if a celebration hadn't ended there a few hours ago.

She could do almost all of it with the ink, except the stage. "The platform needs to be taken down manually. Lyric, darling, maybe you can be in charge of that? I have something I need to do first."

Lyric looked like they were going to argue; their jaw clenched as they bit back a retort. "Carpentry isn't a skill set I have."

"But bossiness is. Use that instead of your hands. I have faith in you." Celia tightened the buckles on her boots and ignored the smell wafting up from her shirt. Good thing she could simply cover it up.

"Are you punishing me?" Lyric said. "Look, I'm really sorry I didn't tell you the truth earlier. I've never had a friend before. I don't know what I'm doing."

Clearly, Celia wanted to say. But she was so tired. It seemed that everyone around her, herself included, was always trying their best, but they were just really bad at it. "Yes, you do," Celia said, sighing and meeting their eyes. "Thanks for bringing Griffin food and water. Thanks for telling me about Zuni. You know how to be a friend, Lyric, and I appreciate it."

Lyric snorted a "shut up" as Celia hauled herself out to the hallway. "Halcyon won't be gone long this first trip, so don't do anything stupid," they called just before disappearing around a corner. Celia wasn't sure where they were going in such a hurry, but with a start, she realized that she trusted them. Either they were going to disassemble the platform or feed Griffin and Zuni some nonpoisonous food.

Xinto buzzed quietly on her shoulder as she crept toward the door at the end of the hall. Her throat closed with the knowledge that she was about to walk among the dead again. Before, she'd entered without understanding what lay beyond. Now it took every iota of willpower Celia possessed to keep moving forward, and she braced herself for the oppressive nothingness of the other side.

The possibility of seeing Anya again made her vibrate with dread and anticipation.

As Celia put her hand on the sunflower doorknob, she paused, going over all the million things she had to remember — a jumbled combination of what she'd found out from her first trip, things Lyric had said, and abstract information Griffin had given her over the span of weeks.

She needed to anchor herself to the door. It was her only way out, and she could quickly get lost in the fog of the nothingness on the other side, even if she didn't plan on moving.

If any of them looked too interested in her — interest of the voracious variety — she had to get the hell out.

She couldn't linger. Time passed strangely there, with the clock winding faster on the side of the living. Moments were minutes, minutes were hours, hours were days.

Halcyon was there, somewhere, and she needed to avoid

him at all cost. If Halcyon caught her, she had a suspicion she'd have a long-ass time to think about her mistakes. She shuddered, remembering what Diavala had told Griffin of her curse's beginnings: her choices had been dying over and over or killing over and over.

It would be a fitting end to Celia's story to have it never end. On and on, body after body, in an infinite loop. If that happened, her only company would be Diavala, for all eternity—the only one who would understand her existence, the only one who could sympathize.

A horrible curse if ever there was one.

She took a deep breath, opened the door, and stepped through. Just as before, the door slammed shut behind her, but her gasp was nothing more than a choked noise in her throat, with no breath to suck in.

Celia made a glowing thread appear from her wrist to the doorknob amid a silence so thick that a heartbeat would have given her away. Then she moved away, only a few steps, and watched the door disappear.

The fog was so strange there: thick but hollow somehow, as if it were made of everything and nothing at the same time.

Immediately, she felt alone.

It was a full-bodied loneliness, consuming her all at once. With no heart beating in her chest and no lungs breathing, there was plenty of space for all that ache, and it filled her from head to toe.

She had something important to do there—a small

experiment, nothing more—but even that was difficult to focus on when all she wanted to do was cry. She must have been running on shock alone, the last trip.

"Okay," she said aloud, trying to chase away the emptiness. "*Ka-thump, ka-thump, ka-thump,*" she intoned, whispering it to herself as she took out her quill and braced it over her forearm.

For weeks she'd been learning how to command the ink into temporary illusion, held in place by tethering it to itself, which was connected to one crucial point in the real world. Something that could be unwound with only a thought because it was always connected to more ink and, ultimately, to herself. But this was a test of her original learning: an inkling making the equivalent of a Divine tattoo, where she would give away the ink rather than hold on to it.

She needed to see if she could fix what Halcyon had broken, and give the ink back.

"*Ka-thump, ka-thump.*" She continued to whisper. With each stroke on her arm, the image grew. It started out as nothing more than a series of lines, but she merged them, shadowed them, imagined them in color: blacks, blues, whites.

She layered even more: one portrait turning into three, stacked one on top of the other. Simultaneously, the portrait was as-yet-nameless little Anya on the day they'd first met, child Anya as they held pinkies and cried in fear, and angel Anya on the day she died.

They were the images of Celia's heart. Part of her didn't want to let them go, but that's what she'd come for: an experiment to see whether she could give the ink away on this side of the door, and whether it would make things better there.

And if anyone could make things right, it was Anya.

Instead of ordering the portraits of Anya to transfer to skin like a regular Divine tattoo, she transferred it to the abyss around her. If ink understood intent, it should understand *be free*. She severed her link to the ink, cutting it like an umbilical cord.

As the lines disappeared from her arms, each one tugged a tear from her eye. Or would have, if her eyes worked properly.

She waited. *"Ka-thump, ka-thump . . ."*

The familiar exhaustion of giving her ink away rolled through her. Or maybe, like the feeling of phantom tears falling from her eyes, she only imagined it.

How long should she wait? How many *ka-thumps* had already passed?

Absently, Celia tugged on the thread around her wrist. It illuminated the fog around her, but barely. Enough to remind her where she was and that she didn't belong there. Not just yet. She needed some sign that it had worked, that it was possible to bring the ink back, let it go, and that something on this side would be better for the effort.

Without any footsteps announcing his arrival, Vincent emerged from the fog right in front of her.

Celia stumbled, choking back a scream. She'd known him as the sad Palidon of the Commedia Follia, but he looked the same as the moment he'd died: wild, puffed hair, gaunt, fever in his eyes. His time being possessed by Diavala and then living with the Touch hadn't been kind to him. It never was.

Twin slashes scraped down the sides of his neck from a mistico's blade, and his white shirt was stained with streams of dark red.

"Vincent," she whispered. She wanted to reach for him, hook her arm under his, and go for one of their quiet walks. He reminded her of comfort, of finding a home.

He was there because of her.

"Is Anya here with you?" she asked in a whisper.

He nodded, and in his mime way, he pantomimed all around him: a miniature play of walking endlessly, of sadness, of darkness and cowering in fear.

Celia squeaked out a whimper. Despite not having a heart beating in her chest, nor air going in and out of her lungs, there was a squeezing going on inside her. A wrenching, twisting ache threatening to choke her. It was Anya and Vincent who didn't belong here, not Celia. "If I could trade places with you . . ." she whispered to him.

Then Celia heard movement. A lot of it and all around her. Vincent had crept up on her without sound, so whatever was coming up behind him was big or many. His eyes widened, and he pointed to the thread around her wrist, gesturing behind her.

He wanted her to leave.

"But did it work?" she asked. "Did the ink I just released help you? I'm not leaving until I know. I have to fix everything. I need to know if this is the right thing to do."

Vincent pointed again, more urgently. Every time he moved even slightly, his trachea bulged through one of the gashes in his neck. Thick cartilage, ribbed and bloody, pushing up to meet her.

A sob burst from Celia's throat, and she met his gray eyes. Had her Palidon been silenced for good, even in the afterlife? "That's not fair," she choked out. "This place isn't right!" she screamed. He'd always been quiet, but how could he not be able to say anything, forever and ever?

"What have you found here?"

The person from all of Halcyon's paintings emerged from the fog. Unlike every other soul Celia had seen there, Martina wasn't bloody and sliced apart. She looked much the same as in every portrait of her that Halcyon had hung in his home: regal, refined. If the dead souls all looked the same as they had at the moment of their death, then hers, unfairly, had been a peaceful one.

Immediately, terribly, Vincent dipped his head and clasped his hands in front of him, as if he were deferring to Martina's authority.

"No, Vincent, look at me," Celia said. She didn't want him bowing to anyone. Ever. Especially the likes of her.

Martina stepped in front of Vincent and reached a hand out, grabbing Celia's trembling drawing hand as she tried to step back. It was so cold despite the oppressive heat around them.

"You called them with it," Martina said urgently. "That means they're coming. You won't leave here if they find you. You gave them only a drop, but they'll want more. They need it."

Celia wasn't scared of her. Not like she'd been of the mistico or of Terrin, the shredded child. As much as she wanted to pull away, hate her, there was an undercurrent of desperation in Martina's grip, as if she needed Celia to listen.

"Answer my question," Celia demanded. "Did the ink I just released help anything?"

"Ink is everything here," Martina said. "It's what sustains this place. With it, we can create our heavens, our hells, whatever we think we deserve. It's done without thought or effort; this place is simply our souls manifest, and it can be very beautiful." She glanced over her shoulder at Vincent, then back at Celia. "At least it's supposed to be. When I first died, it wasn't like it is now. Vincent should be able to change himself, his reality, his memories, however he wants, as much as he wants. A Palidon performing with his troupe, a simple life with a lover and some Kids, an adventure to the mountains . . . or all of the above, because time doesn't exist here. This space was endless potential, adventure, peace. It was magical, but it hasn't been right for a long time."

"But *you* started this with Halcyon," Celia said, trying to untangle herself. "I know about your chest, the door, I know you found a way to steal some ink and leave."

"We made a mistake, taking it away." Martina looked away, as if the confession pained her. "And every moment that passes, it gets darker and more desperate here. Without the ability to change their forms, every soul is stuck in the moment of death. Can you imagine it? Knowing you're dead, remembering every detail of your life, and then being forced to stay in the moment you died and left that world . . . it's an endless curse. They can't create a present or a future, because they're stuck in the past. If it feels like we're starving, it's because we are."

Celia stopped tugging. She looked at Vincent for confirmation, and he stared at her long enough for her to recall his end in detail—being tortured by Diavala's Touch, forced to remember all of *her* pain, and then mistico approaching with blades, the feeling of your neck being sliced open, the wails of your friends singing you to sleep . . .

Vincent nodded. He pressed his hands to his heart and dropped his head. His trachea bulged like a crooked finger poking out of his neck.

With a mewling whimper, Celia grabbed his hand and stroked the blood-soaked bracelet around his wrist that marked him as part of the Rabble Mob. He'd been the one who'd gifted her with the twin around her own wrist.

Anya would have one too: bloodstained, ink-stained. She would have those same gashes in her neck. And worst of all, she would exist for the rest of eternity on a stage where Celia, her best friend, had been the one to kill her.

Celia wanted to scream at the injustice of it. Her fists clenched and her chest tightened.

No. There had to be a way of fixing it. Death was bad enough without being forced to stay within it for eternity. The fact that the afterlife existed proved that there *should* be a future for every soul.

Caught between them—one hand in Vincent's and one in Martina's—Celia turned to Martina.

"Do you hide from him?" Celia asked. Halcyon had been searching for her for a thousand years, yet she'd appeared for Celia on her second trip.

Martina's lips pressed together as she nodded. "He is beyond reason. And without the ink, I have no power here."

"He would give it all to you, on the other side," Celia said. He'd vowed to bring Martina home one day; it was his entire mission in life. Wisteria was full of Martina's favorite things, and he was so determined to get the original Martina that even a near-perfect ink copy of her wouldn't do. "Everything he does is for you."

Martina's lips tightened into a hard line, and she cut Celia off. "He's known my wishes from the beginning, but refuses to hear them. Tell me, why does he go to the trouble of creating a paradise for me with the ink on the side of the living, when he could do it here, where we both belong?"

As Vincent nodded, that struck Celia like a blow. If the ink was the very substance of the afterlife, all of Wisteria could easily exist there.

Instead, he'd pulled the ink out and hoarded it and refused to meet his death. "What are you saying?" Celia asked in a whisper.

Martina turned to Celia again, her eyes piercing her with

their intensity. "Halcyon says it's about me, and I really think he believes it in his heart, but it's always been about *her*. The child who took my chest of ink. The one who foiled his plans. He blames her for my change of heart. She was the catalyst for our moral disagreement, and he will never forgive her for that." Martina looked down then, to the place where her hand rested on Celia's. Both of them trembled.

"She had nothing to do with your death," Celia said bluntly. The timeline now made sense: Halcyon and Martina had started all this a thousand years ago when they'd taken the ink. Diavala's part had only started when she'd happened across a chest of magical ink as a child. She was no murderer.

But Halcyon was.

"The only thing that child killed was Halcyon's dream," Martina said. Her hands had turned clawlike, nearly piercing through skin. "He's always only ever yearned for beauty—to be surrounded by it, to live it, to create it—and in his mind, I was a vital part of that dream. Unfortunately for all of us, he didn't take kindly to me having a mind of my own." Despite the indents from Martina's fingers, Celia didn't feel a thing except the cold. "So now he exists to inflict eternal revenge. His hate overpowered his love a long, long time ago."

A perfectly balanced scale had tipped the wrong way.

Celia didn't feel it even when Martina's nails ripped through and blood bloomed.

Vincent's eyes widened again. He swiveled and disappeared into the fog, leaving his blood on Celia's empty hand.

Martina's nostrils flared, and she didn't look away from Celia's fresh blood. "There's ink inside you." The same hunger for the ink Celia had sensed in the mistico, in the shredded child, was now written all over Martina's face.

Vincent had run from it, Martina was fighting it.

"I want to give it away," Celia said. "If it will help Vincent, help you, take it." She shoved her bleeding hand into Martina's face. "It's okay. I can't even feel this. Take it. I have people here I love, so many of them, and if they need it to make this place bearable and it's all I can do, then I want you to take it!" Her voice had risen alarmingly as all the emotional pain flooded back. She would give away everything inside her if it could only make things better—for Vincent, for Anya, for everyone to come.

Martina shook her head and, with difficulty, let go of Celia's hand. "It wouldn't be enough. Your sacrifice would be for nothing." She looked over her shoulder at the still-hidden masses approaching. The rumbles of conversation, footsteps, shrieks were louder now. Celia was so focused on the conversation, she had managed to forget, for a moment, where she was. "Get out! Leave!" Martina cried.

"What if I can bring you back the chest? I'll steal it from him—"

"Halcyon would never allow it. Don't bother, Inkling. Don't bother. Just protect yourself, and don't come back here."

Then, with a sad look in her eyes, Martina turned and disappeared into the fog.

CHAPTER 24

On the other side of the door, Celia gasped until her lungs remembered how to do their job, her heart remembered to beat. Her eyes caught up—the tears she'd wanted to shed on the other side coming out all at once. With blurry vision she stumbled toward the bird room down the hall. Her footsteps sounded like the pounding of a drum, her nose picked up every scent: wisteria everywhere, candles burning, parchment, and ink. She could smell it, but whether it was from the small wound on her hand, or infused in the house, or the underlying scent of everything around her, she couldn't tell.

Prying the door open, she flung herself in, the birds already screeching at her from every branch.

She swiped her hands across her eyes, trying to clear them, the copper scent of her blood stinging her nose. Collapsing onto a bench under an old oak tree near the back, she put her face in her hands and tried to calm down.

The ink would help them. It belonged there. She needed to steal his chest and take the ink home.

"There you are!" Halcyon stood in the doorway, looking around, as if trying to figure out why his beloved birds were so upset.

Even with the door wide open, the birds didn't try to escape. His gaze landed on Celia, on the wound on her hand.

"I'm okay," she said, wiping her face a little more. The quiver in her voice was too strong. She forced herself to talk low and even. "I tried to pet one of the ravens, but he didn't appreciate it." She held up her bleeding hand as evidence and tried to laugh.

He took one step toward her. Two. His eyes assessed the upset birds and Celia's hand with a shrewd calculation, and her chuckle petered out as the black swirls began overtaking the green in his eyes.

Watching his nostrils flare, Celia remembered Lyric's warning too late: the scent of the afterlife clung like a film. Ashes and dust. Layers of it.

He knew.

Those dark eyes snapped to hers.

"How could you be so foolish?" he growled.

"They'll be fine," she said. If she kept pretending he was upset about the birds, maybe that could become the truth. "I'll stay in here until they calm down."

"Not letting you in there was for your protection!" he said. "There is no life in the afterlife. Not for them and certainly not for you. They would have sucked you dry of your ink and left you a husk, wandering around forever." Halcyon was beside himself with anger. She'd never seen him so unhinged. The whites of his eyes were gone, overtaken by black.

"I told you," he said, shouting now, "to stay out of that room!"

Fine, it wasn't about birds.

She stood, forcing herself not to shrink back from what she saw: the master of something that had caused so much pain, a jailer, a manipulator, a killer.

And a liar. Such a good one, he'd managed to lie to himself for centuries.

"I made a deal that I thought would help my friend," Celia said. "I'd master the ink illusions, look after Wisteria while you searched for Martina, be bound here for the rest of my life — and in return, I've gotten nothing but lies." Celia raised her flushed face and glared. She was glad she didn't have to lie anymore; it made her words hiss and crackle like the fire she felt burning inside her. She could hardly believe she had the spine to take a step toward him, and yet she did. And she kept right on yelling. "I'm alone in this bubble, scrambling around and playing with illusions and not making any difference, while there's a door to the afterlife a few steps away?!"

Halcyon truly looked concerned. "What is wrong with you, Celia Sand?" he said, shaking his head, his eyes roiling. "Do you truly not care what would could have happened to you, or are you that talented at hiding your fear?"

Both.

"I wanted answers, and I got them," she said. "I know you're just like Diavala: treacherous. You manipulate everyone around you, and you like to be worshiped. I've somehow managed to go from one captor to the next."

"I am *nothing* like her," Halcyon hissed.

The lush aviary around them fell away, and the next moment,

they were walking side by side along a forested path. Celia looked down, amazed that her feet were moving without her commanding them. It was high summer, the air hot and dry, the leaves and needles crunching underfoot shed from thirsty trees.

Halcyon paused as a slow snake slithered across the path, twisting and turning to avoid being stepped on. Dead leaves fell around them, one fluttering to land on his shoulder. He didn't notice until Celia brushed it away, touching him without thinking about it. A flush rose into his pale cheeks, and he looked at her, startled.

Perhaps he expected her to be shocked at their new surroundings, but if so, he hadn't been paying attention.

All of Celia's shock had worn off. By then her spine was braced for anything. A new location, a new setting were all part of her life now.

Despite her noncooperative feet and hands, she could match him.

"I was hoping to explain everything over time," he said. He sounded and looked serene, a stark difference from only a moment ago, but his eyes still swirled. He was having a hard time keeping his anger in check.

He inhaled deeply, gesturing for Celia to walk off the path and through the trees. Within a few steps they arrived at a high overlook: a rocky cliff dropping steeply downward. On the horizon, a mountain range looked like an anthill, and below them, rivers snaked like thin worms through wide, quilted valleys of color. It stole Celia's breath, the beauty of it. Even more beautiful than the lake country surrounding Wisteria, and she hadn't thought anything could be more picturesque.

Halcyon looked across the valley, his hair rustling faintly with the wind, his face painted with wistful yearning.

"This was where we were meant to be," he said. "This is a rudimentary rendition of Poclesh, across the Lassina Sea. Such a beautiful land." He swept a graceful hand outward; what he called rudimentary was so pristine and precise that Celia wondered how much more perfect perfection could be. "In life, I was a painter, my Martina was a poet. We met in the afterlife and bonded over our art, our dreams. We both knew this was the perfect place for artists to live — the entire land is a living, breathing muse — and we decided we would get there."

Celia's breath stopped.

She'd been wrong: some things could still surprise her.

She'd thought Halcyon was alive and had found a way to the afterlife, with the ink somehow extending his life as he played with it. The fact that he'd been *dead* for a thousand years almost made Celia vomit all over his pretty illusion.

He and Martina had met in the afterlife and brought the ink out together. The big difference was that Martina had soon realized the wrongness of it all, and had tried to do the right thing.

Celia tried to run, her body in full flight mode, but her feet didn't move.

Dead, dead, dead.

His body should have been ashes and dust. Instead, he was so adept with the ink, he'd crafted a new body for himself, complete with a strange, hard-to-pin-down tenor. That would explain how he could make a tattoo disappear from his skin. It had never been permanent; there was no real skin for it to stick to. It had been one illusion on top of another, and he'd wiped it away.

This would certainly explain why he was hunting for a soul who'd been dead for a thousand years: if Halcyon could exist on the wrong side of the veil, so could Martina.

It seemed as if that had been their plan in the beginning. It was still Halcyon's, even if his beloved had had a change of heart centuries ago.

Halcyon's eyes burned fever-bright as he looked over the cliff. Behind them, a rustling sound grabbed Celia's attention, and she turned.

As if Celia's thoughts had summoned her, Martina walked toward them. She had no tenor, just like ink-Anya earlier, a startling reminder that all this was nothing but an illusion Halcyon had thrown together relatively carelessly.

When Martina got to Halcyon's side, they stood together at the edge of the cliff.

"All we wanted was a simple life," he shouted, his voice barely carrying over the blasts of wind. "A poet and a painter, using the ink as a medium for our art. We made it so far, experimented so much, and that life we yearned for was within our grasp."

Abruptly, he turned to Celia and grabbed her hand, pulling her toward the edge of the cliff, leaning her over. She shrieked in alarm, even knowing it was an illusion. Halcyon held her from behind as Martina looked on. Pebbles fell from under Celia's scrambling feet and pitched over the edge of the cliff into the craggy abyss below. His chest pressed into her back, and she felt his labored breathing, his tight grip the only thing keeping her from following those pebbles. The wind whipped her hair around her face, blinding her as she cried out.

"But can you believe how this story ends?" he yelled.

Martina spoke from the first time, adding an echo to Halcyon's words. "How *my* story ends?"

"Our ink was stolen by a child who had no vision for it, no master plan, and was too clever by half."

"Diavala—" Celia gasped.

They were so far in the past—before Profeta started, before inklings—when the story was just between a poet, a painter, and the child who got in the way.

"By rights, that ink was Martina's, but she gave up looking for it too early," Halcyon said.

"I didn't," Martina said calmly behind them.

"You did!" Halcyon shouted over his shoulder.

"No. I saw the way of things," Martina said. "I accepted my fate."

Halcyon continued as if Martina hadn't spoken. "Martina might have returned to the afterlife, but she *will* join me again on this side one day. With you around, I'll have that much more time to search for her."

"I will never come back," Martina said. It sounded like she'd said the same line many times before.

He laughed in Celia's ear, his breath as hot as fire. "It took me some time to find Diavala, but I did. She was using the ink as a toy, pushing it into others' skin as if it were a novelty instead of art and substance itself. If she hadn't stolen it—hadn't brought doubt about the nature of our work—Martina and I would be in Poclesh, living our dream. And to this day, Diavala acts as if she was blameless in Martina's ultimate demise. I killed Diavala, but as it turned out, death was too lenient. Justice has to fit the crime, don't you agree?"

Celia choked, her tears too thick to see through, everything blurry and undone, unwinding. She already knew what his ultimate confession would be. It was in his breath, his grip, his wind-whipped hair. Telling her this story had rekindled his ancient rage, a rage she understood well, the same one that had fueled her since leaving Asura—the ever-present desire for reckoning against the one who'd taken Anya from her.

She'd been no better than Halcyon. She'd hated Diavala so much she'd broken her own rules, all while telling herself it was for Griffin.

But Halcyon was so blinded by it, he didn't even see that his own illusion was arguing with him: he knew Martina's wishes weren't the same as his, but he didn't care.

"You threw Diavala out of the afterlife," Celia said. For the first time, the words took root inside her. Diavala had been nothing more than a casualty of Halcyon's misplaced quest. "You cursed her to be a dead soul in the land of the living."

The similarities between Diavala and Halcyon were

frightening, but the distinction was all about power. He was skilled enough to use the ink to create a body and sustain the life he wanted. Diavala could not. She faced an eternity of grappling, of struggle, of not having a choice.

"I did," he said. "And it's a perfect revenge, don't you think?"

Celia would have agreed if she hadn't suffered at Diavala's hand. "But why did you let her create Profeta?" Celia screamed. "Why let her be happy at all?"

"I've watched her for centuries, Celia Sand, and she's never been happy. Whenever she was close to getting what she wanted, I stepped in. To drown her, to start a plague, to flog her, to make her believers doubt by creating a senseless war. Until this last time, in Asura, when she was ready to claim a mortal body and be worshiped in the flesh . . . Well, you took care of that for me, didn't you."

Celia shook her head and closed her eyes, her face flushed, throat tight.

"Your game with her was deeply entertaining," Halcyon said, whispering the words in her ear, pressing his cheek to hers. "I almost stepped in more than once when I thought she'd bested you, yet you always recovered and pushed back."

He paused. Taunting. "Right to the tragic, bloody end."

Celia had started crying some time ago, but those words made her gasp out screams.

He was saying that Diavala would have never claimed that stage she'd tried to steal as the Divine.

That, maybe, Anya's death didn't have to happen.

Halcyon would have stepped in and done it all for them if only they'd waited for the Curse of the Divine to do his work.

"My revenge is perfect because it's infinite," he said. "No matter how high Diavala climbs, she will always, always fall."

He let Celia go.

Celia screamed Anya's name as she fell.

And she fell for so long, she screamed her voice hoarse. The wind tangled into her lungs with a force that choked her. Gasping, screaming as the ground rose toward her, expanding in detail as she closed in: the boulder where her skull would shatter, the crag where her legs would twist and snap, the moss her blood would soak into.

Her arms windmilled, as if a ledge made of sky could save her.

A thunderous clap echoed off the hills, so loud that instinct pulled her windmilling arms in to clap her hands over her ears.

Solid floor beneath her body, no more wind.

She scrambled up to sitting, then standing, panting so hard and so violently disoriented that even though her eyes were open, she could see nothing, register nothing.

Her hands flew to her hair and tugged down. A shriek rose out of her throat.

"Celia, I understand how overwhelming this is," Halcyon said, "but you came here because, in the end, we have the same enemy. Diavala took everything from both of us, and I recognized the rage in you because it matches mine."

With her heart still thumping, she came back to her senses

slowly, adrenaline buzzing through her veins. His words disgusted her, they were so misplaced, so willing to ignore collateral damage.

"But the Touch," she gasped out. "You said you could make a cure." The reason she'd come in the first place, the thing she'd bargained everything for. "Is there a cure for Diavala's Touch, or was that another lie?"

He sighed, as if her question were mundane and disappointing. "The only way to avoid the Touch is if you're dead. That's why Diavala couldn't harm me when she came three years ago, that's what I was going to help your friend with. I never lied to you; it *will* give him immunity."

It was one thing to suspect you were working for someone who'd gone mad with his hate, another thing entirely to hear unequivocal proof leave his mouth. Celia tried to bolt for the courtyard but made it only a few steps before she threw up.

She'd bargained for Griffin's death.

Halcyon looked down his nose at her. "Clean that up and meet me at Rian's," he said before stepping over her. "Let's settle our debt so you can focus."

CHAPTER 25

As she ran to Rian's, Celia's imagination spun out of control: Rian killing Griffin and Zuni with some toxic tea, then Halcyon's curses of immortality, scattered around like confetti; or more illusions, tormenting them with their worst nightmares or forcing them to lift daggers to their own necks.

Halcyon could do anything because the ink *was* ever-powerful. It was meant to craft millions upon millions of parallel worlds, each individualized. The sheer expanse of what it was designed to do was amazing to think of. It was creation itself, on a different plane.

But it didn't belong here, so everything around her was wrong. Wisteria was wrong.

The townspeople watched her run. Davi's and Giada's stares from the front window of the Outside Inn were hawkish; Garuld and Rosetta swiveled to follow Celia, Garuld's cane tapping a beat into the stones, increasing in pace when Celia tried to pull away.

So strange.

And, just then, sinister. All claws and teeth. They were in on the con.

Or perhaps they were part of it . . .

Xinto flew beside her, his wings whipping ferociously as he tried to keep up, inconveniently reminding her that she'd created him from nothing, and yet he'd developed a personality all on his own. She hadn't had to command his behavior for a long time.

He'd evolved.

It suddenly didn't feel foolish to believe that Halcyon had stocked Wisteria with ink-people. Their fierce devotion, their willingness to accept even the strangest occurrences. Celia had dismissed this thought before because they all had tenors, but if the ink listened to intent, their tenors could have been their own adaptations.

Michali emerged from their shop, a ream of fabric in their arms, shaking their wheat-colored head and clicking their tongue in disappointment. Celia must have looked a fright, with blood on her face and wind-whipped hair.

With their longer legs, Lyric finally caught up to Celia. Their shouts had chased her for blocks. "What did you do?" they asked over and over.

Celia's eyes stung, and she tried to bat Xinto away. Instead of answering, she swerved down a side street. She could fold herself to Rian's like Halcyon undoubtedly had and lose Lyric that way, but that meant she'd be at Rian's . . . something she wasn't ready for yet. So she had to lose Lyric the old-fashioned way.

"It's me!" Lyric called, desperation in their voice. "Celia, it's just me!" They sounded hurt — why would their first friend run from them like this?

Celia reared to a stop, and Lyric didn't have time to avoid crashing into her. They went down, tumbling to the ground, scraping skin as they went. Lyric's hands were everywhere, trying to catch themself but also, mostly, trying to catch Celia.

They skidded to a stop and lay beside each other, panting and bleeding, their legs snarled up together. Celia heaved herself onto Lyric, straddling their hips, and pinned them down, grabbing their arm. "Is this real?" she hissed. The fresh scrape on Lyric's arm was already a vicious red, speckled with pebbles from the road.

Lyric frowned, panting, and tried to push Celia away. "Whatever you're ranting about—"

"Will Rian heal it?" Celia asked, pressing closer so Lyric couldn't move. "I'm not letting you up until I know you're real. You said you don't know how to have a friend, but a friend would tell me whether they were real or not, Lyric!" Her voice pitched higher. Behind them, Garuld and Rosetta had caught up and were staring at them from the mouth of the alley. Michali was behind them with the bolt of fabric still in their arms, as if they were determined to mend any ripped clothing immediately.

Lyric went from shocked to angry in a heartbeat. "*Of course* I'm real."

"What about the rest of them?" Celia nudged her chin toward the mouth of the alley.

Lyric tried to look away, but Celia pressed closer, chest to chest, not allowing it. "You know exactly what I mean, Lyric. Don't pretend you don't."

All fight left them, and they sagged under Celia's weight. When Celia let up on her grip, worried that Lyric had passed out, it gave Lyric the opportunity to shove their legs up, push Celia off, and scramble away.

But instead of running, Lyric extended an arm to help Celia up. "Everything is fine!" Lyric called to their small crowd. "Off you go!"

Celia groaned, but grabbed Lyric's wrist and hopped up, wincing from the pain of their fall.

"Everyone here is very real," Lyric said. "They're as human as you and me, but they have a certain way of looking at the world because this is all they've ever known. So you can't go around bleating nonsense. They'll haul you to Rian's without thinking twice. Do you want a mob following us?"

Act normal. Act like everything's fine.

But everything wasn't fine. Perhaps the townspeople weren't made of ink, but that only meant they were Halcyon's eyes and ears. On his command, they arranged for visitors to meet their deaths. Did their actions make them culpable, or were they innocent victims of Halcyon's indoctrination because they didn't see how wrong it was?

Celia took a steadying breath. The last thing she wanted was to make this an all-out war. She was severely outnumbered.

Lyric nodded at Celia's understanding, and off they went, side by side, pretending everything was fine. Celia wished she had a mask like the plague doctor's, to make her performance more believable.

Every once in a while Celia looked over her shoulder, expecting to see eyes watching them. They were there—they'd been there since the beginning—but only now did she feel them so strongly.

At Rian's, nothing looked wrong, but Celia became more on guard because of it. She cycled through her options, tried to make contingencies. She imagined Anya barking *Focus!* and stomping lightly on Celia's toes, just as she had when they were younger.

The more normal everything looked, the more the hairs on her neck prickled. The ink in her blood thrummed. She was finally on a level playing field with the master of the ink, she reminded herself. She had everything he had.

Except experience, generations of knowledge, a narcissistic streak, and any idea what her enemy was up to.

Focus! Anya whisper-shouted again.

Even before Celia left the safety of the buildings and trees for Rian's pumpkin patch, she knew Halcyon was there. It was too quiet.

"Come, Celia! Ah, Lyric!" Halcyon shouted. He stood on Rian's front steps, hands on his hips. Rian stood with him, stooped, as if her back would give out at any second. When Celia glanced up, a beaked shadow moved in an upstairs window. Celia's heart sank; he hadn't found Zuni.

"Here we go," Lyric whispered before taking those last few steps to the farmhouse and up the stairs.

Celia was much slower with her approach, walking as if the ground were lanced with explosives set to go off with a misstep.

Eventually she made it. She'd thought that Halcyon had calmed down some, but up close, she could see how wrong she'd been. His eyes were still as black as pitch, the whites overtaken completely by turbulent ocean waves slamming against rocks.

"We have a couple of things to take care of here," he said. "First and foremost," he said, turning to Rian, "I'd like you to explain to me how Celia knew about your role here. You had one job, and that was to hold until I sent word. All you had to do was act normal, Rian. How was it that you still couldn't manage that?"

Rian's milky gaze darted to Celia for a moment before turning again and looking straight ahead. Her spine stiffened. If ever there was a moment where Celia felt some sympathy for her, it was then. She looked like she didn't have the faintest idea of what was going on, but she was steeling herself for the consequences anyway. "I'm sorry," she said.

Halcyon shifted his gaze to Lyric. "Or was it you who tipped Celia off?"

Lyric looked guilty as hell. Celia had never seen someone so red, and Lyric couldn't even meet Halcyon's eyes. Their guilt was written all over their face.

But before Lyric could stammer out an explanation and defend themself, Rian interrupted. "You're a stubborn fool,

Halcyon. If ever I wanted to keep secrets from you, it wouldn't be now, when there was a chance to save my own skin." But her eyes betrayed her as she glanced at Lyric and then quickly away. "I'll take responsibility for my slip-up—I suspect it happened when I lost track of them at the lakes—but I've made it clear before that Lyric isn't ready for this job, and my opinion about that hasn't changed. They're too emotional. Too naive. It would be foolish to hand over such important work to an amateur."

"Ah, there it is," he said. "Now you *are* trying to save your own skin. You think I should keep you around until Lyric becomes more competent?"

Rian flushed, but she nodded.

"I think they're competent enough," Halcyon said, turning his gaze to Lyric.

The next moment, Rian fell to the porch, batting her hands into the air and smacking them on her body, warding off a swarm of fire ants that wanted only her. Her panic was quiet; she uttered no sound as she writhed on the ground, overtaken by an undulating horde of red and black. Her silence was worse than any screams. Celia's skin prickled from the sound of a million legs moving, a million pincers pinching. When Lyric choked out a sob and tried to go to her, Halcyon cleared his throat. "You know what to do."

Trembling, Lyric stepped around their grandmother and went into the house, emerging a moment later with the bottle of poison Celia had caught them arguing over earlier. *Lyric believes I have no heart,* Rian had said. *When everything I've ever done has been for them.*

With great effort, Rian hauled herself to her feet. The fire ants were still after her in a waking nightmare, consuming her methodically. Already, there wasn't much left of her skin, and as they made for her eyes, she inadvertently flinched.

Still, she managed to snatch the bottle from Lyric's shaking hands. She managed to mutter "incompetent, amateur, fool" at them. And she managed to open the bottle and press her tongue to the rim.

She handed it to Lyric, straightened, and stared Halcyon down. Her lips began moving—perhaps she wanted to say something like *You'll regret this*—but the fire ants filled her mouth and she collapsed before any word left her lips.

With one last rattly breath, Rian the Spectator, Wisteria's executioner, died on her own front step. Her last execution had been her own.

The ants disappeared, and Rian's form lay unmarked on the steps at their feet. She looked almost peaceful, her face relaxed, as if she were asleep. But Celia now knew that in the afterlife she would be fighting that fear, and those ants, forever. Halcyon had made sure of that.

"Now," Halcyon said. "Next thing we have to settle is the issue of the plague doctor." The bottle knocked so hard in Lyric's hands that Celia was afraid a drop would fly out and hit her skin. "Calm down, Lyric," Halcyon said when he noticed the same thing. "Don't prove old Rian right."

"It's just that it's almost supper," Lyric said, their voice a breathless whisper.

Halcyon opened his palms and examined them; then he cursed. "You're right. See? You're very competent. Thank you." The praise slid off his tongue so effortlessly, even as he stood over Rian's body. "Lock Celia up, then, and make sure she doesn't have access to a quill. I'll be back in a couple of hours."

He shoved his hands into his pockets and dipped his head to Celia. His eyes had settled to almost normal, as if all he'd needed was someone to die in front of him to calm his nerves. "We'll continue this later."

CHAPTER 26

HALCYON USES SUPPER HOUR TO POLISH THE TOWN . . ."
Lyric said with no inflection in their voice. *Polish the town.* Wisteria was a pretty machine: all cogs and wheels and gears, as cold as metal and just as lifeless.

"It's easier when he knows the people are out of the way," Lyric continued. They pulled their grandmother's body down the steps by the feet, Rian's head thumping with each step. Lyric didn't seem to notice until Celia scrambled over to help.

"I'm so sorry," Celia said.

Lyric had mentioned once, with heat in their voice, that Rian had gambled something important away in a game with Halcyon a long time ago: perhaps it had been her family's freedom. He liked to keep his lines nice and straight. No wonder Lyric was so messed up: any person who happened through the town was quickly dispatched. Their family legacy literally entailed killing anyone new, and Rian had shouldered that burden for as long as she could.

"She didn't actually have to kill too many people," Lyric said, as if apologizing for her and forgiving her all at once. "Most of the time, people changed their mind and just turned around.

Only the most determined could ever get through Halcyon's protections."

Lyric's bleary eyes landed on Celia, as if they'd only just noticed she was there. They snatched at the bottle they'd stuffed into their pocket and, with big eyes, brandished it in Celia's direction. "*This* is *your* fault."

Celia backed away, her hands up in deference. "I'm really sorry, Lyric." Slowly reaching into her pocket, Celia took her quill and held it out. "Here. Just show me where to go, and I'll go. Wherever you want. Do what he says so you stay safe."

Lyric's gaze went from the quill to Celia's eyes to the bottle in her hand to their grandmother. "There is no *safe* here. If anyone ever crosses him, they die. You were supposed to help me get free, but now we're all trapped." They met Celia's eyes. "I'm going to clean and wrap Rian and then bury her, and then I'm probably going to have to bury you and your friends. That's my prison." They nudged their chin toward the farmhouse. "Yours is in there with Zuni and Griffin. For now."

Celia inhaled and nodded. It had never been loyalty to Halcyon holding Lyric's tongue, it had been fear. Celia should have recognized it earlier because they acted much like Celia had at the temple: constantly assessing personal risk, subtly undermining the work, and holding on tight to small rebellions, ones that had little chance of real repercussions. It was the dance of the oppressed.

Then Celia had arrived and made things even worse for them.

At the temple, life had been terrible, but at least it had been predictable. Since leaving, Celia had faced one crisis after another, one tragedy after another.

If she hadn't left, Anya would be alive, Vincent would be alive, Griffin would be plague doctor-y, greeting revelers at the Rabble Mob shows and dancing nights away. He might not have been happy, exactly, but he would have been safe.

And Zuni and Lyric wouldn't be trapped in a town made of death.

All her fault . . . everything. She'd been shackled since she was six years old, and all she'd done was spread her shackles around. She hadn't known they could multiply, or get so heavy they dragged the world down.

Even if Griffin survived, he was more broken than before. At some point, all that brokenness would be beyond repair.

"Xinto," Celia called. Looking at him was painful, feeling the tickle of his legs on her shoulder even worse. His nose kisses along her collarbone didn't feel sinister, but they were made of something that belonged to the dead.

As Lyric wrapped their grandmother behind the farmhouse, Celia inhaled and took out her quill. Whether it was grief over-riding sense or something a friend would do, Lyric hadn't listened to Halcyon and confiscated Celia's quill.

Sitting on the farmhouse steps, Celia pushed the quill to her arm and closed her eyes, imagining what she wanted to create. The size and shape, the texture, the smell, the sound. Everything had to be just right for this last indulgence.

She didn't open her eyes for a long time. Not when she heard the sound of footsteps and a tapping umbrella, nor when she felt the warmth of someone sitting next to her and wrapping their arms around her smaller shoulders. And even when Anya said *Hey, Cece* and gave her arm a squeeze, Celia held her eyes tightly shut.

"I'm too scared," Celia whispered. "I can't do it." She didn't know whether she was talking about what she had to do next or about opening her eyes.

It's okay to be scared, Anya said softly. *Sometimes, surviving is the hardest thing you can do.*

Celia swallowed, her lips pinching together as she nodded. "If I open my eyes, will it really be you?"

Anya didn't answer, but they were in a place where wants became real with wishes.

Celia opened her eyes.

And promptly lost control of them.

"Anny," she squeaked. "You're so perfect." Long black hair, perfectly straight top hat, ocean-blue eyes. Celia knew her so well that even Anya's tenor shone perfectly, pulsing *alive, alive, alive* in familiar red hues.

"He said I could have you again. Just like this. Forever. And I want that so badly, I need it like I need water and air. I can't do this without you." She let the tears fall when Anya hooked her pinky around Celia's and squeezed.

"I'm so tired," Celia said. Her sobs competed with Lyric's. The farm was awash with tears.

I know, Anya said. *I know.*

Celia rested her head on Anya's shoulder, inhaling the warmth and comfort of her other half, her angel. "Every time I try to do the right thing, it blows up in my face. I trust people too much. Everyone always lies to me: Diavala, Halcyon. It doesn't even matter who I'm trying to fight, who's pushing me down—they're all the same. I only ever make things worse."

"It's not your fault that people lie."

But it *was* her fault that she kept believing them.

On a stage in Asura, weeks ago, forever ago, Celia and Anya had devised a plan to defeat the Divine with her own ink. Flawless and meticulously outlined, with other players acting their parts to perfection, the two of them had set everything up exquisitely.

Celia shifted on Rian's steps, tears still coursing down her cheeks, and faced Anya for the first time since watching her die.

"Do you remember our plan?" she said, weeping.

Anya looked down at their clasped pinkies. And nodded. *I remember.*

"It was the best we could come up with, and we both knew it probably wasn't going to work. But that was okay, Anny, because we came up with it together, like we always did. And everything—all the lies and fear—it was going to end with us together. Freedom, together. Do you remember that part?"

Celia only realized she was yelling when her voice cracked in two with her next words. "Do you remember?" She held their linked pinkies up. "This was supposed to be it, Anny! And I was okay with that because I had you. That's all I've ever needed."

Anya's blue eyes glistened with unshed tears and her throat bobbed as she swallowed. She didn't try to pull their pinkies apart, she didn't try to look away.

She nodded at everything Celia said.

"But then you looked at me and said, *Be strong, Cece.* And then I had a dagger in my hand and I pressed it to your neck. Do you remember that? You put that dagger in my hand, Anya. You said, *Be strong and do it. This is the way it has to be.* And like a fool, I did it! Because I love you, because I didn't want to let you down. I did what you wanted, all the way to the end."

Celia inhaled. "And then you were dead, but I wasn't."

She stared at their linked pinkies. "This is all I ever believed to be true, but in the end, even *you* lied to me. Why would you do that to me? I cleaned your blood up. I know what it smells like, what it feels like on my hands and on my face . . .

"Even *you* lied to me"—she met Anya's gaze, whispering— "and I'm so mad at you for that."

Lyric came over, tracks of tears staining their cheeks, and stood with them. Anya, on the stairs of a home she'd never visit, with Celia hovering over her, crying so much it hurt. Her insides were so twisted they'd never untangle. It hurt to breathe, every lungful of air searing her.

"It's okay," Lyric said. "You can let her go."

But Celia didn't want to. Their linked pinkies were

everything. If she didn't believe in them, she had nothing. Nothing but empty hands and an empty heart.

I'm sorry I lied to you, Cece, Anya whispered. *I'm sorry I hurt you. I hope one day you can forgive me.*

Celia didn't know how long she cried, but it felt like she'd never stop.

And she didn't let go of Anya's pinky. They held on tight.

Together.

Until one of them vanished and one was left behind.

Interlude

The plague doctor watched everything transpire outside his window: Halcyon, more than a little pissed off; Rian, more than a little poisoned; Lyric, more than a little promoted; and Celia, more than a little wrecked.

Arms crossed, he peered down at Celia and Lyric as they sobbed together, his throat pinched tight. "I think Celia has said goodbye to her ghost," he whispered. Somehow his own pinky ached from that exchange, a phantom sympathy pain as deep as a scar. "Another dawn brings shadows, full of creeping things and claws . . ."

"Stop staring, voyeur," Zuni barked from the other side of the room. Her small travel pack shifted against her hip as she paced, rattling the skulls inside. Rian had confiscated them from her, and since getting them back, she'd insisted that she wasn't going to let them out of her sight ever again. The plague doctor didn't know Zuni well, but she seemed to be much more upset that her skulls had been taken than about being locked in a basement for the past two weeks. The first thing she'd done when he'd opened the door to her cell was shriek about how thirsty Saccharine—one of her favorite skulls—must have been.

Apparently, some skulls needed to be moisturized regularly. Who knew.

The plague doctor looked back out the window in time to see Lyric help Celia stand on wobbly legs. His heart told him to run down there and scoop her up. His heart also told him to stay put. That about summed up his feelings toward the little inkling ever since he'd first laid eyes on her in a Rover field. Incredible and dangerous.

"Well?" Zuni snapped. "Tell me what's happening!"

"Looks like they're coming in," he said. He hadn't gotten so much as a thank-you after jimmying the lock on her cell and freeing her.

Celia had drawn a hatch under his bed with her ink magic. When she'd managed to do it, he didn't know, but she'd inscribed SASTIMOS FUTURA on it, like an apology.

He'd gone through the hatch, snuck around the endless house trying to avoid Rian (who'd been remarkably keen of hearing) and find another doorless room, and eventually he'd stumbled upon a wee little cell holding a face he recognized from Asura. They'd caught up after he brought her back to the relative safety of his room — Zuni doing a fair amount of frowning and hissing — and then they'd watched as Halcyon burst into the farmhouse and herded Rian outside.

"He's the handsome one?" Zuni had asked in a low whisper.

Pffft, handsome. He'd seen better. He hadn't even justified that with a response.

"I expected . . . horns or something." Zuni had arched an eyebrow at him. "Maybe an ugly mask."

The purple-eyed child brought him back to the present. *"Fo—"*

I know, I know, he thought, cutting Diavala off. *Focus, plague doctor, focus. Your mind is too scattered, etcetera, etcetera.*

He looked over at Zuni and cleared his throat. "It's not too late for you to bolt, you know." As soon as the words left his mouth, he wanted them back.

Damn, but Zuni could throw eye daggers just as expertly as Celia could.

"Forget it," he mumbled.

The door creaked open, and Celia walked in with Lyric. Her eyes landed on him first, then flitted to Zuni. Zuni's tenor, splinters of a million shades of reds and silvers, seemed to pierce Celia and pin her in place like a butterfly under glass.

Zuni lifted her dark, wide eyes to Celia.

Xinto took off from Celia's shoulder and went to investigate the new face, but Zuni didn't shift her gaze away when the giant bee landed on her shoulder.

"Oh—" Celia choked out, her face exploding in tears all over again.

Zuni bumped Xinto off her shoulder, and after a swirl

of movement as she dodged the furniture, she was in front of Celia. She narrowed her eyes. "How dare you leave home without telling me?"

The hard lines of Zuni's scowl melted one by one, and the two of them collapsed into a hug. "How dare you come after me?" Celia asked in a squeak. They dissolved to whispers, and the plague doctor turned away.

"It took some doing to get here," Zuni explained. "At first, Dante wouldn't tell me where you'd gone. He finally spilled when I threatened to break his fingers one by one, which he knew would put a damper on his Marco explorations."

Amazingly, Celia chuckled.

He definitely didn't like Zuni. Or he liked her very much indeed.

"Halcyon will be back soon," Lyric said, thankfully interrupting the reunion.

"And none of us are leaving," he added. "So don't even bother."

He'd said the same thing to Celia earlier, trying to explain devotion—*Once you're in the Rabble Mob, you're in the Rabble Mob*—and it looked like she finally understood it.

She nodded.

The barest whisper of a smile passed her lips, aimed at him, and his heart soared.

Then Celia proceeded to tell everyone what her terrible plan was.

It took only a few minutes. The players included a former inkling, a plague doctor, a skullkeeper, and an executioner who'd never killed. The props included one door, one chest of ink, and the afterlife.

There were a lot of holes in the plan. All of them knew it. Most of it would be improvised. And they would almost certainly fail. "We're not even going to *touch* the chest before he catches on," Lyric said, ever cutting and grim. "But if we run, he'll catch us. If we fight, he'll get the town to fight back. I suppose we may as well go down trying." Lyric was the only one of them who could still back out and continue pretending to be his ally, so even though their delivery sucked, the plague doctor thought it was quite a heartening speech.

"The ink is what helps people make their own heavens or their hells," Celia explained. "On the other side, everyone is an inkling. They can craft the world they feel they deserve. Or they're supposed to be able to, at least." She met the plague doctor's eyes. "Remember the Rabble Mob's take on Passion's tale? Normally, she'd go to heaven or hell, find the angels or live forever with the devils. It was clear-cut. Final. But the Mob's story was that she got neither. She was suspended in nothingness forever—and then the curtain fell."

The plague doctor remembered. He'd written it, after all.

"When I bring the ink back, Passion won't be suspended in nothingness anymore. She'll be able to make her afterlife exactly as she wants."

The afterlife.

If Celia's terrible, wonderful plan worked and they released the ink inside the chest to where it belonged, each soul would be able to write their own ending. They could rewrite the horror of that nothingness with infinite potential.

It was better than a dream.

I know you heard all of that, Diavala. The afterlife. A door. What do you think? He already knew what she thought.

At the lake, as soon as Celia had begun doubting Halcyon, he'd felt the thrill of a new emotion from Diavala, deep in his bones, but until that moment he hadn't recognized it for what it was.

Somehow you knew, he said to Diavala. *That was why you no longer wanted to leave.*

For centuries, Diavala had thought that returning to the afterlife was impossible for her, that her curse couldn't be broken.

"I didn't know," Diavala said. *"But I hoped."*

That was the emotion he hadn't been able to place: hope.

Celia had an uncanny way of staring deep into his

soul even when he had his mask on. She'd been the only one to ever search for his eyes behind the goggles, as if the mask didn't matter. Even then, from across the room, with tinted lenses between them, she found his eyes and held his gaze. "How do we know Diavala won't just bolt for that door and leave us all to suffer Halcyon's wrath?" she asked.

The purple-eyed child in front of him was actually trembling, so fierce was her excitement, but, absurdly, he trusted Diavala.

They'd become a most ridiculous team.

"We don't know for sure," he admitted. "But she's thrilled at the idea of becoming the thief Halcyon always accused her of being."

"And what about you?" Celia asked.

"I . . ." He hesitated. Saying it out loud again—*I know I won't survive*—felt defeatist and terrible. But this would allow him to face the place that scared him, and to make it better for everyone who came after. He'd be a real plague doctor: giving comfort at the end of days.

It was the role he was meant for.

"It's a sad-happy sort of thing," he finally said.

Celia rolled her eyes. "Riddlish."

"And the truth."

He cocked his head to the left and clapped his hands together.

Showtime.

CHAPTER 27

THREE, TWO, ONE . . ." LYRIC COUNTED DOWN THE PRECISE
moment to when Halcyon's "polish the town" time was over,
and the four of them stared across Rian's pumpkin patch, waiting for lightning to strike.

Trying to tame her nerves, Celia turned all the pumpkins
bright purple, erected some bat houses with little misti-bats diving in and out, and stretched out Xinto's wings so he could keep
up with them.

Anything to distract herself from the fact that her ink double
and Griffin's ink double were currently passionately kissing in
the middle of the field of purple pumpkins while ink-Lyric and
ink-Zuni shuffled awkwardly close by.

There were four new ink-people in Wisteria now: Celia's
paranoia had led to inspiration.

The real group stood in a row, hidden behind some shrubs,
watching for the moment Halcyon returned. Thankfully, Celia
was on the end, so she only had to deal with Lyric's comments.
"If this doesn't work because those two can't stop kissing, I
swear . . ." Lyric whispered.

"This is awkward for everyone, trust me," Celia hissed.

The decoys seemed to function well enough, except that

they obviously didn't understand how to appropriately handle impending danger.

"It does look like you're both having fun," Lyric noted.

Celia gritted her teeth and knocked one of the bat houses over, sending a stream of cloaked misti-bats flying for the skies and sending the ink doubles into crouch position.

And just in time too, because Halcyon appeared in front of them the next moment. "What's going on here?" he asked ink-Lyric, gesturing to the fact that no one was locked up. He assessed ink-Zuni with undisclosed irritation, saying, "Celia's not supposed to know about her yet."

"Celia's had time to think about everything, and she's willing to continue the arrangement you made, but she'd like to renegotiate the terms."

"I'm very eloquent," real Lyric whispered.

Celia ignored them, intent on the scene playing out in front of her. They needed Halcyon to buy into this illusion—he wanted Celia to stick around and do his dirty work, after all.

And it looked like it was working. Ink-Celia looked perfectly humbled (if a little flushed from her kissing session), ink-Zuni and ink-Griffin looked appropriately fearful, and ink-Lyric was a good intermediary: capable and devoted to Halcyon's cause.

Although Celia was curious as to whether ink-Lyric could in fact broker a truce, she didn't waste any more time. They'd only needed to know that Halcyon was away from the chest of ink and the ever-important door.

Concentrating hard on both their exact location and Halcyon's front gate, Celia closed her eyes and used the ink to change the town. Like reordering a jigsaw puzzle, she shifted the four of them to the exact spot she wanted. Celia had folded herself many shortcuts over the past days, but she'd never had to move so many people, and so stealthily.

"Did it work?" she whispered. But when she opened her eyes, they were all there: Lyric and Xinto, unperturbed; Zuni and Griffin, highly perturbed.

"Holy shit, Celia!" Zuni said, staring down at herself. "I thought you were making up stories. Damn—to be so enmeshed in a world so bizarre . . ." Standing on the street she'd never seen, but was now miraculously on, Zuni took stock of the gate, then looked back at Celia.

Celia shook her head. Through Zuni's eyes, all this must look so strange. It had been introduced to Celia so incrementally, it had felt quite magical. Only very recently had that magic turned a little sour.

"Let's just get this over with," Celia said, scaling the fence. She could have probably gotten them all closer, but manipulating Halcyon's home felt far riskier—if she got something wrong putting it back in order, or if she inadvertently left some trace behind, he was far more likely to notice.

"Only Xinto and I really know this place," Lyric said as they ran through the tunnel of wisteria. "So whatever you do, don't lose us."

Zuni nodded, patting the bulge in the bag she kept at her hip. "Saccharine likes me well enough, but she's not too keen to have me join her in this bag. Let's make this quick."

"I knew you'd bring a skull with you," Celia said.

"I didn't," Zuni whispered. "I brought two." And her mouth twitched into an almost-smile. "I couldn't abandon Bruno either." She patted another bulge.

Despite the knot in her stomach, Celia laughed.

Then they were inside Halcyon's perfect home, with all its hallways, doors, sconces, and paintings. Zuni oohed at the opulence, and Griffin's mouth curled up with distaste.

Lyric led the way, but it was a disorganized search. They seemed to be throwing open doors at random. "I don't know where he moved the chest, but it has to be here," they muttered.

"Wait," Griffin said, slowing to a stop in front of the aviary. Xinto had flown in first and was buzzing around Zuni's head, as if excited to show the space off to someone he knew would appreciate it.

"I feel like it's this way—" Griffin said, pulling Celia back the way they'd come.

"Why would you feel that?" Celia said. Her insides clenched, bracing for a blow. This was what she'd been afraid of: Diavala trying to sabotage them and using Griffin to do it.

Griffin cocked his head, as if he were listening; then he must have recognized the tight line of Celia's spine. "I imagined her as she was in the beginning," he said, stepping closer. "A ten-year-old child like any other ten-year-old, neither Divine nor

Diavala. She has striking purple eyes though, much like this."
He reached into his pocket, and a spark of his blue and purple
fire erupted in his palm, showing Celia the exact hue of these
imagined eyes. "It might help if you tried that too."

Celia puffed out the flame. "We don't have time for pretend—"

The ground began shaking, cutting her off.

At the far end of the hall, Lyric stopped throwing doors open.
Zuni emerged from the aviary with Xinto on her shoulder and
a sparrow in her palm.

Lyric had been right—they hadn't even touched the chest
before being discovered. Halcyon had already caught on to
their duplicity, and judging by the way the walls shook and the
ground heaved, he wasn't interested in any further negotiation.

CHAPTER 28

FOUR PEOPLE AND ONE GIANT BEE HUDDLED TOGETHER IN the hallway as the lights went out all at once. Pitched into a darkness so absolute, Celia had to put her fingers to her eyes to make sure they were still open. Beside her, Zuni's labored breathing competed with the alarmed chirps of the bird in her palm. Griffin had grabbed Celia's arm, squeezing tight.

Then the breathing and the bird were gone. Griffin's hand was gone.

When she could see again, only Lyric was beside her.

And Halcyon.

He all but hauled Celia and Lyric into the studio. He went over to his favorite puffy chair and collapsed into it, rubbing his temples, as if dealing with Celia was turning into the biggest inconvenience of his very long life.

But he hadn't killed her yet, so she focused on that.

She felt like crying, like curling up into a little ball in the corner, but she definitely didn't focus on that.

With a guttural noise, Halcyon lifted his head. "The expendables have been dealt with for now," he said, his voice hard. All the earlier molten fire in him had hardened to stone. "And I'll keep them hostage for as long as it takes for you to understand the situation here."

Celia's gaze darted between Halcyon and Lyric. She cleared her throat, wondering how much she would regret the question burning at the tip of her tongue. "And what exactly is the situation here?"

Halcyon made more of those noises and Celia hoped he'd choke on them.

"As free-spirited as you've come to be, you are my apprentice. You have natural talent and a vicious streak, both of which I can't help but admire." He tapped the armrest of his chair with his slender fingers, counting out time like a metronome. He looked very much like a king on his throne, dealing with irritating peasants when he'd rather be planning for war. "But your old world keeps distracting you. You should be focused on one thing and one thing only, and that's answering destiny's call."

He stopped tapping and leaned forward, lacing his fingers together in front of his lips. "And you—" He looked at Lyric, who looked like they were trying to disappear into the floorboards, before looking back at Celia. "Such a pity. You were so useful."

After a flick of his fingers, Lyric screamed as they were hauled into the air by an invisible hand. They hit the ceiling hard. Flapping their arms, their hair dangling in their face, they had no power to stop the assault. Over and over again, down and then up, Lyric's back kept hitting the ceiling.

Celia was enraged on Lyric's behalf. If she hadn't had the foresight to think that he might drop them, she would have punched someone for the first time in her life.

"Here's what's going to happen," Halcyon said. "I will make sure you and every one of your friends share Diavala's same fate." He grinned. "You will die, I will find you in the afterlife, and I will push you out. Over and over again, you and your friends will have to find a body, steal it, live as an interloper, die with them or kill them, and then do it all over again. For all eternity, you will do nothing but exist."

The thumps of Lyric's body hitting the ceiling were like heartbeats. They'd stopped screaming and had gone rigid, taking the blows silently.

"Or," he said. "You can simply cooperate, Celia. All I want is a caretaker for my paradise. How can you still be fighting me about this? You're being so infuriatingly dramatic!"

With everything inside her, she tried to overpower Halcyon's illusion. She didn't have the skill to stop him, but she added cushions to the ceiling, trying to soften the blows. Halcyon vanished every one.

To him, there was only one clear decision she could make.

"Wait!" Celia said, grasping, desperate for him to stop. "I saw Martina! I'm just confused because I saw Martina!"

The thumping heartbeat stopped. With her eyes still on Halcyon, Celia inked nonsense on her arm and commanded some cushions on the ground in case he decided to drop Lyric, who'd unstiffened, hair dangling, and was cycling their arms again, trying to get down.

"Liar," Halcyon said.

"It's true." Celia swallowed, unsure what his ultimate reaction would be. But at least he'd stopped tossing Lyric around like a rag doll. At least he was listening. "She was with a friend of mine. She found me."

Halcyon finally let go of the invisible hand, and with a shriek, Lyric tumbled to the cushions, knocking their hip on a workbench on the way. They stumbled to their feet and stood immobile but in a ready position, waiting for the sign that would tell them which way to run.

Halcyon's stillness was eerie. His eyes swirled, and tension had brought him to his feet. He was the picture of a volcano set to erupt. "You would say anything right now . . ."

Did he want to believe Celia, or did he hope she was lying? She had no idea what he wanted to hear.

From the corner of her eye, she saw Lyric nod slightly.

"I can prove it. I know her death was peaceful. She died young—not much more than twenty."

"You could have guessed that from my portraits."

According to those portraits, Martina had changed her hair and clothing dramatically and often, and Celia would guess that in life, her tenor had changed as well. But in the afterlife, she was stuck with both the pronoun and the clothing she'd died in. The idea sent a wave of sympathy washing over Celia:

it wasn't right that something as fluid as identity was stifled for eternity.

And it was Halcyon's fault. Not only was he harming every-one else, he was hurting the one he claimed to love most. Celia swallowed her rage. "She was wearing a green dress the color of emeralds, with cream lace here"—she gestured at her wrists—"and here—" she touched her neckline. "She had a belt made of ribbon, and the dress was a unique cut with open splits up the sides, so I think she made it herself—"

"Enough!" Halcyon roared.

And if Celia had thought she'd made him mad before, that was nothing compared to now.

INTERLUDE

The plague doctor lit some Kinallen powder to illuminate the space, casting Zuni and her bag of skulls in a dim, blueish light. Halcyon had tossed them into what looked like a cellar.

"This is more privacy than I ever had with the Rabble Mob," he said, wondering if Zuni had ever been held in the Asuran dungeon: more rats than people, the smell so strong it wormed in through your nose and settled right behind your eyes, making them water perpetually. This wasn't nearly as bad. Four walls. A floor. A door with a hatch. The hatch could be opened from both sides, likely to pass food and water through. Zuni rattled it open. "You won't be able to squeeze through," she said, examining the size of the opening. "You have"—she arched an eyebrow in his direction—"shoulders."

The plague doctor took off his coat and mask, then carefully balanced the flame on the ground between them.

"I can't believe this," Zuni muttered, putting her head in her hands. "Tossed out of the fight before it even started."

"Don't be defeatist," he said. It was as if Zuni actually believed they were trapped! He felt along the inside of the slim beak of his mask, running his fingers along its length until he found the two metal rods that gave the beak some of its support, no more than two slight bumps. He picked at those little bumps carefully, loosening the ceramic around them. "The inside of my coat will have a few things," he said to Zuni as he concentrated. No way was he ruining his mask, despite the emergency.

Zuni scooped it up. "Like what? What am I looking for?"

"A small braid on the flip side of the breast pocket. Follow the trail of it through the fabric—do *not* wreck my coat, Zuni—and you should get to some treasures along the way." A magnet, money, the braid woven from spun silver, a needle, a small spool of thread, various pockets of Kinallen's fire powder in an assortment of colors (his trademark might have been blue and purple, but sometimes the last thing you wanted was to leave a trail), two buttons . . . "I don't remember everything. Just look until you find the pliers."

"Pliers," Zuni mumbled, feeling along the length of the braid. "You have pliers sewn into your jacket."

"*Move faster, plague doctor,*" Diavala said. "*He won't take kindly to escape plans.*"

"Well, we're *actually* escaping, so it isn't a *plan,*" he muttered. Did no one here appreciate his talents?

"Angeli in heaven, is this a spoon?" Zuni exclaimed, her fingers tracing along a ridge at the bottom of the coat.

"Of course," he said. "But focus, Zuni." The clips in

the mask were almost out; he'd scratched away most of the clay holding them in place, mourning the state of his mask. From perfect to less than. "I need the pliers."

"I found a hammer."

"Is a hammer pliers?" the plague doctor asked, his voice sugary sweet. "But keep it out." He nodded at their growing pile of supplies. "We might need it."

With the rods out of the mask and the pliers finally freed from his coat, he bent and flattened the tips to the shape he needed. The lock on the door was an older style, easy enough to pick, if he could get both hands working it. He wasn't sure of the angle. "I'm glad illusion locks are the same as regular locks," he said.

He still didn't know what was real and what wasn't. Maybe he never would.

Struggling to reach out of the hatch, making a mental note to add an adhesive to his pockets when he had a chance (if he dropped the rods, they'd be in there a good long time), he angled his hands toward the lock. Just barely reaching it. Just barely able to tickle the metal. With only his arms stretched out, his cheek resting on the inside of the door, he couldn't see what he was doing, but he'd picked worse locks in worse conditions. As the clinks and clanks of his work rang through the hallway, he winced.

His shoulders felt the strain of the awkward position, and his hands were beginning to sweat. But the lock clicked open, and though he did his best to catch it, it clattered to the floor. The door swung open easily and silently, the fresh air snuffing out the flame.

"Let's go," Zuni said, yanking the plague doctor's arm.

They quickly walked down the long, dark hallway. On either side was a stretch of bare stone wall.

. . . Until they passed their open cell again, the freshly picked lock lying on the ground where they'd left it.

They picked up their pace. Running in a straight line, without making any turns, they passed the cell they'd just left another three times before rearing to a stop, out of breath.

"Should have known it was too easy," the plague doctor said, surveying the hallway. It was identical in both directions, stretching so far they couldn't see the end. "Other way, then."

They ran in the other direction. With Diavala chanting in his head, he was about to scream when Zuni lurched to a stop and he narrowly avoided bowling her over. "Look," she said, pointing up.

The only difference in the opposite direction was a ladder that began above Zuni's head and, three rungs later, disappeared into the ceiling. No door, no hatch, no marks on the ceiling or wall, just three rungs of a ladder on the wall, leading nowhere, like an ornament or decoration.

The plague doctor knelt down, propped a knee up,

and took Zuni's hand to help her balance as she stepped up onto his knee as if it were a step stool. Pressing her hands to the ceiling and wall around the ladder rungs, wobbling the whole while as she balanced, she searched for a hidden access.

"Just go up," the plague doctor said, his leg straining from holding Zuni's weight. "It's a ladder. Climb it."

"I don't want a concussion, thank you very much!" Zuni said, jumping off. "If it's so easy to climb through a ceiling, be my guest."

The plague doctor put his coat and mask on, stuffed every loose item into his pockets, and jumped, grabbing the bottom rung of the ladder. He hung there a moment, closing his eyes, hoping he was right about this. Without looking, he grabbed the second rung, then the third, and scrabbling up the wall, he reached for the fourth.

Then the fifth.

His foot found purchase on the bottom rung. Still not opening his eyes—because some things were better in the dark, including leaps of faith that made no logical sense—he called to Zuni. "Are you able to reach?"

In answer, she jumped, her hands slapping the rung by his feet. "I'm not Celia-short," she huffed.

Because he'd started the climb with his eyes closed—and that leap of faith had worked—he continued the climb with them tightly shut. All around him was darkness, nothing seeping in, but his other senses became more attuned. He heard Zuni's breathing below him, the sound of his hands slapping the rungs in a steady pace, the clomp of their boots. He smelled stagnant air with an undertone of dampness, as if they were in the belly of Illinia itself, and the smell became stronger the farther they went. Could they be climbing down?

His muscles strained, and Zuni's breathing became more laborious. The climb (or descent) went on and on. Straight up and down. Forever.

He stopped, wrapping his arms around the ladder rungs to give his hands a rest. Zuni rested her forehead on his lower legs.

"Do you have your eyes open?" he asked her.

"Yes." Zuni laughed, the movement rustling his pant legs. "You don't?"

"No." He couldn't shake the feeling that it was the only thing holding him there. Locked in his own darkness, forever climbing.

"Well, there's light coming in from far up, but we definitely don't seem to be getting closer."

"What about around us? Have you seen any ledges?" he asked.

"Holy hell, Griffin, if there'd been a ledge, don't you think I would have mentioned it? No, there's nothing. We're in a tube that extends into infinity."

If they kept going into infinity, their mortal arms would tire. They were close already, shuddering with effort. Once they gave out for good, they would both fall. And if they fell, they would fall far.

Definitely farther than he'd fallen before, that time he'd died. He'd barely been able to shout out before impact that time. This time, he'd likely have time to recite entire play. *Wonder which option's worse,* he thought.

"The long fall," Diavala said.

Wasn't talking to you, Diavala.

"This is the most bored I've been in decades, plague doctor. Even your disregard is better than nothing."

He tilted his head up, trying to sense the light Zuni had mentioned. He didn't. But as he began climbing again, there was a nagging thought at the back of his mind that he couldn't quite shake loose.

A few minutes later, he paused again. "This isn't working." In the stillness and darkness, he felt himself losing touch with reality with every rung he climbed (or descended). There was a madness in doing the same thing and expecting a different result.

"Okay, Zuni, I'm going to let go."

"Excuse me . . . pardon me? What?" she panted below him, reaching up to give his shin a swat, as if to knock the idea out of him.

"That kind of excitement wasn't really what I had in mind," Diavala said.

"What do people do with ladders?" he called down to Zuni.

"They climb them."

"Right, they climb them. And where do ladders go?"

"They go up." Zuni was stretching out her words, long and slow, as if she were answering a child but wanted them to feel heard.

"But are we going up?"

"I don't think we are, no," Zuni said. "But that doesn't mean I want to experiment with forces of gravity."

The plague doctor shook his head, trying to clear it. "What if the ladder is a decoy?" Tentatively, he reached a hand out and felt around him: the stone was damp and slimy, each brick as similar as the one around it. He went up a rung and tried again, looking for anything other than monotony.

Every illusion had a flaw; you just had to find it, and everything unraveled.

His hand landed on a patch of moss.

"How far away is the light up above? Are we any closer?" he asked. At that point he wasn't sure why he was being weird about opening his eyes, but given what he was considering, he could handle only so much experimentation.

"It's still way up there. A pinprick."

"So there's no light around us?"

"No. It's dead black."

He shuddered at her description.

"Then how can moss grow here?" He pulled his

favorite iron hammer from his pocket, hefted it into his palm, reached out, and tapped. Where was the flaw?

The hammer met stone, giving away none of its secrets.

He dropped it.

"Hey!" Zuni exclaimed. The ladder jerked as she hugged closer to it to avoid being hit.

Then they both paused. And listened.

Nothing more than a breath later, it hit the bottom with an echoey *thunk* . . . somewhere on the wall near Zuni's head.

"What the hell?" she mumbled. Griffin heard her fumble around, trying to find it, and a moment later she had it in her hand. "It fell sideways."

"All right, ready? We're going to fall sideways too. On the count of five, let go."

"No, Griffin, this is a foolish—"

"One, two, three—"

"If you die here, I have to take Zuni over, Griffin Kay!" Diavala shouted. *"Our deal is over! This is the end of your story!"*

"Are you mad? We have to figure this out first!" Zuni shouted.

It would work. "Four—"

"If you die, I'll never forgive you—"

"Five!"

He let go of the ladder.

And fell.

Although it wasn't the end of his story, it was still a painful landing. His shoulder hit first, rocking a jolt through him that slammed his teeth together, nearly slicing his tongue in half. A loud thump and a twist, and something or someone—Zuni—landed on his legs, smashing them together.

"*Dia*," Zuni cursed with a moan. And then, "Holy shit. Holy shit! It actually worked!" She scrambled to untangle herself and, he assumed, stood up.

All he tasted was the blood from the cut on his tongue where his teeth had gone through, the sting of it sharpening every other sensation in his body. His shoulder felt like it had been pulled out of its socket.

He couldn't tell whether they'd fallen up or down or sideways, but they'd fallen for a moment and then landed hard, and then the tunnel was no longer a tunnel, the ladder no longer a ladder, and in front of them was a door. Cracked open, revealing the light of outside streaming through.

The jolt had made his eyes snap open. Finally. He could see again.

Zuni rolled her shoulders and helped him stand. In the dim light, he could see her grinning, and he thought for a moment they'd landed in some upside-down world, where gloomy Zunis smiled and happy plague doctors winced.

"I can feel the ink close," Diavala said.

"Follow me," the plague doctor whispered. They were still in Halcyon's house somewhere; the garish parquet flooring was the same. The door in one direction—the way the plague doctor would have gone, given a choice—was the same as all the others. But Diavala instructed him to go the other way, through an archway, around a corner and into a long kitchen, through a dining area, and then into a back storage area. If the main hallway was the heart of the house, this was more like the appendix. The afterthought.

"It's in there, plague doctor."

And Diavala was right. They opened the creaky door, and the plague doctor saw a copy of the chest he'd seen smashed in Asura, glinting out from behind stacks of flour and canned goods. Among Lyric's food stores was the chest that Diavala mourned for.

Zuni pushed past the plague doctor and scooped it up in her arms. "Let's get it to the door."

That was going to be difficult. Not only did they not know their way around (and couldn't count on Diavala sniffing out two things they needed), but when they swiveled to go back the way they came, they heard a shout so loud it rattled the walls.

No, it *was* the walls.

"Don't you dare!" Halcyon's house yelled at them.

CHAPTER 29

THE IMAGE OF HALCYON'S FURIOUS FACE WAS IMPRINTED IN Celia's mind. His eyes had widened, and he'd roared a warning— "Don't you dare!"—before everything around her changed. Yet the warning hadn't been for her—he'd been reacting to something else.

His strategy of dividing them had backfired, and he was now fighting on two fronts.

Celia was on a narrow road, like any she'd traveled in the Illinian countryside, muddy with deep ruts from wagon wheels. The darkness became sky, overcast and moist, arched over by long-limbed, naked trees deep in the sleep of winter. The road extended only a dozen steps before curving into the depths of a forest.

She was about to unravel the illusion, knowing it was only meant to distract her, when from around the bend came a voice Celia recognized, her shout long and drawn out. *"Ceceee!"*

When Anya appeared at the edge of the path ahead and reared to a stop, Celia took a step forward. Then another. It was Anya: long black hair, pale skin, wearing her favorite midnight-blue top hat and a fierce frown. They'd said their goodbyes, so this was particularly cruel.

"You!" Anya roared it, the angry version of her exploding in a flash of movement, running toward Celia as Celia ran toward her. Anya's hands, in tight fists, slammed into Celia's stomach, her jaw, as they met. The greeting Celia truly deserved. *"I'm dead because of you!"*

They tumbled backwards together, a tangle of limbs on the ground. Anya controlled her fists after the first two shots, but she scrambled to pin Celia down. Her hand pressed on Celia's jaw, forcing her face sideways into the mud, but from the corner of her eye Celia couldn't escape the anger and betrayal on Anya's face. She couldn't apologize.

It was part of Celia's biggest nightmare realized. The part where Anya tells her it was a mistake, the biggest mistake, that Celia had misunderstood everything.

Instead of fighting her off, Celia sank under her weight, taking it.

Anya leaned down and whispered hoarse words into Celia's ear, pinning Celia with her entire body. *"What did you gain, Cece? What did you win when you convinced everyone their god was dead?"* She leaned away enough that Celia could see the sneer on her face, her familiar ocean-blue eyes swimming with hate and pain. *"I always put too much faith in you, didn't I? You spent years showing me what kind of person you were, and I ignored every sign."* She shook her head slowly. *"I loved you too hard for too long, hoping that love would smooth your rough edges. But that's impossible, isn't it? That was my mistake. You're nothing but rough edges, Celia Sand. You're sharpened spikes, jagged rocks, nails and thorns and* poison, every inch of you designed to hurt anyone who comes close." Anya pressed closer again, her mouth right at Celia's ear as she whispered, "It should have been you on that stage with two gashes in your neck, bleeding out, dying, dying, dead. It should have been you."

Celia shrieked and pushed Anya off, rolling away into the grass beside the road. With her hair in her eyes and the mud streaking her skin, she clambered back to her feet, holding her shaking hands in front of her toward this version of Anya.

As real as she felt, as true as her words were, Celia knew it wasn't the real Anya. Still, she hesitated before unraveling the illusion. The pain in Celia's gut clenched with want, immediately aching for her friend-that-wasn't-her-friend. Maybe she didn't want Angry Anya to go away. Maybe Angry Anya was better than no Anya.

Was it to be her fate, to have to let go of Anya over and over again?

The hairs on the back of Celia's neck rose as Angry Anya flanked her, a vicious glint in her eye. Celia's hesitation cost her, and she didn't even have the chance to lift her arms in protection before Anya attacked.

A hand slapped over Celia's mouth, cutting off another emerging scream. She was on the ground on her back, flashes of light brown hair in the space above her, a lithe body holding her down. The more she struggled, the more fiery the pain: her eye, swollen from a blow, bites and scratches on her arms, bruises on her legs. Everywhere hurt.

Chest heaving, pain raging, Angry Anya gone, Celia had returned to the room. Lyric had pinned her down, but with Celia's return to the normal world, Lyric slid off her.

Celia gasped out ragged breaths as she inspected her wounds. Aside from some scratches, likely self-inflicted, there were none. Her eye wasn't swollen, her arms and legs were fine. The scent of her own blood was the last thing to fade. As her breathing slowed, Lyric sat back on their heels. "Whatever you were fighting, I think they won."

Propping herself up on her elbows, Celia frowned, her heart still thumping hard and out of control. "Dead best friend," she muttered, pressing her hand to the wood planks beneath her, noting that she was no longer covered in mud and leaves, that there was no blood. Next time Halcyon summoned an illusion trying to bait her, she wouldn't hesitate in unraveling it.

Xinto flew down from the corner of the room and landed on Lyric's head as Celia looked around for Halcyon — *child killer, curse maker, ink stealer, master of death* — but the room was empty except for her, Lyric, and Xinto.

Celia scrambled up and tried the door.

It opened.

She and Lyric stared at each other a beat, clearly neither of them expecting the door to be unlocked and openable.

They peeked out, but Halcyon wasn't in the hallway.

Celia had the good sense to know that he wasn't done with them, but she wasn't going to wait around if there was an opportunity to flee. She and Lyric jogged down the main hall-way toward the front door, Xinto trailing behind. The doors to every room hung open, beckoning her to look in.

"He's buying time," Celia said. "Zuni and Griffin did some-thing he had to take care of." The thought made her excited and nervous all at once. Maybe they'd found the chest.

"Wait, Celia!" Lyric lurched to a stop, grabbing a fistful of Celia's shirt in the process and choking her with it. They tried to pull her into one of the rooms—a light inside casting a pale blue light into the hallway, glowing and icelike.

Celia averted her eyes and tugged back. "If he wants us to look, that means we shouldn't do it!"

"Griffin's in there. *Everyone's* in there."

Celia yanked harder. She wanted to look in the room, but she focused on Lyric's face instead, illuminated by the pale blue shine. "No, they definitely aren't."

Lyric considered a split second more and then nodded. They raced off again.

But they ran for far too long, the hallway stretching forever. Celia tried another passage, continuing to ignore all the open doors even after they started screaming at her that perhaps they were another exit. *Try me, no me . . .*

They passed the door with the faint blue light more than once, and each time, Lyric looked inside and hesitated before continuing on at Celia's insistence. Lyric's pauses became longer and longer, and Celia's resolve got weaker and weaker.

"Celia, it's really them," Lyric said the next time they reared to a stop, panting and holding their knees. "I know Halcyon's illusions. This can't be one of them."

Or maybe he's dipping into an arsenal he never needed before, Celia thought. But she couldn't say it out loud; her lungs were on fire.

Lyric began walking toward the open the door, and Celia barely had enough time to yank them back before they stepped over the threshold. "Devil's hell, Lyric, stop it!" she shouted, exasperated. "It's an illusion!" But as she shouted and wrestled with Lyric in the doorway, she got a peek into the room she so desperately didn't want to see.

Lyric was right. Everyone was there.

At the far side of the expansive room, small cells lined up in a row and stacked on top of one another as in a beehive, each with a door and a hatch. In each cell was someone they knew, and many more were filled with people Celia didn't know. Lupita was in one of the bottom cells at the front, gripping the bars with her wrinkled hands, facing whoever was in the cell beside her. Kitty Kay was talking to Milloni. Marco was curled up in a ball, and Lilac was reaching a hand through the bars, trying to console him.

"Celia!" Griffin was in one of the top cells, up so high she could barely tell who it was. He grabbed the bars and shouted down to her. "Get out of here! Go!"

Celia had to prove that this was an illusion, and the only way to do that was to take it away.

Without thinking about it, she imagined all the ink in the room coming to her. As she'd trained, she'd wiped away hundreds of poor attempts and started over.

She didn't even stop to consider that it wouldn't work.

Her skin quivered. From head to foot, tiny ripples erupted, the sensation so all-encompassing and strange, she quivered from the quivers.

It didn't feel right.

Because it wasn't *her* ink. To date, she'd only added to or altered Halcyon's grand illusion. She'd tethered her illusions to something that was already there; even Xinto was tied to the scents on the breeze.

Everything she'd put out into the world could ultimately come back to her. But this was taking back what *Halcyon* had put out into the world.

It was the equivalent of trying to control another inkling's ink. It should have been impossible, but she felt it responding to her anyway.

"Lyric, stop!" she called out again, hoping it was enough to slow them down. They were almost at the rows upon rows of cells.

A few of the caged people began screaming—at Lyric, at nothing. That, more than Celia's shout, was what made Lyric slow down. Since Celia didn't know how this illusion had been cast, or what, if any of it, was real, she grabbed at everything she could—the people, the cell bars, the ground, the ceiling—searching for a way to unravel it all.

"Holy shit," Lyric said.

Celia had closed her eyes, trying to block out all the visual stimulus in order to search the darkness where the ink might try hiding from her, but Lyric's panicked words made them snap open.

Lyric had lurched to a stop and turned around so quickly, they almost lost their footing, and they were running back to the doorway where Celia stood with a new jolt of energy.

The cells were *melting*. Like candles, they liquified from top to bottom, dripping into vast puddles and stretching toward them.

It reminded Celia of her first attempt with the ink: the exploded bee on the wall of Halcyon's studio, the way it had oozed toward her as if sensing new blood. She'd ducked against the explosion, but the ink had disappeared. Halcyon must have taken it into himself—what she was trying to do now.

But that wasn't what Lyric had reacted to. The *people* were also melting. Their faces washed away first, all color in their skin, hair, and clothing gone as they were reduced to inky black blobs. But still they moved, the ink dripping from their forms, writhing like snakes. And those snakes, dismissed from holding the illusion, felt the warmth of bodies nearby and wanted them.

"Okay, you were right," Lyric said, grabbing Celia's arm. "It's a trap."

Celia planted her feet firmly and refocused. She couldn't leave the ink there like that—free and wild. If it wasn't contained,

Celia had no doubt it would keep going, searching for a host, spreading.

Whatever she'd done to unravel the illusion had created a hungry monster. She needed to calm it down.

"What are you doing?" Lyric said, their eyes wide. "Let's go!"

Celia shook her head. "You have to figure out what he's doing. Find Griffin and Zuni! Get the chest." She yanked her arm away and turned back toward the room. Almost everything had fully melted, only stubs of figures still standing. "Go!" she shouted, and pushed Lyric toward the door.

Then she took a deep breath and ran toward the inky mess. The ink sensed her coming, changing direction so that it was pointed at her. She knew it wouldn't kill her. It wanted to obey. She'd always thought of the ink as parasitic, voracious in its need for a host, but it was more like a desperate servant, needing to please. And right then it was just a confused mess, trying to find answers.

She stopped to meet it, and the snakes of ink slithered over her body. Up her legs, her torso, her arms, around her neck and face.

For many moments she was entirely covered. The inky snakes pushed into her nose and mouth; they covered her eyes and tried to worm their way into her mouth, making her gag. But the ink seeped into her body too slowly, there was too much of it, and for a ridiculous minute she thought she would die, anticlimactically, by suffocation before doing anything of value at all.

But as the last drops of ink fused into her, disappearing and dispersing into her bloodstream, she felt its happiness.

It felt like a sigh. A release.

Celia had Halcyon's ink inside her now.

A lot of it.

She could do more than bring the Chest Majestic full of ink back to the dead. Now she could bring all of Wisteria as well.

CHAPTER 30

WHEN CELIA AND LYRIC EMERGED FROM THE TRAP-ROOM after having sprung it, the house was as it had always been. The hallways didn't stretch forever, the doors weren't hanging open, it was quiet.

That quiet felt more ominous to Celia than if she'd seen Halcyon and his dark, swirling demon eyes. He'd wanted a head start to do *something*.

"He's either torturing them or killing them," Lyric whispered, being incredibly unhelpful.

Walking faster, Celia approached the cherry-red front door. "You were supposed to find them and warn them!" She knew that a few minutes head start wouldn't have mattered, as they didn't even know where Griffin and Zuni were. She punched Lyric on the arm, hoping they'd know what she meant.

"But would he, actually?" Celia said. Halcyon didn't like getting his hands dirty—he hated dirt. "Never mind, I don't want to know. Let's trust they have the chest."

Morning sun crested the horizon in the courtyard, and Celia blinked against it. Robins and larks piped cheerful morning songs, and she smelled the bakery a few streets away where the bakers were already hard at work preparing the day's bread and sweets.

"Morning, Celia. Lyric," Garuld said, waving at them in greeting as they entered the town after leaving the courtyard, wisteria tunnel, and gate behind.

"It's not enough to take the chest of ink," Celia said. "I'm going to take it all."

The chest, the town, even Halcyon himself.

"Are you *mad*?" Lyric hissed.

It was ambitious, but Martina herself had said that Halcyon would never stop. He might lose his chest, but he would find a way to get more. Not only had he discovered enough secrets of the ink to bring it from the afterlife, he now had the wisdom of ages on his side.

Celia didn't have the skill or the stamina or the time to draw in all the ink at once. What she'd done dissolving the cells in Halcyon's home had been desperate and ill-planned. The ink had devolved into its base with her scrambled efforts, and the last thing she wanted was for everything to melt down into uncontrollable puddles and seek out the closest new host: Zuni, Griffin, or Lyric.

Celia needed to be in control at every moment—calling every drop of it back as if she'd been the one to cast it out all along—to make sure the ink came only to her.

Closing her eyes, she reached out with her mind for the ink around her.

Halcyon's illusions were layered and deep. She couldn't break down an illusion unless she knew where it was, and each piece was connected to another piece to another piece and on again. So Celia felt the edges of each one of Halcyon's illusions. She started with the cobblestones because that was an intuitive pattern that extended through the whole of Wisteria. She tugged at one of the strands and felt the ink respond. The ground rippled.

Just as with all the tattoos she'd ever done, she saw how the cobblestones under her feet were drawn in her mind's eye, how they had gone from Halcyon's imagination and become real-ish, and once she had the shape, texture, and scent, she held on tight. *Enough,* Celia told the ink. *You don't belong here.*

And like all those tattoos she'd partially sent into the world with Anya, secret messaging before they even knew what it meant, she called the ink back. She might not have been the one to originally cast it, but now she knew that it would recognize her summons as if she had.

Before, she could only add on to Halcyon's creations with her own ink. With the proper instruction, any other inkling could have done it.

This was more.

This was hers.

In showing her how to build it bigger, how to understand and tend to every corner like a precious rose garden, Halcyon had also shown her how to tear it down.

The cobblestones disappeared, and Lyric jumped at the fresh dirt under their feet.

Wet, loamy, real Illinian soil.

"Wait!" Lyric gasped. They looked back at Garuld, who was donning a sun hat and gardening gloves before heading into his carrot garden. He must have noticed that his footsteps sounded strange, because he stopped and looked down, frowning at the mud on his shoe.

Then he shrugged and kept going.

"The time to consider their feelings is long past," Celia said with urgency. "They might not be evil, but they exist in a world that doesn't belong to them."

Frantic, Lyric looked around. They'd wanted to escape, not to eliminate the only town they'd ever known. "What about Xinto?"

Xinto had been following them at a distance, as he always did, but when he heard his name, he landed on the ground and walked toward them, his head hung low, as if he didn't understand what he'd done wrong or why he was in trouble.

Lyric's mentioning him was a low blow. Xinto would have to be unraveled too. "We don't have time to argue about this—" Celia choked. "This is how it has to be."

Celia looked down at Xinto, who'd arrived at her feet and crawled on top of her boot, staring up at her with big black eyes. "You're such a good bee," she whispered. He cocked his head, listening.

Dia, maybe she couldn't do this. Celia scooped Xinto up, soft, fuzzy, and adorable, handed him to Lyric.

"I have to lure Halcyon through the door," Celia said. "Just like herding river lobsters . . ." she mumbled to herself. Maybe a part of Griffin had known it would have to end like this.

The noise Lyric made was something garbled and confused, as if Celia's insanity had just been confirmed.

"I'll start with the town, and when there's enough panic—" Celia looked at carrot-growing Garuld for a moment. Would the townspeople even react when their town began disappearing? She shook her head and focused. "If there's enough chaos, Halcyon will run toward the familiar, the place he came from. I can *feel* it inside me, how much the ink wants to go back."

Lyric shook their head and backed away.

"The town won't melt or anything," Celia said. *I don't think . . .* "Not like what you saw before." *Hopefully . . .*

"This is far too much improvisation for me. I hate it," Lyric said.

Celia tried to smile. "Welcome to theater?"

Far from convinced, Lyric snuggled Xinto under their chin and stared Celia down.

"The good thing about winging it is that you never make it to the end of your plan," Celia said.

"Not reassuring," Lyric mumbled. But they nodded, tucked Xinto between their shoulder and neck, and hooked their arm around Celia's. "Let's see what you can do, Inkling."

A shudder ran down Celia's spine at the hated title *Inkling,* but she was grateful for Lyric's touch. It grounded her. Reassured her that she wouldn't float away.

And, closing her eyes, she began unwinding Wisteria, piece by piece.

She lost her sense of time again.

She imagined that she was walking from Halcyon's front gate down every road in town, tugging at everything—doors, windows, rocks, the scent of wisteria, the sun on her skin—and wiping away anything she felt responding. She didn't need to tug too hard, and she didn't need to move. The ink wanted to go home. It answered her call without hesitating. Everything was part of Halcyon's sweater, and now that she'd tugged it loose, it unraveled easily, small creeks becoming streams becoming rivers, and all leading to her.

"Are you okay?"

A distant question, far away. Celia was in another place and couldn't grasp it, except that it was repeated and repeated and repeated, a persistent echo. "Are you okay?"

She almost laughed. It wasn't like mixing one and one to make two, it was one and one becoming *other*.

It felt terrible.

And perfect.

INTERLUDE

The plague doctor ran with Zuni, chest in hand, but they made it only as far as the aviary. With every step, the house had heaved under their feet, pulsing like Obi's giant heartbeat within the walls. And it screamed warnings and threats in a voice similar to Halcyon's, but deeper and louder, booming like thunder.

"This is . . . not fun," Zuni had said, panting as she ran.

The plague doctor agreed.

The ink sloshed dangerously inside the chest in Zuni's arms, and Diavala kept shouting at Griffin that they couldn't spill a drop.

Plus, he couldn't tell if the house was booby-trapped or if it was another ink illusion, and that was driving him to distraction *again*.

By the time he'd figured out that the house was herding them where it wanted them to go, it was too late. Halcyon had emerged from his studio, and without thinking, the plague doctor had opened the closest door and pushed Zuni into the aviary.

They stumbled to the back, twisting around trees, shrubs, and angry nesting songbirds. Zuni put the chest down and sat on top of it, earning an affronted gasp from Diavala.

"This is the end, then," Zuni said, trying to catch her breath. "I'm pissed that I'm with you, but happy to be with the birds."

The door burst open, the cacophony of birdcalls dying all at once—not because Halcyon had silenced them, but because he'd killed them. They dropped from their perches and from the air, landing with soft thuds all around. The plague doctor tried to shield Zuni before any landed on her, but he was too late. A small sparrow, maybe even the same one she'd held in her hands earlier, landed in her lap, motionless legs up, beak open.

Zuni shrieked so loud she blasted the roof off the house.

Quite literally.

There was no longer a roof on the house.

Above them was overcast sky, the kind that didn't exist in Wisteria.

He swiveled toward Halcyon, trying to figure out what horror was lined up for them next. A rainfall of dead birds he understood, but why would he rip the roof from his own house? To what end? *This* would be when Obi the Giant made his appearance, and he would be no benevolent fool, tripping his way through life and learning valuable lessons. He would have the sharp teeth of a cannibal and seven glowing red eyes—

"Curse your imagination!" Diavala said.

No Obi appeared, and judging from the look on

Halcyon's face, he didn't know what came next either. He looked just as surprised that the roof was gone as the plague doctor and Zuni.

The walls disappeared from around them.

"What are you doing?" Halcyon asked. His voice was full of panicked wonder, and for a moment the plague doctor enjoyed it. Quite flattering, that Halcyon could think he could do something like this.

He stopped enjoying it when Halcyon retaliated.

"Stop it immediately!" Halcyon demanded. Two long, wide strips of bark tore off the back of the tree closest to the plague doctor and wrapped around him, taking him into a rough embrace. Still connected at the trunk, the bark hugged him close, pulled him in tight. He struggled against it while the tree hugged him with two bark arms, squeezing his chest. Only his head and feet were visible, the rest of him wrapped in a shroud of rough hazelnut-colored bark, with lichen and moss accents. His eyes widened, panic setting in as thin, sharp branches headed toward the goggles of his mask. This would hurt.

"Zuni, you'd better be taking advantage of the new exit—" One small slice of bark ripped away and crept toward the plague doctor's face; then, despite how he tried to twist away, it pressed down, like a palm slapped against his mouth, silencing him.

He couldn't move, couldn't talk, could barely breathe.

One of the slim branches had wedged under his mask at his jawline, and as it extended, the pressure increased until it would either be the mask or his face that ripped first. He put his money on his well-crafted mask surviving longer than his skin.

But he could see all the way to Celia and Lyric, because the rest of Halcyon's lair had disappeared from around them.

Paintings, ornate floor, wall sconces, all gone. Trampled dirt was under their feet, and the breeze hit from all directions. No tunnel of wisteria, no red front door, no fountain or garden. If any of the ink birds had been alive, they would have flown away.

The door with the sunflower doorknob was the only thing left of Halcyon's home. The door they needed to get the ink through.

The plague doctor mumbled at Zuni, loud, trying to get her attention over the people's screams and the chaos of everything falling apart. He had no idea why the tree squeezing the life out of him hadn't disappeared, since everything else in the room was gone, but that seemed to be about his luck.

"*Zu-ni!*" he said through closed, bark-kissed lips. Her dazed eyes met his as his mask was pushed up by the branch, and he pointedly looked in the direction of the door, then down at the chest, trying to say *Take the chest to Celia, there's the door,* with only his eyeballs.

Halcyon had abandoned the empty aviary and was in damage control mode, trying to put everything back just as fast as Celia took it down and yelling at his people to stay calm. They didn't listen.

Shouting above the townspeople's screams, Lyric was giving Celia updates about what she'd managed to make disappear. "The oak trees along the main street," they yelled. "The bakery, the grocer."

"*How a-bout* this *tree, Ce-lee-ah!*" the plague doctor mumbled at her. There was no way she could have heard him, but Zuni did, *and* she happened to have pocketed his folding knife earlier when she'd gone through his coat. As she started sawing at the bark, he'd never been so happy to have been robbed.

He liked Zuni.

Final verdict.

He pushed out as she sliced, helping her, ignoring the few times she accidentally cut into his arm instead of bark, and he pulled away from the tree with a final *riiiip.*

His poor, incredible plague doctor mask hung like a macabre decoration against the bark, the goggles impaled on the branch, where, moments ago, his face had been.

"Don't you dare salute," Zuni said, grabbing his hand.

But it had been a most excellent mask . . .

He shook his head and looked at Zuni. "Grab the chest!" he yelled.

"You're welcome!" Zuni yelled back.

And the plague doctor managed a laugh as they ran through the swirling chaos toward the one who was creating it.

CHAPTER 31

HALCYON WAS TRYING TO PUT IT ALL BACK, BUT CELIA HAD had a good head start, and she simply undid everything all over again. Maybe this would be her purgatory—forever battling an immortal ink-person who'd died a thousand years ago—because that seemed to be about her luck.

"We have the ink!" Zuni called. Then, "Oh no," Zuni whispered, staring into Celia's eyes, then looking away, then looking back, as if she were peering at a fascinating yet grotesque curiosity behind glass.

Griffin was more direct. He looked at Celia so strangely, roaming her eyes, her skin, but she thought he was the strange one: a maskless plague doctor with such pretty, kissable lips.

Leaning closer, he cupped his hands at the sides of her face, creating a tunnel between them, blocking out the rest of the world. Just Celia and Griffin, forehead to forehead. The scent of cloves and lemon hit her, and that familiar tug of *want* came with it. "Oh, Celia." One of his fingers traced a light path by her eye.

Are they black and swirly like his? Celia wanted to ask, but she already had the answer in the way they both stared.

"Does it hurt?" he asked. His hands moved from her upper

arms to her hand, cupping it and turning it over. Black streaks like lightning stained it, disappearing under her shirtsleeve. She stared in wonder as the streaks pulsed and throbbed. It didn't hurt. Not yet. But giving it away on the other side would. Even a complicated tattoo caused exhaustion, and the amount of ink given away was minimal. This would be everything. All of it inside her.

Celia didn't expect to survive.

"Focus, Celia!" Lyric yelled. Their hair whipped around their face as they moved with Zuni toward the door, keeping a close eye on Halcyon as he worked ferociously trying to restore his town. His efforts had slowed, as if he were beginning to realize that casting illusions was more difficult than erasing them, and he wouldn't win this battle.

With the town gone, people were running everywhere, staring up at the sky and at the dirt under their feet. Xinto flew from one person to the next, making confused pips and squeaks. No wisteria, no buildings and homes, no main square. One soul in a bright red suit clutched her dog tight in her arms—so tight the poor thing yipped and struggled—as if she were scared it would disappear.

Celia watched everything as a spectator—undoing anything Halcyon did without thinking, disembodied and weak already. She was ink, and she had to go home. The drive within her was becoming all-consuming. She imagined the sunflower doorknob warm in her hand, turning, pushing the door open: over and over, the same fantasy.

So close to the threshold, she buzzed with need.

With his town in ruins and his people defecting, Halcyon set his gaze on the door.

Just like a river lobster.

Then his gaze moved to Celia.

She shifted her focus to him, her eyes pulsing bright. She needed *his* ink before she could answer the call of the door and finish this. It was one thing to take the ink from the illusions that had built a town, another thing entirely to take it from someone who'd been steeping in it for a thousand years. How could she get him through the door? Celia's hands twitched at her sides, ready to reach for a sword and begin the inevitable duel.

Halcyon staggered as he walked toward her, listing dangerously, as if he'd had too much to drink. The ground rose up to meet him, and he fell on all fours, his head hanging.

A low, guttural moan, as if he were praying to the earth. Beseeching. Apologizing.

Celia hesitated.

Suddenly this didn't feel like a win.

"Don't you dare stop," Zuni said. Her hands gripped the sides of Halcyon's Chest Majestic, and she looked as if she was debating throwing it through the open door.

Celia's veins pulsed harder, the fat, inky lines spreading farther. The ink inside her believed she would lead it home, and it didn't appreciate the delay.

But still, Halcyon looked utterly wrecked. His world had

been so finely crafted; now he crouched in its dust. In the space where a beautiful town once stood were now only a door, trampled ground made of moss and mud, a cloudy sky, frantic, confused people, and one thick-trunked oak tree that had once stood in his aviary but now had the whole field to itself.

"Celia?" he whispered. One word, entirely made of questions. *You've ruined us. How could you do this?* Why *did you do this?*

Halcyon's gaze came up and pierced her, his despair battling with anger. It looked as if he were playing out all the ways he could take his revenge on her, the one who was supposed to be his ally, and trying to land on the right one.

But he also fought to contain his hurt. "You had so much promise," he said. "Why would you do this to us?"

"You need to go back," Celia said. At the moment of desolation, perhaps he could be reasoned with. "Martina will welcome you if you do the right thing."

Halcyon began laughing, deep and full-bellied. "You still claim to have spoken with her? What a marvelous thing! Tell me, in detail, all the things my beloved said."

He stood slowly, and she put her hand out as if to ward him off. If he physically attacked, she had three people who could help her, but if he did something inklike—expand his body to the size of a giant or throw a flurry of knives—she would have no choice but to unleash her own ink attack, and the entire point of this was to bring all the ink home, not release more.

"Martina is full of regret, Halcyon," Celia said. "And she's lived for centuries in that same stark world that you've condemned everyone else to. Think about that for a moment: when you stole from the afterlife, you stole from Martina. If you love her, why wouldn't you want to make things right for her? I'm doing this out of love for the people I've lost, for the people yet to meet their inevitable fate. You should do the same for her."

"I suppose," he said slowly, "you are simply a better person than I." His eyes swirled as he stepped ever closer, and desperate, Celia glanced at Griffin for help. She should have known reason wouldn't work with Halcyon. He was too far gone. Too lost.

He was such a good liar, he was even able to deceive himself.

Then, beside her, someone started screaming. She knew the voice, and she recognized that sound.

She whirled.

Griffin had fallen to his knees, clutching his head and shredding his beautiful megaphone-amplified voice. She'd heard it before, when Vincent fell. She knew that it ended when mistico with daggers descended. But all the mistico were gone and daggerless now that Profeta was dead, so would the sound go on forever? Lyric was the only one who didn't recognize it, who didn't know what it meant, and so they were the only one on their knees beside Griffin, ineffectually trying to help.

"What's happening?" Lyric said, their voice rising. "What's wrong with him?"

In that moment, surrounded by a wall of screams coming from the one person she'd been trying to protect all this time,

Celia regretted every choice she'd made. She shouldn't have trusted Diavala at all, shouldn't have let Diavala manipulate her again. If it was destined to lead her here anyway, to the one thing Celia had been desperate to avoid, she should have done more to destroy Diavala along the way.

Where was Diavala now? The only options were Lyric or Zuni, so her heart shattered in a million pieces.

"Griffin, shhh, it'll be okay." Celia wrapped her arms around him. He babbled loud: screaming nonsense and whispering nonsense. Up and down his voice waxed and waned.

"Water hurts so much more than I could have imagined!" he screamed.

"It's not real," he whispered.

"Are snowdrops sad or happy flowers? I've never been able to tell!" he yelled, then followed it with a high-pitched laugh.

"Diversion," he whispered.

Celia and Griffin locked eyes. And Celia understood.

Love hadn't worked to get Halcyon through the door.

Maybe hate would.

"Get in character, Devil," Griffin said, disguising it as low, nonsense mumbles. "I'll be right behind you with the chest."

Celia had felt herself inching toward death lately. Working with the ink and Halcyon had always felt temporary, even after she'd promised to do it forever. But she still wanted Griffin safe, alive. It had been her only goal for so long; it was supposed to be her redemption. But hers would be a one-way journey. If he followed, his would be too.

And he knew it.

Not only did he know what was coming, he actually seemed *happy* about it.

Griffin had told her once that he'd spoken words about the afterlife aloud, and how wrong it had felt. That those words didn't belong in the land of the living, that by unleashing them, he'd upset a balance. And now she understood it: He didn't want anyone else to live with that fear of what comes next.

The prison of the afterlife was terrible in its vastness and its blankness. Its *nothingness*. No wonder he couldn't talk about it—it was the kind of thing that would make you go mad, knowing that was waiting for you just on the horizon.

But she understood him a little better now. She'd accused him, once, of trying too hard, and she'd been both right and unfair.

Maybe trying too hard in life was the point.

Tears spiked in her eyes, and she didn't know what to say. It wasn't fair that in the middle of him pretending to have the Touch, she had to say goodbye to him. Once they went through the door, it would be over. Given that the afterlife was infinite, they would never see each other again. Celia tenderly kissed his cheek.

"You're ruining my curtain call," he whispered with a small smile. *"Again."*

Celia grabbed Griffin under the arm and hauled him to his feet. Devil's hell, he could be so *loud*. Right in her ear, he wailed, reveling in the performance of the tortured soul. Zuni had clued in — she'd heard the wails of the Touch just as much as Celia had. Lyric and Halcyon, however, were fooled. Lyric had taken the opportunity to unleash years of rage on Halcyon, taunting him with the fact that the town was gone, that he poisoned everything he touched and he deserved this fall.

There was nothing left of Wisteria except for a lone oak tree with an impaled plague doctor mask hanging from it; their horse, Aaro, galloping away in the distance, his hitching post gone; and an assortment of mundane items the townfolk needed to survive: food, clothing, and personal items strewn around like litter. Most of the people had collapsed to wailing or silent shock.

But in those few moments where Griffin and Celia said goodbye and Lyric began their yelling, Halcyon had put some things together.

With five long steps, he was in front of Zuni, forcing the chest from her hands so it tumbled to the ground and grabbing her in a tight hold. *"You,"* he raged. "You *dared* return here?!"

Celia swallowed the lump in her throat. "Tell Lyric and Zuni to destroy that doorknob," she said to Griffin in the lulls of his performance. It was the most important thing, the link between *this place* and *that place.* It had taken the unraveling of everything to find the real-world tether that everything had started from, but it was so obvious now: that sunflower doorknob was the weakest spot and the strongest spot. Every illusion Halcyon had created had been tied to it. "If they don't, Halcyon can walk out and start all over."

Then Celia stood and squared her stance.

And laughed.

This would have to be her best performance yet: taking on the role of the Divine and facing down her curse for the last time.

"I am *so* glad to be free of that one," she said, looking at Griffin. She shook out her shoulders and smiled at Halcyon, who was holding Zuni. "With how long you've haunted me, I'm *amazed* you still can't recognize me!"

He pushed Zuni aside. "Diavala," he said.

"You're pathetic, Halcyon." Celia forced her lips to curl into a satisfied sneer. "A thousand years of torturing me, and in the end, I get the satisfaction of watching everything around you crumble. Beyond that door is my happy ending, and I can't thank this foolish inkling enough for doing all the work for me."

Halcyon's face had contorted into something so ugly he barely looked human. His already long fingers had lengthened even more, ending in dark claws as he tensed his hands, ready to strangle. His eyes had no hint of color left in them; they were black pits in his skull.

With a flourish, Celia bowed at him, smiling self-righteously.

She ran to the open door, stepped into the afterlife, and died . . .

ish.

CHAPTER 32

THE DARKNESS AND FOG ENVELOPED CELIA IMMEDIATELY, but just before the door slammed shut on its own, a huge, buzzing, beautiful bee scooted through. Xinto tumbled to the ground in a crash, rolled a few times, then sat back on his bee bum and stared up at Celia in a daze.

"Xinto! I'm so sorry!"

He looked mighty affronted, as if he couldn't believe she'd forgotten him.

Relief washed through her that she had. She wouldn't have been able to unravel him as she'd unraveled everything else.

They could keep each other company forever now.

He stood on his six legs and shrugged off the fall, then tapped his way over to stand between her legs. He peeked out from between them, unsure of this place.

She scooped him up and ran, trying to put as much distance between them and the door, wondering if she was just moving in circles. There was no way to tell, and before, running forward had always taken her backwards.

The heaviness pushed down, unbearably humid and achingly quiet except for Halcyon's lone voice behind her, calling out. "Where are you?"

She wished she could hear her heartbeat. When things you'd taken for granted your whole life were suddenly gone, the silence was deafening. Lonely.

"That's okay, though, Xinto."

The ink inside her boiled and bubbled, and without any more conversation or doubt, she commanded it away. With a nudge, she sent some to Anya, to Martina, to Vincent, the shredded child Terrin, this soul, that soul, everyone.

The ink listened.

It was a rushing river, a storm inside her. The ink was the only thing close to alive left in her body, and its movement as it obeyed her made her feel that she was made of a thousand snakes wrapped in skin.

It was exactly like a Divine tattoo, but without the quill and the inherent beauty of an image to go with it. Without Celia's inkling knowledge of how the ink worked, she would never have had the capacity to do this.

And it was exactly like one of Halcyon's illusions, but without landscape and texture. Without his tutelage, she would never have been able to project so much at once.

Though it felt like snakes inside her, once it was freed, it just *was*. It existed in and of itself. All around. There were no visible, writhing tendrils leaving her body, no terrible noise as it was freed. The room where everything had melted and pooled had been a mistake: when the ink was confused, it acted more like ink and less celestial.

But released to where it belonged, it was the endless magic of stars, ethereal and whole, but unseen. When it was used for creation, it was an invisible magic, and it thrived in this place. It was infinite potential.

A crowd of souls assembled in front of her as she worked. Ominously silent, their despair was such a force that Celia felt them before she saw them. Though they looked just as hungry as before, Martina was at the head of the group, with her arms out, holding them back without a sound. She locked eyes with Celia and nodded.

Celia kept going. Would she realize the moment when there was nothing left inside her? She'd taken in centuries of it, so maybe this would be a process that required centuries to fix.

Without breath or a heartbeat to warn her, it didn't seem like such a terrifying thought—at least there was that to be grateful for.

With what she'd already scattered and given away, the souls had started creating. The dark of the gray fog gradually lightened, a bird sang a tinny trill in the distance, and the shredded child with the marble had started to sew herself back up, humming as she worked.

The ink *could* be beautiful. Celia had known it, deep down, as soon as Xinto first snuggled into her chest for a warm hug. Its power was as vast as a million dreams. It was wishes that could be made real.

It had just been on the wrong side of the door.

There won't be anything here to be terrified of soon, Celia thought. This would make Griffin so happy. Instead of nothing, nothing, nothing, it would be full of everything. It could be like Wisteria, except with everyone in charge of themselves and their existence, rather than someone—Diavala or Halcyon or her—acting as a shepherd tending a flock.

Other souls had begun to fill the space in front of her. With the ink she'd already freed permeating the air around them, some created tethers to deceased loved ones or imaginings of souls yet to join them, so it became a place of reunions. Others healed wounds or aged backwards to their youthful days. One old soul made themselves a guitar and began strumming madly, as if trying to catch up all at once on an eternity without their music.

Martina watched it all happen, a faint smile tracing her lips.

What will you make, my angel? Celia silently asked Anya. As hard as Celia wished for it, Anya didn't appear. She was probably already on her next adventure, sparing Celia the pain of having to say goodbye yet again.

So Celia imagined it: Anya as perfect as ever, with a wry smile on her lips and a healthy flush to her cheeks. She'd travel to Kinallen, the land of stars, and she'd go by sea, because in this world, Anya didn't get motion sickness—she'd never experienced water torture that made her deathly afraid of water. She had no terrible memories at all.

Anya would love the sea—the fresh smell, the sound of

waves crashing—and the wind would whip her long black hair around her shoulders as she headed toward a new land.

Perhaps there would be a short friend beside her on the prow of that boat; they would be a sprite and a changeling, a mouse and a lion, a stump and a sapling.

I can't wait to see the stars, Anya would whisper. And she'd reach for her friend's pinky finger and wrap hers around it tight as the horizon welcomed them. *I've heard there are so many, you could spend forever counting them and still not count them all.*

And Anya would turn to her friend and smile wide. *I'm going to try, though.*

Celia wanted to cry, but couldn't. She wanted to scream *I forgive you! Do you forgive me?* But imagining Anya counting those fairy-tale stars forever would have to be enough.

"There you are," Halcyon said slowly as he stepped toward Celia. So lost in the giving, she'd forgotten about the one who'd done the taking.

That was her only warning. Halcyon lunged for her, pushing some of the souls who stood between them out of his way, including the one he would call his beloved, his hands contracted into claws.

Halcyon's eyes were wide, his mouth a sneer, everything undignified as he looked upon the one he thought was Diavala, the ancient soul he'd loathed for a thousand years.

Some of the dead souls had stepped closer, intent on the scene. Many of them Celia didn't recognize. They looked like curious birds, cocking their heads from side to side and blinking, much more interested in Halcyon than in Celia.

"Halcyon," Martina said, stepping forward. "Darling, it's me."

It took a long moment before he recognized the voice and turned. Martina held out her arms to him, waiting for him to run into them, but her gaze was fearful, as if she didn't expect that to happen.

As if she expected something worse.

"Martina, love," he said, choking on the words, still consumed with his vicious hatred.

Then he turned back to Celia. Even now, he would go to Martina only after he'd dealt with his archenemy.

Martina's arms fell, and she locked eyes with Celia for only a moment before bursting into movement and grabbing at Halcyon. She didn't charge in violence. It wasn't hate that drove her, Celia saw that in her eyes.

Martina looped her hands into his necklace and yanked it off.

"You've been oblivious to the truth for so long, Halcyon," she said, tossing the pendant so far away it was immediately swallowed by the fog. "It ends here."

Halcyon cried out for his pendant, knowing what the loss of it meant. The afterlife souls would sense he was made of ink.

His gaze began swiveling as he looked for the first time at the souls surrounding them.

"I recognize you now," said one of the souls, staring at Halcyon. "You stole from us."

The shadows of the dead surrounded him slowly. They were in a tight ring, standing shoulder to shoulder with each other, with more ever adding to their ranks. They pushed past Martina and Celia as if they were no longer there.

Celia continued to command the ink inside her to freedom, even more quickly than before, hoping to distance herself from their anger and hold on to that feeling of peace a little longer.

The souls were so close that Halcyon had to push them away, yet they still advanced on him. At first Celia thought they wanted to eat him, and damn, she'd never hated her imagination more. They made pulling motions, as if tugging on invisible rope.

Terror had taken over his anger at her, and he screamed for Celia's help. Her name cut off abruptly as one of the souls silenced him. Somehow.

Celia didn't want to know how. If she didn't get rid of the ink inside her quickly, she would be next.

The transformation was terrible. Halcyon's body began sinking as more and more of the ink left by force and slunk away. She imagined it burrowing into the ground like invisible worms, rising up and disappearing into the fog like mist, and slithering up the legs like fingers. The souls around him took it all in, ready to use it for their own heavens, their own hells, whatever they thought they deserved.

"You won't die," Martina called to him. Perhaps it was the only comfort she could give him. Halcyon wouldn't die, because he was already dead. It was the vessel he'd used that was being sucked clean. He would endure in some other form. Perhaps he'd find a stray bit of the ink he'd coveted for so long and craft his next millennium of existence from it.

You've ruined us, he'd said. But no, he'd ruined himself. He belonged here, and now that he'd returned to the place where wishes became real, some of the souls he'd wronged would make him pay.

Judging by the looks on the faces of those around him, Halcyon would have a lot of demons to outrun. This was only the beginning of his punishment.

Not everything could be sunshine and beauty. There were always dark corners, revenge, and suffering. Wherever souls were, there was pain. Just as there was heaven, there was hell.

Celia kept looking back. She could still see Halcyon's body as the dead souls continued taking any ink they could get, in an almost reverent, peaceful way. Martina stood over the fancy suit, stained and hollowed now. He moved, slightly, and he seemed to be suffering unbearably. In a place of never-endings, how long before his soul could break free?

If he did harness some of the ink around them again, Celia thought, he would never be able to use it for himself. He might have had the luxury of experimenting with it once, to the point of finding a way to build chests to hold it and a doorway to escape through, but never again. There were thousands upon thousands of souls who wouldn't allow it.

And the one with the biggest grudge was Martina, for using her as an excuse for so long.

"Xinto," Celia breathed, turning away. She tucked Xinto under her arm, scratching his chin.

The satiated souls had moved on, new ones had taken their place, and Halcyon's fate was sealed.

Suddenly agitated, Xinto began squirming. Celia took his buzzy hint and backed away slowly, putting distance between herself and what was left of Halcyon. "Shhh, Xinto, it's all right," she whispered, trying to calm him.

But he only squirmed harder, buzzed louder.

Celia loosened her grip, and he flew off, then doubled back, then darted away again. "What is wrong with you?" As fluent as she'd become in Xinto's language, she couldn't tell if he was excited or terrified. Even after Halcyon, Martina, and the dead souls had faded from view, Xinto led her farther. Along the way, Celia released the ink slowly, creating specific items and then dismissing them to the ether: a buttery sweet shirran for Vincent; a gnarled oak tree with perfect climbing branches for her old friends Monroe and Salome; stacks of books for Rian to get lost in.

A sky full of stars for Anya, "So you can count every one," Celia whispered.

Then she honored the living: a bottle of juniper gin for Lupita; a brightly lit stage for Kitty Kay; birds of all sizes and colors for Zuni.

With all sense of time gone, Celia turned each drop of ink inside her into a precious gift.

Then, out of the lightening fog, Griffin appeared. Xinto

flew straight for him, landed on his shoulder, stared at Celia, and *bowed,* as if waiting for applause.

Before Celia could react, Griffin smiled.

Nothing had changed about him: he bore the same strong jaw, dark eyes and hair, tattooed constellation on his temple, long nose, and jagged scar along his chin. Even the way he stood, with most of his weight on one foot as if perpetually ready to run, was the same.

But that powerful smile disarmed her. She'd never seen anything so real.

"Did you finish yet?" he asked.

A rush of something heady—peace, maybe; regret, definitely—hit Celia, and she laughed. "Am I taking too long with my infinity?" She hadn't expected to see Griffin so soon, if ever again. Belatedly, she nodded *thank you* to Xinto.

"Where's the chest?" Celia asked when she noticed that his hands were empty. *Dia,* he had one job . . .

"Gone. I opened it as soon as I stepped through the door. The ink inside is now a garden, an adorable Kid who ran to their parent, some rare parrots Zuni would *love,* a stack of books that stretched up to the clouds, and, quite sinisterly, a set of shackles." His words were thick with emotion, but his smile didn't falter.

"Are you crying?"

"I wish," he said with a sharp laugh. "Nothing works right here." He pulled her into an embrace, wrapping his arms around her shoulders and into her hair. The smell of him: cloves, lemon, and perfectly imperfect.

"I'm glad you're all right, but Diavala . . ." Celia didn't know how to end that sentence. *Where did she go?* In the land of impossibility, what had ultimately happened to Celia's nemesis?

Griffin understood the look on her face without her having to say a word. He clicked his tongue and said softly, "At some point, you either have to let the hate and fear go or let it burn you down."

She rolled her eyes. "*Stop* quoting Ficus. Am I in hell?"

A soft, rumbling chuckle pressed from his chest to hers. "Listen to her, okay? I know you can do it, Celia. Breaking her curse is the last thing, and then we can rest."

"What do you mean?" she said quickly. Griffin was making it sound like the curse wasn't yet lifted . . . His body tensed in her arms, and Xinto flew from his shoulder to hers before trying to burrow himself down the back of her shirt.

Celia stepped out of his embrace as if she'd been burned. "Diavala," she hissed.

"You need to be done," Diavala said, grabbing Celia's arm. Seconds ago, that same hand had been full of tenderness. Now it pinched with festering hatred. "It's been hours now, Inkling, and I sense there's *still* ink inside you."

It hadn't been hours. She'd only just started. "You should be able to create here," Celia said, her anger rising all over again. What angle was Diavala going for now? "You told Griffin this would break your curse, so why are you still here? Leave us alone!"

"You might have to push him out," Diavala said, hauling her forcefully away. "Get ready."

Xinto objected, buzzing in loud circles.

Celia objected too.

But Diavala's grip was too strong, too tight, and Celia couldn't yank free.

"What are you talking about? Push him out where? Stop yanking me!" She was *trying* to listen, but Diavala always made simple things impossible.

"Listen, Inkling, as much as I love the idea of sharing this space with you and tormenting you forevermore, I grew quite fond of your plague doctor. His mind flits around like butter-flies, and he has a devastatingly perfect way of understanding subtlety."

"What does that even mean?" Celia had resigned herself to an eternity in this place, aimlessly walking, or flying, or crawl-ing, as she tried to give back every drop of ink. Again, Diavala was there to change the game.

"Just finish releasing the ink so we can get this over with," Diavala said, irritated.

Celia, trying to wrap her mind around those words, blinked as Diavala stared at her. She asked the same question again, but this time low and quiet, laced with fire. "What does that *mean?*"

"*I'm* going to stay, and *he's* going to go. With the door

between us, my memories will be here with me, and he'll be free."

Diavala had finally wrestled Celia to where she wanted her. With one more hard yank, she let Celia's arm go and stepped back. The door was within arm's reach, a leftover glowing thread suspended in midair, showing Celia the way out. The rose on the doorknob beckoned for Celia to grab it and throw it open.

"Lyric and Zuni were supposed to destroy the doorknob," Celia said, blinking. If they didn't, that meant that Halcyon or anyone else, or the ink itself, could still get out.

"They were," Diavala said, "but I told them he would do it himself."

Celia shook her head.

This didn't make sense. The idea that Diavala would want to save Griffin was world-altering. She could have already crafted a body for herself, and been enjoying a heaven she'd missed out on for a thousand years. The fact that she was waiting in order to try to *save* someone was . . .

No. Griffin was foolish to trust her. He'd known that the cost of his freedom from Diavala would be his life; endlessly roaming the afterlife—alive-ish—his payment. He'd made peace with it.

On the other side of the door, his mind would revolt against the memories Diavala had to leave behind—the Touch would break him. That had been the inevitable truth neither of them could hide from.

Tricking him into that tormented fate, and allowing Celia to help, would be Diavala's final revenge.

"How are you so positive that this will work?" Celia said. *I can't do it, Griffin. I can't trust her.*

Celia felt cornered. This was their dynamic, always: Diavala squashing Celia underfoot, whether she was a small inkling or a runaway rebel or powerful ink master.

"When I came to Wisteria three years ago and possessed Halcyon," Diavala said, "I was searching for the answer to how to break my curse. I learned that the only way was to get to the afterlife again, which at the time I believed was impossible. But considering where we are now . . ."

"Do you feel it?" Celia asked quickly. "Do you feel not-cursed?"

Diavala considered the question thoughtfully, tilting her head. "I feel . . . right."

That wasn't the resounding *absolutely!* or *absolutely not!* that Celia wanted to hear. She wanted a definite answer. One she could understand.

Perhaps she should have known she'd never get that from Diavala.

"I also suspect that Halcyon might not have completely lied to you about how to survive the Touch. Technically, the plague doctor's body has died again. There is no heartbeat, there is no breath. Perhaps the toxicity of the Touch is erased when someone dies."

To Celia's arched eyebrow, Diavala bristled.

"My point is, if one option doesn't work, the other might. It's not like this has ever happened before, Inkling. I can't personally guarantee it will work. You will just have to trust me. And you should at least consider it, precisely because *he told you to.*"

Celia closed her eyes and pulled Xinto in tight. "Do you promise this won't hurt him?"

Diavala, with Griffin's lovely loud voice, laughed. "No. I can't promise that either."

That sounded like the unhoneyed truth at least, a little too sharp to be anything but real.

Anya, should I trust her?

And of course, Anya didn't answer. She was off on her adventure.

Maybe Celia would have to make Celia-like decisions from now on.

If she trusted Diavala, she would either give Griffin life or the Touch. All or nothing. If she decided not to trust Diavala, Griffin would spend his eternity alive-ish, as he'd been prepared to do.

When distilled down to those facts, it was a simple decision. "I don't trust you," Celia said, then sighed. "But I do trust Griffin."

She murmured into Xinto's fuzz as she tried to touch every drop of ink still coursing through her. It felt like there would be enough to do what she wanted. If Diavala was up to anything crooked, this might make her change her mind.

Celia would give the last of the ink back to her. One last gift, not for someone she loved and wanted to honor, but to end this tragic play.

The curtain had to fall; otherwise she was no better than Halcyon. She either had to let go of her hate or let it burn her down. That stupid Ficus poem was right.

In her mind's eye, Celia imagined a young person with tattered clothes and a too-skinny frame. Not too young, maybe ten years old or so. Her tenor is bright red with a thousand hues spiked through it, her cheeks rounded into little apples when she smiles. Her hands are often empty, but she finger-paints in the dust under her feet or with water on dry rock. Celia gave that little soul stunning violet eyes.

One more Divine tattoo, in three dimensions.

When Celia opened her eyes, a young person was standing in front of her, unmoving.

Celia felt empty. Hollow. Every last drop of the ink was gone. "That's it," she said. She looked at Diavala, still in Griffin's body for the time being. "And that's for you." She swayed so violently, lightheaded and weak, that Xinto pushed against her chest, flapping his wings ferociously, as if trying to keep her upright.

"I can't sense it inside you anymore," Diavala said, confirming it. Her words were strangely clipped. Still inside Griffin, she examined her new body. She stared at her face. Her fingers reached up and hovered above her cheek as she tried to recognize herself.

"This is . . . nice," Diavala said, clearing her throat. She wouldn't look at Celia. "Now get ready. I don't know what will happen." It took a beat—one long, stretched-out moment where they stared at each other—and then Diavala closed her eyes.

Despite the warning, Celia wasn't ready. Griffin collapsed to his hands and knees, as if his spine had been yanked out, and as Celia scrambled to his side, he let out a ground-rumbling moan.

Standing above them, Diavala's new body shifted, then spoke. "Now, Celia," young Diavala said calmly. Her voice was higher than Celia had imagined it; up until then, she'd only heard Diavala speak through Vincent, High Mistico Benedict, Anya, and Griffin. Her voice in the afterlife, whole—her true voice—sounded innocent and childlike.

Diavala pierced her with an otherworldly purple-eyed glare. "Push him *out*, Inkling!" Diavala wouldn't help. This had to be Celia's decision.

I don't trust Diavala, but I trust you, Celia thought. *I trust you, Griffin Kay.*

Despite how weak Celia was now, she pulled a staggering Griffin toward the door, yanked it open, and pushed him out. "Remember the doorknob," she said. Her voice was whisper thin and wheezy, and it took every bit of willpower she had to remain standing. If she'd had a heartbeat, it would be slowing down. If her lungs had worked, they would be preparing for their last inhale.

Celia thought of going through the door after him. Of dying properly and returning to the afterlife the normal way.

Instead, she stood there at the threshold, blocking the

doorway in case something else aimed to come in or out. To the end, she would make sure this curtain fell.

"What's your name?" Celia asked.

"I"—Diavala frowned—"I don't remember." That was sad. Celia closed her eyes.

"It can be whatever you want—" Celia started to say.

Forcefully, Xinto was yanked off Celia's shoulder. She turned with his squeals only to see his little legs pumping in the air as the violet-eyed soul held on by the scruff of his neck. She'd changed quite a bit in those last few seconds: taller, thicker, and stronger than Celia had imagined her, with black hair instead of brown, short instead of long. The violet eyes were the same, though. The false tenor, she'd kept that too.

"Xinto belongs here, but I'll take good care of him."

And then Diavala shoved Celia out and slammed the door.

The last thing Celia heard was a tiny buzz, as if Xinto were saying goodbye too.

CHAPTER 33

On the other side of the door, it was raining.

The sky was a violent shade of gray, and the water pouring down had turned everything a mud brown. There was no one else around, not even Zuni or Lyric. Perhaps it had been days, weeks, that they'd spent there. Into each horizon, the line of sight was unimpeded save for an occasional copse of trees or a hill. Nothing except an untouched country landscape in the lake country, with one lone oak tree and a freestanding door with a sunflower doorknob.

And Griffin. Sitting on the ground, breathing hard.

Celia was breathing too. She realized it with such force that she gasped, hyperventilating, as something as normal as *breathing* became the thing that took her most by surprise.

She sat. In the cold mud.

She stretched out and lay down.

Water hit her face with hard pings.

She really needed that nap. On the other side of the door, she'd been tired, but here she didn't even feel human. No thoughts swarmed around in her head, her bees too exhausted to move. There was nothing left to do but close her eyes forever. Dreamless.

She would fall asleep to a lullaby of blessed silence. The screams of the Touch would no longer pierce this world. "I was right to trust you," she whispered. "And you were right to trust her."

Beside her, Griffin had wrapped one hand around his forearm. Then he moved his hands to his temples. Pressed the heels of his palms to his eye sockets, as if he were feeling for humming bones, that ever-present voice, confirmation that he wasn't hallucinating.

With a giant sigh, he collapsed backwards, the mud squelching under his head like a pillow as he turned to face her.

A moment passed as they stared at each other. He said, "Diavala . . . ?" It was both a question and a confirmation.

She was on the other side of the door. For the first time in a millennium, whole. The Curse of the Divine was over.

All this time, the solution to keeping Griffin safe from the Touch had been to heal Diavala. To Celia, that felt both unfair and just. It itched like a bug bite that along with everyone's happy ending came hers. She'd even kept Xinto, which wasn't fair at all.

But it was right.

Griffin tilted his head back and laughed, rain splashing on his face so hard he sputtered. It wasn't his bullshit laugh, it was joyful freedom, gratitude.

He looked at Celia and cocked his head, his lips still smiling.

One bee roused itself to whisper, *Those are very kissable lips . . .*

But just as her lungs and her heart remembered how to do their jobs again, the rest of her body caught up as well. With those kissable lips coming ever closer, Celia's body gave out from giving away all her ink.

Her last thought was, *It's finally over, Anny.*

INTERLUDE

It took three days in a white-hot fire to destroy the door and melt the doorknob. A monstrous feat to undertake in the middle of nowhere with barely any supplies, but they'd all made a promise to Celia, and they had to keep it.

The oak tree had claimed the plague doctor mask, smashing the lenses and snapping the beak. "Celia would say good riddance," Zuni had said as they'd stared down at the broken pieces.

No, she wouldn't be so heartless, Griffin had thought at the time, because it had felt like a funeral.

Three months later, Griffin finally admitted that Zuni had been right.

His new mask fit him so much better.

"I bent over and peered into the dark cave," he said in a slow, low whisper, "only to see *seven* glowing red eyes staring right back at me!" With deft movement he lit some Kinallen powder, and it exploded in his hands, shimmering in red and silver like a miniature firework.

The Kids squealed and leaned back in delighted shock, right on cue, each tiny mouth open in a breathless O. One bright soul in the crowd shouted, "Oh no, Obi! What foolish nonsense have you gotten yourself into now?"

It was a good question. Griffin hadn't thought that far ahead. His Obi the Giant mask had been a gift from Michali—a joke more than anything—and Griffin had only donned it and launched into the story to kill time until the Kids were called to bed.

Griffin laughed and straightened, removing the phenomenally ugly mask with a flourish. He took a bow amid a chorus of complaints. "If you stop whining, I might tell you the rest another time," he said.

Truthfully, he had no idea how the story ended, and it was so much better that way.

He made his way through the camp toward the bright blue wagon, nodding silent greetings to the few people he passed. It was so strange to see only unfamiliar faces; he kept expecting to see Kitty Kay, Seer Ostra, Marco, Lilac . . .

But they were all still in Asura, and though he knew he'd end up with them again, that wasn't the place for him now.

The only familiar faces in the entire Rover camp were Lyric, Zuni, and Michali, who'd recovered the quickest after Wisteria's fall and decided they would follow Griffin anywhere because no one else appreciated leather nearly enough.

Oh, and Zuni's skulls: Bruno and Saccharine.

They'd hitched a ride with that Rover troupe, nothing more, and they were almost at their destination.

All Griffin needed was for night to fall and the stars to come out, and they would be there.

He entered the wagon quietly, sneaking past where Zuni and Lyric were napping. They'd taken to the habit of sleeping as much as possible, their nest of blankets, pillows, and tangled limbs a fresh delight they couldn't get enough of. He would wake them soon, but he had something to do first.

With a hand on his heart to calm its thunder, he knelt at the edge of Celia's bed.

We're here.

They're almost ready for you.

Celia's dark eyes fluttered open slowly.

He stopped breathing.

With a small smile, she fumbled a hand out from under the covers and reached for his face. He wanted that hand to cup his cheek, trace his brow, pull him closer, whatever else she wanted to do with it . . . The blanket fell away, and those full, glistening lips were another thing he wanted. Everything was want—his own mirrored back to him on Celia's features.

"You're so pretty," she said, her thumb gently tracing a trail along the constellation beside his eye. Then, meeting his gaze, she whispered, "I'm nervous."

So was he. Never one to get stage fright, this was the moment that they'd died—and come back—for. Words were entirely stuck in his throat and wouldn't come out.

There was no place for the wrong ones, and the right ones might not even exist.

He took her hand and brought it slowly to his mouth, kissing her palm. He kissed her slowly, the moment turning infinite. It was his imagination, it had to be, but Celia tasted of cherries. Perhaps she'd made friends with the cook and they were sneaking her desserts when no one was looking. She had that way about her.

Her palm was firm and soft at the same time, sweet, dulcet. If kisses were colors, they'd be covered in rich carmine.

His fingers lengthened against the back of her hand, caressing it, and hers stretched to absorb his touch. He pulled away just enough to blow on the skin where his lips just were. If that kiss was color, he wanted it absorbed into her skin. So, like a fresco painting, he mixed himself with the carmine color and blew gently to help it dry. When he was done, the kiss would be part of her, forever fresh and glowing. Despite time, it wouldn't fade.

He kissed slowly again, cupping her hand, then blew. Wet to dry, the sun evaporating dew. Dry to wet, the night dropping it back.

Another play was forming in his mind: *The Night of the Infinite Kiss,* or something equally poetic. He'd be perfect for the role, as long as Celia played the other lead.

And he would have kept going all night, pouring himself into her palm, except that he finally registered

Celia's breathing. It was thunderous: the blanket covering her chest heaved, her lips were parted, her eyes open wider than they'd been in weeks. Giving away all the ink inside her had nearly killed her, and she still wasn't strong—maybe it was too soon for *The Night of the Infinite Kiss*. But when he paused, she whimpered.

He tucked her hand gently across her chest so his carmine fresco rested where her heart beat. Maybe his kiss could reach even deeper, to the soul inside.

"Are you ready to see those Kinallen stars?" he asked.

Already, her eyes glimmered. With tears, with reflected starlight. "I hope you're prepared for a long night," Celia whispered. "I'm going to count them all."

Acknowledgments

I owe a debt of thanks to so many people for helping me get to the point where I could type *The End* on this one. I won't lie, after the third or fourth complete rewrite, I thought there was a good chance I'd never get here. They say second books are hard, and *they* are right.

First and best, to my husband, Johnny. For putting up with my moans and stress cries with measured grace, for always being there to talk out plot problems with me, and for offering never-ending support and encouragement. I wouldn't have been able to finish this one without you, period.

To Ember, who definitely flipped to the back to make sure her name came before her brother's (here you go, darling)—you are my number-one fan, and I'm yours. XO

To Linden, who is so big-hearted and kind he won't even mind that his sister's name is first—you are my inspiration. The world is better because you're in it, and you make me proud every day.

Thanks to my parents for always being there with food, babysitting, and conversation (in that order). And thanks to my brothers, Adam and Dave, and my sisters, Meredith and Emily, for supporting me every step of the way. We're a strange crew, but the best crew.

Huge thank-yous to Daniel Lazar and Torie Doherty-Munro at Writers House. I'd be lost without you two.

My team at HMH has been fabulous in every way, and the biggest shout out has to go to Nicole Sclama, my wonderful editor. I can always count on you for sage advice and healthy doses of cheerleading. I've loved working with you. You're the patron saint of the Rabble Mob.

Special thanks to my sensitivity readers, especially Dill Werner. This book is so much better because of your insight.

Every writer needs a support network, and I've been especially blessed with wonderful friends. Thank you to Rebecca Schaeffer, for reading one of the early drafts and confirming it did, in fact, suck and need to be rewritten. To Jessika Fleck, for always, ALWAYS being there for me. To Sam Taylor, Rosiee Thor, Jade Hemming, and Kayla McGrath, for being awesome in all ways.

And thanks, lastly, to the readers of *Ink in the Blood* for your enthusiasm and support. From the bottom of my heart, I hope you like this one, too.